SMALL CASES YOU SOLVE.

BLOOD RED IVORY

JOHN STAMP

WILDBLUE
PRESS

WildBluePress.com

BLOOD
RED
IVORY

CHAPTER ONE

They were all looking at her. The cops, the five International Counter-Poaching Federation Rangers. The cops gave her sideways glances, some shook their heads in disgust. Some stared at her with open contempt. The rangers in line behind her looked at her with a trepid mix of fear and determination as if to say, "I'm glad we're here... but what the fuck are we doing here?" Not that any of them would ever say that or use that kind of language. They were the first all-female anti-poaching force in Africa. They had been 'invited' to join the Zimbabwe Regional Police in a raid on a suspected ivory stash house. This was their moment, and Sergeant Victoria Jurness was their leader, whether she was ready or not.

Her earpiece crackled, "Go, go, go."

Victoria saw the point man from the Regional Police nod and the policeman holding the metal door handle pulled it open. The two teams were at parallel doors across from a wide roll-up door at a warehouse outside of Victoria Falls. This was far outside Jurness's normal beat. On average, she, and the other women of the ICPF, were on patrol in and around the Phundundu Wildlife Preserve, tracking elephant herds and keeping a wary eye for snakes wherever they stepped.

But this was necessary. The next step in their fight against the poachers and wildlife traffickers that seemed hellbent on wiping great swaths of animals from the Earth.

It was her squad who captured a hunter trying to poison one of the few precious watering holes with cyanide that led to this mission. When they had turned him over to police, he had given up the location of this warehouse in a plea for leniency. Their founder and Lead Ranger Danner Maynard had selected her to lead her squad on this raid as a prize for the arrest.

She remembered how proud she had been in that moment. She was one of the first Maynard selected to train as a ranger. Now, as she gave the signal like the policeman had done and her door to the warehouse opened before her, she marshalled all the excitement she had felt during that arrest and moved forward.

It was dark, a gloomy contrast to the already blazing morning sun outside. Out of the corner of her eye she noted the police contingent in a line paralleling her own squad on the opposite side of the expansive building. Down the center was a long bay of open space of concrete floor and metal support structures. She knew the layout of the building. The police commander had stressed an assortment of offices lining the sides of the building. She scanned left to right repeatedly for any movement. To her left the call of, "POLICE!" echoed through the building. Though she was not one, she had been ordered to give the same warning. "POLICE!" she announced through a cotton mouth. She stopped at a door on her right. Slowly, she tried the knob, but it was locked.

"Locked," she whispered. "Cover."

She moved across the threshold and held her ground while the two rangers behind her kicked the rickety wooden door open. She waited, her eyes scanning the open space and the potential hidden danger in front of her until she heard, "Clear," and felt a pat on her shoulder.

"Moving," she said, then, "Police!" as she made her way to the next office. This one was open, and she traced a slow arc around the door frame, sweeping the small rectangular room with the muzzle of her AR-15 as she moved. Again, pausing on the other side to cover the unknown ahead of them, she waited as the next two women entered and again announced, "Clear!"

Again, the team formed back up and she felt the soft pat on her shoulder. "Moving. Police!" she called, her eyes scanning again from right to left, only this time when she swept back from the center of the warehouse there was a man standing there. He yelled as he raised a rifle in her direction.

BAM! BAM! BAM!

Three shots to the center of his chest. It took her a moment to realize she'd pulled the trigger. Her ears were ringing, she felt blood rushing in her neck. It was all so fast. He had just appeared out of nowhere, now he squirmed on the dusty grey floor. Blood flowed freely from his chest where she... she had just shot him. Her squad rushed past her to control the man's weapon and hyper tense stillness switched to chaos in the blink of an eye. She watched dumbfounded over what had just happened as the man, this stranger with a gun, coughed and shook before her. Sergeant Jurness knew she should be doing something, moving, taking action, something, but it was all a blank. The world just swirled in madness as she watched the man's life run out and his body go still, as she watched herself become a killer.

CHAPTER TWO

Special Agent Tyrone Benhoff walked out of the squat, one-story concrete building that served as the main Police Nationale Congalaise headquarters in North Kivu, Democratic Republic of the Congo. It was going on ten o'clock in the morning and the sun assaulted him, like a flamethrower to the lungs, as he stepped onto the crowded street. He stood still for a second facing the street while people streamed past him. He looked up and down the street scanning faces. The cracked and faded asphalt streets were choked with everything from donkey carts to Mercedez Benz sedans. The sidewalks alternated between dirt paths and concrete walks. They were at once loaded with street venders hocking bushmeat, fruit, or drink amongst the people milling from place to place. Most who passed him were placid, smiling faces going about their business, whatever that may be in a city ravaged by the Ebola virus. After what he'd read and been briefed on regarding the disease, he couldn't help himself. He saw nothing but bleeding eyes and melting internal organs everywhere he looked. These people moved about in groups laughing and talking with all the care given to a bad flu season. Part of him saw a lot of good in that, another part of him wanted to scrub his whole body with a wire brush. Turns out viruses freaked him out.

According to the police chief and for whatever reason, the mayor of North Kivu that just happened to be waiting for him when he arrived; the outbreak was well under control. There was no real danger in Kivu, they told him. Then they went straight into the fees and taxes that would be associated with an official visit from the United States Navy. Ty hadn't asked what their split on those fees would have been. He didn't care, no one from the Navy or any other U.S. agency with any sense was coming to the Congo any time soon. He just needed something to report.

If you looked at his Defense Travel System orders, Tyrone Benhoff, Special Agent, Naval Criminal Investigative Service was conducting a Force Protection Survey of the Democratic Republic of the Congo. Specifically, he was there in advance of a potential mercy visit from the Naval Bureau for Medicine and Surgery (BUMED). That was bullshit. Ty started for the rented Jeep he'd parked a block away from the police station. For a country supposedly riddled by strife, poverty, and a viral outbreak there certainly was a lot of business in the street. The place was packed with people going about their daily lives. Resilient, he thought. His phone chirped in his pocket,

"Benhoff," he said.

"You've got follow on tasking Benhoff,"

"More bullshit?" he asked Supervisory Special Agent (SSA) Thomas Boulden, NCIS Resident Agent in Charge, Camp Lemonnier, Djibouti.

"This comes from the same place your last order came from. It's your ass or it's my ass Benhoff, that's just the way shit goes. You're going to Gabon to conduct a port assessment of some shithole called Port Gentil."

Benhoff scoffed. He was assessing African hot spots like he was writing a travel book for the suicidal. According to the Department of State Travel Advisories he was about to leave one of the most dangerous places on Earth for one of the second most dangerous places on Earth.

Boulden must have noted his silence, "What's a matter Benhoff, you not having fun racking up the miles?"

Ty pictured a woman he knew, sort of knew, who was laying in a hospital bed in Virginia. He could hear an odd mirth in Boulden's voice as he started a fresh jab, "You know I don't know what you did to piss off that particular assistant director, bu...."

Ty hung up on the SSA and sent a quick text, "Any progress?" he typed.

He rounded the corner to find two skinny men wearing grimy tank tops and dirt encrusted cargo shorts. They were barefoot, staring at him. Ty sighed; this was the third time in forty-eight hours he'd had Congolese mess with him. These dudes preferred intimidation. Pestering for change or pulling the 'I kept your car safe,' bullshit to try and extort tourists. The one on the left, bald with a pornstash that did nothing to hide one of the most mangled set of teeth Ty had ever seen, carried a machete. The one on the right leaned against the driver side door.

Ty stopped ten feet out. He thought for a moment about tossing the asshole his keys. NCIS was on the hook for the truck, not him. And at his point fuck those guys. But that was exactly why he was surveying a city choking on a viral outbreak. That's exactly what a certain Assistant Director wanted.

Instead, Ty lifted the Dave Matthews Band t-shirt he wore with his left hand to show the Glock 19 in his waist band, "Fuck. Off," he said plainly.

The two men looked at the gun. The one with the machete and the pornstash backed up a step. The one on the door fixated on the gun. Ty started toward him, reaching for the weapon and the man moved toward the front bumper. Ty popped the door, his eyes still on the two men.

"Wait for the French," he told them as he hopped in, "They'll give you whatever you want."

Ty fired up the sport utility vehicle and pulled off barely missing pornstash with his passenger rear view mirror.

His phone chirped with a text, "She's still non-responsive. Other side, pieces are coming together. Talk soon."

He grimaced as he made his way for the nearest airport.

Gabon, he thought, with a grimace.

Still worth it.

CHAPTER THREE

Three weeks later

Albieto Cruz drove with the windows down. Despite the dust, despite the still raging heat from the day, he guided his rented Toyota Hilux through the winding paths and sometimes paved portions of Zambezi's valley roads. The night was pitch black, the worn and yellow headlights of his pickup truck barely cut a swath through the darkness. All around him was wilderness. High grasses and patches of dense Khaya trees covered a terrain filled with a myriad of wildlife. He could hear them over the engine of his truck. Insects and birds filled the night with a chorus of song, punctuated every now and then by the laugh of a hyena or sometimes when he was lucky, the call of a lion.

Albieto Cruz, a kid from the dregs of Miami, Florida, driving alone, at night, through the hinterlands of Africa. Cruz could only think that his mother would be pissed if she knew what he was up to. He curved his way through a dense patch of trees and passed into a grassland that seemed to cut right through a forest. Cruz slowed as he crossed the grass. This was the fourth time he had made the trip to Zambezi on his own. The last time through, a hippopotamus stared him down. Somehow the massive animal had managed to appear out of nowhere, and it looked at him in a way Cruz had not known before. He had felt like he was at the animal's mercy in that moment. That it was the big creature's decision alone whether he lived or died. It was a very primal sort of experience; one Cruz was hoping not to experience again. But he did want to see another one, which was why he slowed to a gentle crawl. In the night, the hippos abandoned the nearby Angwa River to graze in the fields in this part of the valley. He had to be careful, but he was mesmerized by the life in this area, he wanted to see it all.

He passed the mile or so of grass fields with his eyes peeled, eyes dancing across the dark shifting landscape as much as possible in the steep darkness. He climbed a hill and saw the trees, signaling the end of the hippo grazing area, just ahead. He could have been surrounded by a handful of thousand-pound animals moments ago, but he didn't see a thing. Next time, he told himself. He accelerated back to full speed, or as fast as you dared on the sandy paths that served as roads in this part of the world. Cruz followed a tight curve amongst the trees that would take him away from the river and eventually to the international airport in Harare where once again his escape to this wonderful place would be over. This time two days from now he would be back aboard Camp Lemonnier, sweating and answering phones in his office in Public Affairs. The idea of returning to the desolation of the US Navy base in Djibouti made him think music. He needed something fast and fun if he was going to pilot his rented heap all the way to the airport. His pack rested on the floorboard on the passenger side of the small truck, his iPod hooked to a pocket on the side. As he reached for it, he hit one of the massive ruts along the route and the bounce made the little device leap from his hand.

"Shit." he grimaced, straining for his digital distraction.

Then the windshield exploded.

The resounding chatter of an automatic rifle and the angry pops and tings of heavy rounds dinging against and punching through the skin of the truck took over Albieto Cruz's world. On instinct he smashed the gas pedal and veered away from a blinding set of spotlights that suddenly appeared before him. Flashes that seemed so close he could feel the heat strobe all around him, then WHAM!

The Hilux smashed into an Acacia tree. Cruz smacked his face on the unpadded steering wheel and heard a crack in the bridge of his nose. Silence. He felt like he was moving in slow motion. He clawed for the seatbelt. It fought him like the tentacles of an octopus as he tried to release himself from the vehicle. He had served two tours in Afghanistan prior to his post to Africa. He'd never seen combat, but he'd been outside the wire countless times riding in convoys along some of the deadliest roads in the world. He'd seen a buffalo, the massive troop transports used to mitigate IEDs, take a blast from a roadside bomb. He knew how to dismount a vehicle in an emergency. Finally, the seatbelt set him free, and he flopped with all the grace of a newborn giraffe onto the rust-colored dirt road.

There was yelling, arguing in Shona, one of the native tongues of Zimbabwe, then a flash and a crack came from the other side of the Hilux.

Cruz dashed into the jungle. Scrambling in the darkness. He ran headlong through the brush and grasses in the pitch black with no idea of his direction or how many armed men were chasing him.

Another crack and what felt like a kick from a drill sergeant's boot hit him in the back.

He stumbled but kept his feet. He knew he'd been shot. His back, just over his right hip, screamed in pain, causing him to gasp with every agonizing step as he ran. The tall grass cut at him and snagged his feet, each time a fire sweeping up his leg. He could hear nothing going on around him. Was he still being chased? Were they shooting at him? Why was this happening? Blood rushed in his ears and his heart raced. He saw lights in the distance, maybe a village, or maybe a patrol. The thought of running into an anti-poaching patrol gave Cruz strength. Strength he used to speed toward the light. He found a gap in the tree line and pushed through, rounding between the flat-topped trees, desperately trying to keep one foot in front of another. He didn't see it until the last possible moment and had to strain his injured body against a low hanging branch to keep from running off a steep bank into the river.

Cruz almost lost it. He looked at the rippling darkness and the light beyond. So close he could almost see flames dancing on the village's cook fires. Given the width of the river and the wildlife that owned those waters, the village might as well have been on the moon.

Move! a voice screamed in his head. *As long as you keep moving, you're still alive, the words of a survival instructor, one whose name he'd long forgot, blasted through his head. Move! he told himself, just move!*

He gulped a deep breath, God, he could barely catch his breath. He took one last look at the salvation of the lights across the river and let that hope go. His salvation lived in putting distance between him and his pursuers. He took his first clumsy step downriver and heard a snicker and some mumbled words. A massive flash and an impact to his chest was Albieto Cruz, Second Class Petty Officer, United States Navy's last sense in this world.

CHAPTER FOUR

He wasn't sure if it was an unbridled anger that registered first or the staccato chirping of the iPhone that always caused the hot emotion. All he knew was that he wanted to send the goddamned thing sailing across the room to blissfully smash against the stone wall. He knew he couldn't explain destroying another phone so instead he settled for pounding on the screen until it shut up. When he rubbed his eyes, he noticed light, bright light, then he noticed the arm draped across his chest and the perfectly tanned leg pinning his shins. Long, drawn-out breathing filled his ear. Benhoff blinked away the murk of the night before and focused on the sharp features and blonde hair of the woman in his bed.

This is purgatory, he reminded himself.

He enjoyed the view for only a moment before a hard banging on the front door of his home ruined whatever inkling of a plan he had for the morning. If it was still morning. He picked up the phone and grimaced. It was 0930.

"Shit," he grumbled. He wormed his way out from under the sleeping woman. The banging on the door sounded like a battering ram and reverberated around in his head. His mouth was dry, and he tasted remnants of bourbon. Before heading downstairs, he grabbed a pair of jeans from among a pile of clothing, to include a German Navy dress uniform that was strewn about the tile floor of his bedroom. Anika Guerlitz, Lieutenant, and liaison to AFRICOM, shifted in her sleep, rolling an Egyptian cotton sheet around her like a crocodile doing a death roll. Ty saw no reason to wake her up. He had to address whoever it was pounding on his door. On his way out he slid his issue nine-millimeter Glock 19 into the back of his waist.

CHAPTER FIVE

Ty yanked the door open mid-bang, "Fuckin' what?"

SSA Boulden, chuckled. He entered without being invited and surveyed the swank accommodations Ty was enjoying as the NCIS adjunct to the United States Embassy.

"You don't deserve this place." Boulden said.

"You don't deserve your title, but shit happens." Ty quipped.

"That's cute, you always start your days this late? The day starts at… "

Boulden stopped talking for some reason when Ty turned his back on him and went into the kitchen. The SSA was growing red as he followed.

"Since you're here, you want a cup of coffee?" Ty asked. "And by the way, I've been working all night, in fact I'm still at work, technically."

"Technically, my ass, just because you're on some bullshit detail to… "

He stopped again and looked for the clacking sound coming down the marble staircase. Benhoff was not surprised. He watched the SSA's jaw drop as Anika, stunning despite just getting out of bed and even pulling off the uniform that spent the night on his floor, walked down the stairs. She could walk right into a briefing, and he bet not a soul would notice she just woke up from a night that included a serious bender. Ty wondered if he was getting old because he doubted he looked nearly as good. And he felt like he'd been hit by a truck.

"Lieutenant Anika Guerlitz, meet Mr. Boulden." Ty intentionally left out Boulden's title.

"Nice to meet you, Mr. Boulden."

"He's the reason we had to get up so early," Ty offered.

Anika smiled with innate class. The woman towered over Ty's own six-foot frame, especially in her heels. She took his chin in her elegant fingers, "That is why you should answer your phone when it rings." She kissed him and headed for the door.

Ty looked at his duty phone, "My phone didn't ring." He looked at Boulden who flipped his eyebrows at him, then turned to watch Anika swagger to his door.

"It rang a dozen times." She turned before leaving, "Ty, you sleep like a hibernating bear. I will see you again."

"Hope so," he responded as the door shut. Ty turned to Boulden. Before the SSA could make yet another attempt at dressing him down, he said, "You cock-blocked me, you know that, right?"

"That was work?" Boulden asked rhetorically.

Benhoff went back to making coffee. "Liaison," he said wistfully. "Liaison."

"If you weren't already on the Director's shit list... "

"Technically I'm on the assistant director's shit list. The director is too new, he hasn't gotten a chance to know me yet."

Boulden scrunched his eyes and shook his head, "What? I still don't give a shit. Like I was saying, I would write you up but since you're not actually assigned to me, I don't give enough of a shit to do the paperwork." Boulden dropped a sheet of paper on the counter next to a half empty bottle of Jameson, "Besides, I get to give you this so as far as I see it, I'm still coming out ahead."

Ty looked at the paper suspiciously before picking it up. It was an email from the SAC in Naples, Italy. Then he saw the letters D-S-I, Director's Special Interest. "Fuck is this?" but Boulden was already halfway to the door.

"From the sounds of it, your first opportunity to show the director what a shitbag you are. It's all you, buddy. Dead sailor in the bush of Zimbabwe. You leave immediately."

"The AD got tired of sending me to Ebolaville to do force protection assessments, huh? Gonna need a terp." According to some of the Department of State people he worked with at the Embassy, he was going to places they weren't allowed to go without CIA paramilitary escorts. The grapevine at NCIS HQ had informed him that every one of those assignments had come from the Office of the Assistant Director for Operations Douglas McClintock.

Boulden tossed his hands up, "They speak English, from what I hear anyway."

"Fuuuuck," Benhoff sighed as he read the details, of which there were hardly any.

Boulden was grinning as he paused in the doorway. Ty noticed he was entertained by this game between the two of them. The man lacked any of the style Anika had graced the same space with, "You know, Benhoff, if you don't like your job, you can always quit."

Benhoff smirked, "It's not the job."

That got a chuckle out of Boulden, "Have a great trip."

Ty looked at the email again. Biodata for one Albieto Cruz PO2, town of Karoi, Zimbabwe, and the email originator, Assistant Director Douglas McClintock via Special Agent in Charge Naples Field office. McClintock's name rattled around in his skull like an anchor chain over New England rocks. That asshole could wait until he had breakfast.

CHAPTER SIX

Only dusty slivers of golden light eking through the gaps in the warping wood slats were able to penetrate the darkness of the old shack. Obert Thoomba was blinded by the lack of light and had to wait for his eyes to adjust from the blazing sunlight outside. Though he was momentarily blinded, he could still hear. Gasps of pain and fear, and soft whimpering filled his ears as details of the interior of the dilapidated room slowly came into view. Three of them knelt before him. They were stripped to the waist, a sheen of sweat and blood reflected what little light there was as they tried to breathe through the damage already paid them. He waited for them to acknowledge him; it was a test.

Thoomba was a giant of a man, standing at six feet five inches tall. His broad chest and thick arms bulged even through the massive quantity of linen it took to tailor his suit jacket. His stare was intense as he waited for them to look him in the eye. Slowly, with a primal hesitancy, their heads rose to meet him. First the one on the left, Nathaniel if memory served, followed by John. That left only Muupha, the one who still whimpered in the darkness. When the boy finally recognized him, Thoomba could not help but see the stream of tears and snot etching clean lines down his dusty face. He stared at them for a long time to allow them opportunity to understand the severity of their mistake.

"Whose idea?" he finally asked.

None of the three said a word. Thoomba respected that. But both Nathaniel and John shot sidelong glances at Muupha.

Thoomba crouched before Muupha. The sobbing was intolerable, "Be a man, stop crying. Stop crying right now."

Muupha sniffled but managed to wrangle himself in. The whites of the boy's eyes were huge and stark in the darkness.

"Why?" Thoomba asked.

More sniffling, "He was helping them. Giving them supplies. I thought… "

"You did not think," Thoomba silenced him. "You did not think about the suppliers and their expectations. You did not think about the Americans who will now come to investigate. You did not think," he pointed a finger the size of a cucumber in the boy's face. "You did not think!"

"They kill Kamalla," the boy said quietly.

Thoomba scrunched his eyes and looked to his second, Fannel.

"My brother." Muupha beat Thoomba's enforcer to the clarification.

Thoomba was surprised he did not recall that Kamalla Undess was the brother of Muupha. It had been a long time since one of his operations suffered a loss so big to the authorities. Thoomba knew the repercussions of that loss had yet to be fully realized. It was a problem that made him sweat at night.

He studied the bound man--man? More like a boy. He could not be twenty years old yet.

"Your brother. He tried to outsmart the rangers himself, without my blessing or my order. Your brother died because of his ignorance. His stupidity." He let that set in as he groaned and brought his massive frame back to full height. He studied the three of them, doing a calculation in his head, "You pull the trigger yourself, Muupha?"

Muupha stared at the dirt floor of the shack. He was silent, still.

Thoomba looked at the other two and noted Nathaniel returning his attention. His eyes had the frightened look of an animal in a trap. Thoomba chuckled and kicked a cloud of red dirt in Muupha's face, "You seek your revenge, and when you find it, you cannot even take it yourself."

He nodded in the direction of Fannel and turned to the other two. The percussion of the nine-millimeter pistol in the tight confines of the old shack made his ears ring. The two remaining prisoners started shaking, John moaning pitifully. Thoomba was sure he could smell piss mixing with the odor of cordite and gunpowder that filled the room. He wondered if he were making a mistake or teaching a lesson.

"Muupha is dead because he was foolish, and he threatened our business. You two will bury him, and you will remember this lesson. Let him be an example for you."

CHAPTER SEVEN

The C-130 landed at the Kariba International Airport and taxied to the far end of the terminal for a quick turnaround. The crew chief, Wilson, lowered the ramp and Benhoff felt a wave of thick, hot African heat rush the cabin, making the pack on his back and sea bag in his left hand feel thirty pounds heavier. He noticed Wilson sigh under the heat as well as he met him at the ramp.

"Enjoy your stay, Agent!" he yelled over the idling engines.

"You, too, you lucky bastard!" Benhoff replied. The C-130 and her crew were on their way to Germany for a re-fit that would last a week, and it was Oktoberfest.

"We plan to."

Benhoff had to jump from the ramp as it had already started to raise before he hit ground. That was a nice touch, he thought. He hustled clear of the thick, suffocating trails of exhaust before the big cargo carrier started to taxi for take-off. Once he was clear of the eye watering, rancid cloud, he squinted in the afternoon sun for the terminal. Instead, he found a white man in a black suit and sunglasses standing in front of a black suburban and a grey, hard-top Jeep Wrangler. He nodded in Benhoff's direction and started his way.

"Special Agent Benhoff, I'm Pellano, DSS. The RSO (Resident Security Officer) in Harare requisitioned you a vehicle for your investigation." He handed Benhoff a folded slip of paper and a set of keys for the Jeep, "Your visa is clear for ten days, keep that in your passport. Depending on where you go around here, formal documents don't really impress as much as they do back home."

"I'm sure." Benhoff reached into his pocket for his passport. Once the paperwork was secured in a pocket least likely to get flooded with sweat, he took Pellano's hand, "I appreciate it."

"No problem, need anything before I go?"

Benhoff tossed his pack in the passenger side of the Jeep and looked around the open tarmac and hangars. The terminal was a single building that looked like a mashup of Legos with an oddly squat tower sitting on top, exactly how Benhoff imagined it. "Don't think so, what's the weapons policy here with the local law?"

Pellano smiled, "A, hope not to get in a shootout. B, if you do, drive like hell for the embassy in Harare. Since it's a five-hour drive on a good day, I would do my damnedest to stick with option A. You all they sending?"

Benhoff grinned, "One riot, one ranger, right?"

Pellano cocked his head. "You say so," he turned to his Suburban. "Most speak English here. But you won't know that unless they want you to. Stay out of the bush at night, don't trust any government official you meet, and don't eat anything cooking on the side of the road, it's probably a monkey, and they are the reason we have Ebola."

"Right, McDonald's it is."

Pellano gestured with a seesawing-hand as if to say, Ehh, maybe. "Good luck, Benhoff."

Benhoff nodded, "Thanks again." He watched Pellano pull away and felt torn. On the one hand he had just circumvented customs in a foreign country which meant he didn't have to gamble on his smuggling capabilities since he had the component parts of both his Glock 19 and an MK-18 broken down and scattered through his luggage. He also didn't have to rely on a locally maintained rat trap from the town's rental car facility. On the other hand, he was just warned by an expert on Zimbabwe to stay away from the food, be in when the sun goes down, not to trust the local cops, and that if he got in the shit, he had to cannonball run five hours across the country to find safety. After a moment's care he honestly figured it was a wash and was just happy to have the Jeep.

CHAPTER EIGHT

The Land Rover carrying Obert Thoomba pulled into the dirt-packed alley next to the trinket store he owned in the small village of Karoi. Thoomba sighed when his vehicle parked behind a black Mercedes Benz E-class sedan, which despite the constant dust that kicked up around the village held barely a speck.

"I swear he parks in my spot-on purpose, Fannel," Thoomba growled as the two stepped from his much grittier SUV.

Fannel nodded then paused, his focus drawn to something across the roundabout on which Obert's store sat. Obert followed his man's attention where he saw a Jeep parked in front of the local police station. He saw a man standing next to the driver's door, an American. Everyone knew an American from the other whites that came as tourists to his country. His shirt was a sand brown, and he wore baggy ripstop pants that served as adventure wear in America. His boots were lightweight, and his sunglasses were black Oakley's. Before leaving the vehicle, Thoomba watched the man with short-clipped dark hair retrieve a notebook. American policeman, Thoomba grimaced as he watched him lock the Jeep with a remote and stroll casually into the police station. Thoomba now had no doubt why his brother was in his store.

The relief he felt walking into the somewhat cooler tourist shop was short-lived.

"Do you see this?" Gerald Thoomba, Minister of the Interior for Mashaland Province, Zimbabwe jabbed a long, thin finger toward the front of the store.

"I saw him," Obert answered.

Gerald put his hands on his hips, his eyes wide and expectant. When he took that pose, Obert thought his older brother looked like their mother. "It is taken care of, brother. Do you know who he is?"

"American police," Gerald growled.

"The Fish police?" Obert had a genuine concern for the Fish and Wildlife Police that came from America. Everyone in their business knew of them, knew they could track you back to your ivory, no matter where it went, or how long after you sold it. Obert felt a pit growing in his stomach.

"No, my contact at the regional office tells me he is a Navy policeman."

Obert scrunched his nose, "Navy? Like the ocean, big ships?"

Gerald's eyes flared again, "Yes!"

Obert shrugged his shoulders, "Why do we care?"

"That man your mongrels killed. He was American Navy."

Obert was confused, but the pit in his stomach seemed to dissipate, "I told you that is handled, there is nothing for him to learn about that here."

"No?" Gerald's eyebrows bounced with the question. "You betta be sure." He put a sickle-like finger in Obert's face, "Be sure." Gerald stepped back to look once more toward the police station, then he turned his attention to one of the carved wooden boxes they sold to the tourists that flocked to Zimbabwe every year for safari.

"You feel betta, brother? You worry too much."

"And you not enough, little brother. You must keep your men on a tight leash, they are not fit to roam without direction, or discipline." He dropped the box back on the table.

Obert grinned, "The problem has been dealt with, I promise. The policeman will talk to our police, he will file a report and be gone within the day."

Gerald nodded his head, "What about the other thing? We have important interests depending on us."

"That is delicate, the time must be right. It will all work out."

Gerald nodded to his driver and the man exited the rear of the store. Gerald flattened his suit coat in a decorative mirror on the far wall, "Your confidence is a constant amazement. You know who we deal with, we cannot fail them again."

Obert smiled over the spine twitching rage flaring inside him. Obert and his men did not fail at anything. They were raided, and the material was taken by the rangers. If anything, it was Gerald who had failed to know of the operation. Obert barely escaped the whole thing. He took a deep breath and guided his older brother out of the store, "I do, brother, I do."

He hugged his brother despite the urge to wrap his meaty hands around Gerald's skinny neck and squeeze. He opened the door for him and watched him go.

When Obert returned, he found Fannel watching the police station near the front of the store, "I want to know who he is, where he stays, and who he talks to, Fannel." Obert did not take his eyes off the Jeep across the way, "This cannot interfere."

Fannel nodded, his eyes never leaving the station.

CHAPTER NINE

Lilliana Cartwell gulped hot, dusty air as she and the rest of her six-woman contingent came off the trail near the main office of the International Counter-Poaching Federation (ICPF)/Phundundu Wildlife Park Rangers station. She was dressed in green BDUs and heavy canvas and leather boots. Her uniform was soaked through, so wet that the green was so dark it was almost black. A fifty-pound pack on her back made her wobble on tired, aching legs. She pulled her boonie cap from her shaved head and wiped the moisture from her scalp and neck.

"Here."

A rough, brown hand offered her a bottle of water. Lilliana clawed at the plastic bottle and chugged. The water was cold, so cold it hurt her teeth and froze her throat, but that was not enough to make her stop drinking.

"Easy with that, you will cramp," the soft voice of Victoria Jurness cautioned her.

Lilliana only stopped drinking because she had to breathe. "Thank you," she smiled. The smile was erased by the stoic expression and more importantly the pack, identical to her own, strapped to her field training officer's back. Ranger Victoria Jurness, Sergeant, ICPF, kept her eyes locked on Lilliana's. Lilliana fought the primal impulse to protest what she knew was coming next.

"Finish the bottle in your hand and stow this one." Victoria handed her a fresh bottle. "Now let's go."

Lilliana's sigh was unavoidable. She's just finished a twelve-kilometer march with her team. That fact bought her little in the way of currency.

"You have something better to do?"

"No, Sergeant Jurness!" Lilliana shouted. Her idea of what else or where else she could be gave her no solace in the face of whatever torture Jurness had in mind.

"Move on then, I will join you in a moment."

Lilliana noted Victoria's attention was over her shoulder. Lilliana turned to see the commander of the ICPF, Lead Ranger Danner Maynard. She followed her training officer's orders with a nod to Mister Maynard, as she called him. He offered her a warm smile in return.

CHAPTER TEN

Victoria Jurness watched her trainee shuffle down the path. She was tiny, her pack looked bigger than she was, but she carried it well, walking with determination. Victoria paid particular attention to the way Lilliana held her head. The rookie ranger had her eyes on the path in front of her instead of at her feet. She turned to face Lead Ranger Maynard.

"Cooking your rookie in the hot sun, Victoria?"

"It is Africa, sir. It is always hot."

"True enough," the man said in an Australian accent. Danner Maynard was a former Australian Special Forces Solider who relocated to Zimbabwe to fight poachers. He started the all-women ranger force. Like the rest of the ranger force, Victoria owed everything to the man.

"How are you doing, Victoria?" The question was sincere, disquieting, but not at all unexpected. He looked her in the eye. No matter how badly she wanted to shrivel away from the question, she did not.

"I am all right."

"I told you, you could take some time. Everyone needs time when they face a loss."

Victoria took a deep breath, "There is no place else I want to be, sir."

He nodded. "Okay, that's all right," he paused. "But do not make whatever you got planned for her about you." He let the words set in, "That's not fair to her."

Victoria had to swallow hard, fighting tears that seemed to always be right at the surface trying to get out, "I understand."

"Very good," Danner nodded. "Dismissed."

Victoria tracked her rookie for almost a kilometer before jogging to catch up to her. Lilliana was clearly exhausted, but she continued to put one boot in front of the other. She even offered a weak smile when Victoria came alongside.

"How far are you planning to go?"

"Until you tell me to stop."

"You know why we are out here?" Victoria asked.

"To train," Lilliana answered.

"Good answer." Victoria stopped and faced her trainee. "Ranger Cartwell, we are out here because this job will always demand more. You will be out by yourself. When you are alone you must be ready, always be ready for more. Out here your radio means shit, your credentials as a ranger, assuming you get them, means shit. You run into trouble it is you that will have to get yourself out of it, no one will be able to get to you in time if something goes bad. Always have that in your mind. Be sure from here on out you have that in your mind. When it gets hard, and I promise it will, be ready for more."

Lilliana Cartwell was silent for a long moment.

"Do you understand what I am saying?"

Lilliana nodded, "I understand."

"Good, now give me your pack, Big City." Lilliana had earned the nickname since she had fled Harare, and her husband, to join the Rangers. "Let's go home."

CHAPTER ELEVEN

Tyrone Benhoff was not a patient man. Never had been. His mother attributed it to their German Scandinavian heritage, which she usually blamed when he threw a tantrum as a little kid. The only thing he absorbed from that, however, was that they were part Viking… and that was awesome.

Still, the 'lobby,' more accurately the hallway in the front of the police station, was stifling as he sat with his notebook sketching out his first moves once he finally got a briefing from the lead investigator from the Zimbabwean Regional Police, Detective Tsunga. By the time the rail thin and rangy detective, dressed in a loose-fitting suit that made him resemble more a clothing rack than a police officer, came to find him, Ty had been reduced to listing positives and negatives in two columns, bourbon or vodka, as to what he was drinking tonight.

"Mista Benhoff," the detective tried to accurately pronounce his name and succeeded. Ty rose and the two shook hands. "I am Detective Matthew Tsunga, I apologize for the wait." Tsunga gestured as he held the door for him.

"Not a problem," Benhoff lied as he followed the smaller man down a narrow hall tiled in an odd mint green. The passageway was lit with naked fluorescent bulbs hanging from the ceiling. "Thanks for making time for me."

"Yes." Tsunga showed him to an office and gestured toward a seat opposite an old metal desk which held a relic of a computer Benhoff figured he might have played Oregon Trail on once as a kid. "Can I offer you some water, Mista Benhoff?"

"No, thank you," Ty responded with a grin. What, was this guy trying to kill him?

Tsunga sat down at his desk and leaned toward him with both elbows propping him up, "I want to tell you before we start, I am not corrupt."

Ty fought the multitude of responses zipping through his head. He cocked his head and scrunched his eyebrows. "Is that a warning, Detective Tsunga?" he asked.

Tsunga gestured with his hands, "No, I simply want you to know. Despite all the graft in my country, I am a clean cop." He nodded his head for emphasis and his smile revealed two rows of gleaming white teeth.

Ty nodded; this dude had dealt with foreigners before. "Well, good to know, and me neither," he said as he filed Tsunga's anti-admission away for another time.

"Yes."

"Yes," Ty mirrored him. "Now, the Cruz investigation. I understand you are the lead detective on the case."

"I am, yes." Tsunga spun around in his chair and fetched a file folder, an empty file folder, from a shelf near the office's lone window. He smiled broadly as he handed Benhoff the file, "This is my file, please have a look."

Ty suppressed a sigh as he flipped the file open. He was relieved to find that it wasn't actually empty. There were two scraps of paper waiting for him. One half-sheet of ruled notebook paper had the date and time, and what he guessed was the name of the village where the body was found. The other had a name and what looked like a scribbled signature.

"Can I get a copy of this?" Ty asked.

Detective Tsunga smiled, "Yes, I can make you a copy." The detective reached for what looked to Ty like some kind of form, but Ty whipped out his phone.

"It's all right, I can just do this," he laid the scraps on the covers of the file, sure to catch the title written on the folder's tab, a word he didn't understand, and took a photo of both 'reports'.

Tsunga was looking at him oddly and Benhoff realized he probably just broke some police protocol he didn't care about. He moved on without addressing the detective's concern, "Thanks, that helps me keep things organized. Gives me a good place to start. Can you tell me about the case?"

Tsunga shook off whatever was clearly a breach and recovered the file, "Yes, I responded to the scene yesterday. A village not too far from here named Allassa, a fishing village. The body was found on shore very near the village dock."

Ty didn't respond, just remained silent. The bubble of silence pushed Tsunga on.

"It seems the body washed down river. It was not too damaged."

"What do you mean too damaged?"

"Crocodiles, hippopotamus, and some of the fish in our rivers get very hungry. We were fortunate nothing had truly started feeding on him."

Gross. "How did you identify him as Mr. Cruz?"

"Ah," Tsunga reached in a desk drawer, "I almost forgot the evidence, do you want to see?"

"Please."

Tsunga pulled out a single plastic, gallon-sized Ziplock bag. It contained Albieto Cruz's DOD identification card, what looked like a stick, and a crimped metal bottle cap that was so rusted Benhoff was amazed it was still in one piece. The bag had a pool of yellow water sloshing around the bottom. He took the bag from the detective.

"May I?" he asked.

"Of course." Tsunga smiled again.

Tsunga had no latex gloves to speak of and Ty's were in his kit in the Jeep. Despite his years of training to the contrary, he reached in the bag and removed the ID first. It dripped the yellow water, and the bag smelled of pond scum. He laid it on the desk. The visage of Albieto Cruz was smiling back at him. Ty noted the grin on the dead man's face. Most kids make their ID photo look like a mugshot. Not Cruz, the kid had a big grin on his face. Though he'd never met the man, Ty found himself feeling sorry for what happened to him. He took another picture with his phone then took out the stick and held it up for Tsunga.

"Yes, that piece was found on the body. It appeared caught in his shirt."

Ty nodded. "Of course," he said. He photo'd the stick but for a different reason than the ID.

Finally, the bottle cap. It flexed in his fingers as Ty pulled it out of the bag. He laid that out on the desk and gave Tsunga another expectant look.

"This was found under the body. I wondered if it was holding fingerprints, or DNA." Tsunga said the last part in kind of a hushed tone.

Ty watched as part of the bottle cap flaked off onto the desk. "You never know," he offered. He photographed the bottle cap as well because... why not? He placed the items back in the bag, "Can I take these?"

"If you think they will assist your investigation."

"Oh, I have no doubt," another lie. "What can you tell me about the area?"

"Allassa is a small fishing village, pretty remote. It is just outside of the wildlife park on the Angwe River. Not much happens there."

"They speak English there?"

"Yes, sir, most in Zimbabwe speak English."

"Good, so what do you think happened to Mr. Cruz?"

Tsunga sighed, "I think he slip and fall in the river. He probably drowned. Why would he be out there? What would he be doing?"

Ty shrugged.

"Maybe he take a safari. Tourism is very popular here in Zimbabwe."

"Do visitors usually go off by themselves? I thought most of these tours were guided, you know, for the lions and stuff."

Tsunga chuckled. "It is the hippos that will get you," he shrugged. "It is not common but possible he went out by himself."

"You find a car belonging to him or any witnesses that saw him before he turned up in the river?"

"No, sir, all we have is what is in the file."

Benhoff smiled, that's helpful, "Where is Cruz now?"

"You want to see him?" Tsunga was confused.

"I do."

CHAPTER TWELVE

The morgue in Karoi was that in name only. It was attached to the rear of a small medical clinic that was nothing more than a waiting area and a large empty room lined with gurneys and a couple larger hospital beds. There was a small glass cabinet for medicine and supplies, and it was sparse. The morgue had a walk-in freezer that served for body storage, one autopsy table and a desk. Benhoff was sure to snag a pair of latex gloves from the Jeep before following Tsunga inside. The place lacked the antiseptic smell that accompanied most morgues he'd attended. This one simply smelled of death and dried blood, of which Benhoff noted several wipe-stains on the tile floor. He tried to be careful to miss those. Out of habit from walking into dozens of crime scenes over his time in law enforcement, Ty kept his hands in his pockets. He was surprised when it was Tsunga who opened the freezer--the unlocked freezer.

"The mortician is a doctor in Harare. He is not in," Tsunga said as he gestured for Benhoff to follow him into the freezer. As he stepped inside, he noted four bodies in addition to Cruz lying uncovered on frosted gurneys. Ty also observed what looked like some medical supplies and a tub of ice cream which Ty found not only oddly out of place but a little disturbing. He could not help but think about all the objections and cross-examination questions defense attorneys in the States would have if evidence had come from a setup like this. He slipped the gloves on as Tsunga stopped at one of the gurneys.

"Here he is."

Benhoff didn't touch Albieto Cruz. He took up a Nikon D7000 he had retrieved from the Jeep along with his gloves and a small evidence kit. He affixed a flash to the boot on top of the camera body and started taking photos. He worked all the way around the body and had to balance himself on a frozen wooden stool to try and get an overhead shot of the body. Cruz was still clothed, his facial features looking like they'd been chewed on by fish or crabs as he floated down river. His lips were picked at and torn to the point half of his lower dentition and jaw could be seen. His eyelids likewise had been picked at, and Benhoff noted damage to the eyes themselves. Cruz still wore a pair of cargo shorts that were ripped, allowing him to see the calf on his left leg was missing. Ragged tears of the skin made Benhoff think an animal got him. Another ragged hole on his right abdomen exposed the intestines. The yellowish fat layer between the skin and the pink muscle tissue seemed to seep into the wound prior to being introduced to the freezer. Benhoff photoed the body and the wounds as best he could with the dim lighting in the freezer. He didn't know why Tsunga wanted to keep the body in the cold, but Benhoff didn't argue. The less Cruz thawed before he was transported to Mortuary Affairs in Ramstein, Germany, the better.

Ty was just about to turn Cruz over when something about the gray t-shirt, partly folded over Cruz's chest, caught his attention. He slung the camera and leaned in closer. There was what looked like a dark stain on the front of the grey Miami Dolphins shirt. When he reached toward the shirt, Tsunga held up a hand.

Ty dismissed him and kept his momentum. "It's fine," he said as he gingerly peeled the frozen garment flat across Cruz's body. He retrieved his camera, "You were right,

Detective Tsunga. Albieto probably fell, and he might have drowned. But I'm willing to bet someone shot him before all that happened."

"Shot him? No."

Ty set the camera up and photographed a hole surrounded by a smattering of smaller tears around the center of the shirt, right through the Miami Dolphin's eyes. The main hole in the center of the mess had black charring. Around the rim of the hole, the wicking material of the t-shirt had melted a dark black. Once he finished taking photos of the shirt, he carefully peeled back the shirt to find what looked like not much more than a puncture mark the width of an eraser head. The wound was circular. Ty started photographing the wound, "We're gonna need to turn him over in a minute."

Tsunga seemed frozen in place. "How?" he asked.

Ty placed the camera on the desk and unslung his pack to drop it next to the camera. "Very carefully," he said. "Come on."

Ty leaned in, suddenly very thankful that Albieto Cruz was frozen and not oozing gunk. He reached across the dead man's chest and pulled on his far shoulder. The literal dead weight was heavy and unwieldy. Benhoff heaved and the body rolled in one solid piece like a length of cord wood. Ice creaked and cracked between the body and the metal table. Benhoff watched Tsunga's eyes widen as he turned the body. When he got Cruz balanced on his side, he said, "Come here."

Tsunga shook his head.

"He's not going to hold it against you. Come on, Detective."

Tsunga's upper lip curled in disgust. He shed his oversized suit jacket and finally took Ty's place. He scrunched his face as he touched the body and held his breath.

"Thanks, this'll only take a minute."

Ty left Tsunga who was staring at the ceiling, doing anything he could to mentally get away from the fact he was holding a frozen corpse. Ty retrieved his camera and rounded the body. He stepped back and took an overall photo of the body, then saw what he had expected and muttered, "Shit."

"What is it?" Tsunga asked, alarmed as he strained to keep the body steady.

"The bullet went through him," Ty said as he took several shots of the wound, getting ever closer until a hole the size of a walnut in Cruz's back took up the entire frame of the photograph. On the last photo Ty took another look as he stuck a scale to the moist skin and realized there was a tiny frozen fish still inside the bullet defect. He peered in as close as he could get to see if there was anything left, maybe the round had splintered and left a piece of itself on the way out. Given the size of the hole, and the fact that the local wildlife had gnawed at the wound, he was not surprised when he couldn't see anything.

"Mista Benhoff," the strained voice of Tsunga gasped. Ty looked up to see Cruz's body wavering on the table as if it were a sail being buffeted by a strong breeze.

"Okay, you can put him down."

Tsunga let go and with a deafening Bang! Cruz hit the thin metal of the autopsy table. The sound reverberated around the freezer as the stiff body wobbled before going still.

Ty retrieved his gear and Tsunga was only too happy to get out of the cold room. He was standing by the door waiting to close it as Ty exited while reviewing his work on the Nikon. "You don't spend much time with dead bodies, huh, Tsunga?"

"Not when I don't have to," answered the smaller detective.

"You didn't notice the wound at the scene?"

Tsunga was quiet as he stared at his feet, "It was the patrol that brought him in."

"You were not at the scene then?"

"No."

The two exited the morgue through the clinic. When they returned to the sun-soaked street of Karoi, Benhoff thought he had stepped into hell it was so hot. He tossed his gear in the front seat of the Jeep and turned to Tsunga to see the detective looking across the street. Ty noticed he was checking out an official looking black Mercedes.

"Nice ride." said Ty.

It seemed like Tsunga forgot he was there. He stuttered for a moment then nodded.

"So, I'm no expert but that wound in there is consistent with other bullet wounds I've seen before. It looked like a rifle shot, and from pretty close in. Got any ideas?"

"No." replied Tsunga. The man suddenly looked very tired. He still kept half his attention on the Mercedes parked next to a souvenir shop across a traffic circle that seemed to be the center of Karoi.

Ty took a map from under the visor on the passenger side of the Jeep and spread it out over the scorching hot hood. "Can you show me Allassa?"

Tsunga seemed reluctant. He pointed the small dot on the map next to a bend in the Angwe River, "Right here, why?"

"Gotta knock on some doors, figure out what happened to Mr. Cruz. Want to come?"

Tsunga shook his head, "No, I cannot, my work is here."

"Of course." Ty wondered if the sudden change in Tsunga's demeanor was because he made him hold a dead guy, or something else. He was wagering something else. "Any advice?"

"Do not go out there at night, Mista Benhoff."

"Why?"

"Lions."

Valid point, "Anything else you think I should know?"

Tsunga shrugged. "I don't know," he said, still half looking at the souvenir shop.

Ty pointed toward the souvenir shop and took a step that way, "I gotta pick some things up for my folks back home. This place have good prices?"

Tsunga's eyes widened, "Ye... I mean no. No, do not go there."

"Why not?"

Tsunga was all but reaching for Ty's arm before he reined himself in, "They gouge the tourist, Mista Benhoff. I do not want you taken advantage of."

"Sure." Benhoff rounded the hood of the Jeep and hopped in the driver's seat. "Like I said, you're the expert, Mister Tsunga. Thank you for looking out for me. If you need me, give me a call." Ty handed him a business card.

Tsunga read the card and nodded.

Ty offered his hand and Tsunga took it. They shook but before letting go, Benhoff asked, "You sure there's nothing else you want to tell me?"

"No, sir. If I hear anything more, I will call. You do the same?"

"Will do, Detective Tsunga. Thank you for your time, you've been real helpful."

Ty looked over the souvenir shop with the shiny Mercedes parked on the side as he drove off. Whatever button of Tsunga's he'd pushed, it was a big one. He wasn't sure if it was the gunshot wound or the damn car that caused all the trouble. He checked his watch and figured he only had about three hours of daylight left, and he'd be damned if he was eaten by a bunch of lions chasing leads in the wilds of Zimbabwe. Albieto Cruz could wait until morning. It was time to find a hotel and a drink.

CHAPTER THIRTEEN

Kali Earnst landed the first strike in a three-punch combination on a duct tape-wrapped heavy bag before pausing only a moment to check the caller ID on her phone. She finished her combination and followed up with a low kick and was just about to hit the asshole button on the side of her phone when she realized it would do her no good on this particular asshole.

"Heard you were in Zimbabwe. That still count as purgatory, or did you find a way out?"

"You're out of breath. Gym or…?" Ty Benhoff asked.

Kali grinned and looked over at a pair of active-duty sailors who were struggling to complete a set of respectable deadlifts, "You've been here, Ty, there is nothing smashable on this base."

"So, the gym then?"

"What do you want, Ty?"

"I need you to track some stuff down on my dead guy. Boulden was in such a rush to get me on a plane I didn't have time to do any background. It's getting harder and harder to work for people who have never worked cases before."

"Boulden's not a bad guy, Ty, he's just doing what he's told," Kali said, taking a drink of water.

"I know, but I can tell it gets to him when I fuck with him."

"And you wonder how you ended up in the ass end of Africa," Kali complained.

"No, I know how I got here," Ty replied.

"It was a shot heard round the world, but you haven't learned a thing from it. Now you're crashing my heart rate, what do you want so I can get back to my work out?"

"For starters, can you get me the basics? CLEOC, NCIC, TLO, my connection is kind of rough here. I think I can handle the social media bit. I might have some folks I need you to talk to later on."

"Send it through. I'll get on it after I get done here."

"Sure, priorities."

"Damn right. So, is this a real case or are you just documenting a dead guy?"

"Somebody shot him, so I got something, don't know what I'm going to be able to do with it here, but there's something."

Kali hissed, "Whoa, that's something all right. Why do I feel like there's an international incident in the offing?"

"No way! You should see me out here, real diplomatic so far."

"Uh huh, I'm out. Call you when I have something."

"Sure, and Kali?"

Earnst cringed 'cause she knew whatever Ty was going to say next would be anywhere from slightly embarrassing to bordering on harassment. "Yes, Ty?"

"Remember a one in week one is a ten in week ten, give the good people of Lemonnier a chance."

"You're a dick." Kali hung up before the rebuttal. Before going back to her workout, she did a scan of the Thunderdome, the affectionately named gym aboard Camp Lemonnier. She still wasn't impressed.

CHAPTER FOURTEEN

Thomas Boulden had just clicked off the lights in his Conex trailer when his agency issued phone chirped. It wasn't a loud chirp, or a disturbing chirp, it was barely more than a subtle hum, but it was enough to send his blood pressure skyrocketing. All special agents, investigators, and any law enforcement officer with an issued phone and a standing recall policy dreaded the moments when their phone rang. They always seemed to right before you were about to call it a night, or right before you were about to sit down to enjoy a game, or a kid's birthday party, etc. So when Boulden dismissed the urge to throw the iPhone across the tin can he lived in and checked the message, he found it was from Ty Benhoff. His pride in not destroying government-issued equipment was dampened as he found himself squeezing the electrons out of the tiny, life-sucking device.

There were a series of text messages from Special Agent Benhoff. The first was a photo of two scraps of paper, handwritten. The caption read, 'I got the case file'.

The second image showed a stick, a rusted bottle cap, and a DOD identification card bearing the likeness of Albieto Cruz, all of which were still nestled in a bacterium fermenting plastic bag. The caption read simply, 'collected evidence'.

The third message carried two images, one of a shirt with what looked like a bullet hole, the second showed a corresponding wound in Cruz's back. The caption read, 'gunshot wound'.

This message hurt Boulden's soul. Not so much because the message depicted a bad end for a member of the United States Navy but more that the sleep Boulden had planned on just became a distant memory. NCIS HQ would be open for business very soon and homicides were immediately categorized as Director's Special Interest. This meant there was paperwork and notifications to be made to the executives back in the States, and simple things like sleep were never an excuse to not file timely reports no one would ever read. Boulden sighed and swore as he rolled out of the single, twin-size, springy mattress. It whined like a transmission preparing to blow with every movement. He took a deep breath before looking at the last message Benhoff had sent. It was another photo, a tumbler full of ice and brown liquid in hand was the foreground. The background in the photo appeared to be legs covered in a hotel bathrobe with feet, crossed and resting on a railing overlooking an African sunset. The caption read, 'Off to a great start, have a good night.'

A distant, long-forgotten part of Supervisory Special Agent Thomas Boulden found the last message entertaining, and at one point in his career Boulden might have been tempted to send just such a sinister thing, if cell phones and text messaging had existed then. But that was a long time ago. Now, Boulden simply cursed Ty Benhoff under his breath, threw the phone down on the empty bed and grabbed his clothes.

CHAPTER FIFTEEN

Albieto Cruz's ID sat on the coffee table next to Benhoff's laptop.

"Now who are you, Mr. Cruz, and what the fuck were you doing in Zimbabwe?" Benhoff asked as he activated his system's VPN and opened the search engine.

The screen was blank as a small circle spun, and spun, and spun, until finally a giant 'Connection Lost' sign popped up on his screen.

Benhoff stared at the screen for a moment before taking a sip of the bitey bourbon, cool amongst the ice in his tumbler, before saying to no one in particular, "Never mind then."

He sat back in a brittle wooden chair and examined the town that laid out before him. It was quiet, and dark. The hotel he had found, the Karoi Grand, overlooked the traffic circle near the police station where he had met Detective Tsunga. He was surprised at the amount of foot traffic there was in what he had thought was a sleepy little town. Clearly not the case as at least half of the people wandering about were white. They moved mostly in groups of three or four, Ty figured they were tourists given the amount of wildlife tours that were advertised in the hotel lobby. He noticed a bar a block over from the station he hadn't recognized before. There was some kind of music drifting from the area, but Ty couldn't make any sense of it. Could have been Britney Spears, could have been some Tutsi war chant, he didn't know. He thought about heading for the watering hole. His mind was spinning with all the information gaps and questions he had in the sudden homicide that had dropped in his lap. A lot of answers were sitting right there behind the screen of his laptop, he just needed a signal. It was going to drive him crazy. Starting a new case always did. Open-ended holes in timelines, details about people, their connections to witnesses or subjects, what their last meal was. All of that was needed to figure out who Albieto Cruz was, and why he was here. Who was he with? Benhoff took another slug of the brown liquid and watched a couple of cars, diesels by the sound of them, course their way through the traffic circle.

It was going to be a long night.

CHAPTER SIXTEEN

On the street outside the Karoi Grand, Fannel stood in the shadowed alcove of an empty store front. From the middle of the darkness, he stared intently at the lone occupied balcony where the dim glow of a laptop illuminated his task. His name was Benhoff, a name that meant nothing to him. The man's face was obscured by the iron balustrade surrounding the terrace, but he knew it was the American. Fannel had sources of information everywhere, especially the hotel.

Before locating the American, he had found Detective Tsunga. Called him at his desk and ordered a meet. The detective knew exactly what Fannel was calling on him for and provided the American's business card, then told him everything the two had spoken about. He had no doubt of the policeman's veracity in his details of the meeting with the American Navy special agent. There was no one that held information back from Fannel when he asked. To do so not only meant grave repercussions to themselves and their family, but it also meant the wraith of the Thoomba brothers. To wrong the Thoomba family meant ruin, if not in the physical then the economic sense. Gerald Thoomba controlled much in this part of Zimbabwe; all knew not to cross him. Detective Tsunga had two children, boys, and a wife that he cared deeply for. The mere mention of this in one of their first meetings made him incredibly malleable to Fannel's wishes and in turn the detective had become a trusted source. Tsunga had readily provided every detail to Fannel, including the American's assertion that the Navy man killed by that fool Muupha was indeed a murder. That fact had been easily covered up by Tsunga before the American arrived.

Now, as Fannel watched the American through the glow of his computer, he wondered to what lengths Obert would allow him to go in dealing with his quarry. There were many things Fannel could do to alleviate them of the American's attention. Each one Fannel could imagine was more satisfying than the last. He had a long history with Americans, going back to his boyhood in Somalia. In fact, he had sought out Americans in every location they came to to meddle with their weapons and their soldiers. From Iraq, to Syria, before that Afghanistan. Fannel, not a believer himself, had readily taken the mantle of whatever zealots that was required if it meant fighting Americans, and he had been successful. He prided himself in the fourteen lives he had taken.

Here, with this American, alone, without the technology or the numbers that made them so dangerous, Fannel reveled in the fact he might, just might have an opportunity he had never had before. The opportunity to really make an American pay for the wrongs against his family, and his people. Fannel was like a statue, his features a blank canvas as he watched his quarry. It would indeed be hard to let such an opportunity pass. He was determined to see to it Obert Thoomba recognized the danger the American posed so Fannel would be free to deal with the American in whatever way he saw fit.

CHAPTER SEVENTEEN

The village of Allassa was a little over an hour's drive from Karoi. Benhoff took off from the hotel just as the sun was coming up so that he could get as much done as possible before the temperature rose to be on par with the surface of Venus. He still wasn't quite sure how he managed to spot the narrow dirt road that broke off from the main highway to find the tiny little speck on the map when he rolled to a stop near a line of simple wood docks. A lot of slips were empty with a handful of carved out wooden jon boats rocking gently against their moorings. Ty stepped from the Jeep and looked around. To call the place a village was a stretch. He counted maybe a dozen real, mud structures. A handful more haphazardly built tin shacks were spread out here and there. Goats circulated around the buildings, chewing on whatever they could find. People were scarcer than the goats. Benhoff figured most were out on the river working. Those that were around paid the American in the expensive new Jeep no mind at all. He found that a little disconcerting.

He grabbed his shoulder pack and slung his camera over his shoulder before wandering down toward the docks. He had no photos of where Cruz's body was found, nor did he have any statements from witnesses. In fact, when he had time the night before to really look at the 'file' Tsunga had provided him, he saw that one 'report' was a receipt, too faded to figure out what was paid for on one side and 'Albieto Cruz, Allassa' scribbled on the other. The other 'report' had the date from three days ago and the time, which he guessed was when the body was found, or maybe when it was taken to Karoi? Could have been the date and time they stopped for lunch on the way to the scene for all Benhoff knew. In one sense he enjoyed the absolute vacuum of information he was working in, the possibilities of what was actually going on in the wilds of Zimbabwe and what it had to do with Cruz were endless. That was entertaining to think about. On the other, the absolute mountain of paperwork, endless, pointless questions from NCIS leadership, most of whom had never worked a homicide, much less had any experience working internationally, was like a landfill of future time wasted, and patience lost ever growing, and growing, and growing just over his shoulder. He did take solace in the silence of his duty phone. He had sent one text to Kali this morning before taking off from the hotel. It read: 'The internet blows here; can you help me out with some open-source searches? Thanks, BTW, meet anyone nice last night?' Then he turned the iPhone off just as the first call from Boulden came in.

It felt good to leave what by now was sure to be the majority of senior leadership at NCIS HQ in a panic over the homicide in Zimbabwe, none more than Assistant Director for Global Operations Douglas McClintock. That prick was the main reason why he was serving time in NCIS purgatory. McClintock was the type that liked to yell when things didn't go his way. Benhoff wondered if he'd gotten to Boulden yet, but mentally shrugged and lined up an overall shot of the small marina and the area surrounding the river--the Angwe River, Ty reminded himself. He snapped a couple of photos in quick succession. When he looked at his viewfinder to check his work, he noticed a small figure standing near one of the slips. Great observation skills there, bud. The boy was still standing near the slip. Ty offered him a little wave, but the boy just stared at him. Ty let the camera fall on its sling and took a couple of tentative steps toward him.

"Hi," he said, "English?"

The boy didn't respond.

Ty looked around to see if there was a parent or an adult of some kind to talk to. He spotted a man working on a net three boats down, but the guy didn't even seem to notice he was there. Ty took a step toward the kid, hoping he wouldn't run. He pulled Cruz's ID from the pocket of his cargo pants and held it up, "Recognize this man?"

The kid didn't take off, but he wasn't saying shit either.

Ty looked in his bag. He found a pack of M&Ms of an indeterminant age, and a pack of cigarettes, Camels, of the same vintage. He didn't smoke but always kept a pack on him. Despite the guilt flood in the United States, the rest of the world loved to smoke. He thought about the two options for a moment and thought, *I'm not the kid's dad.* He held out both the candy and the smokes.

The kid studied the two for a moment then took both offerings.

Ty smiled. "Ty," he said, pointing at himself.

"Andrew," the kid said as he tapped the pack on the palm of his hand.

"Nice to meet you. Did you see the body that washed up here a couple days ago?"

Andrew had an unlit cigarette hanging from his lips in what Ty couldn't help but see as an homage to Andrew Dice Clay. He held his hands out expectantly.

"Right, shit." Ty searched his bag and came up with a Bic lighter, then looked around sheepishly for a moment. He thought the kid expected him to light the cigarette for him. Whatever the social norms of rural Zimbabwe were, Ty couldn't bring himself to go that far. He handed the lighter over and the kid flicked the flame on and lit the cigarette like a twenty-year smoker. He then put the pack and lighter in his shirt pocket. Andrew wore baggy, frayed, gray shorts and a similarly baggy blue flannel that had a rip down the left arm.

"How old are you, Andrew?"

"Eighteen." The kid lifted his chin and bowed up a little for emphasis.

Sure. "Good," Ty said.

"So, what happened with the dead body the other day?"

"It wash up over der'. It was eaten a little but not too bad. Police come and take it away."

Ty gestured toward where Andrew pointed, "Right over there, huh? Did you find it?"

"Nah, it was de old men who fish that found it. They out in de riveh now."

"Anybody say what happened to him?"

"He wash down from up riveh, probably drown."

"He was shot in the back."

Andrew shrugged and took a pull on the smoke.

"He was an American, I'm supposed to find out what happened to him. You see him before he washed up?"

"No, never seen him before."

"No? Where do you think he came from upriver?"

Andrew shrugged again, "No place up there but grass and trees." The boy fished in his shirt pocket for a fresh butt and used the still burning cigarette to light the next. When he went to put the pack back, Ty noticed a greenish-blue phone case peeking out of the pocket for just a moment.

"I like your phone," he said, gesturing to the boy's pocket.

Andrew bowed up, "It's mine."

"Can I see it?"

Andrew eyed him suspiciously before showing him. Ty recognized the Miami Dolphins logo on the back of the phone case. It was a newer iPhone.

"That come from the dead man?"

Andrew shook his head.

Ty fished out his wallet and held up a hundred-dollar bill.

Andrew held up two fingers.

Fuckin' snake. He pulled out a fifty and held both bills up.

Andrew tried to eye his wallet again. He must've figured he'd gotten over on the American enough. He grabbed the money first before handing over the phone.

"This came from the man."

"I found it."

"Where?"

"Up de riveh a way."

"Show me."

CHAPTER EIGHTEEN

Ty regretted telling the kid to show him almost immediately. It had to be over a hundred degrees in the open flats of the village. That unbridled sun made you feel like a worm dancing on a frying pan. When the kid ducked down a narrow path into the forest of high-topped trees and chest-high grasses, the ambiance turned to more of an oven than an open stove. There was a thick humidity inside the canopy that didn't exist on the outside. Andrew skipped and jogged down the path on his thong-sandaled feet, shorts, and flannel, while Ty's ripstop cargo pants felt like wet blankets covering his legs, and his lightweight hiking boots felt like they were full of cement. He caught the unimpressed looks from Andrew whenever he would peek back to make sure he was still coming. Ty swore to himself he would see himself dead before the kid smoking cigarettes on the run beat him. Then he prayed that the place Andrew was leading him to was really close.

They must've hiked for almost an hour. A water bottle Ty had stashed in a side pocket of his pack was almost empty, and the ballcap he'd put on to keep the sweat out of his eyes was drenched to the point rivulets of salty fluid were streaming down his face. Andrew had given up on jogging the whole way. Ty told himself that it was because the kid had tired and not the other way around. He was shuffling ahead, kicking twigs from the slender trail and batting at errant stalks of high brittle grass when he suddenly stopped and looked around.

The trail had snaked through the forest, sometimes right along the Angwe River while at other times diving back into the forest. There was no rhyme or reason Ty could see for the deviations, but he also realized this was not his continent, so he didn't question the intentions of whoever it was who had cut the path, whenever that was. Andrew stopped at a tree that leaned haphazardly over the running water. He hung off the narrow trunk over the water. All Ty could think about was the crocodile that was about to burst from the water and eat him like an hors d'oeuvre.

"This is where you found this?" he asked.

Andrew swung from the tree and pointed below toward the water. "It was in de mud der."

"In the water?"

Andrew shook his head.

"How'd you find it?"

"Fishing with my uncle. I have him bring de boat in. I grab it."

"Good eye, my friend." He studied the area for a moment before noticing Andrew creeping his way back down the trail toward Allassa. He nodded his head in the direction of the trail that moved back into the forest. "What's that way?" he asked.

Andrew shrugged, "More trees."

"Uh-huh."

"And elephants."

Ty looked at him.

"And lions."

Ty rubbed the sweat on his forehead.

"And jackals."

Ty looked back down the trail.

"And snakes."

Ty felt his heart skip a beat. He gauged the potential lead against the fact no one back in the world would know if he followed the path or not....

Finally, Benhoff pointed down the trail, "You comin'?"

"No," Andrew scoffed. "I go fishing."

"Seriously?"

"You will probably get eaten, you know dis, yeah?"

Shit... Ty went to catch up with Andrew before he got too far.

The kid had a shit-eating-grin on his face. Ty held up a twenty, "Nothing happens to my Jeep while I'm gone, got it?"

Andrew held up two fingers, and his smile broadened.

"You're an extortionist." Ty slapped forty bucks in his hand.

"You are part of de food chain," Andrew chided before bursting into a jog back down the trail.

Ty patted the Glock on his side before taking another swig of his dwindling water supply, "Let's hope not."

CHAPTER NINETEEN

Obert Thoomba looked at the topological map laid out before him with a grimace. The map was of the sanctuaries and parks around West Mashaland, the countryside he grew up in. A place where he knew every speck of red dirt, every thorny acacia tree and shrub. His family still had their farm on the far side of Karoi, an expansive spread where his hands raised cattle and pigs, and goats, as well as some big cats and cape buffalo for trophy hunters from the West to shoot and feel powerful. Regardless, the map before him had him perplexed. How such a simple thing, a thing he knew backwards and forwards, could stump him left him dumbstruck.

Next to the map were notes and times his men had collected over the past weeks. He knew when the rangers of Phundundu reported for duty. When and for the most part where they patrolled, though the where was one of those things that puzzled him and was too important a detail to ignore. He knew on average how many people the station had and what kind of resources they could muster. He knew a lot but somehow it did not help him. He had drawn a giant X over the spot on the map where the ranger station sat. Surrounding that mark on the map were two concentric circles, one larger than the other. The diameter of those circles represented distance from the station, providing Obert with a gauge for response times related to an idea he had percolating in his mind. It was an extreme thought, though, a massive departure from his normal handling of the ranger force. It was always easier, and less expensive, to operate outside the vision of the wildlife forces. Better to pass on one opportunity with an eye toward patience and longevity. There was always another hunt, another herd, another opportunity. And the rangers could not be everywhere at once.

But these were extreme times. Obert sighed as he considered his fortune in the lucky happenstance, he was not at the warehouse when the rangers and the Regional Police came. Only Kamalla, Muupha's brother, had been present, keeping watch on Obert's very valuable collection of ivory when they'd come. Kamalla went against orders when he attempted to fight them. He was told to flee or to give up and keep his mouth shut. Instead, they shot him down like a dog, and they seized Obert's ivory. The largest take he had ever known, his future as a wealthier man gone in mere moments. And that one decision by a stupid rural boy begat another stupid decision by a rural boy which left three men dead, and an American policeman stumbling around the Mashaland. But that was another problem for another day.

Obert reeled himself back in from his daze. The stress was taking its toll, and he was tired. But he was also on the clock. Neither he nor Gerald had very long before their friends from the East came looking for recompense, and they were not the type to accept wringing hands and excuses. Re-gathering his focus, Obert looked again at the map. Extremes, it was not his nature to go to extremes. However, as he studied the information before him, it seemed the extreme was his only path to survival.

CHAPTER TWENTY

"This was so dumb," Benhoff told himself as he looked back down the tiny game trail.

It had been only a half hour or so since he'd left Andrew at the river. Part of him found it funny that he'd spent almost two hundred dollars to get there, which was nowhere. He swept the area with his eyes while part of him mused about the expression Boulden would make when Ty put in a voucher for the money. "Director's Special Interest," he muttered while scanning the ground both looking for signs that his victim passed through there, and for freaking snakes. If only he hadn't snoozed during that block during the Criminal Investigator Training Program at FLETC where they taught them how to cut signs in the African bush. *Oh, that's right,* he reminded himself, *the Navajos had called in sick that day.*

The trail took him in a relatively straight line from the riverbank into a patch of trees that poked over the grass like columns holding up a dense cavity of green-brown leaves. It was not very long that his trek took him to a rutted, single-track road colored in that rust red dirt you could only seem to find in Africa. He paused at the road and immediately noticed he'd left the oven once again for the frying pan. The sun was brutal, and he suddenly yearned to be back in the baking humidity of the forest. He took a small drink of his diminishing water supply and studied the road before him, noting a crusty tread pattern in the red dirt. At least someone has been through here, he told himself. As far as who, when, or if they had anything to do with his case, there was no way to tell. It did make Ty feel better, though, to know someone might find his body when he finally succumbed to heat stroke.

He wiped his brow and wrung out his sopping ballcap as he looked each way up and down the dirt road. To his right something in the dirt ahead caught his eye. It reflected the burning sunlight then intermittently disappeared if he shifted his eyes just so.

"I've come this far," he told himself.

The mysterious item was near a bend in the road only thirty yards or so from where he'd left the forest. He wandered slowly up the road, watching the faded tire tracks as he went until finally, he came upon a shard of mirror sitting half covered in the rusty dirt. Sherlock, you are not, was his first thought. He backed off the mirror and took a wider view. There was more on the ground. Diced glass from a vehicle window, and he found a couple of chips of green paint. Ty started taking pictures of the general area. There were tracks, skid marks from tires that had come up the road. A vehicle had veered off the road into the grass. He found red taillight plastic as he followed the tracks. Something had hit a tree; he noted a patch of bare wood about bumper height where the thin light bark had been scraped off. Ty started to get a bad feeling when he noticed a couple of pock marks in the tree. Fresh divots in the wood where it had taken a hit. Ty took some photos before prying at one of the divots with his Benchmade folder. He didn't have to dig very far in the soft wood before the fragmented remains of a copper jacket and a fair chunk of lead fell out into his hand.

"Shit," he breathed. He held the mangled round up to the light of the sun and examined it. He wasn't enough of an expert to know what kind of round it had once been, but he had been around long enough to know he needed a crime scene unit out here. He studied the flattened and chipped piece of lead that kind of resembled a broken metal mushroom when he noticed movement in the background, big movement. He shifted his focus from the bullet fragment to a grey giant standing not twenty yards away. A bull elephant with tusks as tall as his own six-foot frame stared at him. Its ears waved slowly in the heat; the snout of its trunk curled in his direction as was all of the massive animal's focus. "Oh shit," Ty Benhoff found himself in a staring contest with an animal the size of his garage back home in Virginia.

"Do not move," the low voice was not much more than a whisper.

The bull snorted and pawed at the red dirt with its front leg.

"He's trying to decide whether or not you are a threat."

"Whoever you are...."

"He's trying to decide whether you live or die. Do not move, do not talk, and whatever you do, do not look away."

"Yup." For reasons Ty could not explain, he found himself raising his hands as if the animal was robbing him.

"I said do not move." The voice was female, and persistent.

The elephant called in a boisterous trumpeting sound and stomped his foot again. Benhoff realized he was shaking, or was that his heart racing? He couldn't tell over the blood rushing in his ears. Then slowly, with an unfathomable silence, several other elephants materialized out of the bush, almost a dozen, to cross the narrow road before disappearing back into the brush. Excruciating moments later, the big bull finally made his decision not to kill Tyrone Benhoff. With a final snort and a wave of the trunk Benhoff interpreted as the elephant version of giving him the finger, the big bull followed his herd into the wild.

Ty let out a long, exhausted breath and muttered, "Holy shit."

"What are you doing here, American?"

Ty's heart leaped for all its worth to reach his throat. That's right, mysterious stranger on my six. He turned to see a very petite woman with dark skin and striking facial features. She stood before him wearing green fatigues and a matching boonie hat. The pack on her back was so big it looked like could double as a tent for her small frame. She also carried an M-16.

"I asked what you are doing here."

Ty again fought the urge to raise his hands, instead he tried humor, "I could ask you the same thing."

"I am with them," she nodded toward the vanished pack of elephants, then bounced the muzzle of the rifle from the ground toward his feet. "Answer my question."

Ty moved slowly, "I'm reaching for my identification, okay?" He pulled his creds and showed her his badge, "I'm a special agent for the American Navy."

She snatched his badge from him, "Navy? There is no ocean here."

"Yes, I know. I promise I'm not lost," *for the most part.* "Can I ask who you are?"

"After you answer what you are doing here," she said, still holding his credentials.

"I'm trying to figure out what happened." He reached again slowly into his pocket, "to this man." he held up Cruz's Navy ID. Her eyes flashed.

"I do not know him." she said bluntly.

Liar.

"You need to go; this is not a safe place." she handed him back his creds.

"I'm...."

"If you are still here after dark, you will be eaten."

Ty looked back at his possible crime scene for a moment. When he turned to ask the woman with the rifle where he was, she was gone just as quickly and quietly as the elephants.

"Why does everybody think I'm going to get eaten?"

CHAPTER TWENTY-ONE

Thomas Boulden felt his head spin when the iPhone he'd been staring at for an hour finally rang. He wondered for a moment if he were in the early stages of a brain aneurism when the static-tempered voice of Tyrone Benhoff tried to speak.

"Where the fuck have you been?" Boulden's voice was like that of a wild animal.

There was a pause and for a moment he thought the connection had been cut, "I was hot on the case, sir. Why, something wrong?"

"You know how…?" Boulden started pacing knowing that anything he said next would be turned back around on him by the son of a bitch in the field, and there was nothing he could do about it. Benhoff was the one person in the world that could get a swarm of empty-suited desk officers, strap hangers, sycophants, and even a goddamned intern at the Russell Knox Building in Quantico, Virginia to leave him the fuck alone. "Where you been, Ty?" For a moment there Boulden felt a sense of pride in his self-control.

"Been a long day, SSA Boulden?"

Boulden saw white and thought he might have lost consciousness for an instant before reality once again materialized before him.

"You have a report for me, Ty?" he groaned.

"Welp, I'm going to need a voucher for 190 bucks, but I recovered Cruz's phone from nearby where his body was discovered." Silence greeted that statement. Ty wondered if Boulden was still simmering or starting to listen, "During that same search I found a location where gunfire was exchanged. A vehicle was involved but was no longer there and the location was almost directly in line with where the kid found the phone."

"The kid?"

"Local kid."

"You gave a local kid three hundred dollars?"

And a pack of smokes, but Ty figured Boulden didn't need to know that. "Two hundred, turned out to be a good investment." Ty heard a sigh. "Look, the clock ran out on me so I grabbed what I could and marked the area. I'm hoping I can find it tomorrow. It's a decent size scene, to do it justice it'll take more than just one person."

"You left a crime scene unsecured?"

There it was, that bit of information Boulden had been waiting for. Ty made a mental note to expect a hearing on this when he got back to Djibouti. "It was getting dark, so I had to get back to civilization. You can't imagine the number of people who told me I was going to get eaten today." Of course, it was only two people, but then again, how many people need to tell you you're going to be eaten by wild animals before you listen to them? "I figured the locals were probably more educated about the local fauna than I was."

Another sigh, "Anything else?"

"Yeah, more people, and a digital forensics expert. Cruz's phone sat in the river for a bit, it's going to need some care."

"You're not getting any more people."

"Then you're nickel and diming the murder of a US Navy Sailor."

"It came from on high, not my call," Boulden's inflection told him they were not far apart on that particular point.

"Where on high?"

"You know where. And you know that means you need to watch your back."

"I knew you cared about me." AD McClintock was always waiting to pounce. Ty wondered for a moment where things stood on that end. He reminded himself to make a call when all this shit was over.

"I just don't want to be in your wake when the toilet bowl gets flushed, Benhoff."

"That's a pretty good one," Ty muttered.

"What was that?" The SSA's question included a practiced edge.

"When's the body being shipped out?" Fuckin' tool.

"Still working on it, hopefully sending somebody down to get it tomorrow."

"Seems like a distinct lack of haste for a DSI case there, boss. Not to mention remains of a US service member."

"That seems like an undue amount of investment from the guy who was pissed about being sent to Zimbabwe."

"I was pissed because you robbed me of a few precious moments with a German supermodel. Zimbabwe is actually pretty cool once you come to terms with the fact things here want to eat you."

"Things in Quantico want to eat you, too, Agent. Remember that. Keep your phone on tomorrow, out." Boulden hung up on him.

"Sure," Ty told the dead line.

CHAPTER TWENTY-TWO

"Where have you been?" Kali demanded.

"I've been on safari all day. What's up?"

"I swear Boulden, the desk officer at RKB, and half the executive staff have been taking turns suffering micro-strokes all day."

"Transient ischemic attack."

"What?"

"Transient ischemic attack, TIA, that's what mini-strokes are."

"Oh my gooodddd."

"I knew that would piss you off."

"I didn't need that to get pissed off at you. Boulden almost paced the building into collapse today."

Benhoff giggled, "Yeah, I actually didn't mean to do that. I was only going to leave my phone off for a couple of hours but then one thing led to another. Saving grace is that there was no service where I ended up anyway, holy shit, tell you about my day later. What've you got?"

"Well, Mr. Cruz worked at the PAO, Public Affairs Office, for the past year."

"He had to be close to shipping out."

"That's affirm, he had a month and a half left."

"He in purgatory, too? Usually, the tour is only six months."

"Nope, I went over there today. He voluntarily extended his rotation."

"There's a big why there."

"Only thing his commanding officer would say is Cruz liked Africa."

"Fair enough, what else?"

"Typical, everyone loved the guy. Never had any trouble, no NCIC, not even as a juvenile, nothing in the Navy's Consolidated Law Enforcement Operations Center Database, TLO, even his financials were clear, he even had a good credit score."

"That's it?"

"For now it is. I'm still digging through his social media. He was one of those guys that selfied his food, selfied waking up in the morning, selfied the sunrise, sunset, and pretty much every fucking thing in between. That's why I'm pissed at you. I'm not even through 2019 yet and I was at this shit all day."

"All day besides the gym."

"Priorities, baby."

"I get it."

"Not sure you do."

"Did the work interviews turn up anything else?"

"A buddy in the PAO mentioned he played pool with a couple of guys from supply. I'm going to head over there in the morning. Did you do anything productive today? Besides bring the wrath of NCIS HQ down on all of AFRICOM?"

"I would consider that a great accomplishment if it were true, but kind of. I found a phone I'm pretty sure belongs to Cruz. Some kid in Allassa had it."

"Allassa, Zimbabwe?"

"When I say it's a little fishing village in rural Zimbabwe, I'm speaking literally. I'm really getting to see the world this week. Anyway, the kid showed me where he found it sitting on a riverbank after a scorching trek through the freakin' bush. Using my brilliant detective skills, I then located a possible crime scene, potentially related to my ongoing homicide investigation."

"Take that, Sherlock."

"Exactly, Watson."

"So, I found this spot on a dirt road where I found broken mirror fragments, taillights, a little paint, 7x62 casings, and some lead buried in the trees."

"Almost sounds like you found a real case. They sending us out there?"

"Not a real enough case for this particular DSI."

"You're shitting me."

"Fraid not."

"They made four agents surge against a recruiter's office in San Diego last week because a girl told a friend her recruiter tried to kiss her. Tried! Didn't even finish the move! The victim even asked a friend of mine why NCIS was making such a big deal out of it."

"That's funny," said Benhoff.

"Someday you've got to tell me what the real reason is McClintock hates you so much."

"All in due time, Watson."

"Not your fucking Watson."

"Sure you are."

"Keep your phone on tomorrow, 'kay?" Kali hung up.

Ty tossed the phone on the bed in his hotel room. "No promises," he said.

CHAPTER TWENTY-THREE

Victoria Jurness leaned against a tree, turning a small pebble over in her slender fingers, near the hut that housed the staff therapist. All of the members of the entirely female ranger troop, each of them a victim of rape, or domestic violence, or some form of assault, were required to see Dr. Bhetto at least once a month when she came in from Harare. Tonight, Lilliana Cartwell was in session. It was her third time visiting the doctor and Victoria wanted to be there when the session ended. From time to time throughout the last forty-five minutes or so that she had been standing in the shadows she'd heard muffled sobs escaping from the thin walls of the hut, but they had barely registered. Victoria had been elsewhere.

"Becoming one with the night?"

The voice was quiet, and so close it had startled her. She did her best to hide it the same way she tried her best to hide the silent tears streaking her dark cheeks. She doubted she fooled Lead Ranger Maynard one bit.

"Do you need me, sir?" she asked.

Maynard emerged silently from his own slice of darkness to stand beside her. "Just want to be here for Lilliana," he said, "and I wanted to check up on you."

"I'm one hundred percent, sir," Victoria announced.

"I have no doubt of that, Victoria." He had his hands in the pockets of his green BDUs in the casual manner he always seemed to carry. Even in the worst of times the man approached every moment with an innate calm that was almost supernatural in her opinion. "But as strong as you are, you have had a bear of a few weeks. You need to recognize that. You need to process that."

Victoria felt tears welling again and felt shame grow with the tide, "I have, sir."

"I'm not sure which is harder, the loss of someone important or the taking of another life. You have experienced both in a very short period. Just know that we are all one here, we are all with you. If you need some time to deal with either, you need to take it. No one will think less of you."

It was nothing he hadn't told her before. But Victoria Jurness could not think of anything she could possibly do other than her job. The idea of leaving the camp, or leaving the wilderness, was a very alien thing anymore. "I am good, sir," she stated, looking him in the eye. Even in the darkness his eyes glinted, capturing even the smallest amount of light.

"Okay."

The door to the hut opened. Maynard put a hand on Victoria's shoulder and gave a gentle squeeze before he turned and disappeared into the night. Lilliana stepped from the light of the therapist's office. She dabbed at her eyes for a few moments before noticing Victoria standing at the foot of the stairs. Lilliana acknowledged her with a small nod of the head and sniffed to clear her nose.

"Are those tears for you or for them?" Victoria asked.

Lilliana looked at her with a confused expression and sat down on the stairs.

"I do not know."

Victoria placed a boot on the first stair and looked for a long moment toward the therapist's office.

"Whatever you left in that life needs to be cut out of you. That is what this is for. It is hard, but it will make you stronger."

Victoria studied her own hands for a moment then she said, "Get some sleep, tomorrow we go, just the two of us, first light."

Lilliana nodded and looked at Victoria with suddenly clear eyes, "Thank you." This would be her first official patrol with the rangers.

"Don't thank me," Victoria said. "This will be no picnic."

CHAPTER TWENTY-FOUR

Ty made it back to Allassa and with a map and the general orientation of the Angwe River somehow managed to find the scene he'd located the day before. Given that he had only as much evidence collection supplies as could fit in his backpack, he had nowhere near enough bags to package everything individually. It killed the crime scene nerd hiding inside him to do it but the potential evidence in the road was marked on a hand drawn sketch, a few photos were taken, and the casings and plastic went into a couple different paper bags. He did find a few tannish paint chips he hoped might have been from a car and some fractured side window glass. He had asked Kali, before he lost signal on the drive out, to try and tie a car to Albieto Cruz if it became a thing. Ty knew he was looking for a green-ish vehicle with blown outdoor windows, taillights, rearview mirrors, and at least one defect to the body. Seemed easy enough. That was of course assuming all the stuff he was picking up was actually part of a crime scene. He did a couple of sweeps and searched as best he could along the road and in the brush, though Ty would admit to anyone that most of his attention was on the lookout for snakes, lions, werewolves, spiders, and anything else his mind played tricks on him with. Every brush of the tall grass, and every flutter of a leaf had Benhoff wondering if he would turn around just in time to see the foot of that bull elephant smashing him to paste. He still couldn't believe how quiet that thing had been. When he figured he'd gotten as much as he was going to find, he turned again to the bullet defects he'd found in the trees. He took some pictures and even managed to get a scale in the frame this time to keep the uproar from headquarters' forensic consultants down to a minimum once they finally got around to Monday morning quarterbacking his work. He had followed the path of three trees and found himself getting deeper and deeper into the woods when he suddenly felt like he was standing at the edge of a rabbit hole.

"Shit," he breathed, looking back at the Jeep, and air conditioning, and his only ticket back to civilization. He took a swig of water, then returned to the Jeep where he grabbed two more bottles of water and the last couple evidence bags he had. He stuffed them all in his backpack and sighed when a little voice in his head mentioned that no one would ever know if he called it right there. Air conditioning, lunch, the pool at the hotel called to him like a modern amenity siren's song.

Nope, he decided. As much as he hated to admit it, he was out there, and would stay out there for one person: Albieto Cruz's mom. In life before NCIS, he'd been the one to make death notifications. Just the unlucky cop who pulled the call for a traffic accident, or a shooting, anything could happen in patrol. There was no way to ever normalize the experience of telling a parent or a spouse that their child or their wife was not coming home. Ty had had to do that twice when he was a street cop, and each time he'd been the one to hold a mother's hand while she cried. He knew that if he ever was asked to speak to Cruz's next of kin about the case, he couldn't do so without being able to tell her he did everything he could. Even if it meant getting eaten by a lion. That sudden thought gave him pause. He stepped around to the passenger side of the SUV and grabbed the MK-18 that he had wedged between the passenger seat and the center console. He then grabbed two extra magazines of the finest 5x56 ammunition the US Navy could provide and started his trek through the Zimbabwe hinterlands, feeling just a smidgeon better about his chances.

It was like following breadcrumbs, if the bread was made from little nuggets of copper and lead. He could see in his mind's eye Albieto Cruz's last moments. From the look of things, it was only sheer luck that he made it out of the truck at all. Ty could see him running for his life in the dark while who knows how many people fired on him as if they were hunting him for sport. As the distance grew from the ambush site, or the 'X' as he was trained, Ty found himself getting angry. The scene on the dirt road looked like maybe a robbery? If he were in the States his first instinct would be gang shooting. Whoever had done it had laid into the vehicle, they seemed to get all the windows and lights, and had peppered the body of the vehicle, if the paint chips were to be trusted. That was one of the reasons Ty had it in his head that there was more than one shooter. What pissed him off was the chase. He could see Albieto sprinting and stumbling around these trees as his pursuers blasted at him with their rifles. He could feel Cruz's fear, his confusion, that final realization once they shot him that he wasn't going home. A robbery in the middle of the night was one thing. It was rural Africa, this kind of thing happened, and it could be chalked up to bad luck. But to pursue Cruz into the trees instead of just taking the vehicle and whatever valuables might be in there seemed personal… almost bloodthirsty. Benhoff hoped he got to meet the sons of bitches who killed Albieto Cruz someday. Not that there was much he could do about it unless NCIS suddenly got a very broad increase in jurisdiction.

Eventually a sort of path through the trees emerged and even when the rounds stopped showing in the trees, a dark brownish-red swipe on one of the light-colored trunks kept his curiosity. He took a couple of photos, one with a scale, then he wet a swab and gathered some of the stain. He opened a blood reagent test kit and dropped a single drop of chemical on the swab. If the swab turned green, then the sample contained blood. When it turned green Ty suddenly forgot all about the one hundred plus degrees and the sweat soaking through his clothes. He even forgot about snakes and lions for a moment.

"Take that, Sherlock," he whispered to himself.

"What are you doing?"

The unexpected voice made him jump like a deer after a rifle shot. He dropped the swab and swept up his rifle while spinning into a crouch. He found himself promptly staring down the barrel of a rifle. He followed the muzzle of the weapon up to the rear sights and a wide eye focused on him. The girl... woman, if she was over twenty years old, it wasn't by much was dressed all in green BDUs. The two stared at each other, fingers poised on their respective triggers. It wasn't until a hand came from the side and lowered the muzzle of the rifle that he noticed the other woman standing next to her.

"Now there are two of you," Ty said, recognizing the other woman from the day before. "Taking the elephants for a walk again today?" he asked, only lowering his weapon slightly.

"You were warned it is not safe here."

"I'm beginning to notice." Ty slowly let his rifle rest against his chest and nodded to the weapon that was only moments ago pointed at his head, "Good news is I haven't been eaten yet."

"You need to leave."

"I'm working. You are in my crime scene."

She looked at the ground and trees around them. The younger one looked at her obvious superior briefly, seeming unsure what to do.

"Who are you two anyway? You're not cops," Ty said, kicking at the swab he'd dropped on the ground. The tip he'd gathered the stain on was a deep green blue. He looked at the rest of the stain.

"We are rangers, anti-poaching."

"That's awesome," Ty said, letting shine his inner tree hugger. "You guys all women?"

"We are not guys, and yes. We are part of the International Counter-Poaching Federation."

Ty searched his memory, swearing he'd heard that before, but he was coming up dry. "This is your beat then?" he asked.

The woman looked at him quizzically.

"This is your area?" he asked.

"Yes, we protect the herds inside the preserves."

"You want to give me a name this time? You know me, I don't know either of you, though we have met twice now under the oddest of circumstances."

"I am Sergeant Victoria Jurness." said the woman he'd met with the elephants. "This is Ranger Lilliana Cartwell." the younger woman only nodded toward him.

"So you are cops, Sergeant." he offered his hand. Victoria was hesitant to take it and he was suddenly reminded of a time he'd almost caused an international incident by shaking a woman's hand in Iraq. It was a point of pride Benhoff kept. Victoria shook his hand, her grip like a vice. Lilliana did the same. Hers was softer, unsure. Ty felt for her, being a rookie wasn't easy.

"Nice to meet the two of you."

"You need to go," Victoria insisted.

"Maybe, but first I want to know if either of you know anything about gunfire starting at the road where my Jeep is and extending through here? I've dug rounds out of trees in a line this way and I just found this," he pointed at the stain on the tree trunk.

"What is this?" Victoria asked, unimpressed.

"Blood," Ty said. "Human blood. I think someone was chased through here, hunted actually. Any ideas?"

Victoria looked like she was having to swallow something from deep inside. Lilliana watched her boss, still looking like she wanted someone to tell her what to do. Ty examined the women's rifles and noted they were M16 variants of some kind, chambered for 5.56. This didn't match the casings he'd found near the road. The ever-suspicious side of his mind whispered suspects based on Jurness's reluctance to tell him whatever she seemed to be choking on. But his gut had doubts. It was an odd feeling regardless, being outnumbered two to one. They had more guns and, oh yeah, they've already gotten the drop on you twice, hero. Ty Benhoff was used to treading on thin ice, but even he had to admit shit was thin at the moment. A silence grew among the three of them. When Ty went to finally speak, Victoria held up a hand.

"Shhh," she hissed.

Ty froze suddenly, thinking there was another elephant looming over him. Victoria focused on something over his shoulder, and he thought about his rifle again. He wondered how a quick draw contest between himself and a five-hundred-pound lion would go.

Without a word, Victoria sprinted deeper into the woods, Lilliana in her wake. Ty looked at the stain then toward the two rangers and had a 'when in Rome' realization, kind of like seeing an EOD guy running. If the bomb guy is running away from something, you want to try and keep up.

He was nowhere near as graceful, or subtle, in his flight through the high grass and narrow trees as the female rangers were. They would have lost him easily if they wanted to. He saw Lilliana's shaved head drop just past a tuft of thick grass. Ty slowed and crouched to join them. He took a knee next to them and couldn't help but note the disgusted look Victoria gave him. They had stopped behind some shrubs overlooking the river. Victoria raised a pair of field glasses to her eyes and looked out over the river. The current was slow and lazy, and in the silence, just over Ty's own breathing, he could hear a boat motor.

Victoria handed the binoculars to Lilliana and pointed down river toward a bend where the muddy water slunk out of sight. She shed her pack and noticed Ty looking at her.

"They hunt the hippos as big game and elephants for their ivory tusks. Sometimes they use the river to infiltrate the preserves. They don't think we watch the water."

A pair of binoculars, American binoculars stamped with a milspec number, were thrust into his hands by Lilliana who turned to help Victoria with a collapsible tripod she had retrieved from her pack. He studied the binoculars for a moment then took a harder look at the two rangers. Their boots were military issue, as was the tag in a boonie hat that flopped behind Lilliana's shoulders. He watched Lilliana set up the tripod while Victoria, to his relief, set up a DSLR Nikon on the tripod. For a second, he wondered if they were going to mount one of the rifles to the petite piece of equipment. The two women moved in synchrony like an artillery unit. He settled into his role as spotter and sighted a twelve- or seventeen-foot center console motorboat round the bend in the river. There were three black males, a white male, and a white female on board. The boat drifted at idle, slowly riding the gentle current.

"I spot five occupants, three black, two white, one a white female."

"Are they armed?"

"One black male is carrying a rifle, looks like a hunting rifle."

Ty turned to see Victoria seated behind the mounted camera, an impressive telephoto lens affixed to the camera body. "Nice," Ty breathed. Victoria gave him a hard stare as if to plainly say, get the fuck out of my way.

Ty slid to her side, out of the view of the camera, and found himself next to Lilliana. "So, you going to arrest them or something?"

"They must commit a crime first," said Lilliana flatly.

Ty could not help but note the rebuke.

"We photo them and keep notes of what they do. I know those men driving the boat. Usually, they just show rich whites where the animals are, but money does bad things to people. We will watch them."

"Makes sense," Benhoff looked over the camera again. The lens had to be a six or seven-hundred-millimeter rig. He noted a couple of dings and scratches to the barrel but still it was a very cool piece of gear. Victoria rotated the barrel to zoom in and he noticed a tag. It was a bar code he had seen countless times in his years of government service--an asset tag. That lens at one point belonged to the US government. "You all are well equipped," he commented. "Where are you based out of?"

"We have a station north of here near Phundundu Park."

"Sssh," hissed Victoria again. Ty wondered if it was to shut her rookie up, or to keep their noise discipline. Either way Ty was pretty confident he knew what he was doing tomorrow.

He gathered his bag and rifle while careful to keep his cover in the trees. When he was sure he had everything, he looked up to see both women staring at him, "What?"

"What are you doing?" hissed Victoria as she clicked off a couple of photos of the interloping boat ride.

"I've still got a scene to process."

"You are a foolish policeman."

"If I was wise, I would have been a doctor," he said with a grin that went unreturned.

"You are going to get eaten by lions or stomped to death by an elephant," Victoria said with an air of confidence Ty found unhelpful.

"You keep saying that. I'll see you guys around."

"We are not guys," they both hissed at once.

"I know, you two are badasses. It was nice meeting you, ladies."

Ty raced back to the tree with the bloodstain and scraped as much as he could into a fold of paper, then secured that in a pharmacist fold and a second paper bag. He took one other look around for any other signs that the chase he'd been tracking had moved on from that spot. He was pretty sure it did but the theory building in his head carried a lot more potential than the trail he was on. He ran back to his Jeep and gunned it for town. He had to talk to Kali.

CHAPTER TWENTY-FIVE

Hassan Rhouran breathed deeply as he watched the fine linen curtains dance in front of the open, floor to ceiling windows of his living room. It was dark and ribbons of white light from the moon traced bluish lines across the marble floors, reaching for him where he sat in an overstuffed chair. He held a nine-millimeter Russian made pistol in one bloody hand and an angry looking knife with a six-inch blade in the other. The pistol was unfired, random hairs and chunks of skin hung from the muzzle and front sight. In his other hand he felt blood dripping in patient rivulets from the blade and down his closed fist to stain the arm of his easy chair. At any other time that would be a problem. If nothing else Hassan Rhouran was meticulous about his home and belongings. Tonight, however none of that mattered. He was done with the mansion he had called home for over six years, done with the furniture that he now stained with every moment he remained seated. Though time was pressing, Rhouran wanted to rest for just a moment and watch the scene before him.

Two of the four men sprawled about his dining room were dead, their still bodies faced the ceiling, wide eyes staring uselessly upward. One of them he'd watch take his last breath only seconds before. That one had succumbed to two quick stabs under the armpit. If Hassan remembered correctly that location offered prime access to the man's heart. He imagined his chest cavity welling with blood, the volume of which crowding out the expansion of his lungs until there was simply no way for the man to take in breath. He was the third of the four Hassan defeated in the space of what he believed could only have been a minute or two. His name was Alec, he didn't know him well but remembered him from an operation they had completed together in Iraq, years ago.

Hassan's eyes were drawn to the spasmodic kick of a leg that was accompanied by a gurgled moan. Tirique Mohammed was dying an immensely painful death feet away and to the right of Alec. Tirique had come at Hassan with a high grasp for his head. Hassan had ducked the attack and using the knife he'd taken from the first man to die, Mustapha bin Saleh, another friend from those hectic times in the early 2000s, he rapidly stabbed Tirique multiple times in the soft patch of his abdomen. No doubt his stomach, liver, and intestines were opened up allowing all the bile, acids, and other unhealthy materials from his gastrointestinal tract to leak into his abdominal cavity. It was said a stomach wound was the worst way to die, and from what Hassan had seen in comrades wounded in such places in the field he believed it to be true. It took a long time for the body to bleed out in that location if a major artery was not affected, all the while that caustic material from the digestive tract attacked all the other moving parts of the man's anatomy.

"What will you do Hassan?"

The voice was quiet and tired. Spoken from the shadows on the opposite wall from where Hassan sat. Hassan could see Mohammed's outline, his feet and legs straight out before him while he sat propped and unmoving against the white wall. Hassan looked on Mohammed with a mix of emotions. He was not surprised in the slightest that the other three had come for him. They were mercenaries at heart, brotherhood meant very little to them when money was involved. Mohammed on the other hand was the closest thing Hassan had ever had to a brother.

"We have bled together, Moha." Moha was Mohammed's nickname while they were fighting the infidels together in Iraq, "I saved your life and you saved mine, you should have had faith in me."

Moha coughed and tried to hide a gasp of pain. Hassan was pretty sure his back was broken. Moha had been the first to attack, no doubt hoping to leverage their relationship into a tactical advantage. Hassan had been ready for the rush. Moha always had the habit of flaring his eyes and stutter stepping just so before striking. It telegraphed his intention in every fight. Hassan had countered by slamming Moha into a stone table that sat in the center of the room. He was immediately charged by the rest of the men, but he distinctly remembered a pop as Moha's body caught on one of the iron pillars supporting the table. The rest had happened so fast he did not know what had become of his old friend until he had dispatched the other three.

"Faith is a luxury saved for better men than us Hassan, you know that."

"That still gave you no cause to come after me."

"I follow orders, just as you should have done," Moha said clenching his teeth.

"I have followed every order I have ever been given," answered Hassan, "no matter the cost to me or my family." He rose with a groan, his body exhausted. He hurt in his joints and a place in his side where he felt blood running. He picked up a small throw pillow from a sofa adjacent to his chair and approached Moha.

"As have I, my friend," sighed Moha.

"I only needed a matter of days, and all would be well."

"There is very little patience where that much money is concerned, my friend."

Hassan took a knee next to the man he trusted above all others, "Yes, I know. Is it your back?"

Moha nodded weakly, his eyes straining against the pain, "I can't move my legs."

Hassan looked at his legs, "A lucky happenstance for me."

"You know it was," Moha had a weak smile. "You know they will not stop."

"I know, my friend. Goodbye."

Hassan pressed the pillow against Mohammed's head blunting the man's last words and pressed the muzzle of the pistol into the pillow before firing two quick shots into Moha's skull. The body spasmed and twitched for only a moment before going slack. Without looking back at his work Hassan Rhouran dropped the pillow and walked over to the gas cans Moha and his men had brought with them. He shook his head at the spitefulness of it all. Men he had served flawlessly for almost two decades, in every part of the world. Holy men, the pillars of his world, were so enveloped by greed, so hungry for the money he'd made them that they not only sent a brother to kill him but wanted to burn everything he owned to the ground. The worst part, a simple mistake by a foolish woman was the impetus of all of this.

Rhouran splashed each of the bodies with diesel and then turned to the furniture, spread it over the floors, the drapes, the kitchen and entertaining parlor, every place on the first floor then left the cans in a cluster among his dead friends. Even when he had told the elders the money was within his grasp. He only needed days to recover it and get them their payment. That was not enough. He flicked a zippo lighter, matte black, trimmed in gold, to life and lit the far end of a long trailer of cloth he'd stuck in the mouth of one of the cans and turned away.

The cloth lit with a whoosh, and he felt the air pressure change around him. He traded the Zippo for his phone and looked at the photo he'd received via text mere hours ago. The face that looked back at him was unmistakable. After all this time he had found her, she had cost him everything, but he had found her. "Soon," he told her image.

Hassan flipped to a number in his contacts that bore no name only a single character: S. He hit the call button and there was an answer after only one ring,

"Did you send them?" Rhouran asked.

"You know I did."

"I only needed a little time."

"Don't we all. I assume they are all dead?"

Hassan felt the heat of the growing fire on his back, "All of them," he said.

"Now I come for you," the voice said, "or you come in and we deal with this honorably, Hassan."

Honorably. They had just sent one of the only men he'd ever called a brother to kill him, "Ha!"

"Very well."

Hassan clicked the call off and tossed the phone into the blaze behind him.

Moments later he dropped into the driver seat of his Maserati and fired up the engine. The night around him was starting to glow with the orange-red light of the fire.

Very soon.

CHAPTER TWENTY-SIX

Special Agent Kali Earnst stood just inside the door of Albieto Cruz's Conex container living space, otherwise known as a wet can, with her hands in her pockets. It was a habit she had picked up her first year as an agent. Her field training officer made her put her hands in her pockets before entering any crime scene the two of them processed. "Cuts the urge to touch anything," mumbled Matt Boros, a gruff old-timer with the humor of a grave digger. The habit stuck.

To her right, Petty Officer Alex Henshaw stared at her. He fidgeted and stepped from side to side, obviously less than comfortable with an agent standing in his room.

She wondered what he was hiding and would save that for after she searched his roommate's side of the can. Kali took her time surveying the twin bed and desk for anything that jumped out at her. There's a big difference in searching someone's residence when you had a search warrant in hand. A warrant implied probable cause and a specificity for why you believe evidence of a crime existed in a given place. In the case of Albieto Cruz, she was trying to figure out how he ended up dead in Zimbabwe. Other than the fact he was shot, she had nothing else to go on. Before Kali slipped on a pair of latex gloves and started digging, she looked at Henshaw.

"Cruz is dead. Was he hiding anything in here I should know about?"

Henshaw looked taken aback and shook his head, "No, ma'am. I didn't know him all that well. He spent most of his time on travel."

"Where?" Earnst asked, slipping on the gloves.

Henshaw shrugged, "Wherever the admiral was going mostly."

"That makes sense." She never had a problem rifling through another person's stuff when on a search warrant. The mess was part of the experience. It was different when you were going through the things of a victim of a homicide. As far as she knew, Albieto Cruz had done nothing wrong and wound-up dead. Not that that was always the case. In her experience, victims often had a role in the bad shit that happened to them. Here, though, she moved with care. She wanted to be respectful, there was always that feeling you were invading their privacy or disrespecting the dead in a sort of way.

She started on the lone bookshelf above Cruz's bed. There was not much there. A picture of him and an older woman. They looked like they were taking a selfie at a game or something. She took the frame off the shelf and held it up for Henshaw.

"His mom, I think," he said, taking a seat on his own creaky mattress. "This going to take long?" he asked.

Kali paused putting the photo back in its place. She fixed Henshaw with a look that unmistakably implied there would be no more stupid questions from his side of the room. When he shriveled up a little, she gently replaced the photo on the shelf, "It will take as long as it takes."

There were a couple of books on the shelf. A textbook on public speaking that she found kind of funny, and another on statistics; she made a note to check if he was taking courses somewhere. She found an original three-book collection of Star Wars which she was relieved to see. Nowadays people compared Harry Potter to Star Wars, and it infuriated her. She flipped through the pages to see if anything fell out, but nothing did. At the other end of the bookshelf was another photo, this of Cruz and another woman. This showed them together, holding hands at an overlook of some sort. She held the photo up for Henshaw.

"Girlfriend, I think. He mentioned her a couple of times after Skyping with her. She's not American, met her on a trip someplace."

Kali nodded and made another note to look for her on his social media feeds. "You guys did not share much, huh? You ever go out on the town? Have a beer, anything like that?"

Henshaw leaned back, supporting himself on his hands. He shook his head, "Like I said, he wasn't around much."

There was a notebook to the side of the picture of Cruz and the girl. It was dog-eared and the spiral binding had loosened on one end. She quickly flipped through it and saw it looked like a journal with dated entries and a couple of sketches. They were rough sketches of animals, elephants, a jackal, and a couple of landscapes with waterfalls. There were a lot of entries so she put it aside so she could take it with her.

Once finished with the shelf, she moved to the twin bed with the standard metal frame. The bed was made crisp, just like they taught at boot camp. She started with the pillow, squeezing it all over for foreign objects… nothing. Next, she felt along the top of the mattress with no result. Careful to preserve the care it took to make the bed, she pulled up the mattress and looked over the box spring. The thin cloth cover had holes in places but there was nothing hidden inside or under the mattress. Under the bed she was greeted by dust, lots of dust, but nothing else.

She decided to cover the narrow closet before the writing desk at the other end of the bed. Uniforms hung neatly in order, one service dress uniform, and several working uniforms separated by blouses and pants. She ran her hands down each item, turning up nothing. Two pairs of boots and a pair of Nike running shoes were also dry holes. A small shelf above the hanging bar showed nothing but more dust at first. Then toward the back she noticed a glint of light. She reached in and retrieved a bottle. It was sealed bottle of Grey Goose vodka, a violation of General Order One, not that she cared. She had a bottle of rum stashed away in almost the exact same place in her wet can.

Finally, she turned to the desk and started with the chair. It was wood-framed, heavy, with a cushioned seat and back. She checked it for holes, or hollows, before flipping it over and doing the same on the other side--nothing. That left the desk. Three drawers, no laptop or tablet, which was no surprise. She made a note to ask Ty about the devices next time she talked to him. In a shallow center drawer just below the writing surface she found a few scraps of paper. Receipts mostly for beef jerky and Monster from the Exchange. Beneath the pile of receipts was a 128gb thumb drive. She added that to the notebook she'd found earlier and made a note of where she'd found it on her pad. In the last drawer she found three more notebooks, spiral-bound and worn like the first. They were also full of scribblings and sketches. This made her sigh, realizing she would have to go through each one without the benefit, yet, of a clue to what she may be looking for. She added the three notebooks to the rest of her take which totaled four notebooks and a thumb drive, then looked over the rest of Cruz's side of the can.

"Anywhere else I need to look?" she asked Henshaw.

He shook his head while eyeing the bottle of vodka which told her she would find much the same stashed away in his closet if she cared to look. Last she checked, though, she wasn't the booze police.

"Anything you can think of I need to know about Cruz? Girlfriend on base, friends?"

"He hangs out with a couple of dudes from the supply warehouse, but I don't know their names."

Kali nodded, "What do they look like?"

"I've only seen them at the bar with Cruz once. One was a big white guy with red hair. The other was Hispanic, I guess. He had dark skin anyway."

Helpful, "All right, I'm done then." She slipped him a card, "If anything comes up, give me a call." Kali took Cruz's notebooks and stowed the thumb drive in the pocket of her 5.11s. As she turned to leave, Henshaw followed her out.

"You think I'm going to get another roommate?" he asked.

Kali wanted to chuckle. Even if the question was a little cold given the circumstances, for the moment Petty Officer Henshaw was one of the rare enlisted aboard Camp Lemonnier with private quarters. Still....

"Not my department," she told him.

CHAPTER TWENTY-SEVEN

Ty gave Martell a wave as he passed the front desk on the way to his room. Martell gave him a warm, welcoming smile like he always did but Ty passed by with a nod and "How's it going, Martell?" and kept moving.

Ty swore he could smell himself. He could feel the sand and dust between his neck and his t-shirt, his boots felt like they were full of mud. He didn't want to expose the ever-pleasant hotel manager to his rankness. And he was not interested in speaking to anybody until after he got a shower and was able to scour his body clean of the African grime and his own funk. He didn't even wait for the elevator on the off chance another guest in the sparsely populated hotel happened to be in there. He trudged up the cement staircase the three flights to his floor, his pants, boots, his overstuffed pack, and the unwieldy paper bags full of evidence getting heavier with each step. He was so tired of being hot and uncomfortable that he almost missed that his door was open just a crack. He stopped and looked at the lock and the gap between the door and the frame. It was just wide enough to allow a sliver of light to pass between the wood and the brass locking mechanism.

As quietly as he could, he set all his bulky burdens on the tightly carpeted floor. He tried to be quiet but the folding and popping of the bag sounded like thunder in the wide vacant hallway. It made him cringe. He straightened and drew his gun. Ty stood quietly at the door and listened for any sound from inside the room. It would be great if the cleaning lady, whom he'd yet to meet but knew existed due to the cute towel origami he found waiting in his bathroom every night, was just running late getting to his room today. He looked up and down the hallway, and maybe she didn't have a cart? He doubted that. It also occurred to him that maybe his door just had a shitty lock. Either way silence from his room gave him no indication of what waited for him behind the door.

He took a deep breath before slowly pressing forward. He pushed the door open slowly with his toe and swept himself around in an angle at the threshold which helped him get a view of the inside. Doorways sucked, tight hallways sucked, stairs really sucked when it came to clearing a place. If there was a bad guy waiting for you inside, they had all the advantage. They could hear you coming, they could choose the best place to ambush you from, and in a place like Ty's hotel suite, they knew where he was coming from. Unless they had scaled a three-story stone façade, they had come in the same way he had. It was all bad news for Ty as he took his first steps into his hotel room. The first area he had to worry about was the T-intersection where the entryway opened to the main room. That was the most obvious place in his opinion. A close second and third however were the bathroom to his left about five feet into the hallway, or a closet with a sliding door at the same distance to his right. It was dealer's choice what area he tackled first. He chose the bathroom and with the image of a boogey man watching him from the slits in the wood lattice just waiting for him to turn his back before attacking, he did a quick penetration of the bathroom, just enough to see there was no one waiting for him before returning to the hallway. The closet was a tight little space, so he stood at an angle and swept the door open.

Nothing.

He centered himself in the hallway and stood silent with his weapon trained on the open area before him. Ty reviewed the lay out of his room in his mind and considered where someone could lie in wait for him. The other side of the break where the entryway met the greater room, there was a small bar which he'd be able to see behind once he got passed the hallway. All the furniture in the suite was so light that no one could hide behind it. Ty slipped toward the right side of the hallway to give him a better view of the left side of his room. He took his steps slowly and eventually was able to see the foot of the bed, then the wall. He crossed the hallway again and his eyes scanned what he could see of the room until he was only a step from the threshold. In a smooth movement he cleared the remaining hallway corner and was in the open floor plan of his suite.

Though now there were more areas where someone could spring an ambush from, Ty felt better being in the open. Where the hall was effectively nothing more than a big barrel, and he was the fish. Now that he was in the open, if someone did open up on him, he'd at least be able to move and fight back. Ty eyed the rest of the hotel suite in silence for a moment before moving toward the one remaining area where someone could be hiding, the counter area separating his small kitchenette from the modest sitting room. He noted the balcony could be in play, but he also saw the glass door was latched. He stopped for a moment to consider the balcony when sudden movement out of the corner of his eye to the right. A wiry black man sprang from an alcove between the living room and the kitchenette. Four feet away from him, a machete poised over his head. Ty tried to pivot and get his gun on him, but the guy was too close. The man grunted and yelled something guttural as he chopped at him with the blade. Ty side stepped and hooked his heel on the wicker framed sofa as he moved and went tumbling to the floor, his gun spinning from his hand.

"Fuck," he breathed in an octave higher than his normal voice as the wild man with the machete loomed over him, closing in for another strike. Ty grabbed a chair and threw it at his attacker who smacked at it with the blade as if it were a baseball on opening day. Ty struck out with this boot and smashed the man's knee with all the strength he could muster. He felt an odd pop come through the thick tread of his boot and the man let out a howl.

Ty rolled out of the way of the blade and found his footing, his gun unfortunately nowhere to be seen. What was readily available however was the old rotary phone sitting on an end table to his right. Ty grabbed it by the cradle and closed on the hobbling home invader. The man tried to get his weapon up again, this time more in a weak means of defense than anything else before Ty smashed through the man's elbow on his way to bashing the man across the top of the head with the heavy old phone. The first blow dropped him to his remaining functional knee, the second caused the man to drop his machete and crumple to the floor. Ty kicked the weapon away and watched the man squirm drunkenly at his feet, blood flowing into the hideous black and gold area rug covering the center of his floor. The offense to interior design depicting a smiling cheetah in a tree or something. Ty dropped the phone and the man looked up at him. He said something in mumbled gibberish and reached for him,

"Oh no you don't," Ty said, before dropping him with a straight punch to the temple.

***

Ty watched Detective Tsunga enter his hotel room. He did so slowly, immediately locking eyes with the man hogtied on the floor. Tsunga looked horrified when the prisoner tried to say something through the towel jammed in his mouth.

"Special Agent Benhoff, are you okay?" he asked, he couldn't help but look a couple more times at the prisoner.

Benhoff was leaning on the countertop near the kitchenette. His Glock in his hand but down near his right thigh. Ty swirled the bourbon in his glass and watched the detective for long enough without responding that Tsunga looked away from him and stepped back.

"Better than him," Ty finally commented. "Anybody you know Detective Tsunga?"

Tsunga scrunched his eyes and studied Ty's words for a moment. Benhoff knew the question got to him. Tsunga sighed and looked at the man, "I do not know him, why do you ask?"

Ty shrugged, "Small town and all. Seems odd that I'm here not even three days and somebody takes a run at me. A cop, in my own room."

Tsunga took a step toward Benhoff, "You also happen to be the only American driving a shiny new American Jeep here in Karoi. And you are by yourself." Tsunga kept his voice controlled but his brow was strained.

Ty was impressed the detective was standing his ground, at least a little.

"You want to press charges Agent Benhoff?"

"Would it do any good Detective Tsunga?"

Tsunga looked around the wrecked furniture and the man squirming on the floor, "It may, was anything taken?"

Ty tapped the blade of the machete that rested next to him on the counter, "He wasn't here to steel from me detective Tsunga."

Tsunga stepped to the counter and studied the blade, "This thing ring a bell detective?" asked Benhoff.

"What do you mean? What bell? It is a machete."

Benhoff blinked trying to process the man's statement, "I mean that the weapon seems to mean something to you."

Tsunga looked from Benhoff to the weapon and back, "It seems an odd choice is all."

"How so?"

"It's not what I would have expected here in the city. When people are robbed or killed here it is with a knife or a gun. Not a blade like this. This is a farmer's weapon."

"And?"

Tsunga looked at the man trussed up on the floor, he watched him intently. Ty noticed the fear on his prisoner's face, "I will talk to him, identify him, and find out why he did this. He will be charged with making an attempt on your life. Are you injured?"

"I'm not." Now Ty was confused. Tsunga seemed excited to him. He didn't trust him worth a damn, but he didn't feel the detective was a threat to him, which was exactly what he was feeling the moment Tsunga stepped in the door. Now the man seemed like any other cop with a lead. He seemed excited in an odd way.

"Good," he said and snapped his fingers. Two uniformed police came in and snatched the hog-tied machete wielder under the elbows which elicited a sharp yelp of pain from the man. Ty noticed Martell standing just inside the room as the uniforms passed by. He could feel the rage radiating from the hotel manager.

Tsunga stuck out his hand and Ty took it immediately which kind of surprised even himself.

"I will call you and let you know what I find out, Agent Benhoff."

Ty watched the two uniformed officers leave and found Martell standing, hands clasped at his waist looking down at the disturbed hotel room, "Martell, I didn't see you come in," he said.

"I am very sorry this happened, sir."

Benhoff saw anguish in the man's eyes and tried to remember if he had ever once seen anyone in the states with that much dedication to their job. The man looked like he was about to shed a tear.

"Any idea how he got in?"

Martell shook his head, "I will find out, sir. It will not happen again."

"I hope not."

His voice kind of caught in his throat, "So will you be leaving us then, sir."

Ty sighed for a moment and took in the room, "There any place else to go in Karoi Martell?"

Martell shrugged half-heartedly.

"That's what I figured; I'll be staying. Wouldn't mind the room getting a quick once over though."

"Immediately, sir." This time it was Martell's turn to snap his fingers. In quick response, two women scurried into the room and began cleaning.

CHAPTER TWENTY-EIGHT

It was almost seven a.m. Virginia time when Assistant Director Douglas McClintock fired up his computer. It wasn't often he was in a rush to get to work at NCIS Headquarters but an opportunity he had been waiting on for quite some time had suddenly dropped in his lap. He had to look up the number of SSA Thomas Boulden before making a call. He checked his watch; it should be around two in the afternoon in Djibouti. The phone rang several times before it was answered.

"Boulden."

"SSA Boulden, AD McClintock, where is the sit rep for the Albieto Cruz case?"

There was a pause, "Sir, Special Agent Benhoff reported in last night and indicated he was experiencing connectivity issues on the ground in Zimbabwe. He issued his report via the phone."

"So, you are the reason the director's office has no morning briefing related to this DSI case, is that correct, Mr. Boulden?"

Another pause, "No, sir. I filed the report through the chain last night. It should be with the desk officer, if not the director's assistant."

"I was not copied on the status update, Mr. Boulden."

"No, sir."

"Why was I not updated on this case, Mr. Boulden?"

Another pause. McClintock's fury at what was becoming readily apparent, that he did not hold the opportunity he believed he did, was not belied in the slightest by the unease of the Resident Agent in Charge (RAC) in Africa.

"Sir, you are not in the notification chain for updates."

"I AM THE ASSISTANT DIRECTOR FOR OPERATIONS, BOULDEN! I WILL BE UPDATED ON WHATEVER I SEE FIT TO KEEP MY EYE ON! SEE TO IT I AM INVOLVED IN ALL REPORTS FROM HERE ON OUT! DO YOU UNDERSTAND, BOULDEN?!"

Boulden cleared his throat, "I do, sir. Won't happen again."

"See that it doesn't, SSA Boulden." McClintock slammed the phone down on the cradle and leaned back in his chair.

McClintock took a deep breath. It was just a matter of time. He knew all he needed was the slightest break in policy and at the least he could have Ty Benhoff recalled to the States in disgrace and put before a review board. He doubted that would be enough to get rid of the man who dared to defy him, but it would be a start. Boulden already had a minor victory over the prick in forcing him to the armpit of Africa in the first place. But Tyrone Benhoff had to be gone from the ranks of the agency before McClintock would be satisfied, there was no room for that kind of disrespect. Not after how much McClintock had invested in the position he held, and the added benefits he deserved. It was only a matter of time, he reminded himself.

CHAPTER TWENTY-NINE

Special Agent Kali Earnst walked into the cavernous warehouse and yelled, "Where's Chief Berry?!" at the first kid in blue fatigues she saw.

The third-class petty officer had earbuds in and stared at her for a moment, she noticed his eyes drifting vertically up and down her petite frame. She was amazed how often that happened, especially when she wore baggy 5.11 tactical pants and a baggy polo shirt, but then again this was a base with eight eighteen to twenty-five-year-old dudes to every female. Might as well have been a prison as far as available women went. Most of the time that worked in Kali's favor. "The chief!" she barked.

The kid pointed toward a row of clapboard offices haphazardly constructed on the left side of the building. She found the first one occupied and knocked on the bare two-by-four door frame. "Chief Berry?"

The beefy man looked like a bear sitting on one of those tiny unicycles at a circus as he huddled over a small desk, hunting and pecking on a keyboard. He looked up at her with a you're already wasting my time look on his face. When he noticed the golden badge clipped to Kali's hip, his normal instincts deflated to resignation. "Who is it? And what did they do?"

"It's not like that, Chief." Kali entered and offered her hand, "I'm working a death investigation and there are a couple of S-4 guys I need to talk to about the deceased."

Chief Berry raised an eyebrow.

Kali swayed her head back and forth. "Strictly a witness thing," she told him.

Ten minutes later, a second-class petty officer named Chavez, and a first-class named Franks met her outside an empty office. They both looked at her with blank expressions you could only learn while completing drill exercises in boot camp. She could also tell they were thrilled to be out of their bunks since they had come off night shift only a few hours ago. It seemed like witness interviews always happened that way. When she mentioned Albieto Cruz's death, Franks shook his head and looked at his feet.

"Nobody's told us what happened to him," Chavez said.

"He was killed. In Zimbabwe," was all she would say.

Kali once more showed her creds to the young sailors. She asked Franks to have a seat while she interviewed Chavez first. Hector Chavez was a Mexican national who enlisted through the INA 328 program that would result in a green card when his tour was up, a fast-track to citizenship so to speak. He was from Calexico originally but had been brought to the States when he was four by his parents when they skipped the border and settled in Nevada. He was guarded, and suspicious. Kali got that, he had reason to be. Anyone from his background might be a little hesitant to talk to law enforcement, much less a guy without status, living in the United States for most of his life. Kali tried to find common ground with the guy. Prior to heading over to the S-4 supply shop, she checked the base roster and found the only six-foot three redhead assigned to the unit, and three Hispanic males. She'd spent time researching the sailors' social media feeds. She decided Chavez was the Hispanic she was looking for when he and Franks were together in every third post on his Instagram. She also found a post with he and Albieto Cruz. Chavez was into pool and cars, two things Kali Earnst could give a shit about. She tried to get him talking about the re-issue of the Toyota Supra and made a little headway, but as soon as she circled around to Albieto Cruz, Chavez clammed right back up. The lone post with he and Cruz together was at the bar aboard Lemonnier, pool cues in hand. If there was something he was hiding about Cruz, a baseless if, he gave up nothing.

Next up was Franks. This kid, she noted, he was twenty-seven to her thirty-two, which hardly put her in the position of referring to the guy as a kid, but it was something that had stuck after her initial assignment at the Pensacola Naval Air Station where most of her cases involved trainees messing up during A-school. Franks was built like a brick shithouse, and not the chiseled gym rat type of build but the solid farm build. He had earned his beef bailing hay and wrestling pigs or steers, or whatever the hell you did on a farm. His complexion was so light she wondered what level sunblock he needed to survive in the African desert without bursting into flames. He had red hair and if he had maybe a handful more freckles on his cheeks, he would have been the walking, talking approximation of the Alfred E. Neuman.

Franks was shy but diligent in answering her questions. He had that humble, honest country style that she relished after the void of information Chavez turned out to be. He knew Cruz mostly from playing pool at the bar. They'd gone out in Djibouti City a few times, but he didn't report anything that made her think they were real tight. When she asked why Cruz was in Zimbabwe, Franks straightened in his chair and stared at his hands like he was suddenly sitting in front of an admonishing parent or something. Kali smiled inside. Finally, she thought.

"You want to know about the stuff then?" he asked sheepishly.

"Yes, Petty Officer Franks, I want to know about the stuff, and remember." She said softly, "Agents never ask a question they don't already know the answer to."

Franks took a deep breath and sighed, "You know it was all in disposition anyway. We were just going to destroy it all or throw it out."

"What, specifically?"

Franks shrugged, "I don't know, whatever he could get to help his girl out. Mostly uniforms, some radios, I remember a ghillie suit, I thought that was kind of weird. Ended up being four ghillie suits, some boots, some field packs, binocs, some expired medical stuff…."

Holy shit. Uniforms, radios, medical supplies, a fucking ghillie suit. Kali's mind raced searching for the last time she read a threat report for Zimbabwe, but nothing came to mind. "This was all for a woman?" she asked, cutting him off.

Franks paused, "Yeah, he has, sorry had, a girl in Zimbabwe. Met her on some PAO trip with AFRICOM a while back. He was way into her, never stopped talking about her."

"You get a name?"

Franks looked at his hands again then shook his head. "Don't recall, am I in any trouble in all this?" he asked.

If this chick turns out to be some Al Shabab whore, you have no idea.

"I don't know the regs on giving out stuff slated for de-mil to just anybody, but you are being really helpful, Franks, that will go a long way." She reached out and put her hand on his. She spoke softly, cultivating a motherly tone that could soothe a pissed off alligator, despite the fact the idea of having kids herself sounded like a living hell. She slid a notebook and pen across the desk, "Now I need you to write down everything you ever gave to Albieto, and I need to know everything he ever said about this girl. Can you do that for me?"

Franks stared at the blank page for a long moment then pursed his lips and took up the pen. Kali tried to hide her relief then sat back in the chair and started texting furiously. It was possible Tyrone Benhoff was traipsing around a terror cell in Zimbabwe like the Lone Ranger.

CHAPTER THIRTY

"The American is looking for a killer?" Gerald Thoomba was apoplectic.

"Yes, he is. Fannel has talked to some people. He has nothing because there is nothing to find."

"He has spent the last two days in the bush. He is clearly looking for something." Gerald spiked a thin finger at the ground.

Obert weighed his words carefully. Though Fannel had talked to his sources at the hotel and with the police, there had been only so much he found out. The idiot detective should have never shown the man the body. The police should have sent it to Harare or delivered it to the Americans long before this Navy man had a chance to see it. Obert could think of options to deal with the American, but each carried risk. Risk and attention, two things he could not chance at the moment. He was close to being able to fulfill his plan, so close. He simply lacked the one thing that could gain him the time he needed to make things work.

"There are things I can do, brother," Obert offered.

"You have done enough; I will show you how to get rid of this American."

Obert was silent in accepting his older brother's false superiority. "It will all be all right, brother, please, you must trust me," he said with a smile.

"I will trust you when we are out of this mess."

"We will be, we will be." Thoomba put his large hand on his brother's brittle shoulder, "There are only minor details to be considered before we move. We could not rush such a thing and risk being unable to fulfill our commitments." *Commitments you made without my counsel*, though Obert left that unsaid. He glanced at his map once more and Gerald followed his attention.

The older Thoomba brother studied the map for a moment, "You will use the herd?"

Obert shook his head, "No, there is not enough certainty the herd will behave as we need it to. We are working on something else."

The front door to the shop opened and Gerald's head snapped up like a meerkat looking for a hawk. He slid a sheet over the table in his office before the two men walked into the display area. A tall, lean Yemeni man wearing a light, linen suit and leather sandals was waiting for them in the center of the collection of carved wooden statues and ornate boxes. He had a tightly manicured beard and wide eyes that tracked the two men as they approached.

"Mister Rhouran, I presume," Obert stated.

"Where is she?" Rhouran asked plainly.

Thoomba gestured toward Gerald, "Mr. Rhouran, this is my brother, Gerald."

"Older brother," Gerald clarified, reaching out.

Rhouran returned the handshake while not taking his eyes off the younger Thoomba.

"Mr. Rhouran's wife ran from him. He is from Harare and operates a quite successful precious stone business. I asked him to join me in Karoi when I heard through mutual friends of his problem. I believe I can be of assistance to you."

"Yes," Rhouran commented. "Now as I said, where is she?"

CHAPTER THIRTY-ONE

Ty Benhoff had to get out of the hotel. He had done nothing but hike through the African wilderness, paperwork, and make life hell for certain low level NCIS managers. He was bone freaking tired. It seemed like the sun was closer to the Earth here than anywhere else in the world. The constant roast just sucked the life out of you. If Benhoff had learned anything during his time in Africa it was that he would never be Superman, in fact if Clark Kent was charged and got his power from the sun, Tyrone Benhoff was the polar opposite of Superman. It was kind of a shame to realize that, but that was neither here nor there. Tired or not, Ty could not take one more look at his laptop, nor could he bear sitting around in the odd, wicker-like hotel furniture in his room. He had to escape.

He stepped off the stairs into the lobby. Martell, the desk attendant who Benhoff was pretty sure lived there, was standing attentively at the desk the same way he had been every time Ty had walked past.

"Martell!" he announced while noticing there were two other gentlemen in the lobby. They stood near a bay window that overlooked an interior courtyard. He gave them a nod and burned their images into his brain, just in case.

"Yes, Mister Ty," Martell responded with a broad smile.

Ty leaned against the desk, "Two things, my friend, actually three things. What the hell is wrong with the phone service around here? It's been out almost the whole day, I'm freakin out a little bit. Two, where's the coolest bar within walking distance? And three, do you want me to bring you a drink when I return? Seems like they don't let you out much."

"No, no, no, sir, on the clock," Martell swore with his hand over his heart. "I can only say welcome to Karoi, sir, regarding the phones. But I could suggest a nice pub a couple blocks down. You looking for dancing… women… something else…?"

"Bourbon, maybe a country singer."

"Haha, they have bourbon, not sure about the singer, sir. Two intersections to the right of the hotel and on the left."

"Good enough. Thanks, Martell."

"Any time, sir."

Ty wondered how it was the desk attendant could hold a grin that long without his cheeks seizing up. He also wondered what was up with the dude he'd dubbed, 'Kid,' clocking him through the reflection in the bay window. The other one, a bit taller and light-skinned, Ty had dubbed him, 'Play,' was a little smoother. He looked to be checking his phone, despite the fact the fucking network had been down for the better part of the day. Ty was wondering if he was going to get a chance to try that pub at all as he strolled into the roaster of a Zimbabwean night.

***

Fannel watched Tyrone Benhoff leave the hotel from across the traffic circle. There was no way the American could see him in the shadows. Fannel shifted on his feet ever so slightly. Like a big cat whose focus was alerted by a fawn taking one step too far from its mother. Not big enough to get excited about, but enough to fill the need if nothing better came along.

It was interesting to see Benhoff outside of the hotel and an opportunity that would surely be missed given Obert's reluctance to deal with the man. He didn't see him as a threat. Fannel noted this as simple naivete. Americans were always a threat. They'd proven such time and again, leaving nothing but bodies and destruction in their wake. Obert would learn, sooner or later, Fannel would be sure of that.

CHAPTER THIRTY-TWO

Benhoff left the hotel and took a right. He remembered a gap in the wall that bordered the hotel about halfway down the block. He considered ducking into the darkness to see if Kid 'n Play were following him or if he was paranoid but decided against it. The rule was, when operating in foreign countries, to just expect surveillance and live with it. In some places active countermeasures like surveillance detection routes, or sweeping your hotel room for bugs, or even trying to shake a tail could trigger an espionage charge. Besides, if Kid 'n Play were a ground team, and worth their awesome eighties rap reference, they would have at least one guy set up in a car just in case Ty went mobile. So, Ty simply strolled, hands in his pockets, down the cracked and dusty sidewalk bordering the street in the hopes he was following the direction Martell meant for him to go. As he passed a couple of cars on the street, he used the rearview mirrors and reflections in the windows to check his six. They were back there a ways and did not seem to be in any hurry to catch up to him. Ty kept his pace casual and after about ten minutes of strolling down the street in the oven-like heat he found the bar he was looking for. Well, at least it was the bar Martell told him about. The sheer amount of eighties pop music screaming through a vintage juke box gave a stark warning that this was not his kind of place, but he ducked through the batwing doors anyway.

This was definitely not his kind of place. It was packed with an interesting slice of what looked like western tourists and locals. The dance floor was full, and a crowd was gyrating to what Ty believed was the theme song to Weird Science. There were a couple of tables scattered around the periphery, but nothing gave him a view of the door until he found a stool on the backside of a bar that stood like an island in the middle of the open space. He slid onto the stool next to a solid looking white guy he guessed was around mid-forties. He had dusty brown hair that was relatively close cut and didn't acknowledge Ty as he sat down. To his right was the corner of the bar where a folding top guarded access to the barkeep's workspace. Past that was Ty's first avenue of escape if Kid 'n Play or any of their friends looked a little more than curious about them. A young African wearing a loud, baggy Hawaiian shirt and a pair of roomy cargo pants nodded in his direction.

"Bourbon," Ty gestured with three fingers. "Rocks."

The bartender nodded and went about filling his order while Ty kept an eye on the front door. He was pondering whether or not he was paranoid, or would his supposed tail follow him into the bar when his phone vibrated in his pocket, making him jump.

"Shit," he muttered as he read the screen. Nine missed texts and thirteen missed calls. He scrolled through the call log and noted the international numbers as probably Boulden, there were ten of those. He also noted with an arched eyebrow three calls from a 5-7-3 area code. "They are never going to believe me," he said to himself. Somebody at Quantico tried to reach him. He could only guess it was McClintock or one of his cheap-suited minions.

Ty heard a chuckle from the guy next to him. When Ty looked in his direction, the man asked, "That statement was either for your wife or your boss. Either way it don't sound good, mate." The man had bright blue eyes, an Australian accent, and a grin that told Ty he wasn't mocking him.

"Not married, but I'm not sure which would be worse," Ty sighed, scrolling to his text messages.

The guy took a swig of his beer, "Depends on how much you like your job I reckon."

Kali had texted him nine times. Ty read the first one and said, "Fuuuuck."

"That don't sound too good."

Ty's stomach had fallen to the floor. "It's not," he said. "Love the job," answering the guy's comment. "It's some of the dipshits associated with it I have a problem with."

The guy nodded, "I feel your pain."

Ty read Kali's messages and his initial fear melded toward confusion, "No way."

The bartender set a tumbler containing ice and a generous pour of brown liquor in front of him. He studied the glass for a moment and flipped the guy what he considered a large denomination bill of Zimbabwean currency. He had no idea how much that bill was worth in Zimbabwe, but in US terms it might have been a couple of bucks. The bartender gave Ty a look that said he also realized Benhoff had no idea what Zimbabwean denominations meant.

"Keep it," Ty told him. He looked at the drink again, maybe this is my kind of place after all.

His new drinking buddy eyed the bourbon. "That medicinal?" he asked.

"That or conciliatory," Ty commented, cringing through a long sip. Whatever was in that glass was no Pappy Van Winkle. The fluid bit hard and had a rough aftertaste. But then again everything, even Pepsi or Coke, had a different taste depending on the country you were in. When in Rome, Ty figured, taking another swig. He took another look at the front door and saw Play scanning the crowd. He searched faces in the roving strobes and disco lights of the dance floor and noted Kid on the far side of the entrance looking around just as Play was on the other flank. Play locked eyes with him for just a moment before turning away. He took another look at Kali's last text. It was all caps: YOU ARE GONNA END UP ON YOUTUBE ASSHOLE.

Ty felt like a mouse dropped into a snake pit given the theory Kali had about Cruz and the mystery woman he had in Zimbabwe.

"Either you're really popular round here, pal, or I am," the Australian said.

"You know who they are?"

The Australian straightened, "I look like a local to you?"

Ty shrugged, "More local than I am. I've only been here three days."

The Australian watched the two men filter through the crowd, trying to appear not to be watching Benhoff. "They look familiar."

"Good guys or bad guys?"

The Australian cocked his head, "Depends on the scale you're using to measure. Everybody's a little grey around here, 'cluding the tourists."

Ty nodded. He really hoped the gasoline he was drinking wouldn't be counted as his last drink. He tipped the tumbler and cleared the liquor in one final wincing gulp. "What's their game?" Ty asked.

"Guides one day, ivory hunters the next. Their kind sorta follows the money, if you know what I mean," the Australian said with a wink.

Ty studied the two men and their path around the bar. They weren't pros, he was sure of that, but that didn't mean they weren't dangerous. They had him outnumbered and he was on their turf. Still, Benhoff couldn't get over the odd feeling that they represented a lead. It's not like he would be known around Karoi for anything else than the Cruz case, if he was known at all. They could also, according to

Kali, be extremists hoping to cut his head off for a million likes. They could also be a couple of thugs looking to rob the American. Ty watched them openly now. He could tell it made them uncomfortable.

"Decisions, decisions…" the Australian muttered.

"I kinda get the feeling you're enjoying this, mister."

"I am, boy, I am. Need some help getting out of here?"

Ty grinned, "Nah, they seem harmless enough." *Yeah, right,* he thought.

Benhoff stood and strode directly toward Kid. The man looked at him sideways, trying to be subtle then did a double take as he locked eyes with Benhoff. He kept his eyes locked on the other man and the two stared each other down as Ty passed the man less than an inch from his shoulders. His tail was frozen as Ty passed him, clearly thrown off by the American's behavior. Benhoff saw Kid trade glances with Play as he watched him through a large mirror on the wall near the door. Kid turned to follow, and they were nearing the door when Ty spun again right before he exited and wrapped an arm around Kid's shoulder as if embracing a long-lost friend. With his free hand he jabbed the muzzle of his Glock 19 into Kid's crotch. In the darkness of the bar and the throng of people coming and going, Ty just prayed no one saw the gun.

"Feel that?" Ty spoke directly into Kid's ear.

Kid shook his head after a moment of shock passed.

"Back him off," he said.

Kid gestured with a free hand for Play to back down.

Ty retreated a little so the two men could look each other in the eye. The eyes of the man he'd dubbed Kid were someplace between embarrassed, pissed off, and scared shitless. "Wallet."

"Huh?"

He shoved the gun a little further into Kid's groin. "Two kilos of pressure," he said. "Wallet."

Kid reached behind him, and Ty pushed a little harder with the weapon to reinforce the severity of Kid's situation. Kid held a neon yellow wallet made of nylon and Velcro in front of him.

Ty eased up on the pressure just a touch, "I don't want to see you again. I know who you are, I know where you live. Understand?"

Kid nodded in short, staccato beats of the head.

"Say it."

"You know who I am." Kid's voice had a quiver to it.

"That's right." Ty returned the gun to his shirt and released the man while grabbing the wallet in one smooth motion. He winked at Kid as he turned and found Play standing right in front of him. Benhoff held a finger up to his lips as he passed the man who carried absolute hatred in his eyes.

Ty reached the stifling night air, his ears splitting from the decibel level inside the bar and the blood and adrenaline surge rushing to his head. He secured his pistol in his waistband rather than the holster behind his right hip, so as not to draw any attention from the stream of tourists and locals heading for the bar, and hot-stepped for the hotel. *I can't believe that worked*, was the only thought that came into his mind as he scanned the roadway and every nook and cranny among the buildings leading back to the hotel. When he reached the front door of the hotel, he fumbled with the Victorian style door handle because his hands were still shaking. He nodded as confidently as he could at Martell who smiled back from his station at the front desk.

"Great place, Martell, you're the best," he said, as he disappeared into the elevator. He needed another drink.

***

As Benhoff entered the hotel, Fannel rounded a corner from across the traffic circle. He had been watching the buffoons tailing the American. He did not know them but vowed to find out. In his experience, they looked like government stooges of some sort which made Fannel automatically think police. He was no more than a few meters from the American when he moved on the one. Fannel had to admit he had a newfound respect for the American's moves. He was fast but careful, able to threaten a man's life, dozens of people surrounding them, and none the wiser. If you knew what you were looking for, and Fannel did, he had seen the gun in his hand, witnessed the direct aggression that so many people lacked, and to do so while outnumbered and in a strange land was impressive. Fannel made a note to discuss what had happened with Detective Tsunga in the morning, and to give the sternest of warnings to Obert Thoomba. It was too early to hope but Fannel might have just witnessed enough of this man to convince his employer the man was a threat and that he needed to be dealt with. Modest hopes, Fannel reminded himself. He had been so close to the American he could have cut his throat and the man would have never seen him. But that was no way to take down such a prize. No, Fannel would have his moment with this American. And the man would know who it was that was killing him.

CHAPTER THIRTY-THREE

It wasn't the hand around her throat or how blurry things got when he choked her right to the edge of consciousness. It wasn't the bruises he left on her body that could be covered up by her traditional dress, or the one time he broke one of her ribs when he kicked her in the stomach after yet another failure to give him a baby. It was the fury in his eyes that caused Lilliana Cartwell to wake night after night whimpering, bathed in sweat and tears.

Five years it took her to wonder if what he did to her was right, was it to be expected, that a man would 'discipline' his woman in that way. That was what he'd called it, 'discipline.' Women were a simpler sort he would tell her, usually after an assault. "Your kind requires a strong hand, my wife," he would say. "That is why I do this, because I must."

Five years it took her, living in a big house in Harare after a lush dowry secured her from her village in rural Zambia. She instantly went from a goat herder's daughter of fifteen to the woman of a massive house in Zimbabwe's capital city. She had servants and clothes and jewels she had never dreamed of. He was a gem trader and the precious minerals he showed her time after time made her head spin. In her quiet, calm moments she wondered if the initial shock of her circumstances caused her such a long span of confusion. Five years it took her to realize the way he treated her was not right. It was not her fault they could not have a baby. Her doctor told her during a rare visit where he was distracted by a phone call that she was healthy in that way. That it was he who could not do his part. She never dared to tell him such a thing, of course, but the information seemed to cause a break in her fugue.

Five years, until that one night, a mere moment of that one night when he grabbed her by the throat and pulled her to face him. His rage was this time sparked by a conversation she had joined during a social for some western clients, Canadians as she remembered them. She had not begun the discussion, she had been keeping to herself, enjoying some of the art in the gallery where he held the event when a nice couple, older, with the congenial way Canadians have, approached her to talk about the piece. She tried not to say too much. Tried not to over play her part as he put it. None of that mattered. She was trembling when the tall, heavy front door shut behind her. She had barely removed her shawl when he backhanded her. She remembered crashing over a floral arrangement she had designed herself and been very proud. Then he dragged her to her feet, his fist constricting her throat like a python. Lilliana didn't even remember the words he had spit at her. She only recalled his eyes flaring like a madman, and flecks of saliva spattering her face while darkness grew over the periphery of her vision. She often wondered how long that moment had lasted, a second? Maybe three? Whatever the case it had been enough. He had left her there gasping for breath, her head swimming, and simply went to bed as if nothing had happened. Lilliana stayed where she fell, lying among her destroyed floral arrangement, thinking, planning.

He went to work the next morning and she did the same. She knew she had a time window of mere minutes between when his driver picked him up and when the staff arrived. In ten minutes, Lilliana had a bag packed and her jewelry collection stowed in several places among her person and hidden in clothes within her bag. She was just working up the final nerve to commence her escape when she noticed his office out of the corner of her eye. It was a place forbidden to her. A place she never had any interest in going, yet today the dark place called her. She rushed the room and started a frantic search for anything valuable. It was when she opened the top drawer of his expansive and ornately carved wooden desk that she found a set of numbers, a combination....

It was almost another ten minutes before she found the safe. It was in a hidden panel below a bookshelf she just happened to bump into with her hip. When the concealed door swung slowly open toward her, she thought she might lose her resolve. A click and creak from the front door signaled the arrival of the cleaning staff. She spun the combination lock feverishly and failed on her first two attempts. Finally, on the third, the heavy locking mechanism gave way and she strained against the metal door. What it revealed was such a simple thing. A single, unmarked, ebony case about the size of her hand was the lone occupant behind all that security. She didn't even try to open it. Lilliana simply threw the case into her bag and closed everything back up as head servant Bavella called her name. Her heart pounded as she scampered her way out the rear of the residence and over the compound's stucco wall.

She didn't know what to expect when she finally got around to opening the box. She had rented a hotel room in Karoi with the last of the cash she took from the house. She remembered sitting on a musty mattress and staring at the thing, trying to work up the nerve to open it. When she did, she found a deep purple velvet pouch containing a dozen single-karat stones and a flash drive. She had expected the diamonds; Hassan would be angered by the loss of the diamonds. But the thumb drive. The little device filled her with a dread she had never known. She wondered if she should throw it in the lake right then. But what if he came for it and she did not have it? She had no idea what was hidden within the tiny device, she only knew that if it was important enough to sit in that box full of diamonds, he would want it back. He would be looking for her.

Now, as Lilliana studied the beams of her small hut she wondered if that was how she came to be a ranger. Was it that all the women of the ICPF were like her? Or was it that she hoped the wilds of the nature preserve would be the last place Hassan would look for her? Either way the damned thing robbed her of peace, robbed her of her sleep even more than the dreams. She took the box hoping she would find something of use, some mechanism to aid her escape. Instead, she found herself more a prisoner, a captive of a single little thing.

CHAPTER THIRTY-FOUR

On the other side of the ranger compound, Sergeant Victoria Jurness found herself similarly deprived of sleep. She was seeing the face of a man over and over every time she tried to sleep.

Kamalla Indieon. A name she will never forget. A face she could not put out of her mind. She relived the scene night after night, sometimes even during the day, eating breakfast, on patrol. It was as if the ghost of the man was still with her. And why wouldn't he be, she'd been the one to kill him.

Victoria knew when she became a Ranger that guns and violence were a part of being a ranger. That was why Lead Ranger Maynard taught them to shoot their M-16s and why he taught them how to fight. She was one of the first of the broken women Danner Maynard recruited to his 'experiment' as everyone called it. An anti-poaching force comprised wholly of women, abused and discarded women at that. She had survived his training. She had performed hundreds of patrols and made arrests and seizures of animal parts and ivory. She had done all of this peaceably, all the men taken under arrest, they never fought her. Until three weeks ago.

Victoria rolled, shifting from one side to another on her narrow mattress, hoping the physical movement would interrupt what she knew was coming. Was it the fourth time that night, maybe the fifth the memory had forced itself to her conscious mind? She felt the... nothing. She didn't feel a thing in that instant when he charged from the hall to her right. She saw the weapon in his hand. Heard his voice yelling like a madman. They were mere feet apart, almost close enough to touch. He raised the gun and in that millisecond she fired. She could feel the subtle bump of the rifle butt against her shoulder and the flash, like lightning in the dim warehouse, lit up his face. She saw his expression alter from one of rage to surprise before he slumped all at once to a clump at her feet. She truly felt nothing but the weapon's recoil. Victoria had simply reacted.

She told herself he had made that choice. She had never led a raid before that night but when they received word that there was a stockpile of illegally harvested ivory and animal parts in a nearby village, they had to act. The source had told them the poachers had made a sale and the ivory would be gone by morning. Danner had given her the honor of leading her squad along with the regional police into the warehouse. Wide open and dark, the police had taken the left side and her squad the right, and out of nowhere Kamalla appeared, and it was over. She remembered the policeman who slapped her on the back, his broad smile wide on his face as he congratulated her. She remembered being confused by that. When Danner appeared at her side, he had taken the rifle from her hands. She was still holding it on the dead man. He had put a gentle hand on her shoulder and led her out of the warehouse. Even then, even when she saw the soft expression on his face, she still felt nothing. He told her the same. That it wouldn't feel real. That the impact of that moment would not hit her at first, and to come to him once it set in, and it would. The words he used were regret, and remorse, and guilt, and that confused her, too.

It was three days later when reality hit. She had a sudden realization of... wrongness. She felt so alien, she knew she had killed a man, but out of nowhere could not reconcile with the fact she had taken another's life. Victoria would never forget the first time that feeling struck her. When those feelings Maynard warned her of really set in. She was on the range preparing to fire a qualification with the very rifle she had ended a man's life with when she froze. She could feel it and smell that warehouse all over again. She remembered shaking and trying to hide the onslaught of guilt and sadness from her troops. She had to force every squeeze of the trigger like she was trying to pull an ornery rhinoceros. That was almost three weeks ago and Victoria Jurness was still stopped in her tracks at the most random times of the day and night reliving that single instant. She sighed and wondered if the waking nightmare, or those feelings, would ever stop.

CHAPTER THIRTY-FIVE

"That doesn't seem right," Ty declared after Kali finished summarizing what she learned from Franks.

"What do you mean, doesn't seem right? The guy's been siphoning off military cargo to the rurals of Zimbabwe. What else could a woman need a ghillie suit for?"

"I've seen her in the ghillie suit. I met this woman twice. She doesn't give me an extremist vibe."

"Know a lot of extremists, do you?" asked Boulden sarcastically.

"A couple," answered Ty. "But then again I haven't been to church in a while," he added that last part because he knew Boulden was a die-hard evangelical.

"Can we stay on point here?" Kali interrupted. She rolled her eyes and Boulden, who was sitting across the speakerphone from her, put his hands up and mouthed, 'What?'

"I'm just sayin', she was following a herd of elephants. I think she's a park ranger or something. And she's had the drop on me twice. If she had wanted to cut my head off on YouTube, she probably could have."

"What about the other two dudes at the bar?" asked Kali.

Ty flipped Kid's ID around in his hands, "Lucious Carrevan, I thought he and his boy just wanted to jack me at first. But they were definitely on me for a reason. No meathead follows a mark into a club, they would have just moved on to some other chump."

"We'll put him through some databases and see if anything shakes out."

"Probably'll come out to jack shit. Did anything turn up on Cruz's wheels?"

"Not yet," Kali sighed. "Getting a hold of rental car companies in Harare is kind of a bitch. Nobody calls you back."

"So, you're still tracking the car, running Carrevan, what else you got lead-wise so I can brief HQ when they call?"

"I'm heading out to see if I can pin down the female, see if she will actually talk to me after I show her the pic you sent me." Ty zoomed in on the photo Kali had skimmed from Cruz's Instagram account that showed him and the ranger who had introduced herself as Victoria. "Only the one post, huh?"

"That's it. I don't think the kid ever ate a meal he didn't take a picture of or make it through the day without at least one selfie, but he and the girl, only one shot from over a year ago."

"Huh, what's that tell you?" Seemed weird to Ty.

"Given what Franks said it's freaking odd for sure. If Cruz was so big on this chick and spends all his leave with her, how is it there's a picture of every burger he's ever eaten but not her?"

"Hopefully I can let you know when I get back."

"You're really going to gamble she's not an Al Shabab honeypot whose day job just happens to be babysitting elephants?"

"That would not be the strangest thing I've ever heard. I'm out, gotta get on the road by dawn. I only called tonight 'cause I knew you would be freaking out."

"You need to answer your damned phone from now on," Boulden glowered. "If you knew the shit I had to explain to almost every empty suit in the RKB yesterday...."

"That's why you get the big bucks, SSA Boulden, but I swear the phones were actually down across the entire freakin country. It wasn't me ignoring you that time, promise."

"That's bullshit," Boulden stated flatly.

"Whatever," Kali interrupted again. "If I don't talk to you again have fun at the terrorist training camp. Hope they don't rape you before they kill you."

Click!

Ty stared at his phone for a second, "That was hurtful."

CHAPTER THIRTY-SIX

Obert Thoomba was not a man accustomed to feeling fear. He was a man who instilled fear. He was a man who used fear as a means of control. However, Obert Thoomba was becoming intimately familiar with true fear. He found it odd that the face of his fear could be something as simple as a note, a message on his phone that contained nothing but an image, and a date and time, 'Friday-midnight.' The image was of his store front in Karoi. A simple message but one that could not be mistaken. It had come from an unknown number, but Thoomba did not need a directory to know who had sent the devilish little message. Niphong Wei, a quiet restaurateur out of Victoria Falls who also happened to be the local representative for the Chinese Triad syndicate operating out of Southwestern Africa. Wei provided logistics for moving ivory out of Africa to distribution channels around the world. He paid well, and for the use of his resources he and the people he represented expected their agreements to be kept, no matter what.

That was the reason Thoomba had not left the table in his office for the last two days. There was so much to be addressed, so many variables to be managed. So much risk to what he had to do. He shuffled through a stack of photos Fannel, and a couple of his most trusted men, had taken as they watched the ranger compound near Phundundu. His men were good, expert trackers and hunters, and he trusted Fannel like no other. He came across one particular photo that he'd been looking for as part of his side project. His distraction as he had classified it in his own mind. He expected Rhouran to be onboard after he saw the photos Fannel took of the woman. Whatever Rhouran's issue with the woman was, Obert did not care. Hassan Rhouran was not a man he thought much of. The Arab carried himself in such a pompous, elitist way Obert immediately disliked him. But necessity created strange bedfellows and as long as Rhouran served his purpose, Thoomba could manage his aversion a bit longer.

Obert heard the rear door to his shop open and the hard slapping of fine leather soles on the tile floor. There was only one man who had access to the store who would wear such things.

"I understand you received the same message I did, brother," Obert commented as Gerald hustled into his office.

"You do not disappoint these people, Obert." Gerald was sweating and pale. His tailored suit looked ruffled, like its wearer. Obert felt for his older brother. He had not been meant for a life such as this.

Gerald Thoomba, being the first-born son, was put on his path to power at birth. Fine schools, educated in Europe, placed on the staff of influential officials, he was put on the path to political success by his father who had been one of the greatest landowners in the country. Farming made the Thoomba family successful if not even wealthy by some estimations. As such, Gerald was meant to build on the Thoomba name while Obert was expected to be a farm hand. Both played their respective roles until Father died. Mother had long since passed when one day Obert realized Gerald was far too engrossed in matters of politics than he would ever be in farming. Obert hated agriculture, hated every aspect of the role he'd been forced to play.

Obert began to chase another natural resource, Africa's trophy animals. At first, he started out running a guide service for wealthy westerners and he even converted some of the family's extensive farmland for use in these hunts. He maintained a herd of antelope and could even release a captured big cat onto the property if such a thing were requested by his customer. All that required hard work, as hard of work as tilling the land. Eventually Obert found himself harvesting ivory. It was easy and almost a thousand American dollars per kilogram. Obert found that by dropping an elephant or a rhino he could almost double his cost to profit ratio than he ever could as a guide. There was only one problem--the law. That was where Gerald came in.

Gerald Thoomba, Minister of the Interior for Mashaland Province. Influential, powerful, and perfectly placed to know if law enforcement, state or otherwise, were looking into the local ivory trade. Gerald feigned repugnance at first but soon was convinced of his little brother's potential. It seemed one look at a roll of American bills equal to one of Obert's mighty fists was all that was required to turn Gerald Thoomba to a life of crime. That's not to say he did not voice his concerns; he even made some demands. He was open to acting as an intelligence source for a percentage. He was open to the use of parts of the family property for processing and logistics. He was not open to violence. He would not get his hands dirty, as he put it. Little did he know Obert had no use for his brother when it came to the darker side of the ivory business.

Obert was not an overly violent man. He did not take particular pleasure in such things, but he did not shy away from them either. Entry to the ivory trade and the territories to hunt was not an easy thing. There was great resistance to his first venture into rural Zimbabwe to harvest his precious commodity. He remembered several individuals in particular who opposed him. Obert remembered the void he found in himself when he shot his first man. He, Fannel and a couple of others he trusted made the decision there was no reckoning with the men of Laiall, so they followed them for three days until they located a load of more than a hundred and fifty kilograms of tusks and horns, they were preparing to bring to market. They waited until the men from Laiall were preparing their load for transport before they moved on them. Three men, three bullets. Obert remembered the look on William Quantoi's face as he put him down. The man who had stood so tall and even threatened his life on one occasion died sniveling and begging for his life. Obert often wondered if he truly had no compunction with the death of another human being, or if the unbecoming behavior of William Quantoi in those final moments soured him on human resolve. Quantoi was the first, but other men followed, three prior to having to put Muupha down for his recklessness. Obert wondered how many more would die as a result of the predicament they now found themselves in. However, many it took was the simple truth.

"You sent a man after the American the other night, didn't you, brother?"

Gerald huffed, "Just to send a message, convince him to head home."

"Did that work out as expected?"

"The buffoon I sent was not successful."

Obert chuckled.

"I'm happy to amuse you."

"Maybe we try my way now? One less thing to worry about would be quite nice."

"You kill one American; many more will show up and you know it."

Obert waved a hand casually, "So you say. He will find nothing, no matter the fact."

Gerald decided it was time to change the subject, "You have made progress, are you almost ready?"

Obert studied the plan laid out before him, a mass of photos and maps. "I believe Mr. Rhouran provides the last piece I was waiting for. Maybe another day or two to allow him to get his own plans in order."

"A day or two could likely be the difference between life and death, brother. I do not like it."

Obert quenched a flare of irritation with his older brother, "Failure is a guaranteed death sentence. I will gamble with a day if it increases likelihood of success."

Another creaking of the rear door to the shop and the sound of heavy boots signaled his man Guillone had returned from the past night's surveillance. Obert covered the map and his collection of photographs with an old shirt and waited expectantly as Guillone and Rhouran, both dressed in drab dusty clothing, entered the office.

"I did not see her," Rhouran stated flatly.

Obert handed over the photo he had set aside for Rhouran. "She is there, my friend, as I said she would be."

Rhouran studied the photo. Obert saw an unsettling intensity in Rhouran's eyes, further ingraining his dislike for the Middle-Easterner, "Guillone?"

Guillone handed over a Nikon camera, "The herds are roaming on the far side of the preserves. According to my source, she is scheduled for a patrol tomorrow night as expected."

"Very good. So, what do you think, Mr. Rhouran? Will such an opportunity suffice?"

Hassan Rhouran did not answer at first. He was still staring intently at the photograph of his wife, "Tomorrow will be acceptable."

"Good," Obert said with a broad grin. "I hope…," he paused as Rhouran turned slowly and left the office. Obert watched the man go, feeling utter disgust for the rude Arab. When he heard the rear door close, he turned to Guillone. "Despicable man," he spat.

"He did not say a word all night," Guillone noted as he watched the door.

"You will take him along with Nathaniel and John tomorrow."

"Understood," Guillone said.

"Good, tonight we go to the encampment one more time. I want to get one more look."

"Yes, sir, though I assure you, there is nothing we do not know about the location at this point."

Obert studied Guillone Beniised for a long moment. In many ways he looked on the man, now in his late twenties, as his own creation. As a boy, Guillone had shown up time after time looking for anything he could do to hunt, to make money, and support his family. Obert had started him out as little more than bait for the lions. But he had proven himself time and time again, no matter what Obert asked of him. Eventually he had earned his place as one of Obert's best hunters, and one of his most trusted men. Obert snorted, "Then it will be a boring trip."

CHAPTER THIRTY-SEVEN

After a quick wave to Martell, Ty Benhoff was just out the front door of the hotel when his phone chirped and without even seeing the number, he knew his day was shot. He looked and saw the international dialing code for the US, and a 7-5-7 area code. "Son of a bitch," he mumbled. "This is Benhoff," he said flatly when the call connected.

"Special Agent Benhoff, hold for the director's office."

Benhoff rolled his eyes and thought, they aren't buying that the phones were down the other day. As a Director's Special Interest (DSI) case he was supposed to brief the director's straphangers every twelve hours. He had a feeling he was about to be sent a message. When the phone picked up, he heard a very familiar voice.

"Special Agent Benhoff, this is Assistant Director Douglas McClintock," *the man who put you in purgatory*, Benhoff continued the AD's statement in his head.

"Uh-huh," he said and imagined the absolute hate his answer was generating in the AD.

"I'm here with the Deputy Assistant to the Director's Executive Assistant and—"

"Who?" asked Benhoff.

"This is Charles Drapnier, Agent, and we have some—"

"Why do I know that name?" asked Benhoff, interrupting them again.

He heard an exasperated vacuum of sound on the other end of the line. He imagined the two 'executives,' and in agency terms executive simply meant 'suit,' usually an empty suit, in Ty Benhoff's humble opinion.

"You should—" Drapnier sputtered.

"You're the guy who sent all those classified laptops through FedEx, aren't you? I knew I'd heard of you before."

"Listen!"

"Good to know that little scrape didn't hurt your ascendance to the upper middle."

"Agent Benhoff!" McClintock bellowed.

"What can I do for you gentlemen?" he asked coolly as if the last bit of insubordination had never happened.

He heard a mumbled, "Motherfucker," in the background followed by a soul-centering sigh.

"Agent Benhoff, you are a hair's breadth from being relieved of duty," McClintock breathed.

"Why?" asked Benhoff, "I've got a DSI to solve, wouldn't that seriously jeopardize the investigation?"

"Well, there's—"

"I mean it would take you at least three days to get someone out here and up to speed on the case, plus I've already established a rapport with a suspected close associate with the victim. I discovered the victim's cell phone through an expertly conducted elicitation operation and a possible location where Cruz was not only initially ambushed but subsequently killed. I did the latter at great personal risk to myself, by the way. Also, I discovered during an examination of Cruz's body that he was in fact shot instead of suffering an accidental drowning which was the official story from local law enforcement, and I was just about to initiate several delicate interviews of potential witnesses and/or suspects in what was possibly the funneling of US Navy property to persons unknown here in Zimbabwe, a situation related to the case. I understand there has been a degree of frustration with the timeliness of my DSI reports, however, there is little connectivity near the location of the suspected crime scene, and the nation's communications infrastructure is prone to outages such as the one that happened yesterday. This made providing summaries to headquarters impossible at times. I apologize for any inconvenience; however, if there is nothing more, I have a critical time frame in which I need to accomplish the very important interviews I have planned for today. So, if there is nothing more, I would like to get going."

Silence followed for a prolonged period until finally a new voice joined the conversation, "You were the only agent sent to investigate this death, Mr. Benhoff?"

There wasn't much that could cause instant dread in Tyrone Benhoff, except, as he recently discovered, a stare down with a massive bull elephant, and hearing that the Director of the Naval Criminal Investigative Service, Alexander Tenever, had just heard him verbally throttle one of his 'suits.' Pushed it a little too far again, dipshit, he told himself. McClintock didn't scare him; Ty had his own plans for that piece of shit. And Drapnier, or whoever, didn't even register on his radar. But the director could make him disappear from the rolls of the agency with the snap of his fingers. Benhoff braced.

"Yes, sir," he answered in the most professional way he knew, using as few words possible.

"Whose decision was it to send you out alone to such a remote location on such an important investigation?"

Benhoff grinned, "I was told that decision came from headquarters, sir. The local SSA seemed reluctant, but he was following clear direction as it was explained to me."

"That so?" the director asked.

"Yes, sir."

"Well, you be careful out there, Special Agent Benhoff, and if possible, try to get those reports in within policy."

"I will, sir."

"Go forth and be safe, Tenever out."

The line went dead. Benhoff stood on the street outside the hotel pondering the chances several men in suits were not at that very moment plotting his eminent NCIS demise. Not that he didn't deserve it, technically. There was a lot of leeway for a spiteful manager when it came to insubordination. He wasn't worried about McClintock; the AD had had it in for him for a little over a year now.

CHAPTER THIRTY-EIGHT

LITTLE OVER A YEAR AGO

The apartment was a wreck. That was his first impression. He nodded to a rookie agent whose name he could not remember. The woman, who didn't look old enough to drink much less carry a gun and badge smiled and wrote his name down on the crime scene log seemingly content in her crap role on the crime scene team. Ty put his hands in his pockets and stood in the doorway taking his time to observe the scene around him. He started at the door frame that was spotless, same for the outer door handle to the first-floor apartment. Inside, eyes training to the left he noted a small kitchen area with a table that looked more like a wooden ramp. Only two legs remained, propping half of it up like something he would have jumped a bike over as a kid. A smattering of mail covered the off white, linoleum floor. Cupboards, a countertop, stove, and fridge wrapped around the kitchenette ending at a sink where a couple of bowls sat unwashed in one basin, what looked like a shattered pot, soil, and a cactus of some sort lay on its side in the other. A chest high island stood over the sink creating a break between the kitchen and a living room area. Ty studied the floor for a moment before stepping inside.

"Definitely not a he said/she said with this one."

Ty took his eyes off the human sized dent in the drywall over a leather sofa and watched Marty Lenders, head of the Norfolk Field Office Major Crimes Response Team carefully exiting the bedroom.

"You pull this one, Benhoff?" he asked.

Ty nodded, "Yup, my spot in the rotation. I just wanted to take a look at the place before I head to the hospital."

Lenders offered him a pair of blue nitrile gloves; Ty removed his hands from his pockets to show the pair he already wore.

Lenders nodded his approval, "Promise not to touch anything and I'll give you the nickel tour. Heard the victims not doing too good."

"Unconscious but alive," Benhoff responded. He looked around the living room as he joined Lenders and noticed some blood on the pointed corner of the bar separating the kitchen from the living room. There was more on the interior door frame and a couple of drops on the wall he hadn't seen earlier."

"Somebody whooped her ass." Lenders watched Benhoff.

"Maybe she gave as good as she got," said Ty.

"Since she's the one in the hospital, I doubt it."

"Forced entry? I didn't see anything at the front door."

Lenders shook his head, "Only other access is a sliding door off the bedroom but it's locked and a wood shaft is in the frame, looks like it's been there a while."

"Maybe she knew him?"

"That's what the statistics would say."

Ty grinned and nodded. The entire field office knew that if Marty Lenders was on scene there would be no speculation on how the events unfolded until all the facts were in. That is of course unless he was the one speculating.

Lenders gestured with a pen, "Living room and kitchen look to be where most of the action happened. If you look closely, you can see a few blood droplets from the front door to the hallway here outside the bedroom. The carpet doesn't do us any favors on the directionality but there's a wipe on the corner in the hallway that feathers down the hall." He dropped yellow placards at each droplet he pointed out as they made their way through the scene.

Ty saw a red brown smudge on the corner where the living room gave way to a hallway leading to a bedroom on the left, another down the hall to the right, and a bathroom on the right in between. The heavy smudge turned to a lighter red smear in the direction of the bathroom, the stain trailed off in kind of a feathered pattern which indicated the direction whatever deposited the blood on the wall was travelling. Lenders stopped four steps down the hallway and put another placard down near a congealing stain a foot or foot and a half in diameter.

"This is where the paramedics found her, naked, curled up in the fetal position, unconscious."

Ty studied the spot for a moment and couldn't help but feel the fear and pain the woman he had not even met had endured. Ty only had a name, Alexa Wilshire, black female, age twenty-two, a Third-Class Petty Officer from Oakland, California. According to the preliminary check he'd run on her, she had only been out of boot camp nine months before this happened. He felt a heat rising in his chest that he knew from experience there'd be very little chance of letting loose on the deserving party.

Lenders stepped back toward the living room and pointed toward a couple different items, "We've got a blouse that looks torn by the sofa, and a skirt on the opposite side near the tv. On the other side of the room toward the back wall you can see a bra back by the bookshelf. A set of panties with what might be blood are crunched against the wall at the end of the hallway."

Ty didn't say anything but in his mind's eye, he could see her being chased around the central room in the apartment. He poked his head in the first bedroom and noted at first glance that the area was pristine compared to the rest of the place.

"Nobody heard anything?" he asked.

"Somebody called it in as a disturbance. Uniforms asked around once we got here to take over the scene. I'll have them give you a call once they check back in."

Ty nodded taking another look around, "Anything else?"

"I had just finished my preliminary walkthrough and gotten the first round of photos when you walked in." Lenders looked around the apartment until something caught his eye, "There was some blood in the sink in the bathroom here." He led Ty into the small bathroom where from the doorway he saw some smudging on the faucet."

Ty's eyes lit up; Lender noticed.

"No one gets in here until I can check everything floor to ceiling."

Ty silently begged the forensic gods for his unknown subject to have been dumb enough to clean up after the attack.

"You saved that for last?" asked Ty.

Lenders shrugged, "Don't you worry, no stone left unturned."

***

Hospitals were not Ty Benhoff's bag. Nothing good ever happened there, the place always smelled of antiseptic, and Saturday at two a.m. was never a great time for a visit. Before going in he took some notes on what he'd seen at Wilshire's apartment and a couple of questions that popped in his head. Inside the emergency room two police officers waiting to either side of a drunk who swayed dumbly on a chair. The two uniformed men had the forlorn look of men whose night would be unalterably wasted babysitting a moron at the hospital instead of being out running the streets. The prisoner's head was bandaged over his left eye and Ty noted mud covering the first six inches of his jeans. He was also missing a Nike. The other one was still there but likewise covered in mud. Ty guessed the idiot had tried to run from the police but hadn't run fast enough.

At the desk he was directed to the trauma floor where he was then directed by another nurse with a general wave of the arm toward Wilshire's room. He finally wandered into another junior agent, this one a black male who introduced himself as Ricardo. He was posted outside her door.

Ty looked in to see Alexa Wilshire laying in a bulky hospital bed, unconscious, intravenous lines running from her left arm to a couple of bags on a stand above her. Several leads connected her to monitoring equipment stationed on the near side of the bed. Then he saw the guy in the dark suit watching him from the far side of her room. The two of them locked eyes for a moment and the suit headed his way,

"She say anything?" Ty asked.

Ricardo shook his head, "She was unconscious when the medics brought her in. They're keeping her under to monitor her head wound."

"Who's the guy?"

"Her lawyer?"

Ty had no time for a follow up as Wilshire's door was wrenched open. The lawyer stepped into the hall with a form in his hand.

"I'm Ms. Wilshire's attorney, James Ennis Jr. of Bergins, McCloud, and Ennis. Ms. Wilshire will be filing a restricted report on this matter."

"Will she?" asked Ty. Partly entertained by the feigned bravado he found was so common to the legal class. For the life of him he could never figure out why every lawyer thought he or she was better and smarter than everyone else around him.

"She will." Ennis proffered a piece of paper which Benhoff glanced at for only a moment but did not accept. "She tell you that?"

Ennis stumbled in his boldness for just a second, "Did your client tell you she wanted a restricted report on whatever may or may not have transpired tonight?" Ty elongated his words as he spoke.

"Uh, she didn't have to I have been appointed-"

"By who?" Ty interrupted just to keep him off balance. His spidey sense alerted to something really wrong all of a sudden.

"I'm not at liberty to—"

"Wrong, if anyone other than Ms. Wilshire, who to my knowledge hasn't said a word since the police found her in her apartment, or her family did not personally acquire your services you have no business here. Can you tell me either of those things happened?"

Ennis took a breath, his nostrils flaring. Ennis' eyes, under a bald, polished scalp grew wide as he tried to come to terms with this 'normal' speaking to him without the proper deference, "I…."

"Get out," he turned to Ricardo, "Special Agent, this man will not be allowed access to Ms. Wilshire's room until he can show official grounds for being here. Is that clear?" Ty jabbed a finger at the lawyer while issuing the order to the rookie.

"Ye—" started Ricardo.

"You are on the wrong side of this Agent."

"Benhoff."

"Benhoff." Ennis finished his threat with his voice low. He held an odd grin upon his face.

Benhoff leaned in toward Ennis. As he did so the attorney shriveled just a bit, and blinked, "Believe it or not I've been told that before by tools just like you. I'll be waiting."

Ty's phone beeped three times, but he ignored it through two annoying cycles until Ennis backed off. Benhoff grinned and turned his back on him, "Benhoff."

"What are you doing?" it was Eva Hill from Virginia Beach Police Department. A detective that Benhoff had worked a pretty good joint MDMA case with a while back.

"I'm discussing legal theory with a new friend, his names Ennis." Ty spun to watch the lawyer who was moving down the hall, his own phone to his ear. Ennis turned at the sound of his name and Benhoff waved at him with a smile.

"Sounds really boring for closing time on Saturday night."

"That why you called me, like a last call thing?"

"Funny," she scoffed.

Ty found himself just a touch self-conscious about the way she said that.

"No, I'm covering night shift for a friend, you guys working an assault at the Boddington Apartments?"

"I am, standing outside my victim's hospital room. She took a bad one."

"Yeah well I got a call from patrol who pulled a DUI stop a couple blocks from there. The Subject is a pilot, and aside from being drunk off his ass, he looks like he's been through the ringer himself. They called me after they got a look at him thinking there might be something more to his story."

"That's interesting. My victim has a pretty solid head wound and her apartment was trashed. There was some blood at the scene."

"He's got some blood on the back of his shirt and on his jeans, a couple of scratches on his arms. Maybe a black eye in the making."

"How do his hands look?"

"Uh, hold on."

"You're out with him right now?"

"I was already in the car following up on something else, so I joined patrol out on the street. Hold on." The phone was muffled but Ty could hear her asking to take a look at his hands. In the distance he could hear some muted protests coming from who he guessed was her subject. After a moment Hill was back on the line with him, "Hands are clean."

"I would very much like to talk to him."

"Then can I interest you in a cup of shitty coffee downtown?"

"I think so."

"What's going on here?"

Ty looked up to see a fortyish white male in jeans, and a polo shirt. His close-cropped greying hair and 2x4 straight spine, and the way he jutted his chin out in Ricardo's direction screamed he was an officer.

"I'll see you in a minute. Pretty sure command just showed up."

"Don't forget to open with a joke," said Hill. "They like that."

"I don't think that will work here," Ty said. "See you in a little bit." He clicked the phone off and joined the officer and Ricardo, "You are?"

The officer was a good five inches or so shorter than Benhoff's six-foot frame, "Commander, Alexander P. Smoltz, Wilshire's Commanding Officer." Smoltz put a fist to either hip and tried to stretch to get in Ty's face.

Ty extended his hand, "Agent Ty Benhoff, NCIS, how are you this evening?"

Smoltz eyed the offered hand but didn't take it. He was in the zone apparently, "I'm confused Benhoff. This girl is filing a restricted report. Which means you." He glared at Ricardo, who for his part looked a mix of confusion and shock, "Neither of you should be here."

"Yeah, that's not what that means," Ty said.

"The hell."

"Lt. Commander, was it?"

"Commander!"

"Sure, yeah you're the second person to tell me that a woman, who no one from the time she was found in her apartment to where she lay in that room over my shoulder has seen conscious, filed a restricted report on an assault. That is a physical impossibility."

"I-!"

"Right, so if you have that report I need to see it and talk to the person whom Ms. Wilshire specifically stated her wish to file a restricted report to. I'm going to need a statement from that individual. Are you that person, mister...?"

"Commander, Smoltz, Alexander, and...."

"Also," Ty kept his voice even and harmless, "that statement will be given under penalty of perjury, so who do I need to talk to?"

Smoltz seemed at a loss for a second.

"Right, so." Ty offered his hand again, "Would you like to start over?" Ty showed Smoltz his credentials and badge, "Ty Benhoff, NCIS." He flipped his creds shut and dropped them in his back pocket. Then he opened his portfolio and started writing, "Smoltz, so you were the last person to speak with Ms. Wilshire?"

"Well, n-"

"If she mentioned a restricted report and it was before EMS responded, then you were at her home pretty close to the time of the incident, is that correct?"

"No."

"No?" Benhoff stopped writing, "So you weren't with Alexa Wilshire just after her assault?"

"No, goddamnit."

"Ok then, can you tell me your whereabouts this evening, specifically in relation to Alexa Wilshire?"

"No, I wasn't..."

Ty made a gesture of writing another note, "So you didn't see Ms. Wilshire tonight."

"No," he blurted.

"So, all that hardcore bullshit was a lie told to two federal agents?"

Smoltz was silent.

Ty closed the gap between them and lowered his voice, "In that case Mr. Smoltz, I think we need to talk about why you were trying to scare me off this case, and who told you to go with the bullshit restricted report gag."

"What do you think you're doing?"

The vaguely familiar voice boomed from behind Ty. He noticed Ricardo's eyes flare and turned to see the Executive Assistant Director for the Atlantic, Douglas McClintock striding down the hall, his eyes locked on him. The EAD wore a grey fleece, a pair of crisp jeans that looked like they were starched and pressed, and a pair of leather loafers. To say it was odd to see a member of the NCIS executive team at a victim's bedside, a little over an hour after an initial incident would be a bit of an understatement. Yet here he was. Ty was about to mention the same when McClintock blurted again.

"I said what do you think you are doing?"

"Sir, how's it going?" said Ty again offering his hand, and again having it ignored, "I'm interviewing a witness?"

"This is a restricted report."

Ty didn't respond. It was still a hunch, but the world felt like it had just flipped on its head all of a sudden.

"So why are you badgering the victim's commanding officer?"

Ty watched McClintock close the distance on him and found he was more curious at the encounter than intimidated, which was what he figured the EAD was going for.

"Answer me Agent?"

Ty had the feeling like opening the front door of a single wide trailer when there was a tornado on the porch. He wasn't sure what was about to happen, but whatever it was, it was going to happen quickly, "Well," he said, "the victim has been unconscious since she was found by first responders which makes it impossible for her to have filed a restricted report."

McClintock went to speak but Ty kept his momentum, "And even if she had, that doesn't mean we don't investigate." For some reason Ty heard Inigio Montoya from *The Princess Bride* saying, "That word, I do not think it means what you think it means..." but now wasn't the time for impressions.

McClintock crossed his arms over his narrow chest, "Agent?"

"Benhoff, Ty Benhoff." Ty forced himself not to roll his eyes. *Here we go....*

"How long have you been with NCIS, Special Agent Benhoff?"

"Three years."

"Right," McClintock commented with a slight turn in the corner of his lip. "Agent Benhoff, you have been advised by command what the status of this investigation is. I am now confirming to you, in as plain of terms as I can that same status. Do you have any questions?"

Several, thought Benhoff. *When does the command ever dictate the status of an NCIS investigation for starters? About as often as the EADLANT shows up at a victim's bedside.* He held McClintock's eyes with his own, "No, sir," he said.

"That's good. You show real potential there," McClintock said sarcastically while his eyes flashed over his shoulder to Ty guessed, Commander Smoltz. Ty choked down the little voice in his head urging him to do what only would effectively end his career: open his mouth.

Instead, he decided he needed to get to Virginia Beach PD as quickly as possible.

"You're dismissed," McClintock finally said.

Uh-huh, "Yes, sir." Ty shared a quick look with Ricardo, who looked like he was about to pass out. He stepped past the EAD without shoulder checking the man despite the urging of that odd little voice and took off down the hall at as fast a casual pace would allow. As soon as he rounded the corner, he put his phone to his ear. When Eva Hill answered he said, "Keep an eye on your drunk pilot, I'm on my way."

***

Eva Hill met Benhoff at the back door of the police headquarters building. "I wouldn't have thought much of this guy had he not been so close to your victim's apartment," she said.

"Yeah, at some point tonight you might start wishing you had just kept driving," Benhoff commented as the two entered the detective bureau. He followed her toward the observation points connected to the interrogation rooms, "I've had three people, a lawyer, the victim's CO, and the Executive Assistant Director for the Atlantic all tell me within the last hour that my comatose victim filed a restricted report. It's been an odd night."

Hill showed him into an observation room where a two-way mirror overlooked a single room bearing only a metal table and three metal chairs. In one, backed into the far corner sat the man he'd come to see. Short black hair, medium, healthy build, crumpled grey polo shirt, and a pair of shorts. He couldn't help but note the shorts were absolutely the most un-masculine shade of mauve he had ever seen. The man's eyes were closed but an almost imperceptible shake of his left canvas boat shoe covered foot betrayed his sedate affect.

"I'm pretty sure I know why you've drawn so much attention tonight," said Hill. She handed him a DMV printout, and an attached sheet detailing his Facebook profile.

Robert Pretaul III, of New York, "Why is that name so familiar?" he asked.

"Probably because his father is Robert Pretaul the second, head of the Senate Appropriations Committee."

Benhoff looked at her, "Oh shit."

"I'm no Special Agent, but I had a feeling that was what you were going to say."

Benhoff studied Pretaul through the mirror, "He invoked yet?"

"Hasn't said a word," Hill said. "If anything, he's acted as if he were bored... prick."

Benhoff felt like he was a moth who just noticed a shiny, inviting flame. The worst part was he happened to be the sort of moth who realized exactly what he was looking at. He thought of the sailor laying in the hospital bed, alone, "You mind?" he asked.

Hill looked at him as if she were sizing him up. He could feel it, she was thinking the same thing. After a moment she said, "Your case," and stepped aside.

As he headed for the door, he tried to come up with a game plan. Normally he would go in soft, take as long as he needed to put the guy at ease. He'd had hours long conversations with child abusers talking everything from football to professional wrestling just to break down their defenses. Here he was on the clock, he maybe had a handful of minutes before the cavalry in the form of legal representation came to save Robert Pretaul the Third. He thought about hitting him hard, tell him the victim is dead, try and spin him up, something to put the guy on his heels. Maybe he would tell him she was awake and identified him by name. But bullshitting a subject seldom worked in the real world.

When Benhoff entered the hallway, he came face to face with the dark suited cavalry. It was Ennis, again, the leach was grinning as Ty's phone started ringing. The two stared at each other for before the lawyer said calmly,

"You should probably take that. I'll wait."

Ty looked at his phone. It was the Special Agent in Charge of the Norfolk Field Office. He looked back at Ennis, "This isn't over."

Ennis handed a folded document to Hill who appeared at Ty's side, "Yes, it is." He grinned and handed hill the document, "I have been retained as council for Mr. Pretaul. He will not be speaking with any sworn law enforcement officer, nor will he be providing any potential biological evidence without service of a search warrant."

Ty turned away as the lawyer started. He'd heard it before, and ninety-nine percent of the time he was all in favor of a subject exercising their constitutional rights. In this one instance though it made his skin crawl. It was too normal, too practiced. Like this Ennis guy was on standby for Pretaul at any given moment. He clicked on his phone and put it to his ear, "This is Benhoff."

He recognized the SAC's voice. It was utterly devoid of any sort of mirth, "My office, seven a.m."

The line went dead before Ty could respond.

Ty turned to see Ennis enter the interrogation room. Through the door he noticed Robert Pretaul III, now fully awake, a big smile on his face. Pretaul nodded in his direction an instant before the door closed.

"Motherfucker," Hill said slowly.

Ty nodded, that was about the whole of it.

"What happened?"

"Pretty sure I have an appointment for a legendary ass chewing in the morning."

"For this," she observed dryly. "I don't get you feds," she said. "Sometimes you go to the hilt for bullshit that wouldn't even draw a ticket in the real world. Other times you fold in the face of an actual bad guy."

**

Ty had not gotten a call from his supervisor on Sunday, which he found a little haunting. He would have imagined the appearance of the EADLANT at a victim's hospital bed after midnight on a Sunday morning might have caused a stir in the ever-jittery ranks of NCIS management. But not a peep. It wasn't until he had just stepped from his G-ride to go into the office Monday morning at a little after seven a.m. that he figured out why.

Like all bad things, this one started when his phone rang. The Assistant to the Executive Assistant Director Atlantic Operations, a very nice older sounding lady who spoke as if she was confirming his spa appointment advised him that EADLANT wanted to see him in his office.

The SSA, ASAC, and SAC, along with McClintock were waiting for him. Ty was shown into a long conference room but wasn't even asked to sit down.

McClintock began, "You need to know your place, Special Agent Benhoff. From what I gathered from these *leaders* you are confused as to the chain of command."

When Ty tried to speak, McClintock yelled over him.

He stood and pointed to Ty's SSA, Georgia Stanson, "You cut an open on the Wilshire investigation. Your SSA was good enough to approve it this morning."

Ty didn't respond. He watched the EAD while he paused for effect. An effect Benhoff denied him when he failed to stammer and grovel. His silence had the desired effect.

"WELL WHAT THE FUCK DO YOU HAVE TO SAY FOR YOURSELF!" roared McClintock. His voice was so loud Ty noticed the conference room windows rattling.

"It's an important case," Ty said blankly. He noticed Stanson shake her head slightly like it was an involuntary tick when he started talking.

"It is a restricted report. A fact that was explained to you multiple times last night by her command and others more familiar with the circumstances. This includes me!"

Ty considered arguing with the executive. Especially when he saw Stanson flinch like she did. In fact, every one of them, the ASAC Rob Davis, and the Special Agent in Charge (SAC) Pete Marks, looked petrified. Well maybe not Marks, Ty thought. The SAC just looked pissed.

"You took it upon yourself to defy your chain of command. And you tried to intimidate a high-ranking member of the flight community. You are a Special Agent of the Naval Criminal Investigative Service, Mr. Benhoff, not a one man show. I don't know where… "

"Syracuse." Benhoff finally got a word in. He couldn't help himself. He'd been chewed out by way better chumps than this guy before.

"Excuse me?"

"I came from Syracuse, New York, sir." Benhoff said.

When the EAD suddenly stopped mid-rant and blinked Ty felt a warmth grow in his chest. Plain and simple distractor, verbal judo one oh one, and it worked like a charm in tongue tying the suit. Benhoff had joined NCIS after spending time as a city cop in Syracuse, New York. In many ways he missed pushing a cruiser around the frigid city in the rust belt. Then again there was the fact Syracuse was the closest thing he'd ever seen to frozen hell. Now he lived in Virginia. Where if it does snow, at least the precipitation has the decency to melt. Ty realized he'd gone on a mental tangent when he realized McClintock had rounded the table and got in his face. Ty didn't so much as blink.

"I don't give a shit where you came from! Bottom line, you want a future with the NCIS, you get with the program and learn to follow orders. Get out of my office!"

Ty remembered Stanson looking at him sideways, not with derision, or scorn, but with true fear, like trapped on a plane as it fell out of the sky kind of fear. He looked at ASAC Davis who wouldn't acknowledge him. The man looked like an Auschwitz gate guard at his Nuremburg trial. He kind of twisted in his seat like he knew something was up he didn't quite agree with. But he didn't want to piss off the SS either. The SAC, Marks, just looked bored now, maybe a little entertained. He didn't acknowledge Benhoff either, not for any real reason other than that a street agent didn't rate that kind of attention.

"I said get the fuck out! Think about your future while we decide what to do with you."

"Yes, sir," said Ty, keeping his voice calm and rose slowly from his seat. He followed orders, though at his own pace, and left the room. He even considered his future, at least his near future. He smiled at McClintock's secretary, as if he'd just joined the EADLANT for coffee. She looked at him as if he were mad. As he left, he texted Eva to meet him after work. He had gone into that scorcher of a dressing down suspicious of what had gone on over the weekend. Now he was straight up conspiratorial. McClintock's rage seemed kind of practiced, like in the mirror practiced, not really having led men kind of practiced. That bolstered Ty's suspicions, but as he was leaving McClintock's conference room, he noticed the flight suit hanging from a coat rack in McClintock's adjoining office. Benhoff checked McClintock's bio on the NCIS website and chuckled. The asshole was a reservist, and he served under the same wing as Smoltz and Pretaul III. It was funny, but only so funny.

Shit.

Ty paused at his G-ride as it all sank in. In writing the opening report he'd declared war as far as Douglas

McClintock was concerned. He also set himself up for an insubordination charge, no matter if it was bullshit or not. To top it all off not one of his immediate chain of command even considered backing him up, or defending NCIS policy, clearly put him in the right. All the righteous bullshit he'd been feeding himself when he cut the opening report, knowing he was in full defiance of one of the most powerful men in the agency was gone now. Replaced by nothing but uncertainty, and maybe a moment of dread. All that ended when a wave of pure wrath vaporized any doubt about what had happened Saturday night.

"Motherfucker!" he barked spontaneously while standing in front of his car, no one else around... like a crazy person. He needed to talk to Hill.

Fuck Doug McClintock.

CHAPTER THIRTY-NINE

Ty felt a sense of urgency that night as he and Eva Hill shared a six-pack and a couple of tacos on the trunk of his car. They met at a quiet stretch of shoreline that overlooked the lights of the Port of Norfolk. He told her what happened.

When he caught her all up, she said, "No shit? What an asshole."

He took a sip of beer and appreciated her ability to curse.

"So, we're fucked?"

There she goes, he thought. "Maybe," he said, "maybe not." Ty Benhoff had been an NCIS Special Agent five years and two months prior to walking into EADLANT McClintock's office. He considered his next words carefully with the understanding his career could very well not survive the investigative option he was considering. He re-lived McClintock's tirade over again and the decision was easy. That guy was a douche, and it didn't matter if Ty got fired for his next move. As far as Tyrone Benhoff was concerned, the piece of shit suit was playing for the wrong side. "I got a guy," he finally said.

CHAPTER FORTY

"No fuckin way, Benhoff!" said Clarence Green while leaning on a stained counter holding a tapestry of junk food and coffee pots.

"Come again?" asked Benhoff, arms crossed as he stared up into the eyes of the six-foot-six former Division One basketball player turned computer analyst.

"One commands an air wing, the other is in charge of half of your own agency. Do you not see how bad an idea this is?" Clarence had his hands in front of them, shaking them in front of Ty as if trying to drive the point through his thick skull.

"Don't forget about their phones, we're gonna need all that, too," offered Eva from Clarence's right where she was picking at a bagel.

Clarence popped a thumb her way and huffed, "What?"

Ty uncrossed his arms and held them out to his sides. "Dude, you owe me for one, and you're not doing anything wrong for two. There is no reasonable expectation of privacy on those systems, you know this. Remember the sabotage case on the Wasp last year? You were the reason I got those guys. You got me their email history, laid out the whole case."

Clarence shook his head.

"And don't forget about that other thing," Ty added.

Clarence huffed again and shifted on his feet like a trapped animal, "That was one time."

"One time and a butt load of classified shit, drone footage and missile cams. Your ass would have been rendered to a black site in Egypt, or Yemen, or some shit if it wasn't for me. So, chin up, work it out."

"You're gonna get me fired."

"I could have put you in jail."

"For what?" asked Eva.

Clarence shook his head as Ty chuckled, "He hacked the fleet's Aegis system looking for UFO footage."

"Noooooo," said Eva in a hushed voice. Her eyes wide, a grin creeping over her features.

Clarence dropped his head.

"Now seem like a good time, buddy?" Ty asked, patting him on the back.

"I hate you."

Twenty minutes later, the three of them were huddled around Clarence Green's workstation in the darkened Information Technology cell of Naval Base Norfolk. Ty sat scrolling through his emails, most of them related to various investigative reports filing through automated systems, while Clarence and Eva went through a list of people whose email she wanted a look at.

"I can't believe it's this easy."

"I couldn't believe it the first time I used it either. But according to the geniuses like Clarence here, and the military court system, this is all legit."

"That's awesome."

"I'm glad you guys are enjoying yourselves," muttered Green.

Ty was casually reading the titles on emails, skipping most of the ones from his management chain. He'd decided those people were in his own personal penalty box until he and Eva made some gains on what was up between McClintock and Smoltz.

"Come on, Clarence," Ty scoffed. "Don't you like the idea of pursuing justice?" He was waiting for a snide remark from his source when he saw his name in the title line of a GEN ADMIN. He opened the email and scrolled. As he read further and further, he realized the impact he'd had on his management chain earlier in the day.

"Ohhhh fuck."

"What?" Clarence and Eva both bolted up as if they had been found sneaking around in the middle of the night.

Ty barely heard them, "Tell you when you're done."

"Okay?" said Clarence, pulling a thumb drive from his workstation.

"You're done?"

"Yup."

"Already?"

Clarence blinked behind his thick glasses, "Yes."

"It would take me hours to save something like that at my desk."

"You don't work in IT," Clarence said flatly.

"What's going on?" asked Eva.

Ty sighed, "I'm being transferred to Africa, Liaison to the State Department in Djibouti."

"Wow, you have a way with people. You better keep my name out of it," warned Clarence with no small bit of menace. He turned to Detective Eva Hill, "And you should run."

"They can do that?" asked Hill.

"They," Ty paused for effect, "can do a lot of shit. Pretty sure there is only one 'they' in this case, though," Ty said, scanning the email again.

"When?" she asked.

"Says here immediately. I'm going to stretch the definition as long as possible though, just to be a dick." He sighed and looked at Eva Hill. "Looks like you're on your own."

Eva looked mad, "We'll see."

CHAPTER FORTY-ONE

After the impromptu meeting with the Director of NCIS, Ty slowly made his way to his Jeep. He wondered if the director would have any follow-up questions for McClintock or if he'd just made a new enemy. Three men rounded a corner between him and the vehicle. Two of the men he recognized, one of them did not look happy. He sighed as he saw Kid 'n Play post themselves in front of his driver's side door. I am never going to get shit done today, he told himself.

"Special Agent Benhoff?" the third man, older and in a nice suit carrying a leather satchel, stepped forward and offered his hand.

Benhoff kept his eyes on Kid 'n Play. He let the other man approach him to give himself a little distance from the other two. "You are?" he asked.

"My name is Captain James Hanswei of the Zimbabwe Republic Police Minerals Flora and Fauna Unit. I was hoping we could have a moment of your time."

That is a hell of a title. "You could have gotten a moment of my time without sending your boys after me the other night," said Benhoff. He shook Hanswei's offered hand.

Hanswei smiled and looked back at his two associates, "Yes, Inspectors Billa and Vong meant no harm. This is dangerous territory for us. We needed to be sure of who you were before making contact. Operational Security is the term I believe you know."

"I'm familiar. How'd you know I was here?"

"We have friends here, few but some good friends. If you have a moment, may we talk somewhere... less public?"

"About what?"

"Albieto Cruz, sir."

Benhoff considered Hanswei for a moment, then studied Kid n' Play who he now knew as Billa and Vong. He couldn't help but smile when he realized he'd mugged a police officer. He looked at Kid, "I suppose you want your wallet back?"

Neither of the two investigators seemed impressed with his generosity.

CHAPTER FORTY-TWO

Detective Matthew Tsunga stopped short at the front door of his cramped bungalow on the outskirts of Karoi. A hasty tug at his suitcoat and a, "I wan' hug," made him smile and drop everything without a second thought.

He turned and pulled his two-year-old boy up by the shoulders. He tried to avoid any drool or fruit droppings around Mathais's mouth as he wrapped the boy in his arms and squeezed just enough to elicit a squeal. "How was that, my favorite boy?"

"Good," said Mathais as he was set back to the stone floor.

Tsunga ran his hand over the boy's puffy frock of black hair. "You listen to your mother," he said before turning and forcing himself out the door over more pleas for a 'big hug.'

The detective skipped down the four steps from his home and was reaching for his keys when he noted a tall figure leaning against the rearview mirror of his dusty Mitsubishi pick-up truck. He tried to keep his calm as he recognized Fannel. The lanky Thoomba enforcer was relaxed, like a leopard lounging in a tree as it waited for the next antelope to wander by.

"What are you doing here, Fannel?" Tsunga asked coolly.

"The American, have you spoken to him recently?"

"No," Tsunga shook his head. "He has not contacted me since our first meeting." Tsunga felt a burning in his stomach and not because of the not-so-subtle attempt at intimidation by the thug showing up at his door. What bothered him more was that the American thought him dirty and didn't trust him, and it was to a point Fannel's fault. "Why?"

"He had a run-in with a pair of men last night at Kosuba's place. They were following him, for a time."

"Probably just locals trying to push on a visitor, happens every day." Tsunga shrugged and inserted his key into the driver door lock.

"I did not recognize them, and they did not seem the type," answered Fannel.

Tsunga placed his leather satchel in the passenger seat and focused on Fannel as he leaned on the door frame. The two were almost nose to nose, Tsunga was sure to stare the poacher in the eye. "And?"

Fannel looked toward Tsunga's house. That infuriated the detective.

"They stank like police," Fannel said, returning his attention to him. "Do you know if there are any outside police in Karoi?"

Tsunga shrugged again, this time forcing himself to maintain eye contact. Truth was he was only too familiar with the outside police, as Fannel put it. Tsunga had seen the opportunity to alert a particular man in Harare after meeting with the American. After realizing the Navy man was murdered. It was all part of the greater scheme. One he and the men from Harare had been working in the shadows to effect for a long time. Too long a time.

"If there are any other units operating here, I have not been notified."

Fannel studied his response. Tsunga bore the scrutiny though it felt like sandpaper on his last nerve. Finally,

Fannel nodded. "I see, it would be a good thing to know though, no?" asked Fannel.

"It would."

"Yes." Fannel turned on his heel, "It was good seeing you, Detective, keep in touch, yeah?"

Tsunga watched the man's back as he stepped away. He wondered what it would be like to put a bullet in the man he knew to be a murderer many times over. "Fannel," he called from his perch in the frame of the truck's door.

Fannel turned, an odd curiosity on his face.

"Do not come to my home again, Fannel, you understand?" Tsunga stated.

Fannel took another brief look toward the bungalow and gave a curt nod. "Be seeing you, Matthew," he said.

Tsunga watched him go for a while, a primal sense of danger reminding him not to take his eyes off the man for a second. When Fannel entered the passenger seat of a sedan two doors down, he finally took a long breath and looked at his home. He froze as he noted the tiny round face in the front window, Mathais's little hand resting on the streaked window.

Too close, he told himself, too close.

CHAPTER FORTY-THREE

Ty guided the men back into the hotel and found an unused meeting room on the first floor. The four of them spread out around a conference table, Captain Hanswei taking up station at the head of the table.

"Before we begin, Agent Benhoff, Detective Tsunga wished to express his regret at not being more helpful. He is under constraints in his position here. After meeting with you the other day and realizing the nature of Mr. Cruz's demise, he reached out to my unit and referred me to you."

"Why would the Flora and Fauna, and... Mineral? Unit be interested in my case? No offense but your title does not sound like you work many homicides."

Hanswei smiled again, it was a knowing smile, like he was explaining orange juice to an alien. Somehow Benhoff did not take offense. The slight black man held a latent wisdom, and a patience Ty did not find in most people. "In Africa, most everything can be associated with murder, Agent Benhoff. Sadly, that is just the way of things."

Not for the first time in the last few days, Benhoff found himself as the true stranger in a strange land. He realized that in his American law enforcement career, though he'd done some things, seen some things, and survived some things, he and his peers could seldom grasp the nature of law enforcement in other parts of the world. In the States, and even in his posts with NCIS abroad, he still had the Constitution, Bill of Rights, and the like that kept him constrained to an objective path, one where the subject was innocent until proven guilty, at least, that's how it was supposed to work. In the different parts of the world where he'd worked with locals, he'd noticed the legislative constraints on what law enforcement could and could not do tended to be a bit murkier or were simply shunned in lieu of corruption and greed. In Africa there were countries where the entire infrastructure was about as sturdy as a house of cards from one day to the next. Forget laws, forget protocols, cops in places like that not only had to deal with the average bad guy, but oozing corruption at all levels of bureaucracy, criminal enterprises and poverty that bred generations willing to kill for a buck just as soon as make eye contact on the street. Hanswei's demeanor was simple in its process, but the man radiated an experience that was foreign to Tyrone Benhoff.

"That's unfortunate," Ty said.

Hanswei shrugged. "Now, why we are here?" he said. Opening his satchel, he withdrew a file folder and handed it to Benhoff.

Ty flipped open the cover and was greeted by two photographs.

"Obert Thoomba is the big one. His older brother Gerald is the other. These two men have dominated the illegal ivory trade here in the Karoi region for some time now. We believe Obert started the business, transitioning from a farmer to use his land as a guide and a hunter before being drawn in by the money exotic wildlife trafficking can offer. He owns a tourist shop in town, he also manages the family estate out in the bush. Gerald," Hanswei gestured to the photo in Ty's right hand. "Owns the family estate as befits his elder status. He is also the Regional Interior Minister. You can now understand maybe why Detective Tsunga was not able to offer you much help. Where there is that high a level of corruption, there are many eyes on an honest man such as him. There is very little he can do here."

"But you can?" asked Benhoff.

Hanswei stood straight, "We are based out of the capital. None of my men have ties here. All of my men have been tested and tried and they are honest men." The tone of Hanswei's statement offered no little bit of challenge. "We have been watching the Thoombas for some time now. We even believed we had them just over a month ago when we struck a storehouse, we believed belonged to them."

"Dry hole?" asked Benhoff.

"No, just the opposite. We seized ivory equivalent to 1.2 million of your dollars, sir. One subject died in the raid, no trace of the Thoomba brothers could be linked to the contraband. Which brings us to your problem."

"How does that touch my problem?" Oh shit, the kid was in on it. Ty pleaded to the universe that Albieto Cruz had nothing to do with wildlife trafficking. If his victim did, Ty Benhoff might as well buy a house in Karoi and put up a white picket fence, 'cause he would never get out of there.

"Flip to the next photo, please."

Ty did as told and found himself looking at an increasingly familiar face. "I know her."

Hanswei stopped short in his casual pacing around the front of the table, and Kid 'n Play looked at him oddly.

"You do?" asked Hanswei.

"Yeah, I met her out in the bush, some wildlife cop or something."

"Exactly right, Mr. Benhoff. She is a sergeant of the rangers in the Lower Zambezi Valley named Victoria Jurness. She shot and killed a Kamalla Indieon when the warehouse was taken down. We believe your mister Cruz was killed because of her."

Benhoff found the photo of Kamalla Indieon in the folder behind the photo of Jurness. It was a death scene photograph. Indieon's eyes were open and unfocused. She had K-5'd him right through the heart. A cop shoots a bad guy, and her… whatever gets killed? "She was with Cruz?"

"We believe so, yes."

"You're not sure?"

"She was reluctant to speak of him, but we discovered enough to link the two."

"And what, Indieon's boys came after Cruz out of revenge?"

"That is correct."

"Who shot him?"

Hanswei sucked air through his teeth, "We have no direct proof, but Kamalla's brother disappeared shortly after the shooting."

"Like he ran?" asked Ty.

"No, like he disappeared."

Ty pondered that for a minute, damned shit was serious around here. All for a bunch of horns.

"So, what now?"

Hanswei grimaced, "Now things are sensitive. We watch and we wait."

"Wait for what?"

"An opportunity. We need them both, Gerald almost more than Obert due to his influence. There is nothing connecting Gerald to the ivory trade."

Benhoff thought about all the variables going into Hanswei's case, and how personal the consequences seemed from the outside looking in. He wondered what would happen to the man if Gerald Thoomba found out he was under investigation. The three men sitting around the table were brave and dedicated. Ty realized he'd misjudged them, but he also appreciated he was literally no closer to solving the murder of Albieto Cruz than he was when Boulden first put him on the plane for southern Africa. Shit. He studied the pictures and reviewed his own findings in his head. "You guys have a forensics lab?"

Hanswei tilted his head, "Of course we do."

"Back home we have a record of fingerprints. Do you have something similar?"

"I know what you speak of. Zimbabwe's is not as robust as the American AFIS. Why, do you have something?"

Ty rose from his chair. "You guys hold tight, I'll be right back."

Ten minutes later, Ty returned to the meeting room with his pack over his shoulder and a handful of sealed paper bags in his arms. He dropped the bags on the table and looked at the three Zimbabwean investigators. "Bear with me a moment," he said, organizing the bags and retrieving his laptop from the pack. He brought up the photos of the suspected crime scene he'd found in the middle of nowhere. "Okay, let me show you what I got."

CHAPTER FORTY-FOUR

Gerald Thoomba eyed his slate grey suit once more in the multi-angle full-length mirror of his immaculately organized walk-in closet. He then inspected the sheen of each of his black loafers for any sign of scuffs. Finally, he leaned in and plucked any errant strand of the short mat of increasingly greying hair that covered his head. Two hairs required a delicate pluck before he was prepared to start his day.

The scent of pressed Ethiopian coffee greeted him as he descended the marble staircase to the first floor of his villa on the outskirts of Karoi. Out of the corner of his eye he noted his plump, elderly head servant shewing a far younger and quite desirable maid to assemble the final aspects of his breakfast on a sterling silver tray. They flitted around the kitchen at a frenetic pace until the very moment she placed the last item and took the tray in her hands. He ignored the head servant's final inspection of the meal and strode casually to the veranda overlooking the end of Karoi and opened into the drifting greens and browns of the Zimbabwean countryside. He was not quite seated when the girl, Maris, set the tray before him. He did not acknowledge her as he reached for an ornate porcelain cup of the steaming coffee doused with heavy cream and sugar. He waved her off as he smelled the brew and tentatively lifted it to his lips.

"I hope we are not disturbing you, Minister Thoomba."

Piercing heat of spattering coffee prickled his skin and burned through his lap as Gerald jumped at a voice that had no place at his breakfast table, much less his home. He dashed from his chair, knocking it to the ground, as he patted instinctively at his burning groin before the sight of his intruder made him freeze, the heat of the coffee forgotten in an instant.

"We?" he asked. "Mr. Wei, what are you doing here?"

The diminutive Chinese man standing to his right was flanked by two much heavier built Asians of the same descent. Wei, dressed also in a suit, though his of a more casual linen and brown sandals, had a passive smile on his face. Gerald looked toward his kitchen for the staff who had betrayed him.

"No, please, do not blame them, they did not know we were on the premises until this very moment."

Gerald looked to Wei, then back to the interior of his house, and back to Wei again.

Wei gestured toward the table. "Please sit," he took a chair himself.

Gerald knew he had to compose himself though he felt like a hen who'd stumbled into a viper pit. He cleared his throat and dabbed once more at the coffee staining his lap. "Would you enjoy a coffee, Mr. Wei, some food perhaps?" Gerald righted the heavy metal chair and sat with a cautious glance toward the two men accompanying the ivory trafficker.

"No, I thank you, Minister Thoomba, but I have many engagements this morning. I was hoping for an update on our pending transaction."

Transaction is an interesting choice of words, thought Gerald. It implied payment for something in return. That was not his understanding of what was to occur between the two men. "I was under the impression, Mr. Wei, that we had another day to deliver your shipment."

"That is the agreement, and I apologize for the intrusion, however, in my occupation there is need to avoid potential prying eyes. The front door is not always the most efficient way of attending a meeting."

"I… I understand."

A silence billowed between the men, one of the most agonizing moments of Gerald Thoomba's life. Wei sat across the table, legs crossed, hands resting in his lap with the same peaceable expression on his face. Finally, Wei leaned forward, "Well? What is the status of our agreement, Minister Thoomba?"

"The merchandise will be delivered on time as agreed upon," Gerald Thoomba said with a petrified stoicism.

"Very good, Minister Thoomba, very good. As you can imagine, I will be in the area." The most congenial smile drifted across Wei's face, and he nodded slowly, as if encouraging a child through a difficult math problem. "I will await your call."

Wei stood and Gerald scrambled to his feet. "Certainly, certainly." The two shook hands slowly, Wei staring deep into Gerald Thoomba's eyes. Gerald couldn't bear it, "May I show you out?"

"No thank you, Minister Thoomba. We will show ourselves out."

Gerald Thoomba did not realize his hands were shaking until after he watched the last of Wei's men disappear into the interior of his own home, like the boogeyman going back to a child's closet. He was not sure how long he watched the empty corner of his terrace and the doorway that led through his study. When he finally collapsed in his chair, Thoomba had no more appetite for the fine breakfast that laid before him. He simply leaned on his hand in a slump and stared blankly at the countryside.

CHAPTER FORTY-FIVE

Assistant Director Douglas McClintock entered 1789, on 36th street and tried to act like he belonged. He took in the rich wood interior, high windows, and brass accents that gave the restaurant a classic feel without being too obvious about it. This was the kind of place he couldn't afford to even walk past when he was first starting out in DC as a street agent. This was the land of the heavy hitters, congressmen and senators, lobbyists, and influencers; the kind of place where things actually got done inside the beltway. He subconsciously checked his tie as he stepped to the hostess stand. The woman, maybe twenty years wore the standard white blouse, black tie, and matching slacks of servers in most upscale restaurants in DC. Her auburn hair was pulled back in a tight knot. Diamond studded earrings glistened in the subtle lighting of the establishment and seemed a little out of place. McClintock recognized the weight of the carats she wore, his wife, estranged wife, had a pair just like them. She smiled warmly in the practiced way of the service industry.

"Good afternoon, sir. Do you have a reservation?"

McClintock stumbled a little with his words, "Ye… yes, I'm meeting someone: Doug McClintock."

"The party your meeting is Doug McClintock?"

He laughed and caught himself, what the hell? "No, miss. I am Doug McClintock, I'm meeting…"

"There you are," said Ennis stepping from the bar. He shook McClintock's hand, "He's with me, Carrie," he told the hostess brusquely before leading McClintock from the entryway.

McClintock struggled to keep up as Ennis wove his way through tables and easy chairs filled with politicians, Republicans and Democrats sitting in small clusters, chatting, or smoking, or playing on their phone. McClintock noticed one congressman he recognized from New York actually playing Candy Crush in one of the most expensive establishments in the nation. McClintock couldn't help but recall the man was also one of the loudest voices on the dangers of screen time for children.

Ennis guided them though a pair of open, intricately carved double doors to a table near the back of the dining area. Ennis gestured for McClintock to sit. Ennis did so himself while simultaneously working on a text. The two sat in silence for a moment while a server dressed in same crisp white shirt and black apron over black slacks as the hostess poured them both water from a crystal decanter. The server followed with two fingers of liquor, McClintock guessed scotch, in a tumbler also of a heavy crystal. He turned to McClintock expectantly, but McClintock waived him off. Not for fear of NCIS policy on booze during the workday, but more because he had no idea what to order and didn't want to sound unsophisticated or cheap.

"Walker, Black, Marcus," said Ennis without looking from his phone.

The server who McClintock now identified as Marcus flashed a practiced smile and disappeared.

"I appreciate the meeting... "

Ennis looked up from his phone, "Yes, Douglas, the Senator was very pleased in your decision to seek the appointment. He likes to reward his friends when he is able. You were of great assistance in the earlier matter. I trust that has been properly handled?"

"It has, the procedures were solid, and the right people were...."

Ennis put a hand up, "I'm sure it was all very well done." He started to stand.

McClintock looked around and stood as well but Ennis waved him down.

"No, no," he said without looking up from his phone once more, "I just got an urgent call from Senator Pretaul, and I have to go."

"Oh," said McClintock, "I was wondering about the confirmation, the position."

Ennis grimaced as he broke away from his phone, "Yes, a staffer will call you with all the particulars. The Department of Transportation Surface Transportation Board is generally a pretty simple process, very important mission." He stuck out his hand.

McClintock had felt stronger grips from corpses over the years, "Than—"

"Yes," Ennis said. "Welcome aboard, call us with anything you need." He smiled briefly and spun on his heel, returning to his phone as he dashed from the restaurant

McClintock watched him go realizing he'd just been blown off, and that he still had no idea what the DOT Surface Transportation Board did. He'd never even heard of such a thing. And he'd been in government over thirty years. When Ennis called with the offer of a presidential appointment McClintock immediately said yes. After all that was how things worked. He had provided a service to one of the nation's most powerful leaders and was due his just reward. Surface Protection Board? McClintock turned back to the table and Marcus, appearing like a ghost, was waiting with his drink which McClintock took and down in one gulp. Inwardly he shrugged, presidential appointment is still a presidential appointment. He looked around at some of the figures in the room and ignored the little voice in his head telling him he had no business being there. Then he sat down and asked Marcus for two things: another scotch and a lunch menu.

CHAPTER FORTY-SIX

The camp was quiet. It was after dark and the platoon or so of rangers had retired to their respective thatched huts some time ago. Secreted amongst the high grasses and gentle hills outside the compound, Obert Thoomba covered the glowing dial on his wristwatch. Precisely twenty-five minutes ago. He made such a notation on the small notebook that laid next to him and returned his eye to the reticle of the night vision scope he had trained on the headquarters of the International Counter-Poaching Federation. His men had had the ICPF compound under surveillance for the better part of three weeks, watching, taking notes, and reporting back to him every morning. They had learned as much as they could watching the location and every detail was needed for Obert to pull off such a stunt as he had planned. He knew the overall workings of the compound, the training and patrol schedules based on the repetitive schedule the ICPF's female rangers followed.

Obert suppressed a snort, women wildlife officers. The idea was preposterous, despite the attention and the legitimacy they had garnered from the national and regional governments. Gerald had managed to provide him a list of the ICPF personnel with pictures from the Ministry of the Interior. This he'd provided to his men and soon they were able to identify which of the women were patrolling when, a detail of little significance until Hassan Rhouran had come to his attention.

No small bit of luck was involved in the way he and Rhouran came to meet. Obert was frantically trying to arrange transport for the ivory the ICPF and police had not found. It was a meager amount compared to the treasure trove that was seized at the warehouse. In searching his contacts, he was told that Rhouran had put feelers out relating to his wife who had fled from him. When the man had forwarded him the picture Hassan was showing around, Obert immediately recognized the woman. Obert's mind had always been good like that, remembering the small things. At the time he had paid the small detail little thought. Then, as the plan to retrieve his seized merchandise came together, he realized Rhouran could fill a vital gap in his plan. Obert had forwarded the picture he'd received from Gerald's office. Though the girl's name was different, Obert knew it was her. Quite frankly, even if it hadn't been the right girl, Obert cared little as long as it was enough to entice Hassan Rhouran to fulfill his role. Within minutes of forwarding the photograph he received a call from Rhouran himself. The man was brusque, almost to the point of insult. He wanted to know where she was, and how to get to her. All in good time, Obert had assured him.

That time was very near, and the fact left Obert with an incessant hole deep in his guts. So much had to come together to make this work and to save his skin. Now that Rhouran was with him, the man added another stress-- his incessant demand to retrieve his wife. Obert took his eye from the reticle and looked over to where Rhouran lay prone, focused on his own set of binoculars. Retrieve was not the right word. He wanted to get to his wife, the man had said nothing of his plans after. Obert mentally shrugged at that. Those were details he cared little for, with any luck Rhouran would be taken care of during the operation itself. Obert could care less what the Arab did with his woman. As if on cue, Rhouran broke the silence of their surveillance post with yet another demand.

"We should go now, it is quiet," he hissed.

"It is quiet, yes," said Obert. "But every person in that camp is armed with a rifle. Would you rather have two women to deal with, or twenty?"

His logic once again seemed to temper Rhouran's impatience. The man huffed but said nothing further. The question of why he cared so much about a single woman rested on Obert's lips, but he didn't bring it forward. He knew enough Arabs to know they held women in an odd category. To Obert it was an odd blend of pedestaled jewel and chattel. It was not his place to care about his motives, only that the job got done.

Obert settled back into his vigil. He was growing confident that all was in place. Every detail had been addressed, that he and his brother would in fact deliver to the Chinese on schedule and mitigate their wrath. There was only one more variable Obert wanted to see for himself. Something his men had yet to report to him. He searched the headquarters building. A single light still shone through a window toward the rear. His watch vibrated silently on his wrist, signaling another hour had passed. Midnight, Obert had made a note each time the piece vibrated. They had moved in just after dark when his reports told him the majority of the ICPF staff took their final meal of the evening. He'd spotted his quarry then, the head of the ICPF Danner Maynard traversing the camp from his office to the canteen, and back again when the meal was over, and the female rangers started to disperse. He appeared to hold a meeting with a couple of the more senior rangers before he was finally alone in his office. Obert needed more assurance of Maynard's movements. He had checked up on the man, by all accounts he was very dangerous. Obert had to ensure Maynard fell for his diversion when the time came. He was awake at midnight, if that was a natural practice then Danner Maynard would be alerted to the emergency call and if the background information on the former Special Operations soldier and mercenary were accurate, more than likely a man like that would run to the aid of his people. Obert felt a surge of anticipation and fear as he saw in his mind the chaos that would overwhelm the camp once his attack on the patrol began. He saw Maynard and the others loading into their trucks and fleeing the meager gates in a rush to help their compatriots. Obert hoped then that the camp would be deserted. He would prefer to succeed without bloodshed, but he and his men were prepared to act if violence was required. He would sweep into the camp in trucks, including the large cargo vehicle he had procured from Harare. Minutes to load their treasure and disappear into the night. Straight to their transfer destination and liberty for he and his brother once the shipment was in the air. Obert let out a long, slow breath. It would all be over so quickly, all his planning, and agonizing, the hell of the past weeks would culminate in what could be a matter of minutes. Could be, he reminded himself.

CHAPTER FORTY-SEVEN

Since McClintock moved to Quantico, he was a little out of Eva Hill's grasp. She still had plans for him, but he was far enough out of pocket to make a direct investigation of him too difficult. Ennis, the lawyer was out simply because he was legal representation for Pretaul, though in her estimation, the slimy bastard seemed more an old-time mob consigliere than an actual attorney. That left Commander Alexander P. Smoltz as her best lead.

Clarence had been spot-on with the emails and phone records from Smoltz and McClintock. The treasure trove of information was a rare thing in law enforcement, when something so good came so easy; and those emails were good. Smoltz and McClintock served together. McClintock was a pilot in the Navy reserves and assigned to Smoltz's wing. It was clear neither of them understood or remembered the warning banner on their home screens that advised every computer user accessing the United States Navy network they had no reasonable expectation of privacy. There was a string of emails that showed how nervous Smoltz was with the Pretaul case. The man sweated every detail from the medical reports to the victim's advocates, who, after reading a couple of forwarded emails between Smoltz and a tenacious Victim's Advocate named Pressley, Eva Hill became a fan. Pressley had Smoltz on the ropes citing emails and phone calls where she pushed DOD policy and instructions in an effort to figure out what the hell was going on with Alexa Wilshire. Some of the emails mentioned Wilshire's family in Oakland and in Pressley's words, the vacuum of information they were living through. In emails, Hill found out Wilshire's mother, Anna had come to be with her daughter. In a panicked series of text messages between McClintock's government phone and Smoltz Clarence swiped from the server system governing the NCIS communications it was clear Anna Wilshire scared the living shit out of Commander Alexander Smoltz. "We're blown!" was the first text Smoltz sent after meeting Mrs. Wilshire, "Wilshire's mother showed up, she knows something's up. We're fucked!"

McClintock's response every time Smoltz panicked was the same, 'There's nothing anyone can do.' 'Nothing points to any wrongdoing by either of us,' 'you have nothing to be afraid of,' 'just keep your eye on the prize,' and finally when Smoltz's paranoia even got to be too much for McClintock his advice was: 'go get a drink, calm the fuck down.'

Time was Eva Hill's friend in this case. Alex Smoltz was cracking under the weight of his own failure. He failed as an officer, he failed as Alexa Wilshire's leader, and he failed as a man, and he knew it. She had Clarence pull Smoltz's phone location records to see what towers his phone pinged on. Most people never thought about it but the cell phone in your pocket can give anyone who looks a map of your life. Whenever that phone is turned on it is reaching out to cell towers every so often to ensure a connection. Just to say hi, did I miss any calls? So, to speak. The data Green provided was nothing more than a series of numbers on an Excel spreadsheet. But when that spreadsheet was fed into a mapping system all of Alex Smoltz's movement, as long as the phone was in his pocket at the time, was there for her to see.

Ninety percent of the information displayed on the map was incredibly simple and expected. His home in

Ocean Front to the NAS Oceana, to the squadron, to the gym, DFAC, blah, blah, blah. But it wasn't the ninety percent Hill was looking for. It was never the ordinary in any investigation. Especially for fine upstanding citizen like Commander Alexander Smoltz. No, it was in the fine details that show what could be nothing more than a momentary lapse in judgement, just one bad day, to give Eva Hill what she needed.

Funny, she thought, but for someone who was supposed to be a bad ass fighter pilot, in her opinion, Alex Smoltz did not handle stress very well. His life before the night Alexa Wilshire was attacked was pretty much rinse and repeat. Work, lunch, work, gym, home, repeat, an endless cycle of suburbanite boredom, save the fact this particular suburbanite happened to fly extremely fast war machines for a living. Two weeks after Alexa Wilshire was attacked things start to drift from the norm for Smoltz. It was first the random excursions in the middle of the day that she noticed. It looked like Smoltz was meandering around the base in the middle of the workday. It didn't look like meetings or anything official and it wasn't every day. But here and there he would jump in his car and circle the perimeter of the Navy base or drive out in town for twenty or thirty minutes. Normally that wouldn't mean anything to Hill or anyone else. Here it was a deviation from the norm and something to keep an eye on.

It was a month after Smoltz started doing his traffic therapy, as Hill like to call it that Smoltz started to drift from his norm again. Where he spent his nights, especially on Fridays and Saturdays started to get really interesting. It wasn't every weekend, at least not at first, that Smoltz began running around the College Park area late at night, but as time progressed Smoltz started making it a more and more regular thing, and he was giving Hill places to investigate when he made stops for sometimes hours at a time. Six months after Alexa Wilshire's attack, Hill had a decent list of places Smoltz liked to frequent on the weekends and she set to work.

She decided to refer to Smoltz's new behavior as deviations. Since the data she had only showed where Smoltz's Navy phone was pinging off cell towers, drilling down to where he was actually going took some work. With maps of the towers in hand, along with dates and times Smoltz was in the area, she took to the streets. One of her first stops was a business park a little outside of downtown where Smoltz had stopped three times for about an hour each. She explored a little and found that the business park was primarily outpatient offices catering to everything from plastic surgery to mental health. When she pulled traffic cam footage using dates and time stamps for reference, she found that he was parking on the side of the building that held a children's behaviorist, a pediatrist, and a psychiatrist. Smoltz was by himself when he visited so she narrowed it down to either he was dealing with a mean case of trench foot, or maybe he was seeing a shrink. Eva admired the new BMW 8 series coupe Smoltz was driving, she also wondered how he could afford it on his salary. The fact that he was seeing either specialist on the economy instead of through Navy medical facilities on base also piqued her interest. Why pay for special medical treatment when you could get it for free? She was bolstered a little by the idea that a career naval aviator probably would not want anyone knowing he was seeing a shrink, it would probably jeopardize his flight status or something, who knew. She made her notes and moved on.

Smoltz's next two new hangouts were interesting but got her nowhere. Each cell tower he pinged off of twice on a couple Friday and Saturday nights. Both were strip clubs on the outskirts of the city. Not a great look for a career officer of a relatively high rank, but for her purposes didn't do much for her plan. There were two others on her list that gave her some hope. The first was in a mostly forgotten strip mall near a distribution plant. Half the traffic cams in the area were busted but she was still able to put Smoltz parking a half block away at a gas station and walking to a 'massage spa' in the dilapidated old strip mall. She made a note that he was stopping by in the middle of the day and that he was out of uniform. Why would he shed his normal business dress for shorts and a polo shirt in the middle of the day if what he was doing was on the up and up? The final deviation Hill tracked down made her smile. She recognized the place as soon as she rounded the corner and confirmed the cell tower. The Angel Lotus Massage Spa, Detective Eva Hill knew the place well.

***

Alexander Smoltz locked his BMW and looked around the gas station parking lot. There were a couple people filling up, one with a plumbing service sign on the side of his truck, the other was an old lady with an even older Saturn sedan. On the side of the building some bum was sitting in a hunch against the concrete wall. He looked like he could have been sleeping, or on the nod, chock full of heroin. None of them seemed to pay him any mind so Smoltz didn't either as he started down the cracked and crumbling sidewalk toward the spa. During his block long stroll down the dreary urban street, even in the sunlight the place looked like it lacked the color of anywhere else Smoltz frequented. It was depressing but he wasn't there for the scenery. He wasn't there for his guilt either, which reared its ugly head with a little voice in the back of his mind warning him he couldn't do it… again.

It was the same every time. That stir in his stomach, adamant he was going to get caught. The utter fear of his face splashed across the evening news along with any number of pathetic bastards when the place got raided. Add to that the fact that the squadron was due to ship out on maneuvers in three weeks and what was he going to do then? But the little voice couldn't dissuade him. There was nothing else that worked to keep him sane anymore. No matter what Smoltz did, he couldn't make it more than a couple hours a day without knowing in his gut Alexa Wilshire was going to sit straight up in her hospital bed and scream rape. He hated himself for not being able to handle it. Not like McClintock, or the lawyer, Pretaul, or Pretaul's father who was a senator for Christsake. If a senator wasn't sweating crushing a rape investigation, why should he?

Because you're the one on the hook for it, asshole? The little voice was always there to remind him. McClintock had told him that wasn't a possibility, so did Ennis. He knew Bob Pretaul, that piece of shit, for sure would tell him the same thing if he could. But Smoltz had shipped Praetal off to the West Coast the first chance he got. Even got the scumbag promoted in the process, to his own amazement. But regardless of the political fixer, or the NCIS executive, Smoltz knew in his bones that if the girl ever pushed for an investigation, if she ever woke up and pushed for an investigation was more accurate. That little detail was like a knife in Smoltz's heart, the little part of him that, as a leader, knew he had failed one of his people. He knew if that ever happened, he would be the one to fall. And soon, with McClintock getting the appointment from the senator, there would be no one left but him to fall. The rest of them would all be untouchable. And all he had to show for it was a new Beemer, fucking idiot. He reached the metal door with the faded sign depicting a lotus blossom behind grubby, grime covered glass and sighed. Then he went in, just like he always did.

There was nothing worse than having to sit in the waiting room of a dirty massage parlor. Like lingering in front of the jock itch medication at the pharmacy. Every second you spend there is one more opportunity for you to be seen by somebody your folks go to church with.

It seemed the old Asian lady who ran the place thought the same thing, or she didn't want a guy to have too much time to think about what he was doing before his 'appointment.' With a warm smile and barely a wave of an arthritic, wrinkled hand she gestured for him toward a doorway covered only by a thick curtain of beads. Before he reached the threshold a tiny, what he figured was a Thai girl appeared on the other side of the beads and reached for him. He recognized her but did not know her name. The little girl, he hoped was at least twenty or so took his hand in hers and lead him through the divide. She wore a tissue paper thin tank top with no bra which allowed him full sight of her pert modest breasts and very alert nipples. It was tied off at her mid-rift exposing a tight belly. She wore a pair of cut off jean shorts trimmed so her ass cheeks hung out of the bottom. She smiled as she showed him to a room, empty for anything save a massage table, and a coat rack behind a tri-fold curtain. Soft music piped from a blue tooth speaker in the corner near a series of candles. Smoltz noted the sounds of a harp and simulated rainfall one would expect at any given spa. Here however the music meant to set a mood did little more than creep him out. She did not say a word. Smoltz remembered trying to talk to her during his first visit. It got awkward quick, so he didn't even bother this time. She gestured toward the screen, handed him a towel, and tried to smile helpfully.

There was no small part of him that was not ashamed as he stepped behind the screen and took off his clothes. The spectre of the world seeing him arrested for this hung over him like a storm cloud. What his wife and two little girls would think? What the squadron would think? But none of it was enough. He hung his shirt and pants on the coat rack and wrapped himself in a towel and focused on what was to come. Then he stepped out from behind the screen and instead of finding what's her name with the see-through shirt and strong hands he found a redhead in a blue police raid jacket,

Commander Alex Smoltz yelped a quick, "No," and shifted on his toes like he was doing an old box step on the dance floor. It was an inadvertent, automatic response to a situation that in no way coincided with what Alex Smoltz could allow his life to be. His body reacted like it was trying to escape the situation while in his mind Smoltz tried to process what was happening to him.

The redhead had a pistol in one hand resting against her thigh and a pair of handcuffs in the other, "Yup," she responded. Taking a step forward she shut the door behind her, "Now sit down."

CHAPTER FORTY-EIGHT

McClintock was studying the stitching on the suit he'd had made for his confirmation hearing with one hand and eyeing a draft of his retirement announcement in the other. The suit, a severe dark blue, and custom tailored by Geoffrey Lewis hung in his office next to his flight suit. It was expensive, the most expensive suit he'd ever purchased, but it was a special occasion, actually a couple special occasions in one, and he deserved it.

The piece of paper in his hand however was another matter entirely. A career was a tough thing to capture in an email. McClintock needed the announcement that he was leaving NCIS after twenty-five years of faithful service to carry the proper gravity his future appointment demanded. This single message had kept him up at night for months. How do you leave the proper, lasting impression in the minds of the people he commanded without bragging? He had done everything in the agency, volunteered for some of the toughest duty stations and assignments, which in turn had led to some of the swiftest promotions the agency had ever seen. To word that right was the thing, nothing seemed to capture it. He'd sacrificed two marriages to his career, and he had a son in San Francisco that he hadn't seen in three years. But when he looked at the words on the page, they seemed hollow, just didn't get what he was trying to say.

His phone buzzed on his desk, shaking him from his fixation. He snatched the thing off his desk in frustration, the mere sound of the thing vibrating on the polished wood grated on his last nerve. He looked at the number and had mixed feelings. He considered hitting the ignore button but another part of him needed to get an update. Smoltz had been a little flaky in the past, McClintock hoped maybe he'd gotten his head on straight since the last time they'd talked.

"Smoltzy," McClintock answered. "Shouldn't you be underway by now?"

"Couple weeks," Smoltz answered in a quiet voice.

McClintock sighed, here we go. He was about to start the long process of calming his friend. The guy he'd known since flight school, almost thirty years ago when….

"He called me."

"Who called you?"

"That agent, your agent, you told me you took care of it."

McClintock could see Tyrone Benhoff's face in his mind's eye. He felt his neck warm, and he wanted to break something, "Whoa, Smoltzy there's no way Benhoff called you, I sent that little shit packing. He's in goddamned Africa for Christsake."

"He said he talked to the family. They say she's going to wake up. Doctors think a full recovery. When she does… we gotta get ahead of this."

McClintock was already working on the narrative justification for the insubordination charges against Benhoff. He hadn't even heard Smoltz's last whimpering nonsense. He'd have that prick on a plane back to the states by nightfall, a civilian within a week, when he heard Smoltz whisper, "We gotta tell somebody."

"You don't have to tell people shit," McClintock hissed. The time for nurturing his old friend along was at an end, "You're going to hold your line just like I am. Even if that bitch wakes up, it doesn't matter what she says. She's been in a fucking coma, her heads all fucked up. Who gives a shit what some doctor says? There's nothing she can say that we can't get around. And as far as their family? What are they going to do against Ennis and all his people? They'll be bankrupted or paid off if they're smart. Either way, snap the fuck out of it!"

"But it's me, I'm the one at the point of all this."

McClintock rolled his eyes, "I told you I have your back. We can handle it only as long as you keep your shit straight. Haven't I been there so far, from the beginning?"

"Yeah."

"And didn't Ennis and the senator come through? Just like they said they would." With cash you dumped on a stupid car you dipshit. McClintock didn't add that last part.

"They did."

"That's right, now get yourself straight."

"Yeah." And the line went dead.

***

Smoltz put his phone down on the massage table and watched Eva Hill like a scolded five-year-old waiting to be sent to his room. She ignored him and replayed the recording to make sure they'd gotten it. Satisfied she dropped the recorder in her jeans pocket and turned for the door.

"What about…."

"What about you?" she finished his question.

He was still sitting on the chair, half naked but for the towel wrapped around his waist. He was in shock, staring slack jawed, his eyes glassy.

"I've got you," she said, her eyes circled the small room as she leaned in closer. "I hold your pathetic life in the palm of my hand. With all this." She gestured to the cringe worthy circumstances of the parlor, "You sell me out, go running to McClintock, or the Senator for that matter, all I have to do is write an affidavit and walk it to my favorite judge. If I were you, I would get my shit together, be a good little sailor, do everything I could for Alexa Wilshire in the event she ever wakes up, and hope we never meet again."

"Bu…" but Commander Alexander Smoltz was speaking to the empty air. Eva Hill was already gone.

CHAPTER FORTY-NINE

Ty Benhoff shuffled into the dark hotel room just after one in the morning. After he'd showed Hanswei and Kid 'n Play the evidence he had collected--he couldn't remember their names though he knew that if he didn't figure them out quick, he was going to end up calling the duo of investigators by the hip hop group's name and that would be embarrassing--the three Zimbabwe cops were so excited with the evidence he'd collected. They wanted to take the cartridges to their lab in Harare and process them as soon as possible. Hanswei also wanted to process the blood Ty pulled from the tree in the middle of the forest but without a control sample from Cruz himself, Ty explained to him that any sequence they developed from the blood sample would be useless.

It took a lot of explaining but Ty was eventually able to get the excited investigator to put a pin in the DNA testing. All this processing of 'his' evidence meant a four-hour drive from Karoi to Harare, he forgot how many hours he stood sentry at the lab making sure not only that his chain of custody was intact but that the processing was done right. He was impressed by the Zimbabwe National Police Crime Lab but being as OCD as agents were when it came to their cases, he didn't trust the techs who immediately broke out powders of all kinds. He suspected part of their exuberance was for his benefit. A means of impressing the American with all the pretty colors. Ty explained that the powders were cool but what they really needed was to fume the cartridges with cyanoacrylate first before doing anything else, but he didn't have nearly enough of the chemical to get the job done in his expedition kit. That slowed everybody down for a while and he was able to replace the excitement of working on 'the big international murder' as Hanswei put it with process to make sure they got the best results they could.

Ty knew NCIS HQ would blow their top at the idea of processing NCIS evidence at another country's lab, which was why he waited until he was satisfied with the lab tech's plan to fume, and dye stain the cartridges, an accepted process at the United States Army Criminal Investigations Lab (USACIL) back in the States, before he called in his status update to Boulden in Djibouti. He thought about calling directly to McClintock just to piss the AD off but thought better of it given the knee-weakening impromptu phone conversation he'd had with the Director of NCIS earlier in the day. For his own part, Boulden flipped his lid when Ty filled him in but at least the SSA was willing to concede that access to the Zimbabwean version of the Automated Fingerprint Identification System (AFIS) would get them results lightyears ahead of the normal process of sending everything to USACIL in Atlanta, Georgia.

"Sooner or later this shit is going to get you skinned alive, Benhoff. You know that, right?" was the last thing Boulden said before hanging up on him.

Ty in fact did realize this, which was why he didn't mention his next call which was to Pellano at DSS to see if he had a Cellebrite system. The Cellebrite was a forensic tool that could scrape all the data off Cruz's phone, if it wasn't destroyed by the river where the kid in Allassa found it. Pellano brought the system over and while the cartridges were being worked, he and Ty tried to get the phone to charge. The hardy little iPhone started charging but the going was slow. When it eventually was able to turn on, much to their surprise, the Cellebrite started copying the data, bit by bit, from the phone to a laptop. That process added a few more hours to the day. When the phone was finally done downloading it was almost eleven o'clock local time. The latent prints lifted from the cartridges were still processing through the database, and how long that could take was anyone's guess. Pellano was a life saver in that he agreed to take over the chain of custody for the evidence so that he could store it in the DSS evidence vault at the embassy instead of Benhoff's super-unsecure Karoi hotel room. Benhoff knew he would answer for that, too, but by the time Pellano had signed for the goods he didn't care what big NCIS thought, he'd had enough fun for the day. When they were finally finished at the lab, the three Zimbabwean investigators and Benhoff started the long trek back to Karoi.

He kicked off his Merrells and dropped his shirt and cargo pants in a wandering trail before flopping on the soft, enveloping king-size bed. He wasn't sure but he might have enjoyed a second or two of deep restful sleep before his phone beeped. It was a subtle beep, but like every special agent and cop in the world would attest, it sounded like a bomb claxon blaring in 1940s London. He picked it up without raising his head from his pillow.

"If this is another call out to the deep dark reaches of Africa, I gotta tell you, my commute is going to be a bitch."

"What?"

That wasn't Boulden. Ty's eyes sprang open, "Hill?"

"Fuck, you're still in Africa?"

"Zimbabwe actually. It's really nice when you get past all the animals who want to eat you and the bugs with diseases that can melt you from the inside out."

"You have really pissed him off, haven't you?"

"It's a continuing process. You know what time it is here?"

"You know how much I've been busting my ass here? It's game time."

Ty bolted upright, "It is?"

"We've got'em, we're serving warrants on your buddy tomorrow morning."

"No shit," Ty breathed. He was suddenly torn. It was a big case, a really big case, and he hated sitting on the bench on another continent. He wanted to be a part of it, but at the same time he was on the cusp of breaking the Cruz murder wide open, he knew it.

"And no one at NCIS knows this is going down?"

"They had their chance and left you out to dry. You having second thoughts?"

Ty shifted on the mattress. "No," he sighed. "Just coming to grips with the fact I gotta find a new job."

"They can't do anything, and you know it."

"You don't know the DOD," he told her. "Doesn't matter, somebody'll hire me." Ty felt a surge to get the Cruz case closed. He was never going to get any sleep in what was left of the night. There was too much left to do, and all those things would be banging around in his mind all night long.

"This is too big to put a halt to, you know that."

"I know." He couldn't stand the sudden guilt he felt. It wasn't that he'd spontaneously grown a strand of empathy for that asshole McClintock, it wasn't the agency. The agency would be better for it once that asshole was gone. Ty was going to miss the work. He was working a murder in the middle of Africa for god's sake, how many American cops could say that?

"Good luck tomorrow, Eva," he told her. "Send McClintock my regards." Might as well get it over with. It wouldn't take long for headquarters to figure out all those original emails came from him and Clarence anyway.

"Bold," Eva commented. "I'll let you know how it goes."

"Awesome, talk to you tomorrow." She clicked off and he muttered, "Fuck." He checked his phone and realized it was three o'clock in the morning. Technically he could still get some sleep. He flopped back on his pillow and started debating whether he should try and go to another federal agency once NCIS was done crucifying him or go back to being a city cop where he could have some fun. That debate didn't last long. He went on to counting ceiling tiles until finally placing bets with himself on how long it would be before someone sent a C-130 straight to Karoi to shuttle him directly back to the RKB for his interrogation. He decided he would know who killed Cruz by that time, and know how to get them, whatever it took.

CHAPTER FIFTY

He breathed in the dry, burnt smells and sickly-sweet odor of charred flesh that permeated what was once Hassan Rhouran's home. Black charred chunks of furniture and melted rugs crackled under foot. The man, wearing a flawless black suit over a glowing white shirt and likewise black tie stood between two black husks of once very capable men. Though they were not good enough to work for him he knew their individual pedigrees. Knew the violent histories that lead these men to a life such as this. They were extremists born for robbery, execution, kidnappings, combat. Sam Heim turned to study the other two bodies that he could make out amongst the destruction. White skulls, cracked from the pressure created by boiling internal organs as they roasted amongst the inferno made them easier to identify. Liquified remains of brain and other matter oozed from the fractures. There was not much left to tell the tale of how these men met their fate. Heim felt there was fighting involved, not firearms. The bodies were oddly scattered around the room, and despite the pugilistic effects of the bodies shriveling inside a raging fire they remained posed in a way that said hand to hand combat.

He found satisfaction in knowing his target could still be a challenge. When he had received the call regarding Rhouran he chose these men specifically, and with the blessing of their masters to be his first wave. He knew it would be a good test of Rhouan, to gauge whether the man still rated the attention of someone like him.

Crunching of black coal behind him took him out of the realm of speculation and into his present charge. He looked to a younger man, dark with olive skin and tightly trimmed facial hair. He too wore an expensively tailored suit. All who served him presented themselves properly. The man simply shook his head no.

"Find him and find the wife." Sam Heim looked through scorched frames that used to hold tall, regal windows. The city of Harare laid out before him. Wisps of smoke still danced from time to time off the rubble surrounding him to wash over his view of the city.

Rhouran had come to rest on the wrong side of very powerful people. People who exclusively turned to him when in need of a correction. Hassan Rhouran's time was growing short.

CHAPTER FIFTY-ONE

When Obert entered his office and found Gerald sitting in a dark corner, he felt immensely more tired than he had at any point on his long watch over the ICPF camp. "You know if they could find you at home, they know where I stay as well, right?" he asked rhetorically while rubbing the stubble on his face with a massive hand.

The look on Gerald's face told him his older brother had not thought of that. Obert sighed, "We go tonight, brother, be at ease."

Gerald stood and took a tentative look around as if waiting for the boogeyman to jump at him from other dark corners around the office. "Ease?" he hissed. "They were waiting for me in my own home. The staff did not even know they were there!"

So you think, thought Obert.

Gerald got in his face and jabbed a slender finger at the dusty tile floor. "My own home," he emphasized. "You do not know what that is like."

Obert suddenly had an urge to make a joke about his brother needing a new suit but thought better of it given the way the man was shaking, "These people expect results, brother," said Obert, putting on a brave face though he felt every bit of the fear his older brother suffered. "Imagine Wei's position. You think his fate will differ in any way from ours if we fail?"

"I don't give a shit what happens to Niphong Wei!" Gerald spat in a hushed tone, his eyes cruising the office.

"I know, I know, brother." Obert sat at the table and pulled the cloth covering off his plans. "I would put you at peace, big brother, though I know the only way to ensure that is to be successful. Tonight, the ICPF will receive information that a group is hunting the herd at the far northern points near the pools. My men have been tracking the elephants in that direction. Hassan's woman will respond, and even if she does not it will not matter. The man is obsessed, whoever the rangers are in that area will suffer his wrath, which is all we need to get a response from the main camp. Once that happens, we move, recover the ivory and go straight to the transfer point."

Obert spread his hands out on the table, studying his operation for any weakness.

"We complete our end of the bargain, brother, then you can know peace once more." Obert looked his older brother in the eye. Gerald tentatively returned the stare. Obert could see the man's resolve hanging by a thread, the price of a life focused on administrative power and standing, versus a life of struggle as Obert understood it.

Gerald slumped in the chair opposite his younger brother and also surveyed the table, and the plan he did not understand. He nodded an understanding toward his brother and wondered how he ever ended up in this mess.

CHAPTER FIFTY-TWO

Lilliana Cartwell found she didn't know how to act. Tonight would be her first scouting mission with Sergeant Jurness. Part of her felt an excitement that was hard to describe. Another part of her was afraid to look at anyone in the eye as she made her way to the mess hall. She was scared. Not scared of the mission or the wild animals that could be just as dangerous as any poachers they could run into. In the end she was afraid of disappointing Sergeant Jurness. As much as tonight would be her first step into becoming a real part of the ICPF, it was also a test. Victoria would be watching her alertness, her endurance, her weapons control, and she expected the senior ranger, one of the first recruited by Danner Maynard, to make her navigate their way through the bush. What if she missed a sign in the soft red earth that put them off course and made them lose the herd? What if she bumbled right into the herd and scattered the animals, or worse yet caused them to turn on them? All these things rattling through Lilliana's head caused her to stumble right into another ranger at the entrance to the mess hall. She felt a hot splash of bitter smelling coffee drench her BDUs.

"So sorr--" she froze when she noticed the surprised expression of Lead Ranger Maynard looking into an empty coffee mug. His hand and wrist were covered in black coffee. Lilliana felt her insides melt despite the grin on his face.

"Mornin', Ranger Cartwell," he said, shaking excess coffee from his hand.

She remembered to stand at attention after a moment of scattered floundering. "Good morning, Lead Ranger Maynard," she stated.

"How's the coffee this morning?" he asked.

Lilliana felt the coffee soaking through her uniform, but she kept her face expressionless.

Lead Ranger Maynard opened the door and held it for her, "Come on, maybe that was a bad joke. I need a refill all of a sudden, after you."

Lilliana jumped and stepped through the door. "Thank you, sir," she said. "I am very sorry."

He waved her off, "No worries." The two started walking toward the food line. "You got a night mission tonight, right?" he asked.

"Y-yes, sir."

"Nervous?" The question seemed rhetorical.

She smiled, "A little, yes."

"I can tell. Anyway, don't be, Sergeant Jurness and the others have trained you well. Just do what feels natural and you'll be fine."

"Yes, sir," she responded.

Maynard broke off to go refill his coffee, "And try to get a nap or something today, you're gonna need it."

Lilliana nodded and watched him go before grabbing a plate and working her way through the line, taking portions of fruit and some nuts for breakfast. When she exited the serving station, she noticed Sergeant Jurness watching her. Lilliana approached her table and Jurness moved her water glass to make room for her. Lilliana set down her tray and sat across the table from her.

"Good morning, Sergeant Jurness."

"Good morning. You ready for tonight?"

"I think so, yes."

"Don't think so. You are ready or you are not."

Lilliana thought about what Jurness said. She was ready… wasn't she? She must have drifted off because the sergeant's words were sharper when next she spoke.

"Ranger Cartwell."

Lilliana snapped back to the mess hall, and her training officer's appraising stare. She suddenly realized she was holding the small velvet bag containing Hassan's diamonds and flash drive between her fingers.

"You are ready, or you are not." It wasn't a question.

"I'm ready, Sergeant."

Victoria watched her for another moment before returning to her meal. "Be in the present, Ranger Cartwell. Everyone here has a past, and that past is respected by everyone here. But when we go out there tonight you will leave the past at the gate, understood?"

"I do, Sergeant."

"Good, what is that anyway?" Victoria gestured toward her velvet bag.

Lilliana shoved the little parcel back inside her uniform that now smelled of coffee. "It is nothing."

"It is something. As long as it is not a distraction it is of no consequence to me. Perhaps it will bring you luck."

Lilliana thought about the precious stones and the horrid mystery of the electronic device. She found herself wearing the package around her neck out of fear she might lose it. She found more and more that she depended on the very thing that was her only connection to her old life. Like a single strand of a spider's web that just wouldn't let her go. It was so very odd, but Lilliana felt safe in some weird way when it was near her.

"Perhaps."

Sergeant Jurness nodded, "I am going for a run, then I am finalizing an operational plan for tonight. I want you to do the same. We will compare our plans at dinner before we strike out. See if we are both on the same page."

"Yes, ma'am," Lilliana said, suddenly bolstered by the fact she had already drafted her own plan for the night patrol on the off chance Jurness asked for such a thing. The small victory gave her a glimmer of confidence going into her first mission.

CHAPTER FIFTY-THREE

Ty sent a text to Boulden in lieu of his DSI report just before leaving Karoi for the ICPF compound. The place was as close to the middle of nowhere as he'd ever been. Ty had a Zimbabwean road atlas he could sort of read sitting on the seat next to him. The temperature was nearing one hundred and twenty degrees--even in the shade. Ty rubbed his weary eyes and covered them in Oakley's as he merged onto the highway, leaving the small tourist town.

He got zero sleep after talking to Eva Hill the previous night. Regardless of the case, and it was a righteous case McClintock shielding his flight-suited, Maverick-wannabe buddies. That prick deserved everything he got for embarrassing the badge Ty and fifteen hundred other agents carried all over the world. The shit Eva Hill was raining down on NCIS and the United States Navy right now was honorable, good, and the right thing to do, in the end the agency would be better for it. But Tyrone Benhoff knew he would never survive it. That wasn't the way the bureaucracy worked. He saw the face of Melanie Lottis for what must have been the thirtieth time since getting off the phone with Hill the night before. There were several ghosts from Ty's past that looked in on him from time to time. Hers was one that hurt the most.

Melanie Lottis was a five-star collegiate swimming prospect out of West Gennessee High School in Syracuse, New York in 2006. She was being courted by the University of Connecticut, University of Florida, and the University of Miami for full-ride athletic scholarships when she met Frank Wentworth at the junction where Interstate 90 met I-81 in Liverpool. Melanie was cruising at the speed limit, heading home after a long night of waiting tables at her uncle's restaurant on in North Syracuse. Wentworth was doing eighty going the wrong way on the off ramp. He was driving a Cadillac Escalade that virtually erased her Honda Civic from existence when the two met head on.

Ty was the first officer on scene. He's pretty sure he was the last thing Melanie saw before her body stopped trembling and her eyes dimmed. Ty had to say pretty sure only because her head was smashed, her skull like an eggshell beneath matted red hair. One of her eyes was destroyed by glass and metal from the wreck. Ty recalled seeing that one remaining brown and gold flecked eye focus on him for just a moment before the light went out. An unspoken question forever frozen in that eye as her body paled under a massive loss of blood. When he was sure she was gone, he turned from her to look for the other driver amongst all the chaos and smoke. That's when he saw Frank Wentworth stumble like any good drunk driver--unscathed--from what remained of the front end of his Escalade. An Escalade and a face Ty had met only two hours earlier that night.

"Motherfucker!" Ty remembered was the only thing he could say as he charged toward the drunk and took him off his feet with a leg sweep. He had the piece of shit by the throat when the next officer, a patrolman named Tate, arrived. Ty still didn't know what Tate witnessed when he arrived but to his credit Tate gave Benhoff a light shoulder bump to bring him back from the brink. Benhoff stood and watched as Tate took Frank Wentworth into custody, his eyes shifting back and forth between Melanie Lottis' decimated vehicle, her still form crumpled within, and

Frank Wentworth, the man who had been allowed to drive away from a DUI stop two hours earlier.

Ty wasn't the one to pull Wentworth over. He'd heard a traffic unit call out the stop on a Crosstown Highway and decided to back him up. When he'd arrived, Officer Burnham, a long-time traffic cop he'd run into a couple of times, was standing just behind the frame of the driver's side door. It was dark, almost midnight, chilly in late fall. Ty took the passenger window and flashed his light on the interior of the cab. The passenger window was up but he could still hear Wentworth talking over Burnham.

"I told you who I am. I live right around the block, come on!"

Burnham had that deadpan, 'just the facts' delivery that Ty never felt he really nailed when talking to the public. "I said step out of the car, sir."

When Wentworth threw the door open and lunged out of the car, Ty was already rushing around the front grill, positive the driver was making a move on the traffic officer. He looked at Burnham who deftly slid a step backward as Wentworth stumbled from side to side for a moment as if he were a character in a Looney Tunes reel. Burnham had the slightest grin on his face. "Step around the rear of the vehicle, sir," Burnham said calmly. "I would hate to see you get hit by a car."

Wentworth did as he was told but not without stating, "I think you should call your chief and see what he has to say about this."

"I'll think about that, but first let's talk about how much you've had to drink tonight."

Ty took a flanking position on Wentworth and watched him. He started mentally checking off all the indicators that showed Wentworth was inebriated so he could document the encounter in his report later on. The man was clumsy, had a confused affect, his speech was slurred, he stank of alcohol, and had a disheveled appearance. Burnham's radio chirped with a response from dispatch related to Wentworth's license plate. Burnham excused himself with that stoic, unflappable touch and stepped back toward his unit. That left Wentworth and Ty standing together. Ty was entertained by the way Wentworth seemed to be trying to focus on him.

"You know this is going nowhere, right?" Wentworth sneered drowsily.

"If that's the case, there's nothing to worry about."

"Nothing to worry about for me. For you and him, probably a little more to worry about."

Ty prickled at the veiled threat. "Do you mean me harm, sir?" he asked the practiced question.

Wentworth chuckled. "Don't have to," he nodded toward the cruiser pulling up behind where Ty had parked. "It's been real," he said as he leaned against the rear of his Escalade.

Ty turned to see Lieutenant Haime, Night Watch Commander, walking up to Burnham. Ty noticed Burnham stiffen as Haime talked to him. Ty couldn't hear all that was said, but he did catch Burnham say, "Fuckin' bullshit," which immediately impressed Benhoff. Burnham shuffled on his feet before straightening and nodding. In the flashing blue lights Ty could see Haime looking at Wentworth.

"Who are you?" Haime asked Benhoff as he and Burnham approached. Burnham's eyes were dark, and his fists were clenched, but he remained silent standing just past Haime's shoulder.

"Benhoff, sir."

"Benhoff, escort Mr. Wentworth to his home." Haime addressed Wentworth like he was giving a press conference, "Mr. Wentworth, we are letting you off with a warning. Patrolman Benhoff is going to see you to your home. Do not get back behind the wheel again tonight. Is that understood?"

Wentworth grinned and made sure both Burnham and Benhoff understood the meaning of his mirth. "Thank you, Officer."

"It's Lieutenant, now be on your way and give a little more thought to your actions in the future." Haime turned on his heel without giving his two officers any more attention.

The three men watched the lieutenant pull away from the curb.

"Like I said, it's been real, gents. Next time maybe we can cut out the middleman, huh?"

"If I find you like this again, I hope you're wrapped around a tree," Burnham growled as he turned to walk away.

Ty was still in a state of shock over what he'd just witnessed. It had all happened so fast. The highest-ranking officer on duty in the city of Syracuse personally issued a get out of jail free card to a drunk and let him get back behind the wheel. Ty literally didn't know what to do. "Burnham?" but the older officer was already in his car. "What the fuck just happened?"

"Shall we?" Wentworth asked casually. "I don't have all night."

Ty looked him over. His first thought was to shoot out his tires and leave him on the side of the road. Then he thought about taking the prick's keys and throwing them into an alley, he'd actually seen that done before.

"Whatever." Wentworth turned to his SUV with a wave. "You coming or not?" he asked.

"Don't you fucking move."

Wentworth froze in obvious surprise, Ty gathered that the man was not often spoken to that way. He turned and crossed his arms, "I get you're new, but you have to have seen the name Wentworth around town. My family built this place. My dad was the mayor's best man. My uncle runs the biggest bank in the city. We own half of downtown. This is how it works."

The asshole couldn't be more than a few years older than Ty, but he talked to him like he was a child. Ty turned toward Frank Wentworth but was stopped when a car came to a halt not six inches from his hip.

"There something wrong, Benjamin?" Haime was back, like this drunk's white knight.

Benjamin? Ty put his head inside the passenger window, "Sir?"

"How long you been on the job, Benjamin?"

Shit, Ty thought. "It's Benhoff, little over two years, sir."

Haime put an arm over the passenger side head rest and sighed as if the conversation were boring him, "If you want to see a day past a little over two years you will be in your car following that piece of shit in the next two minutes, that clear?"

Ty wondered looking back if he'd even had the urge to lash out at his superior or if he'd just dumbly acknowledged the order and turned on his heel. Regardless, he'd followed the order. He remembered his first sight of Haime when he arrived at the crash site. Ty had barely a step in the command officer's direction when he was washed aside by the wake of another dark blue suit, Burnham. The older traffic cop closed on Haime. Haime had an instant to put a handout to try and calm the enraged officer when Burnham dropped the lieutenant to his knees with a straight right to the jaw. Responding officers, civilians, fire, paramedics, the entire menagerie of people populating the travesty on the onramp froze as time suspended itself. Ty heard Haime coughing, blood spewed from his nose and mouth. He tried to say something, but Burnham had him by the scruff and the Sam Browne as he dragged him like an unruly child to where Melanie Lottis lay among the detritus her crumpled vehicle.

"Open your eyes, motherfucker!" Burnham's coolness was gone. His voice was like a wildfire.

"This is on you. LOOK AT HER!" Burnham kneed Haime in the gut and banged him off the bent frame of the car before two other officers could break the two up.

Ty remembered seeing Burnham only once more after that, during the investigation of what happened that night. He remembered the man's hollowed eyes, his shoulders slouched as the two sat among others in the second-floor conference room at headquarters waiting for their turn to be interrogated. Haime was crucified, almost did time for a color of law violation, but enough time had passed, and the public forgot about Melanie Lottis enough that they could just drum him out of the department. Burnham left, too, but without a reprimand. Ty wondered if the moment he could have gone against Haime's order to let Wentworth go haunted him like it did Ty.

Ty sighed, trying to put Melanie Lottis out of his mind. Part of him felt a little better about blowing up his NCIS career after thinking of her. He remembered the moment when she was extracted from the car and zipped into a body bag. He told himself then he would never let bureaucracy or shitty politics keep him from doing his job. He had promised himself the next time he ran into a 'Haime' he wouldn't fail his job and his oath like he had that night. Too bad for McClintock he was the next 'Haime.'

CHAPTER FIFTY-FOUR

Obert returned from the café several blocks from the store with coffee and a bag of pastries to find Hassan Rhouran standing in his office, leaning over the table where his operation was on display before him. Obert hardly had time to register what the Arab was looking at before Hassan's voice rattled him to the point he almost dropped his coffee.

"Are you setting me up, Thoomba?"

"What are you doing in my office?" Obert asked, masking the seething rage in his chest.

Hassan pulled a pistol from his waistband and pointed it at him. "You are setting me up," his voice started to grow louder as he took a step in Obert's direction. "You think I am one to be used as a pawn!"

Obert set the coffee on his desk and dropped the bag of danishes next to it. He reminded himself he needed this animal for everything to work out. In mere hours everything had to work out. "Mr. Rhouran, what you see here is an opportunity I understood would benefit us both. Look again, tell me you do not see this." Obert held his hands up around his shoulders to placate the Arab with the gun.

Rhouran spat, "What I see is that you have a plan to attack this outpost while I retrieve my wife here." He jabbed a finger on the map. "Written in your own hand: diversion. A diversion!" Rhouran said as he stabbed the air with the gun.

Obert nodded, still keeping his hands up as he took a step toward the table. "Does this serve me?" He pointed at the word scrawled on the map. "It does but look at the rest," Obert stated, stepping toward a pile of notes. "My men have watched this camp for weeks. They have documented all of the women there, including your wife. When I heard of you and realized it was she you were seeking, I saw an opportunity. Truth is we would have ambushed her and her partner at that point in the field with or without you. It just so happened that there was opportunity for the both of us." Obert traced his finger between the planned ambush point and the camp itself. "Look at the distance," he said quietly. "An attack on your wife's patrol will draw help from the camp, this is an advantage I need for my own ends. However, look at the distance, they cannot get there in time to stop you. You will have one of my best men with you and a fast vehicle. You have all the advantage here." Obert stepped back. "You will get what you came for, Mr. Rhouran, we will both get what we need out of this."

Rhouran kept the gun leveled at Obert's massive chest. "Why? Why this assistance when you could have simply handled this all yourself?"

"I know who you are, Mr. Rhouran. I know your connections; I know your business. I have need of skills you possess. You can move assets and currency in ways my brother and I cannot. I knew I would not gain your respect or your services without being of service to you. I plan to call on you one day, sir, when I no longer need this place and want to disappear with my livelihood for more stable climes."

Rhouran did not lower the gun. The two men stared at each other, one over the front sight of the weapon while the other looked past the muzzle. "You had best hope you are not betraying me, Mr. Thoomba, especially since you know who I am and what I can do."

Obert grinned, "You will not be disappointed, Mr. Rhouran." Obert turned back to his coffee and danish, leaving the man holding the gun on him. "Danish?" he asked.

CHAPTER FIFTY-FIVE

Gerald Thoomba huffed as he stepped from his Mercedes and felt his loafers slip into the soft, dusty red soil of the driveway. He fluttered his jacket and buttoned the suitcoat while taking in the stillness of the rural property where he grew up. The large white house to his left was lit from the inside as was the barn offset behind it. Such an odd choice of meeting places. He wondered if Obert was trying to be dramatic in bringing him back there. Though he still owned the sprawling plantation. He had not been there in years. He had outgrown such a place. He had never had the aspirations to be a farmer, nor had his father wanted that for him. His trajectory was much higher in life. The mere sight of the place made him yearn for his plush home overlooking Karoi. A place where the dirt could not reach him.

"Brother."

Gerald started just a bit. He had not seen Obert standing on the veranda. The massive man was so quiet when he wanted to be. He imagined it was one of the things that made him so good a hunter.

"Taking a moment to relive old memories?"

"Why did you call me here Obert?" Thoomba asked, tiptoeing through the soft dirt of the drive until he could reach the stone walkway.

Obert lumbered down the steps, the old wood creaking with great strain. He stepped off into the dirt and waved him to follow.

Gerald looked to the house and then to his brother who ambled into the night, heading for the barn.

"Where are you going?"

"I have to show you something," his little brother said without looking at him.

Gerald followed cringing at the dirt surely clinging to his shoes and soiling his pants, "I have no wish to go walking into the night Obert."

"It is important. Don't worry I brought a light for you to see." Obert flicked on a flashlight and handed it to Gerald.

He followed his brother behind the house and passed the barn toward the open pastures. When they rounded the barn, Gerald noted another set of lights in the distance where the first pasture gave way to the bush. The plantation his father had built was massive. The field was only the first of many interspersed among the wild forested area Obert once used to guide his hunts. It had been so long he could not remember the acreage encompassing the property, he only remembered it was massive, larger than some cities as he recalled. They seemed to walk forever before the lights finally appeared to grow closer. Walking in the tall grass he began to feel moisture from the night's dew filling his shoes and his suit pants began to grow heavy as the tall grasses transferred their moisture to him. When he finally reached the lighted area, he found two men digging a hole.

"What is this Obert? I don't have the ti-," Gerald stopped at the edge of the deep hole when a sweet, and at the same time noxious smell assaulted him.

He waved a hand at the offending odor trying not to gag. Then he noticed the tangle of a dusty black corpse laying in a pile in the bottom of the hole. All at once the urge to gag was overwhelmed and all Gerald Thoomba could do was twist away from the sight before his stomach contents washed the surrounding grass in bile and chunks of digesting food. He wretched uncontrollably, the entire world dizzy and bleary in his watering eyes, "No!" he finally yelled, "Why would you show me this?" Gerald turned around wiping at the sour taste in his mouth to find Obert looming over him. He was backlit by the flood light illuminating the pit. He was nothing more than a dark, hulking shadow.

"I told you, brother, that I had the Navy man situation handled. But you did not trust me. You sent a man after the American policeman, and he failed."

"We discussed this," Gerald said.

"Then why did two more men accost the American again?"

"What?"

"Fannel saw them tracking him."

Gerald stepped back, "I did not send anyone else after the man…"

Obert grabbed Gerald by the scruff, and he felt his soaked toes scrambling for purchase as his little brother dragged him toward the pit.

"Obert!" he shouted. Gerald found himself staring directly into the pit. The face of a young man, his sloughing skin mangled in a horrific expression, wide eyes covered in red dirt the only thing he could see.

"This is the man who killed the sailor, Gerald. He will never be found, will never speak to anyone. Can never be linked to me or you. This is a mess that was finished and would have forever been lost to the police." Obert's voice was dark as he growled in his ear.

Gerald was wrenched back to stand at the threshold of the grave. Obert let go of him.

Gerald was quiet. His insides shook, "I… "

"No!" boomed Obert. "No more! You brought the Chinese to us and look where we are! You sent a weakling to kill a man, and again with two more men no better than the first, now look where we are! You do not have the mind for this sort of thing Gerald. You stay out of it. You think to try one more thing without my consent and this fool will not be alone in his hole. Do you hear me brother?" Obert's eyes blazed, his giant fists clenched, "Do you hear me?" he repeated.

"I-I-I hear you," Gerald managed to whisper.

Obert reached out for him, and Gerald flinched. His legs shook so that he could barely keep his feet underneath him as his younger brother smoothed out his jacket for him.

"Good. Now go brother. Go back to your car, and your office, and your big house. Leave this to me."

Gerald only nodded and turned to start the long dark walk back to his waiting car. He'd made it only a handful of paces on his wobbly legs when he heard,

"Brother?"

"Yes?"

"Do not let us have this conversation again."

CHAPTER FIFTY-SIX

Doug McClintock was smiling a broad, satisfied smile. He was reading over the latest field report regarding the Cruz case from the RAC in Lemonnier.

He had him.

The single greatest thorn in his side for the past year had done himself in, just as McClintock had known he would. Tyrone Benhoff abandoned the integrity of his evidence, leaving it to a 'crime lab' in a third-world country. It was a simple violation of policy. The NCIS Manual dictated evidence was to be maintained by the evidence custodian, or in this case the case agent, until properly entered into the NCIS evidence management system. He read the paragraph over a second time just to be sure it really was this easy. While he did so he noted the lack of accusation, or condemnation in the narrative submitted by SSA Thomas Boulden. McClintock made a mental reminder to ensure that managerial oversight was addressed once Benhoff was off the board. Between the violation and the clear insubordination, he would document himself during the last conference call with the director. McClintock knew that was more than enough to force Benhoff into resignation in lieu of a massive smear on his record. McClintock had to acknowledge that in the federal government even he lacked to ability to summarily dismiss a special agent even under the gravest of errors. But there were other ways of dealing with that, ways he'd perfected over his twenty years as a manager. He hit print and listened to the hum of the spooling printer as he sat back and walked the disciplinary process through in his mind. He was reaching for the phone, it was time to recall Special Agent Tyrone Benhoff, when a knock at his door interrupted his train of thought.

His assistant, Gwen Soreano, a middle-aged federal employee of thirty years, stood in his doorway.

"Not now!" he lashed out.

"But... "

McClintock looked up, ready to let loose on the woman, when he noticed the fit looking thirty-something female in a pantsuit standing in Gwen's place. She held a form in her hand. She was clearly an agent but if she was an RKB regular, he didn't recognize her.

"You are?"

The woman flashed a badge, not the NCIS golden chicken either. He didn't rise from his chair, his hand still on the phone.

"Assistant Director Douglas McClintock, Detective Eva Hill, Virginia Beach Police Department," she strode across his suite with her credentials out for him to see.

McClintock felt his insides quiver, suddenly all too familiar with why she was there. She handed him a search warrant.

"Sir, I have a search warrant for any and all documentation related to the sexual assault of Alexa Wilshire."

McClintock stared at the warrant in his hand wondering why he had accepted it from her. Then he looked at the softly glowing screen of his desktop. His email was open, the first words on the screen he managed to focus on read: T-y-r-o-n-e B-e-n-h-o-f-f.

"No." he breathed.

Hill stood at his side. She must have seen the same name he had. "Yes, sir," she said, slamming the screen shut. She removed his DOD identification card and held it out for him. "And Special Agent Benhoff asked me to send his regards."

McClintock couldn't focus, couldn't concentrate, he could only think of the little shit he'd sent to Africa.

"I'd like to ask you some questions, sir. I understand the conference room on this floor has been made available."

That brought him clarity. She had already coordinated to use the conference room. She had already told someone she was coming. He looked around his office and noticed two more dark-suited agents in the doorway. How many people knew about this before he did?

"I'm not saying a word without a lawyer," he said in a cold, distant voice.

Eva Hill smiled. It was a smile McClintock had seen and shown many times before in his own career.

"That's probably a wise choice, sir," Eva Hill said.

CHAPTER FIFTY-SEVEN

Danner Maynard exited his office and skipped down the steps to meet the blistering morning sun. He carried an American-made 5.56 caliber AR variant by the stock in his left hand while a bulging day pack was slung about his opposite shoulder. A Land Cruiser carrying three of his senior rangers waited for him. They were heading out to meet a couple of trackers visiting from South Africa. He had arranged it so that some of his people could get some advanced training in cutting sign. He had been looking forward to it all week as a way to get away from his desk which, as the female-led, anti-poaching model continued to grow, seemed to be harder and harder to break free from. He was about to toss his bag in the front passenger seat when a cloud of dust started rising over the access road to the ICPF compound. That was not out of the ordinary. Visitors came and went from the compound where, in addition to their patrols and other anti-poaching duties, the ICPF did a lot of community events and hosted tours. What was out of the ordinary was that the Jeep, as it came into view, was travelling like the driver was trying to break an axle on the erratic dirt roads that crisscrossed the Zimbabwean bush. Only Americans drove like that, he realized. Danner Maynard sighed as a grey Jeep with diplomatic plates downshifted before stopping at the entry checkpoint.

"Sorry, guys," Maynard said as he retrieved his pack, "I'm going to have to join you later. Better get going."

He dropped his pack on the step leading to his hut but kept the rifle in hand as he waited for the Jeep to clear the checkpoint. He watched as the driver parked right in front of the mess hall so everyone coming and going from the busy wooden building had to walk around the dusty vehicle. Definitely American, he told himself. He grinned ever so subtly when the driver got out of the SUV. He recognized him immediately, even over the black-framed Oakley's, cargo pants, untucked polo shirt, and backwards ballcap sporting some kind of a team he'd never heard of before. The tactical backpack was also a dead giveaway. The driver of the Jeep looked around for a moment before looking at his phone which suddenly went off in his hand like an air raid siren.

CHAPTER FIFTY-EIGHT

Ty was not sure where to park so he just found a place. He as much didn't know who to talk to so he kind of just hovered for a moment getting his bearings. He couldn't put a number on how many women were there, he guessed a dozen, maybe twenty. Each of them gave some variation of the 'why are you here,' look Victoria Jurness showed him both times they met. He noticed what looked like bunkhouses made of thatched roofing and wood. All the buildings looked the same as far as he could tell. The same rectangular design on posts three or so feet off the ground. Gravel paths wound through the red dirt and sparse grass, coursing through the buildings like veins on a massive reddish-orange beast. There were a couple of administrative buildings, and he could smell a mess hall prepping something he couldn't quite identify.

His phone went off, he grimaced when he recognized over a dozen calls. Six were from Lemonnier, the other six had a Quantico prefix. Still nothing from Hanswei or the crime lab.

"They always do that, mate," a white man carrying a rifle called from a dozen paces away. "We have the only service tower for almost twenty miles in any direction."

Ty recognized the face of the man approaching him but couldn't quite put a finger on it. The man, for his part, seemed friendly enough. He looked around the collection of huts of various design and noticed the uniformed women, many with shaved heads, crisscrossing the complex.

"This the International Counter-Poaching Federation?"

"ICPF, that's us. I'm Danner Maynard, Lead Ranger, and you are?"

Ty pulled out his creds and showed his badge, "Ty Benhoff, Naval Criminal Investigative Service, US."

Maynard didn't miss a beat, "Well if you go far enough in any direction, you'll eventually hit an ocean, mate, but that could be quite a hike. You lost?"

Ty broke a smile. "That's a good one," he said. "No, unfortunately I'm here to talk to one of your rangers I think." Ty pulled a print off of the lone Instagram post Albieto Cruz had that included Victoria Jurness and handed it to Maynard. "Recognize her?"

Maynard looked at the photo, "Yeah, Sergeant Victoria Jurness, can I ask what this is about?"

"The guy in the photo is a US Navy Sailor named Albieto Cruz. He was killed outside of Allassa a few days ago. I found her on his feed, I need to ask her if she knows anything about what happened to him."

"Yeah, we heard about that. Albi seemed like a good kid, shame that," said Maynard. "She's around here somewhere, want some coffee or tea while I round her up? We can find some shade, too; I don't imagine Zimbabwe is the most comfortable place you've ever been."

"That'd be great. I do feel like I've been slow roasting since I got to this country."

"I know the feelin'." Maynard waved him to follow and the two climbed the stairs toward the lead ranger's hut. As he did so, he stopped a woman wearing green BDUs and asked her to round up Sergeant Jurness.

Ty watched closely and appreciated that he didn't caveat his request that the police were here to see her. That never went well and gained Maynard a few positive points in Ty's ledger.

Maynard held the door for him and the two entered the office where a window-mounted AC tried to fend off the heat. Maynard crossed to a table and started filling two cardboard cups of coffee. Ty watched with a mixed conflict. Part of him had no interest in adding any more heat to his body. Another part would do anything for caffeine after the long drive through the bush on very little sleep. He took the coffee and immediately relished the bitter smell of the brew as the two sat at a rectangular conference table. "So, you guys have jurisdiction in Zimbabwe?" he asked.

"Not really," Ty replied. "I've been working with the Regional Police some. I will forward any findings to them, but really I'm here to figure out what happened to Cruz." He sighed, "Ultimately, I'm more here so I can tell his mother what happened to him than anything else."

"Seems a lot of effort for one dead sailor."

"You sound like you know what you're talking about."

"I been around a time or two. Former Aussie Service."

"So how did you know Albieto Cruz?"

"He and Victoria have, excuse me, had a thing. He came out here every chance he got. He was a good kid."

"She know what happened to him?"

"Things spread pretty fast out here. I'm actually surprised it took you so long to get out here."

"It wasn't for lack of trying." Ty watched Maynard tip back his coffee and it suddenly hit him where he knew him from. "You knew who I was that night in the bar."

Maynard laughed, "I didn't think you recognized me. Victoria mentioned running into you out in the bush. Said you were in a bad way with some elephants." He continued, "So that night, you got that trouble sorted out obviously."

"Just a little misunderstanding, that's all."

"That guy almost shit himself when you put your gun to his cock."

Ty put his coffee down, "You saw that?"

"I've seen worse, kid. It was a good move for what it's worth."

"Honestly it just came to me."

"Good instincts, I guess."

Ty nodded his head and was about to respond when there was a knock at the door. Ty stood to greet Victoria Jurness. She walked in at a brisk clip and offered her hand.

"Sergeant, this is Ty Benhoff, US Navy policeman?"

"We've met."

"We have, no need to show you my creds again I presume."

"No, sir."

Ty turned to Maynard, "Sir, you have some place I could talk to Sergeant Jurness alone?"

Maynard spread his arms wide, "Mi casa, su casa, or something to that effect. I'll be out and about."

"Thank you."

Maynard left the hut and Ty gestured toward the table, "Have a seat?"

Victoria watched him for a second before doing so.

Ty did the same and retrieved a notebook from his pack. "It's nice to finally meet you without a gun or a big scary animal involved."

Jurness did not respond, she watched him with big eyes that constantly took measure of him.

Ty smiled, "That was supposed to be a joke."

"Yes," she replied.

"Yup, anyway, I want to talk to you about Albieto Cruz." He held up the same photo of her and Cruz that he'd shown to Maynard. Jurness seemed to shrivel just a bit at the sight of the photo. "I understand you and Petty Officer Cruz were close. I'm sorry for your loss."

"Thank you," she said quietly.

Ty left the picture on the table in full view, "Yes, so when we spoke out in the forest--"

"The bush."

"The bush?"

"That's what we call it, yes."

"Okay, when we spoke in the bush, I mentioned that I was there investigating his death. Even showed you a picture of him. You denied knowing him, why?"

Jurness shrugged, "I do not know you. I see an American in the bush while on patrol. This is very unusual. I do not need to tell you anything."

"Fair enough." Ty commented on his pad 'American gear', so he'd remember to swing back around to that later. She was already a little defensive, no need to piss her off right out of the gate. In the back of his mind Ty heard a little voice whisper, that's not like you. Oddly the voice sounded like Kali Earnst. "So, can you tell me about you and Cruz? How'd you meet?"

Victoria took a deep breath that was a little thready on the back end. "He came here with his boss and a delegation from your military. They wanted to meet us and see what we did."

"You being the ICPF?"

"Yes, but more specifically people come to see us, females doing ranger work. This is very unusual here."

"I believe it, are you the only female anti-poaching unit?"

"There are others, we are the first full unit. Lead Ranger Maynard created us, recruited us, and trained us."

"That seems like a great thing, and not an easy thing."

"It has not been easy. We have gone through a lot."

"Well, I for one am glad you are here, I don't think that thing with the elephant would have gone so well if you were not there."

Victoria smiled, and her eyes traced down to the picture of her and Cruz.

"You met him on an official visit. Then what happened?"

CHAPTER FIFTY-NINE

Victoria felt goosebumps bristle the fine hair on her arms as she remembered the first conversation between she and Cruz. It had been after hours. The delegation, except for him and another Navy man, a photographer named Treach, had returned to their hotel in Karoi. Albieto had been ordered to stay behind and accompany Treach for a military news article. She and another of the more senior rangers took the Navy men on a tour of their area of operation. They stopped by the Mana Pools for a packed lunch, she remembered his odd reaction to the vegan meal of fruit, nuts, and some hummus. But he was polite, he asked her opinion of things, which was not a common occurrence where she was from. When they returned to the ICPF grounds, it was too late for him and Treach to leave and make it back to Karoi safely. They stayed in some of the guest quarters but neither she nor Cruz slept a wink that night. They sat on the edge of the camp and talked. All they did was talk. When he left the next morning, he asked if he could come back and take her out to dinner. Victoria remembered the odd sensation of fear and a desire for more time with him twisting in her chest. She left that part out as she answered the Navy policeman's questions.

"How often did he visit?" asked Ty.

It was a month after his first visit that Cruz returned to Zimbabwe. He had called the ICPF out of the blue and asked for her. Victoria did not receive many phone calls as she did not have any family left that acknowledged her. After leaving her husband and joining the rangers, she was a scandal in her hometown of Pfueava, Mozambique. She had no one other than the rangers at the ICPF. She remembered thinking she heard relief in his voice when she heard him speak. "I told you I would be back," he'd said. "Still up for dinner?"

She was. Lead Ranger Maynard was happy for her. He had given her time off, a few days he'd offered with a raised eyebrow. She was stern in her request for the day. She met Cruz in Karoi and the two again traveled the countryside. They drove to Victoria Falls and acted like tourists, falling in with a couple of groups as they hiked around the massive series of waterfalls. Cruz snapped photos both with a very nice digital camera, and with his phone. The photo before her of the two of them was taken toward the end of that day while they walked around the lakeside back in Karoi. At the end of the day, he thanked her for seeing him. It was such a sweet gesture; Victoria couldn't help but give him a kiss before leaving for the ICPF. He was so different from any other man she'd ever met. He treated her as if her enjoyment in their time together was his priority. She felt as if she were a princess that day.

"He sounds nice," Ty commented. "I never met him."

"He was nice," she responded, eyes glistening.

"He came back?"

"Many times, yes."

"Would you say the two of you were dating, serious?"

It had become serious the fourth time he came back; he had told her about his mother then. How he had told her about Victoria. She remembered how she had found that information frightening. Why, she still to this day could not quite explain. Maybe it was such an alien thing. A man seeking approval of a woman from his mother. That was not the custom where she came from. She stayed with him in his hotel that time. Memories of that sleepless night, and the long day of pleasure and laughter that followed drew a tear from her moist eyes.

"We were dating, yes."

"For how long?"

"Over a year." Victoria looked at the photo some more and sniffed.

"Did he ever have any problems with anyone here, or in Karoi when he visited? Do you know of anyone that would want to do him harm?"

Victoria felt a wave of heat spread from deep in her chest, her fingers were suddenly tingling. She nodded, "It was not him they wanted, it was me. It was my fault."

Ty peeled a travel pack of tissues from his backpack and handed them to her. "How do you mean?" he asked softly.

Victoria Jurness, this fearsome woman he'd met in the wilds of Africa, cried freely in front of him.

"I know this is hard and I'm sorry. But I want to get the guys that did this, however I can."

"Us too, mate." The voice boomed across the wooden structure. "Problem is we can't get to 'em around here. And there's nothin you could do about it anyway." Maynard stood in the doorway. The bright sun from outside backlit him so he loomed in silhouette.

Ty bristled at the material fact Maynard blurted out. He used to hear the same thing from mothers and grandmothers when he would canvas with the detectives after a shooting. 'You all can't do nothin,' they'd say, or 'You all don't care about another boy dying in the streets.' Sometimes it seemed like they were right, depending on who you talked to. But that never meant you quit trying.

"None of that's a reason not to try," he shot back.

Maynard seemed to chuckle a little, "I think she's had enough, and this is pointless." He put a hand on Victoria's shoulder and guided her from the chair.

"I'm not done."

"I don't give a damn," Maynard shot back, his eyes hard, leaving no question to his resolve. "You got no authority here." Maynard saw Victoria to the door and turned to face Benhoff, "What's the point in dragging her through this all over again? She has a patrol tonight. Getting this stirred up in her head will do no one any good. You should get the hell out of here before it's too late."

"That a threat?" Ty asked.

"I don't care how you take it, kid, just get outta here."

"I still need answers."

Maynard grimaced, "What does it matter now? He's dead."

"I'm looking to fill gaps, and I won't leave 'til I do." Huge bluff. Truth was there wasn't a damn thing he could do if Danner Maynard literally threw him out of his office at that moment.

"Christ," Maynard breathed. "All you wankers this thick?"

"I'm denser than most," Ty retorted.

Maynard nodded, "All right, but you lay off Victoria."

Ty put his hands up, "You got it." At least he wasn't being kicked out.

"Grab your pack, I'm gonna show you somethin'."

CHAPTER SIXTY

Ty followed Maynard out into the staunch heat and hoofed it to keep up with the lead ranger. They walked down a slightly raised wooden walkway amongst dirt and rocks, past several wooden buildings the same as his office, before Maynard stopped in front of one of the larger ones Ty had seen. It was no more distinguishable than the others save for a woman with a rifle posted at the front door, a massive padlock securing the entry. Maynard nodded at the guard who stepped aside as he retrieved a key from a lanyard around his neck.

"That's an awfully big lock, whatcha hiding back there?" asked Ty.

Maynard dropped the lock to the dust-covered wood porch and pushed open the door, "You'll see."

The room was dark as Ty entered. Ribbons of dusty light drifted in from a row of vents lining the junction between the walls and the roof. A harsh, musty odor, almost an odd mix of decay, soil, and horse feed, hit him like a wall in his next step. He coughed against the caustic scent. A central line of lights flashed on down the center of the room and suddenly Ty Benhoff forgot about the smell. He stood between two massive elephant tusks. Whites and browns ran throughout the pieces, each a foot and a half longer than he was tall.

"Jesus."

"Jesus ain't lookin' here, mate, or if he is, he's not payin' attention."

The room was full of ivory horns and tusks, skins, and skulls of all kinds. The material was stacked and piled in some places almost to the ceiling. He noticed tags, looked like evidence tags, on almost all the animal parts.

"This?" Ty started.

"All poaching, all this year," Maynard stated flatly. "What you see here is almost two million of your dollars in illegally harvested animal parts."

"Two million dollars." Ty parroted the words in disbelief.

"Everyone gets stuck on the number. What's more difficult to think about is that there used to be an animal, a rare animal, attached to everything in this room. These beasts are killed and left to rot so some dick can play chess on a really expensive board."

"That's despicable." Ty felt himself getting mad.

"They poison their watering holes with cyanide, or they just shoot them. The old, the young, doesn't matter as long as there's a payday attached to it. Victoria took Albieto on a couple of patrols with her team. It wasn't regulation but he had the ear of AFRICOM. In this business every little bit helps, right? We got no congressional mandate here. Albie saw this firsthand. He was with them when they found the remains of animals butchered while they were still alive. He got pissed and yeah, he snuck us some gear."

"Guns, ammo?"

Maynard shook his head, "No, I got my own people for that, don't ask any more."

"Sure."

"He got us some comms, uniforms, stuff like the binocs you saw, mosquito nets and tents, that sort."

Ty sighed, he kept finding himself a fan of the kid. He wondered if they'd ever passed each other at the gym or the DEFAC (cafeteria) on base. Probably, it wasn't that big a joint.

"There's something else," Maynard broke his thought pattern.

Ty looked at the lead ranger. His lips were pursed, his fists on his hips.

Maynard gestured around the room, "This whole lot here came from one raid about a month ago now. I put Victoria and her squad on the entry team. She'd earned it, I knew she could handle it. During entry, she shot a fella. He pulled on her first by all accounts. We think Albie was mixed up in a hit meant for us when he was killed. He left in the night even though he knew better. We tried to get him to wait 'til mornin' but he had lost track of time and might've ended up AWOL if he were any later. It was only a couple of weeks since the shooting. The gang we hit had some pretty firm local ties. Victoria thinks this more than the rest which was why I broke it off in there. She's having trouble. You don't need to add to it."

Ty nodded, "I'm sorry for that, what she's going through."

"You ever done it? Killed a man?"

Ty shook his head, "Nope, thank God."

Maynard nodded, "Well thanks, but you got no idea what she's dealing with."

There was a long silence as the men stood amongst the expensive remains of slaughtered animals.

"So was Cruz in it for the woman or for the cause?"

Maynard crunched his eyebrows, "What?"

"Smuggling this gear from the base in Djibouti out here was stealing from the US Government. Even if this stuff was scheduled to be destroyed, he still would have been drummed out of the Navy for it. He was risking his career; I just want to know if he was doing it for Victoria or for the wildlife."

"Both."

The two men snapped up to see Victoria Jurness standing at the door.

"Victoria, ya okay?" asked Maynard.

"Yes, sir." She took a tentative step inside the storage room as if she hated the very thought of being amongst those trophies. "Albieto loved me. He told me as much, and said he wanted to take me to Florida to meet his mother. But he also loved our work here. He called it his mission, too, a righteous mission. He talked about joining us here after his time with the Navy was over."

I like this kid, thought Benhoff. He wanted more than ever to find the man who pulled the trigger on him.

"The men who killed him. They shot him thinking he was me or one of us. They wanted revenge."

"How do you know that?"

"The man I killed, he was from a family known for trafficking. He had brothers, I know."

Ty studied a rhinoceros tusk at his feet. "Even if I can't bring them to justice in my country, I'm going to find out who did this to Cruz and I'm going to do everything I can to see they face justice." Ty didn't mean to say that. You never make promises to victims or their families, but the words just seemed to tumble out of him.

"Can you tell me about the family, the gang?"

"I have records in my office. We can go through them."

Ty nodded toward Maynard, then he looked at Victoria. "Thank you for talking to me," he said.

CHAPTER SIXTY-ONE

As Ty Benhoff and Danner Maynard left the storage room, Fannel, lying prone in his hide a half a mile away from the ICPF camp, dialed a number on his satellite phone.

"What is it?" asked Obert on the other end.

"The American is here."

"The American cop?"

"Yes."

"He means nothing. Leave one man to continue watching and come back here, we have much to do."

"Yes," said Fannel, ending the call. He turned to face the man who was sleeping on a mat beside him and elbowed him in the ribs.

"Uhh." The man was not much more than a kid, maybe seventeen years old. Fannel had not bothered to learn his name yet. "You keep watch. The American leaves, you tell me. I catch you sleeping out here, I will stake you to the ground and leave you for the jackals."

"Yes, sir," the boy whispered, blinking sleep from his eyes.

Fannel backed out of the blind on his belly and began his crawl down the long path to his camouflaged vehicle. Fannel seethed. He had told him and Obert had not listened. The big poacher did not understand. Americans were a danger even when there was only one of them, Fannel had seen their impact in places like Kenya and Afghanistan where he had gone as a mercenary just for the chance to kill them. The American needed to be taken seriously. The man would have been dead already if Obert had only listened to him. Though Fannel disliked the presence of the American, he now hoped the man would not leave. Before long the two of them would be inside the same fence, penned in together. When that moment came, the need to ask for Obert's permission would no longer matter, nor would the need to kill him quietly and hide his every trace. Fannel left the observation point and started back to Karoi, suddenly energized for an operation that to date he had cared very little for.

CHAPTER SIXTY-TWO

Ty was staring at a large three-ring binder almost four inches thick and absolutely bursting with loose sheets of paper. These are your files? he thought. Maynard had left to hold a debrief of last night's patrol. He'd told him he could use his office for the time being. That's as far as Ty got. Maynard gave him the binder and a place to read through it, even gave him a family name to start with. When Ty left, he made the mistake of looking at the messages on his phone.

All caps from Boulden: 'ANSWER YOUR PHONE!'

There was another one from Kali: 'I THINK YOU MADE THE NEWS, AND NOT IN A GOOD WAY.'

Ty had to admit that he'd somehow managed to forget his career was blowing up today. As he scrolled through his missed calls it looked like he was combusting in an amazing fashion. Six calls from Lemonnier, four from the Russell Knox Building, two from Eva Hill, and two more from a couple of his buddies that he went through NCIS Special Agents Basic Training with. He thought about calling Kali first to get a feel for Boulden, but he didn't want to get her in trouble. He called Boulden first.

"You never cease to amaze me, Benhoff."

"Thanks?" Ty answered, but Boulden talked over him.

"Technically you're not even under my command, but you have managed to make yourself the bane of my existence."

Ty didn't respond to that one. Was that a sign of growth?

"I don't even give a shit anymore. Bottomline, there will be a C-130 to pick you up at Karoi International tonight at 1800, don't miss it."

"I'm in the middle of nowhere, breaking this case."

"What part of 'don't give a shit' did you not understand? Earnst is coming to replace you, you can brief her then."

"I can't make any promises." So much for the maturity.

"BECAUSE OF YOU THE RKB MIGHT AS WELL BE ON FIRE! AND ALL THOSE FRANTIC CALLS ABOUT YOU ARE COMING TO ME! ME! I DON'T GIVE A FUCK ABOUT A DEAD SAILOR, AND SINCE THIS MORNING NO ONE THERE DOES EITHER! GET YOUR ASS ON THAT PLANE!"

Ty's phone vibrated showing another call coming in. It was Hanswei from the Rocks and Kitten's squad as he'd come to think of them. Ty's heart skipped a beat. Boulden was still screaming into the phone. "I just got a call, Tom, I'll call you right back." He flipped over to Hanswei just as Boulden's shouting climbed another octave.

"Captain Hanswei."

"Special Agent Benhoff, I hope you are well?"

Ty shrugged, "All things considered, got some good news?"

Hanswei paused for a moment as if considering his words. "I think we do. We have a fingerprint match on one of the cartridges you collected outside Allassa. That is good news, yes?"

"It is very good news," said Ty.

"Yes, it is," Hanswei agreed, then... nothing.

Ty waited. Then he waited some more... and... "So what's your next move?" He couldn't take it anymore.

"It is a sensitive matter now," Hanswei said with a bit of a hush to his voice.

"What does that mean?"

"It means the individual related to the fingerprint is linked to some very important men in West Mashaland."

"No sh-kidding."

"No, there is no kidding."

"What are you going to do?"

"I have my team watching for him in the areas these people are known to frequent, we will find him, and talk to him."

Ty checked his watch and his eyes bulged out of his head. It was almost four-thirty in the afternoon. How much time did he need to get back to Karoi before the sun went down?

"Can I get his name? I'm at the ICPF, I might be able to get some info from them if he is who you think he is."

"Not over the phone. As you know, this must be dealt with very carefully. What I really need from you is a DNA sample from Mr. Cruz to compare the blood from the tree to a known sample."

In other words, you need me to get help from big NCIS and the Naval Medical Command. Ty sucked through his teeth, today was not the day for that sort of request.

"Agent Benhoff?"

"Yeah, Captain, I'm just trying to figure out how to make that happen for you." Ty's mind spun, dead man's DNA. An already packed and shipped body full of dead man's DNA. His sleep-deprived mind blossomed for a moment, "Does it have to be official from the Navy, or will a sample from one of his possessions work?"

There was a long pause. "I honestly don't know; can you get his DNA from one of his possessions?"

"I could try, let me make a couple of calls."

"Very good, I will be waiting."

Before the line disconnected, Ty spoke up, "Wait, Captain Hanswei?"

"Yes?"

"You've been to the ICPF, right?"

"Not personally, but I know the area."

"Great, how much time do I need to get from the ICPF compound to the international airport?"

Hanswei was silent for a moment. "In Karoi? Depending on roads and season, I would say at least three hours, Agent Benhoff."

Ty looked at his watch and breathed, "Shit." He wondered if Boulden would call in a drone strike on him if he cost him one more ass chewing from NCISHQ. "Thanks, one more thing?"

"Yes?"

"Is it really too dangerous to drive around out here after dark, or is just something to say to the tourists?"

Hanswei didn't need any time to consider the question. "For you, Officer Benhoff, I would say driving around the bush out there after dark would be a very, very bad decision. Please do not do so."

I'm fucked. "Thanks, Captain, let me see what I can do about your DNA sample."

"You have a great day, Officer Benhoff."

"Will do."

CHAPTER SIXTY-THREE

Ty stared at his phone. He had Kali's number on the screen and cringed as he started the call. The phone rang for what seemed an eternity. Ty was pretty sure she was ignoring him until finally the line clicked.

"I don't want any part of some sick career suicide pact, Benhoff."

"That bad, huh?"

"You haven't seen the news? By news I mean you can take your pick, Fox, NBC, CNN, you've made all of them today. Boulden is pissed. I heard him curse your name twice today and I'm two offices away from his."

"I need your help."

"You're supposed to be getting on a plane in a little over two hours. Not the time to be running leads in Zimbabwe."

"Yeah, don't think I'm going to be making that plane."

"You really are trying to get fired."

"Pretty sure I'm already fired. I'm just trying to clear this case. The cops here matched a print I picked up in the bush. They need a sample of Cruz's DNA to compare to a blood stain I picked up at the scene. You know if the base has already cleaned out Cruz's can?"

"What do you want, the guy's toothbrush or something?"

"That would work."

"Fuuuuck, call you back."

***

Earnst was a fan of running. She did so almost every night in Djibouti… after the sun went down. It was a hundred and twenty-four degrees on Camp Lemonnier when she burst out of the office door and took off in a sprint down the main thoroughfare that stretched down the center of the base. Sweat poured from you when you simply walked around Camp Lemonnier during the day, much less running through it. By the time she reached the long stretch of consolidated housing units, or CHUs, which were nothing more than Conex containers with linoleum flooring and if you were lucky running water and a toilet, she was drenched. Cruz's living quarters were the third row in from a gravel roadway about halfway down the quarter mile stretch of containers. She knocked on the door hoping that Cruz's roommate, whose name she'd forgotten, would be in. She was just about to shimmy the lock with her DODID card when the door creaked open. Second-Class Petty Officer Henshaw stood before her wearing blue shorts and the golden t-shirt that was the official PT gear of the Navy. He looked confused.

"Special Agent Earnst?"

"That's right," Kali answered between gasps of desperate breath. She wondered if she were about to have a heat stroke while also cursing that she did not keep her time as she ran from the office. She felt a touch of pride, she was really moving.

"You okay?" he asked.

She waved dismissively and cringed as Henshaw jumped, struck with errant impacts of sweat droplets flying from her fingertips. "Cruz's stuff still here?"

Henshaw looked back into the can for a moment before shaking his head, "No, ma'am, Mortuary Affairs picked it up yesterday afternoon."

"Don't call me, ma'am. Of course they did, thanks."

"You sure you're alright?" Henshaw asked again, no doubt still wondering why this NCIS agent stood dripping sweat outside his door.

"Yup, as you were," she said with a wave. Without another word she walked off in the direction of her own can, and a shower. Mortuary Affairs, she thought, I probably could have just called. She scrolled through her phone until she found Benhoff's number. "No luck," she texted. "Good luck with the rest of the crusade."

***

"Shit," Benhoff stated flatly. Maybe NCIS would work with the Zimbabweans once he was gone. He wondered if big NCIS would give enough of a shit to follow up. Technically he had no jurisdiction in Africa, all the desk chumps at headquarters really needed was paper for the file so when the family or a congressional office called to see what they'd done about the death of a servicemember, they'd have something to tell them. The idea of leaving Zimbabwe without at least trying to get something for Hanswei, something to give Albieto Cruz's mother a sense of closure, left Ty Benhoff tracing a rut in the floor of Maynard's hut. He was pissed, there had to be something. He grabbed his backpack and shot out the door.

CHAPTER SIXTY-FOUR

Victoria inspected Lilliana's rifle and found it spotless. "A little more time brushing the chamber next time, yes?" she chided the new ranger anyway.

"Yes, ma'am," Lilliana replied.

Her uniform was clean, her pack in order, Lilliana Cartwell was organized. The look in her eye told Victoria she was nervous, that was also good. She finished inspecting her trainee and took up station standing shoulder to shoulder with her.

Maynard stood with his arms crossed observing the process. When Victoria took her position, he grinned. "Good, Ranger Cartwell, you look good." He turned to the map with a series of concentric circles with a funnel-like curve running through it. The map depicted the parks and preserves around the greater West Mashaland. The circles and the drawings across the parks showed the relative travel of the resident elephant herd.

"All right, you ladies are going to join the herd around zone twelve, it's where we last spotted them. Trail them for the night. Radio for pick-up once they seem to settle. For whatever reason they've been on a bit of a walkabout as of late. You might be in for quite a hike tonight. Intel gives us some light chatter about known customers in and out of the area, but so far there is nothing about active hunts. Regardless, this lot," he gestured toward the drawing showing the relative location of the herd, "around twenty strong are well within the preserve. As long as they stay that way, they're safe. We get any news about a hunt or anything suspicious, you'll be the first to know."

"Yes, sir," stated Lilliana.

"Yes, sir," joined Victoria.

Maynard looked over Victoria's shoulder and muttered, "What's this now?"

Victoria turned to find the American policeman approaching, his eyes fixed on hers.

"All done, headed back to civilization, mate?" asked Maynard.

"I wish," the policeman said, still with his eyes on her. "I just spoke with the Minerals and Fauna Unit in Harare. We've been working together analyzing the evidence I found the day we met out in the woods."

Bush, thought Victoria.

"The crime lab in Harare processed a fingerprint from one of the rifle casings I recovered. They have matched the fingerprints to a subject."

"Case closed," spouted Maynard.

Ty grimaced, "Not quite, I have an individual firing a weapon out there. I have Cruz's phone recovered in the general area, but the two are not close enough to link definitively."

"What does that mean?" asked Victoria.

"It means I need more," said Ty. "Now, do you remember the day you found me wandering around near the river?"

"Yes."

"I was tracking a trail of bullet defects through the area. On that trail I found what I believed to be a blood stain on one of the trees. I collected a sample and the lab in Harare was able to process it for DNA. I have a DNA profile that could be Albieto's. But without a sample of Albieto's DNA to compare it to, it is not proof. I apologize, I know this is hard, but I've got nothing else to go on right now. Victoria, do you have anything of Albie's, anything like clothing, something that might contain his DNA?"

"The Navy will have his profile. Why not get it from them?"

"You know as well as I do what kind of red tape something like that will generate. It could take a very long time. I'm trying to get it done. Get some closure for not only Sergeant Jurness but Cruz's family. They deserve that."

Ty was puzzled as Maynard seemed to find a sudden calm. There was an almost imperceptible nod of... appreciation?

"I think I might have something," said Victoria in a small voice.

CHAPTER SIXTY-FIVE

Five minutes later, Ty was standing in the doorway to Victoria's hut. She knelt over a worn footlocker at the end of her bed. She opened the lid and stared for a long moment, as if working up the courage to reach inside. When she did, she retrieved something and cradled it in her arms. In the dim light of the room, she carried the precious item toward him as if she were about to present him with a newborn baby.

It was a hat, green and orange colors with the U symbol of the University of Miami. Ty had latex gloves on his hands as she handed it over to him.

"I was afraid to touch it since I found out what happened," she said in a shaky voice. "It is all I have of him."

"I promise I will return it as soon as possible."

Victoria nodded.

He put the hat in one of his last remaining paper evidence bags and sealed it with red evidence tape. "Thank you for your help," he said to Maynard and Jurness. "Be safe on your patrol. I will call you with any updates as soon as I get them." Ty hoped he would be able to keep that promise. A lot of that depended on what was to come after he returned to the NCIS's waiting bureaucracy. He slung his bag and headed for his Jeep.

"Where ya goin'?" asked Maynard.

"Harare." *Got a lead, man, can't lose the momentum.*

"Not tonight you're not."

Ty looked at his watch and tried not to cringe, "Why not?"

"You got only a couple of hours before dark, mate. You head out now if the hyenas don't get you some thug will. You might as well be driving a polished ruby in that flashy Jeep of yours."

"I can handle it. I gotta get back."

"You will, in the morning," Maynard told him flatly. "Don't worry, happens to people all the time. We got room for you."

Ty looked at his watch again. He thought about McClintock, thought about Boulden, wondered how Hill was fairing. All people who wanted something from him and none of it good. At least he would have good news for Hanswei. He looked at the sun that still seemed high enough in the sky and suddenly felt like a sissy, scared of the dark. A little voice in the back of his mind told him he could make it. A bigger voice scolded him for laying up when he had a break in the case. He stood by and watched while Maynard talked to his two rangers.

"It's been a tough day, someone else can cover tonight," he heard him tell Jurness.

"I want to be in the field," she told him. Ty saw the subtle poise the woman carried. She had already impressed him when she got the drop on him... twice. Here he saw a stoic determination. The woman was dedicated to her cause, and it was a good one.

"Okay, check in at regular intervals. Watch each other's backs." He shook each of their hands, "Pay attention to her, Ranger Cartwell."

"Yes, sir," the younger of the women said.

The three separated and Maynard joined him in watching them go. Ty looked around the rest of the camp. "An all-female unit, that's what Jurness told me," he said.

Maynard gave them a final wave then looked at Ty with an upraised eyebrow, "You hadn't heard of them?"

Ty shrugged, "Not from around here, I guess."

"No shit." Maynard started walking back toward his hut. "I put this group together a few years back. I wanted a way to fight poaching. I was also pretty disgusted at how women are treated in this part of the world. Every one of my rangers is either a divorcee, widow, victim of domestic violence, or sexual assault. You know what kind of life there is for a divorcee in some places on this continent, not to mention whose fault it is when a woman, or a girl, is raped?"

"I've been around, I know how they're treated. Kind of hard to miss."

"Right, well, I can't stand that shit, so I started the ICPF, and I started recruiting some of those very women."

"An anti-poaching unit made completely of women, how'd that go over with the powers that be?"

"At first, like a juicy fart in church. I got denied permits in a couple of different places before I landed here in Zimbabwe. Problem for those blokes was they didn't know me. I trained all these women from the ground up in fitness, discipline, weapons, and hand fighting the same way I would train any military unit."

"Who were you with?"

"Aussie SAS. You serve?"

"Nope."

"Huh, you missed out then."

Ty agreed, "That's what I hear."

Maynard guided them closer to the source of the food and as the unfamiliar smells grew in intensity, Ty realized he'd forgotten the last time he'd eaten. "Anyway, we were shut out of a lot of meetings, no one wanted to really work with us. Then we started making progress. Caught a few fellas here and there. One group of assholes we nabbed right before they poisoned a watering hole with cyanide."

Ty still couldn't fathom Maynard's last statement. Who would do that? He didn't care how much a tusk was worth. "What kind of asshole poisons a water source?"

"The greedy and desperate kind. Had to control myself a little bit more than usual that day."

"I bet."

Maynard stopped in front of the dining hall. "So, long and short of it, we won them over for the most part. That's how we ended up on the raid I told you about when Sergeant Jurness had to shoot a man." He sighed and looked over the camp for a minute. Ty wondered if he saw a shred of regret in the former soldier's eyes.

Ty let the silence continue.

Maynard finally opened the screen door leading to the food, "I'm going to get some grub. I told you it is too late for the likes of you to traverse this ground. Once you lose the sun, navigating here is a whole different ball game. I've got a bunk room for visitors I can set you up in." He nodded toward the food, "How about some chow?"

Ty nodded and was following Maynard through the screened door when his phone chirped. The number was from NCIS Headquarters. This could be interesting. He shrugged at Maynard. "I think I liked it better out on the road," he commented. "Headquarters."

He left the mess hall and answered, "This is Special Agent Benhoff."

"Special Agent Benhoff, you were instructed to meet a plane at the Karoi International Airport 1800 your time and you refused."

"Who is this?" It was the EAD Drapnier, but Ty just wanted to ask the question.

"Charles Drapnier, answer the question."

"There was no question, as to your previous statement there is no place I'd rather be than on a bird back home, but I did not refuse the order."

"You say."

"I informed SSA Boulden I was on a lead in a remote location. That I have a tentative identification about this DSI investigation. I just gained potentially identifying evidence linking subject to victim. That evidence just so happens to be in a place that makes getting to Karoi International by 1800 an impossibility. I can probably make it tomorrow, but the pick-up will be better suited in Harare."

Ty heard nothing on the other end of the line. This was where Boulden would be screaming. This was where McClintock for sure would have popped. He wondered if Drapnier was more controlled than either of them. Or maybe he was just confused, a headquarters executive who'd never supervised more than his own cubicle while climbing the corporate ladder one PowerPoint presentation at a time. He was, after all, an Executive Assistant Director. Ty waited another moment, trying to gauge his next move. He was getting tired of being a wise ass, a state he didn't even think was possible. Tormenting empty suits had been one of his passions ever since joining the federal government. There were just so many of them to pick on.

"So, tomorrow night, Harare, then say 1800?"

"Special Agent… "

"Also, this counts as my DSI brief, correct? You'll pass that along?"

"Special Agent Benhoff!"

"Or is he there again?" Now he could hear the heavy breathing. It wasn't as satisfying with Drapnier, though, for some reason. Ty kind of felt bad for the guy, he was clearly out of his league.

"Special Agent Benhoff, you will get on that plane as ordered, and you will return to headquarters where your conduct is under review, is that clear?"

"Which one?"

"What?" Pure confusion is the only way to explain the tone of the single-word question.

"Which plane?"

A quick intake of breath.

"And which plane? Harare?"

The phone clicked in his ear as the line went dead.

CHAPTER SIXTY-SIX

Obert Thoomba was tired of staring at the table covered with a map, notes, photographs. He couldn't stand the sight of any of it anymore, but at the same time he could not look away. The conglomeration of plans, hopes, worries, and contingencies was the only chance he had of surviving the next couple of days. His eyes centered on the ICPF encampment, on the specific building that held his treasure. Then his eyes drifted, tracing a line from the camp into the bush. A straight-line dashing across the countryside for a handful of kilometers where a dot and an empty circle on a map was the only interest anyone in the history of man ever had on that spot. It was freedom, the finish line for he and his brother. His task fulfilled, his debt paid, his only prize would be his continued existence. Thoomba was surprised as a single droplet of sweat fell with a splat on that exact mark. He blinked and watched the ink smudge under the drop. It was time.

In a wide storeroom in the rear of the trinket shop stood fifteen men, some barely more than boys. Men with nothing he did not provide for them. They ate and were able to feed their families at night because of him. They owed everything to him, and they knew the price for failing him. Each held a rifle in their hands. Fannel and Hassan Rhouran stood to the side. Fannel had a coolness to him that Thoomba had depended on since childhood. Rhouran held a look of disgust. He had wideset eyes that seared into Obert as he approached the group.

"Shoot anyone who tries to oppose me. Get into position, do not move until I say." He eyed each one of the men, lingering for a moment as he stared at them to measure their resolve. They did not fail him. He had chosen each one himself and provided a plentiful bonus on the promise of success, they would not fail him.

"Go."

He waited for them to clear the room before approaching Fannel and Rhouran. "I am fulfilling my end of the bargain. Consider this when I approach you with opportunities in the future." He stuck out his hand.

Rhouran studied the meaty paw before taking it. "We will see," was all the man said.

Thoomba nodded to Fannel who showed Rhouran to the vehicle where four men, including Guillone, were waiting to take him to the site. When Fannel returned, he said plainly, "I do not trust him."

"Nor do I."

"The American is still at the encampment."

"Then all your dreams have come true, my friend. As long as it is not a detriment to the mission, he is yours to deal with as you please," Thoomba said with a fatigued resignation. He had no room left in him for any more contingencies. "We go."

CHAPTER SIXTY-SEVEN

Kali Earnst ripped her ID card out of the laptop and slammed the lid shut. She had come to the realization that if she read one more email with an NCIS lead request in it she would throw the goddamn thing through the metal wall of her office. The NCIS office aboard Camp Lemonnier was nothing more than three metal container units stacked on each other like so many Jenga blocks. She was fairly certain she could at least punch a hole through the wall with the computer if she really wanted to. Tonight, she really wanted to. It was one of those days where she had come in to work with a list of things, she needed to get done to keep up with her own case load but ended up almost immediately covering everything for everyone else. There were three other agents and an Air Force Office of Special Investigations Agent assigned to the NCIS office, all of which managed to be somewhere else on a 'force protection' survey which was nothing more than an officially covered boondoggle surveying local hotels and scamming free meals from restaurants that wanted U.S. servicemembers' greenbacks.

First came the suspicious package. At 0830, prior to her finishing her first cup of coffee - even in the pit of hell an agent needed her coffee - the Explosive Ordnance Disposal Unit was called to a backpack on the perimeter road of the base. Boulden had simply banged on the ceiling of the lower deck and yelled the name of the security chief who called it in. By 0900 she was sizzling in the mid-morning Djiboutian sun while the bomb techs sent a robot rolling in a high-pitched whirr to investigate. She and at least a dozen officers, contractors, and enlisted watched the little guy she'd dubbed Johnny Five study what turned out to be a poncho liner containing a smuggled half-bottle of Southern Comfort, and a half dozen condoms. This led the assembly to speculate with great comic relief that someone's 'romantic' interlude was interrupted the previous night and in their flight from a roving security patrol they'd ditched their precious cargo. She almost laughed in the face of three officers when they asked her if she was going to take the evidence for her investigation. They were calling it a date kit. All she saw was a sexual assault allegation in the making. By the time she cleared the 'scene' she was soaked in sweat but before she was able to escape to her quarters for a change of clothes, Boulden lit up her cell and sent her to give an onboarding brief to Camp Lemonnier's newest group of candidates for heat stroke.

Whenever a new group joined the base, they were given an onboarding brief. This consisted of an overview of base SOPs, a threats brief for the area of operation, a health and welfare brief, and a sexual assault brief. At some point an enterprising SSA, years before Kali came to the searing dot in the horn of Africa, decided the sexual assault portion of the onboarding briefing was NCIS territory. This even though the base had a cadre of victim advocates and Sexual Assault Reporting Coordinators (SARCs) whose job it was to do just that, communicate and render aid in the event of a sexual assault on base. Kali had to wait for the Command representative, some Ensign, to give a practiced though not quite polished intimidation brief on the rules and regulations governing life on base. This was then followed by an intel specialist who provided a similarly, though much more refined threats brief. The First-Class Petty Officer had the new additions afraid of every goat and rock along the roads outside the gate before he was done. When it was Kali's turn to give the sexual assault brief, she was just that, brief.

"Don't shit where you eat. No means no. Keep your dirty freaking hands off your co-workers. Also, don't lie, just because he's not into you anymore, or doesn't call you back, doesn't make him or her a rapist. If you follow rule number one you will be fine. If you do not heed rules two and three, know that you will be meeting me under difficult circumstances, but that is only if you survive the incident. Be warned that every person on this base that I have given this brief to has been advised to use the most incapacitating force in their arsenal in the event they suffer an attempted assault."

Kali noted the blank stares from not only the assembled group of newcomers but also the disapproving looks from the Victim Advocates. "Now, everyone bow your heads."

The audience shared quizzical looks.

"Are you disobeying a lawful order? Bow your heads!" she bellowed.

Everyone in the audience immediately did what they were told.

"Now, with the power vested in me, I hereby grant each one of you the authority to commit great bodily injury upon any such person who without permission grabs your butt, your boobs, your package, blows on your neck, or attempts to enter any orifice without first gaining specific verbal approval from you at the time of entry. You may lift your heads."

The room was deafeningly silent. She let the pause linger for a moment before closing, "There, now you have the same freedom to defend yourself everyone else on this base has. Doesn't that feel good?"

Kali exited the command brief without another word, amazed once again that there was a need to explain to grown adults that they cannot rape or grope their co-workers. She was heading in a beeline for the office to finally make some headway on her own workload when Boulden once again yanked on her digital leash. His text read: "Base emergency management policy meeting, fire department, 1030hr." As she read the message, she realized it was 1025hr. A passing blue digital-clad sailor jumped when she motherfucked her phone in the same tone she'd ordered two dozen other sailors to bow their heads.

On the bright side, the policy meeting had very little to do with NCIS's role aboard Camp Lemonnier. Though the meeting included the contract fire department staff, EOD, the medical command, and a couple of the CO's straphangers, she was not compelled to make up some NCIS stance on any given topic. Her biggest challenge at surviving the meeting was staying awake.

Once that bit of bureaucracy finally came to a graceful conclusion, she raced by the dining facility for her usual lunch of chicken and broccoli, then raced back to her office to finally get on a case she hoped to close. Her laptop had barely flared back to life before a high priority lead assignment flashed across her email.

"You're fucking kidding me," she swore to the empty room. She read the email message again. The Camp Pendleton Field Office wanted to know if a third-class petty officer assigned to the medical unit was involved with the subject of a domestic aggravated assault that occurred a week before in California. There was nothing else, the case agent wanted to know if a third-class in Djibouti was friends with a second-class in Pendleton who had a thing for beating his wife. That was it, no context, no hint at what the case agent was really looking for.

"Pfft! Two hours of my time that could be covered with a goddamned phone call, my priority is higher than yours, pal."

All she wanted was a couple of hours to file some ultimately useless paperwork no one would ever look at so she could close a couple cases, update an operations report, and update a source record. A bogus high priority lead could wait. Kali turned off her email, put her phone on silent, not vibrate, and set to work abusing her keyboard. One after the other, boom, boom, boom, she was churning through the bureaucratic shuffle that unfortunately was the sad truth in the life of a special agent. When she started on the update for one of her sources, she started seeing the light at the end of the tunnel. She saw herself bombarding Boulden's inbox with her mountain of paper then fleeing her live-in Jenga puzzle for the Thunderdome. It was shoulder and back day, a nice leisurely workout followed by an easy run once the sun went down, then a glass of Cabernet Sauvignon from the secret stash she kept in her can.

Then the phone rang.

She looked at the phone then looked at the clock and all her hopes died a withering death. Somehow, she'd fallen into a time warp because it was 1620hrs, almost the end of the day but not quite close enough. Not that time mattered in a place where you worked seven days a week, but if it were at least 1630 she could legitimately say she was on her way to the gym or something. The ID read Boulden. If it was anyone else, she could ignore it and flee, but he knew she was there. She didn't even have the energy to swear, Kali just sighed. "Yes, sir," she said as she answered the phone.

"Get your shit and get to the flight line," Boulden said, his voice was brusk and held a dark tone. For whatever reason she immediately thought Ty Benhoff had something to do with whatever came her way next.

"Why?" she asked

"Benhoff's shit has finally caught up with him. He's being relieved and you're up."

"Fuck."

"What's that?" Boulden asked sharply.

"Nothing, what time do I need to be on the flight line?"

"Ten minutes ago."

"Yes, sir."

"Great, and Kali?"

"Yes, sir?"

"You were right the first time, you just got fucked, thank Benhoff if you see him."

She hung up the phone and slouched back in her chair. "This just isn't my day," she told herself. "Wait... if I see him?"

CHAPTER SIXTY-EIGHT

Lilliana Cartwell watched the old Land Rover disappear in a cloud of red dust and once again reminded herself to calm down. She'd been out this far into the bush before. But that was with a platoon of trainees like herself. She'd even been on multi-day patrols, sleeping in a small tent hoping the lions and the hyenas were not paying attention. But this was different, tonight was for real. She was an ICPF ranger, and she was out there alone with Sergeant Jurness. She observed the red-orange sun low in the sky for a moment. It flirted with the Acacia trees, turning them to shadow. She retrieved her map and compass from her thigh pocket and got her bearings. The vehicle dropped them at a pre-established point, but she knew Sergeant Jurness would ask her where they were. It was rule number one out in the wild. Drilled into her and the other trainees relentlessly. If you don't know where you are, no one can come to your aid. Figuring out your spot on the map during an emergency is time wasted, and seconds could mean the difference between life and death.

She studied the topographical map and compared it to what she saw around her. As she turned, studying the geography, her eyes found Sergeant Jurness watching her. She froze for a moment.

"Are we where we should be, Ranger Cartwell?"

"Yes, Sergeant."

"Very good," Sergeant Jurness smiled. "Now for the rest of the patrol I am Victoria and you are Lilliana. Will that be all right?"

"Yes, Ser-- Victoria."

"Good, have you found any sign of our charges?"

Lilliana's breath caught in her throat, oh no. She studied the ground and the sparse trees and bushes covering the landscape. She wanted to look like she knew what she was doing, as if she'd already thought of it. A panic grew inside her as time wore on without her finding anything. A stray look back at Victoria was not something she meant to do. The sergeant was not looking at her, though. Her eyes were at her feet. Lilliana did the same and realized her right boot was standing in the middle of a massive circular track. The animal sign dwarfed her own footprint. Her cheeks flushed with heat.

"Take a deep breath," Victoria told her. "You can't do it all in the first five minutes of the mission. We will be out here for three days."

"Yes-- Victoria."

The sergeant nodded, "Do a comms check and we will catch up to them."

Lilliana did as she was told and received a static-laced confirmation and a, "Good luck," from the ICPF communications room. When she finished, she looked at Jurness.

"After you," she gestured with a wave of her hand.

Lilliana gave the massive pack on her back a shake. Cinched down her shoulder straps and assured that they did not interfere with the sling on her rifle. Then with her eyes roving for the next track, which was obvious now that she saw the huge prints, she started after the herd.

CHAPTER SIXTY-NINE

Ty watched the sun set over the grasses and trees of the Zimbabwean countryside as he and Captain Hanswei confirmed plans to meet at the crime lab in Harare in the morning. It really was pretty out in the wilds of Africa, if only there weren't so many things out there that wanted to kill you, Ty mused. He hung up with Hanswei and studied the list of calls and text messages he hadn't responded to. Boulden and Earnst, and a voicemail message from Hill indicating McClintock had already lawyered up. She did also mention that she'd heard the assistant director curse his name while being escorted out of the Russell Knox Building. That gave Ty a little bit of a pick me up, though not one that could diminish the 'your career is over' alert ever present in his mind. He'd even caught himself wondering what his next move was going to be. He was going to clear the Cruz case. Even if he didn't get to slap cuffs on Albieto Cruz's killer, he had found the evidence and put the case together that would bring the case to an end he hoped Albieto's mother could find closure in. Well, Cruz's mother and Victoria Jurness, that was. Then what? Back to the PD? Maybe surf usajobs.gov and hope word hadn't spread so far, he couldn't get on as an agent somewhere else. Fuck, who knew?

He checked his watch again. It was almost six. He wondered what the flight crew had been told when they were sent to Karoi, nothing good, he was sure. When his phone vibrated in his hand, he expected to see an international number. The crew chief or pilot or something wondering where he was. Instead, it was Kali.

"I figured you'd be at the gym by now," he answered.

"Not funny, asshole, three guesses where I am."

"Bermuda?"

"Nope."

"Kabul."

"God no." She scoffed.

"Djibouti?"

"Flight line, Camp Lemonnier, your plane and mine took a shit during the final walkthrough."

Ty actually felt pretty good for a moment, "So I didn't miss my flight?"

"Cut it out, I don't have it in me for bullshit banter anymore, Benhoff. What the fuck did you do?"

Ty sighed and thought about the talking points he'd been rehearsing over and over in his head for when he finally met the disciplinary board that would be charged with drumming him out of NCIS. He knew what he said wouldn't matter but he didn't want to go out like a chump either. Now that he had a chance to practice his closing argument with another agent, the words in his head sounded stupid, even to himself. "McClintock pissed me off one day so I helped the local PD out with a case he was trying to shut down."

"You did an end run around an Assistant Director?"

"Yup."

"What did you do?"

"I put the lead agent in touch with one of my sources in the IT shop aboard Norfolk. He gave her emails from the air wing command, and McClintock."

"Huh."

"Huh?"

"You have no survival instincts at all do you?" she asked.

Benhoff sighed, "If I told you, it was the principle of the thing, would that matter?"

"You and principles seem kind of mutually exclusive, so not really."

There was a silence then until finally Ty broke the pause. "So Boulden sent you to walk me to the gallows?"

"No, I'm your replacement, so you can add me to your list of victims. Looks like you've got a stay of execution, though. I don't think this thing is lifting off any time soon."

"Good."

"You got this Cruz thing wrapped up then?"

"I think so. I won't be in Karoi tomorrow, though, I've got evidence I've got to get to Harare. Might want to float that to Boulden, maybe he's calmed down a little by now."

"Doubtful, I think you represent a diminishing possibility of him ever seeing GS-14 if you are around."

Ty chuckled, "That's funny. You know what the plan is?"

"For you?"

"No, for the other four assholes who put NCIS on the national news today."

"Touchy. I know Boulden has orders to get you back to the motherland and do it fast."

"Yeah." Ty felt the weight of inevitability.

"Yeah, well, I will call you if I hear anything else. In the meantime, I'm going to see what's up with theses flyboys malingering on my base."

"That sounded dirty," Ty told her.

"It may be."

CHAPTER SEVENTY

Rhouran liked the tall grasses. Creeping through them reminded him of another life, one he'd left but never truly left behind. The stalks were tall and brittle, and he followed the man in front of him as the two belly-crawled to their first checkpoint. They knew the rangers had been dropped off and were tracking a herd of African elephants by the radio chatter that they were able to listen in on thanks to some very creative though simple electronics gear the Thoombas employed against their main enemy in their poaching efforts. Rhouran had immediately recognized Lilliana's voice as she signaled the ICPF their position and directions. A cold anger grew in his chest as he was reminded of the disrespect his wife had shown him. The embarrassment of having to find excuses for her absence from public events. That would be addressed soon enough. The biggest question in his mind as he followed the poacher through the brush was the wallet. Not for the first time did he wonder if the woman even realized what she had in her possession, what it meant to so many people, people Hassan Rhouran could ill afford to disappoint. If it had been simply the diamonds, he would have let her go, there were plenty other women for a man of his means, and as far as he could tell the whore was barren anyway. But she could not have left well enough alone. She would learn from her mistake, Hassan knew, just as soon as he once more had the cryptocurrency wallet back in his possession.

Ahead of him the poacher stopped and waved him forward with a gentle flick of the wrist. Hassan crept slowly so as not to disturb the high brittle grass and came to a stop shoulder to shoulder with his guide. The man had a pair of binoculars to his eyes. He rested them on the soft ground and pointed forward and toward his left.

"You see them?" he asked. "In the trees."

Rhouran put his own glass up to his eyes and searched the direction the poacher had indicated. He missed them at first until he noticed the trunk of a juvenile whip toward a low hanging branch.

"Whoa," said Hassan. They were so big; the lumbering herd of elephants were massive animals. But the adults were so still inside the tree line he could barely make them out at first look.

"Yes, there is a water source over the next rise. We wait here, the rangers should find the elephants here soon."

Hassan was watching the beasts swaying softly inside the trees, "Why do they not go to the water?"

"They wait for the bull. He decides when it is safe."

"Safe?"

The poacher nodded. "Yes, they have young." The man spoke like he was explaining something to a child. Rhouran found himself incensed.

"What if they come this way?" he asked, fearing the very idea of being trampled by a herd of elephants.

"They will not come this way."

"How do you know?" asked Rhouran, thinking the African was a bit of a blow hard.

The poacher pointed to the biggest animal. He stood further off to Rhouran's left. Still, he estimated two hundred meters away at least. As he focused the glass on the big animal, he found it odd that it looked like the bull was watching him. The poacher might have read his mind.

"The bull knows we are here. He can probably smell us. He won't let any of the others approach us. If he approaches, it will be only because he intends to kill us. Then we run."

"Run," said Rhouran.

"Yes, run, absolutely."

Rhouran studied the big bull elephant who was definitely looking in his direction. Then he considered the AK-47 laying next to him and the pistol strapped to his chest. "Run," he breathed.

CHAPTER SEVENTY-ONE

Obert stood in the spacious bed of the cargo truck he had procured for the night's operation. No registration, no identifying numbers, and a counterfeit license plate made the vehicle a ghost. He'd had the truck delivered to the family plantation the week before last where it had sat quietly in one of his many outbuildings waiting for just this moment. He watched the sun drifting lazily behind the flat-topped trees and tall grasses. The horizon looked like it was on fire, the sky was so red. He studied his men. They were disciplined men, if not trained by himself to be silent and patient hunters, trackers, and guides, then men recruited by Fannel for their reputation in other matters. The dozen or so lounged in the shadow of the truck or the stand of trees they used to mask the vehicle's stark profile. It was quiet, serene in the moments before an action that would be unprecedented in the quiet war that men of his kind had waged against the wildlife police for decades. He wondered as he watched them waiting if it was not he who seemed the most nervous of the entire group. His plan had to fall into place like the gears in an expensive timepiece for him to make his final delivery and to once again know peace.

Obert took a deep breath as he watched the last shreds of light yield to a starfield as clear and as breathtaking as ever he'd seen.

He looked in the direction of the International Counter-Poaching Federation. He was miles away, trusting his scouts, nestled like ticks in the wild surrounding the encampment, to do their job and alert him of any last-minute variables he had not seen. The radio was quiet, just as Thoomba hoped it would be. Time grows short, he told himself. Time grows short.

***

The darkness was complete by the time Lilliana called a halt. She could barely see enough in front of her to keep from walking into an Acacia tree, so she stopped and took a knee. Victoria, facing the other direction, took a knee next to her.

"What is it?" Victoria asked as Lilliana shuffled with her belt.

"I cannot see enough to keep sight of the tracks," she commented as she retrieved a red filtered light from her hip.

"Keep it low, we only use the light when we have no other choice."

Lilliana froze for a moment before shaking her head. "Night vision?" she asked sheepishly.

"Yes," said Victoria, retrieving her own device.

Lilliana grabbed a night vision monocular that was mounted on an awkward harness that never seemed to fit her. She flipped her boonie cap back, so it hung from her neck and slid the harness over her head. She closed her eyes as she flipped on the light absorbing goggles to protect her natural night vision, if only for a moment. As she opened her eyes, the world shifted into a spectrum of light greens and black. She looked at Victoria whose eyes glowed as she studied the night vision goggles in her hands. Lilliana did not say anything. She knew what her superior was thinking about. The fantastic technology had come from her American sailor. She let her have her moment and instead searched the ground for the next track. It didn't take her long. There were more animals in a tighter herd now. If it was daytime the track she was following might have looked almost like a paved road. Lilliana searched the trees ahead and noticed several sets of glowing eyes swaying near the treetops.

"Found them," she whispered.

CHAPTER SEVENTY-TWO

Ty was standing outside the small, one-room hut he'd been assigned, holding a cup of coffee, and staring up at the sky. He had never seen so many stars. It was brilliant.

"It's the light pollution," Danner Maynard said.

The voice from out of nowhere spooked him a little. "Huh?" Ty asked.

Maynard put his hands out and gestured around the camp. "We are in the middle of nowhere. We have no streetlights, as you call them, so," he looked up, "every night is a spectacle. Especially when a city guy like you shows up."

Ty looked at the stars again, "Actually I grew up in the country."

"Yeah, get back there much?"

"Not enough," Ty paused. "What about you? How'd you end up out here?"

Maynard didn't look at him as he answered. Ty could tell he'd been asked the same question by countless people countless times.

"Found a passion and I ran with it. I did my time in the sandbox, and I liked it. I liked it even better when I started going to the same shitholes to do the same job but got paid three times a soldier's rate for it."

"The contractor's life."

"Yep, and I enjoyed every part of it. There were two years when I would leave Iraq or Afghanistan, maybe

Yemen a time or two, and instead of going home I would run off to Macau or Vegas and burn through every cent I made at war. I would go broke just before jumping on a plane and flying back to the shit. Gambling, girls, blow, whatever, livin' that life."

"What happened?"

Maynard smiled to himself, "My dad got sick. I got home just in time for him to take my hand and tell me to find something more, to live my passion. Drops that on me and dies right there in the bed. Leaving me bleary-eyed and hungover, wondering what the fuck he was talking about. I was livin' the dream. I went back and six months later I return to his empty house and a box, like a shoe box. In that shoe box were letters and photos of him building houses, digging wells. There were letters from the Red Cross, the Department of State, a medal from the Australian Ministry of Interior for his efforts building a school in East Timor."

"Good guy."

"Yeah, but I didn't know he did any of that stuff. To me he worked nine to five as a bank executive in Queensland, took care of me, my brother and my mom, rinse and repeat. That's when it hit me. I was passionate about money and a good time. He meant for me to find a passion that made the world a better place so, here I am."

Maynard went silent, looking back up at the sky.

Wait, thought Ty, *that's it?* "So how did you end up here leading an all-women anti-poaching unit?"

"I like animals, and I hate it when women are treated like second-class citizens. Seemed like a good fit."

True, Ty had to admit.

"Now for my questions."

Ty looked at his host.

"What's the US Navy doing in a landlocked country investigating a crime they have no jurisdiction over?"

Ty chuckled, "You'd think I'd have heard that one before, but you're the first."

"Sure."

"Officially I'm here to find out what happened to Albieto Cruz so I can report back to his command, they can further it up their chain, so that a paper trail that no one is ever going to read exists just in case," Ty sighed.

"So now for why you're really here."

"I didn't know Albieto Cruz. The Navy Casualty Assistance Officer has already probably told his mother he died in Zimbabwe, but they can't tell her why. In the end I could give a shit about some Navy bureaucrat being able to tell his boss what happened. But Cruz's mom deserves to know, and more importantly, given the way he was killed, she needs to know I did everything I could to make sure his killer faced some kind of justice. Whatever that looks like in Zimbabwe."

There was a pause while Danner Maynard digested his words. Then the ex-soldier commented, "Never thought of it like that. I always thought you investigative types were just out to get us raggedy soldiers so you could make rank."

"I'm a civilian, I don't make rank."

"Civilian? Even better."

Ty looked at the stars again, choosing his next words carefully. Truthfully, he had no interest in asking but the matter of the US gear in the ICPF camp was going to come up. "I've got another question."

"I'm an open book, mate."

"I noticed a few Navy identifiers on some of Victoria's gear. How did she get it?"

Maynard chuckled again, "You don't miss much."

"Hazzard of the job."

"All that shit came from Albie. He'd show with pelican cases full of it. I try to outfit my girls the best I can but, in the end, this is a non-profit. Every little bit helps."

"He ever say how he got it?"

"Yeah," said Maynard.

"So?"

Maynard looked at him sideways, "It's not what you think, mate."

CHAPTER SEVENTY-THREE

Victoria felt the familiar sensation, kind of a tickle in her chest as she watched the dozen or so elephants standing inside the tree line. The adults watched the surrounding area patiently and still. They barely moved. It was amazing that so many massive animals scarcely made a sound. She scanned the herd as her eyes adjusted to the soft green light in the goggles. She recognized most of them, even in the grainy distortion of the night vision. Looking more toward ground level, she counted two additional sets of eyes that blinked in and out as the two calves, Mojo and Jenna, shifted a little more restlessly than the adults. That was her herd, eight females, two calves, one juvenile male, and she looked more intently until she found Kanja, the big bull elephant who led them. She'd been following them, watching out for them since she joined the ICPF. It took her a moment and she felt a pang of fear growing slowly in her gut until she was able to see a massive ear, backlit by the ambient light streaming through the trees, undulate as it swatted at a fly. A moment's relief was fleeting as she realized Kanja was not focused on her, but somewhere over the next rise.

It wasn't normal. Kanja always saw the rangers, or anyone else, coming before they could get too close. Kanja was no more than a couple of hundred meters away, half that to the water source that was obviously the herd's intended destination. She kept watch on him while scanning the direction that held his attention. The big bull's first priority was the safety of his females and his young. The fact that he was keeping them secluded in the trees and ignoring her was unsettling.

"Do you see them?" she whispered.

"I do," Lilliana affirmed.

"How many?" Victoria quizzed her rookie while she kept watch on the bull and scanned the surrounding area.

"Nine... no, twelve," she corrected herself. "I did not see the calves."

"And where are we in relation to the watering hole?"

"Umm."

Victoria was continually drawn from the bull to whatever it was he was so focused on. A pack of hyenas or lions would not dare go after a full-grown elephant, but a calf would be fair game and worth keeping an eye on. Even worse, a couple of humans were a lot higher probability prey than a herd of elephants. If there were predators around, they needed to put eyes on them. Victoria could tell the big male elephant was ignoring her and Lilliana, there was no way of quantifying that feeling, her gut just told her there was something else out there. If the herd was being stalked, it might be poachers. It could also be a pack of hyenas. Either scenario put them in danger, but that was the job. She was about to ask Lilliana once more about the watering hole when a sudden flare blew out the right side of her goggles.

"No," she hissed. "Kill that light!"

CHAPTER SEVENTY-FOUR

Every muscle in Hassan Rhouran's body tightened as a red light reached out like a flare in the pitch darkness.

"It's them," he murmured, disengaging the safety on his rifle.

"No, no," his guide, Guillone, whispered, tamping the ground with his hand. But Rhouran was already moving. It was her; he knew it. They were too far away yet. He had to get closer.

"The bull watches us."

Rhouran could give a shit about an elephant.

***

Victoria blinked to clear her eyes. The grainy greens and blacks flittered around until finally resolving back to a clear picture of the night. She held her breath while she watched the herd. There were several hoots and low trumpets and the body language changed. The herd seemed to step from side to side in a frenetic nervous dance as if only waiting for Kanja's permission to escape into the night. When she finally found the big male again, she saw his glowing eyes towering above the rest of the herd. He was out in front of the pack, just outside the tree line. She had his attention now but not for long. She noticed his left ear, the ear opposite her position, was up and alert. She realized he was positioned to keep an eye not only on her but on whatever had piqued his interest prior to Lilliana's folly.

Victoria's voice was barely a whisper, "You could have caused a stampede. They are on edge."

"I am very sorry."

"You can prove it by never doing that again." Victoria was leery of taking her eyes off the massive elephant, but something drew her attention. In the distance she noted a kind of scramble in the grasses. Nothing definitive but in the stillness of the night the dry stalks shook off to Kanja's left. "Left of Kanja, one hundred meters," she breathed.

To her credit Lilliana was still, barely moving as she trained her night vision on the area.

"Watch the grass."

***

"Move your men around the herd. Drive them to me," Rhouran hissed, pointing toward the position he'd last seen the red light.

"We cannot," said his guide. "The bull knows we are here, to move at all could cause a stampede, or for him to charge."

"Do what I say!" Rhouran whispered. He had to control himself to keep from snatching the man by his grimy field jacket. It was as if he were being ordered around by a child.

***

"Did you hear that?" asked Lilliana, but Victoria was busy trying to process.

Voices, a voice coming from the direction Kanja was so interested in. The great elephant bellowed a stern warning and stomped a massive foot in the red dust. She could not make out the words but someone was out there.

"Don't take your eyes off Kanja," she ordered her trainee. Victoria felt the hairs on the back of her neck stand on end. She studied the area where she had seen the disturbed undergrowth move and waited as she considered radioing the ICPF.

***

Rhouran studied his options. A watering hole sat between him and his wife. To one side, in the trees, was the herd of elephants his cowardly guide feared so much. To the other was far too much open ground. Even in the little light that there was they would be seen if they tried to approach from that direction.

"Back out," Rhouran ordered. "Into the trees, do it now."

***

Victoria forced herself to breathe. Just as Danner had taught her, in for a count of four, hold for a count of four, out for a count of four, repeat. It calmed her and helped her to think clearly. Something was not right here, she felt it.

Call it in, a voice in her head told her.

She looked at Kanja again. The elephant had lost interest in her and Lilliana and now watched the distance, but not where he had before. In the green-black view of her night vision she could see the big animal's eyes flitter in and out as he turned his head, using his wide ears to zone in on the humans she'd heard. She followed the general direction where he was so intently focused.

"That way," she whispered, gesturing off to their right. "Watch the tree line to the right."

CHAPTER SEVENTY-FIVE

"There's no way," said Ty.

Maynard put his hands out at his sides. "It's the way it is, man," he said with a grin.

Ty took a moment to process what the lead ranger had told him, "The admiral?"

"As I said, sent Albie back with his blessing and a couple crates of gear. It was set for de-mil, or destroy, whatever you Americans call it."

"Huh." Oddly, Ty found himself kind of impressed. He'd met Admiral Whillet a couple of times when he got guilted into joining his protective detail by a buddy who just happened to be Whillet's Protective Service Agent. Ty always thought the guy was a little standoffish, hard to read, so Ty had written him off as a suit. Who knew the guy would have a soft creamy inside?

***

She spotted just a flash of silhouette skittering through the green fog of ambient light, then another. There were five of them.

"I count five men at our nine o'clock moving through the trees," she whispered. Victoria heard a nervous gasp from Cartwell. She slipped her rifle from her shoulder. Victoria nodded, thatta girl. "Keep an eye on Kanja, let me know if he starts getting jumpy."

Lilliana nodded her head. "What does he look like when he gets jumpy?" she whispered.

"You'll know it when you see it," Victoria replied. She was intent on the trees ahead of her. Another flitter of movement. They were getting closer to her position. They moved in the general direction of the water hole, but something was off. Their movement was just... off.

"What's Kanja doing?" she asked.

"He's gone. They are all gone."

Victoria felt a pit in her stomach. "Get down!" she yelled just as a piercing crack split the silent night. Victoria jumped as a heavy bullet smacked the trunk of the tree, she was lying next to, peppering her with wood splinters. She heard Lilliana scream and without a moment to process what had just happened, she leapt to one knee and fired back in the direction where the shot had come from. "Call it in!" she cried. "Call the base!"

***

He was mad. That was the only possible explanation Guillone could think of. This Arab was mad, and he was going to get them killed! Guillone ran after him, trying to keep one eye on the big male elephant while at the same time trying to get the crazy Arab's attention.

"Sir," he hissed. "Sir!"

The others raced to keep up, eager to be a part of the action, whatever it was. He dropped to one knee when the Arab finally stopped. "Not yet, it is not time yet."

The Arab was leveling his weapon. "I do not work on your timetable," he said as he squeezed off a shot. Guillone was blinded by the white flash from the muzzle of the AK-47. He grabbed the man by the arm and was dropped by the butt of the Arab's rifle when it crashed into his face. Guillone was blinking away stars before he recognized the smoking muzzle pointed at his face.

Guillone stared at the smoking hole in the end of the barrel as time stretched before him. He did not know whether this Arab was going to shoot him or let him live. Before the foreigner got the chance, a volley of return fire from the rangers caused him to dive for cover.

"Get me those women!" he screamed.

Guillone rolled with his own rifle to hunker beneath the meager trunk of the nearest tree. He saw flashes in the distance and felt a couple of rounds pop in the air around him. The Arab squirmed with his rifle as the ranger's fire forced him down. Guillone considered dropping the wild man right there. Let this all be over. Keep the rangers occupied long enough for a response force to clear out of their compound then just disappear into the night, let the animals deal with the lunatic. It would be so easy right here to do it. Guillone actually felt his finger slipping toward the trigger when he came to his senses. Obert Thoomba gave him orders, gave this asshole protection. Guillone Beniised would rather deal with a crazy Arab than a disappointed Obert Thoomba any day.

CHAPTER SEVENTY-SIX

Grace Seraceh startled when the radio crackled and Lilliana Cartwell's frantic voice broke over the communications center speakers. A black hole opened up in her chest.

"Help! Rangers Jurness and Cartwell taking fire!" The transmission was garbled and interrupted by staccato of weapons fire.

Seraceh had to force herself to breathe. She felt tears welling in her eyes. She had to remind herself after a moment to press the alarm. It took an amazing amount of effort to force her limbs to respond. When she finally did, the squawking over the entire compound was deafening but it broke her paralysis.

"Jurness, report position and situation," she ordered.

***

The sound of the alarm carried from the compound to his position over a kilometer away. It was so distant at first that it barely registered. No, he thought.

"No, not yet," he spoke more to himself than any of the gunmen leaping to their feet. He looked at his watch. It was too early. He looked around at his men, then at his watch again. Everything required the perfect timing; if they went now the plane would not be ready. Obert could see himself sitting in the middle of nowhere with over a million dollars in ivory waiting on a plane. He cursed himself, and Rhouran. He should have known better than to trust an outsider. "Fuck, we go on my say," he told his men. "Be ready!"

CHAPTER SEVENTY-SEVEN

"What the hell is that?" Benhoff heard himself say the words even though he knew exactly what the clipped frenetic cry coming over the radio meant. Any cop who'd ever heard an officer in distress call over the air couldn't forget something like that. Maynard ignored him as the two raced for the communications room. Barging through the door, they found three other rangers crouching over the radio operator who had her hands over her ears, trying to hear information to relay.

"Get your gear, ladies," Maynard said coolly. "You have thirty seconds."

Benhoff watched the women scramble for the door and followed them on instinct. He sprinted for his Jeep where he ripped a heavy plate carrier from his pack, a belt holding several magazine pouches for both his pistol and long gun, and a hip holster. He slipped the heavy carrier with plates for his vitals, back and chest on over his head and clipped the belt around his waist. He loaded several full 5.56 magazines into the belt and slid his Glock into the thigh rig. Lastly, he grabbed his blowout kit that would also hang on the belt and slung his rifle over his chest. He met Lead Ranger Maynard outside the comm shed just as two Land Rovers full of armed rangers slid to a halt in front of them. Maynard was slinging his own body armor over his shoulders when Ty fell in beside him on his march to the waiting vehicles.

"I'm going with you," he said flatly.

"Watering hole ten-B," Maynard told the driver. Without looking at Benhoff, he jumped in the front passenger side of the Rover. "No, you're not. I don't know you, and we can handle it."

"That's bullshit! I'm coming."

Maynard didn't acknowledge him as the driver spit red dust and gravel as the two vehicles sped for the gate. They didn't let up as the sentry on duty barely got the security bar raised before the lead truck raced through the exit.

"Fuck!" Benhoff raced inside the shack. He would get the coordinates himself, fuck Maynard, he wasn't sitting on the bench if someone was in trouble. "What's the coordinates?" he asked the operator as he barged through the door.

The woman was leaning over her terminal. She looked at him but didn't bother to engage him.

"Come on," he told her, trying to control his voice, "I'm going to help. Where are they?"

"Go away," she whispered.

"Yeah, I'm trying, those fuckers left without me. Give me a map and show me how to get there."

The comms officer reached out and slammed the thin door in his face.

CHAPTER SEVENTY-EIGHT

Get off the X!
Victoria heard Maynard's voice in her head. "Move! Move!" She grabbed Cartwell by the shoulder strap of her pack and dragged her away from their attackers. Victoria had no idea where she was fleeing to, she only knew that there were many men out there and they were all shooting at that spot. She stumbled through the night looking for cover and found a stand of trees to their left. Shots popped and ripped the air all around her. She felt Lilliana flinch as a round buzzed by. Then after a moment she batted away Victoria's hand and started running with her.

"The trees, go!" Victoria pointed before pivoting and dropping to one knee. She scanned from left to right and counted three muzzle flashes before she was able to zero in on one and fire back. Keeping her rifle on a single shot setting, she fired three rounds at each of the places she saw muzzle flashes and turned to run. As she did, the report of a rifle shot hit her like a bomb going off. She ran through the unsettling shockwave and was heartened to see Cartwell in position firing back at their attackers to cover Victoria's retreat. Lilliana had paid attention during Maynard's bounding exercises, that kind of poise by an untested ranger gave Victoria a shred of hope. She sprinted past Cartwell and another ten meters before she repeated the process and covered Cartwell's escape. Cartwell did the same once more and the two disappeared into the low brush and trees.

***

"No, get them!" Hassan Rhouran raged as he fired round after round at his fleeing targets. As much as he wanted to kill his woman for how she betrayed him, he needed the wallet more, which meant he might need her alive. The men knew that but as he studied the two closest to him, he noted their wild handling of their weapons. Especially when an errant round from the rangers came close, or even seemed close, the poachers would flinch and fire their weapons undirected into the night. Rhouran noted most of those shots would be far above the women's heads by the time they crossed paths. And that was only if they were on target.

He tracked and fired at the two shadows as they fled into a stand of trees. The flashes of light in the darkness messed with his vision and hurt his aim. After a few moments the shooting died down and the women were gone. Rhouran felt heat in his chest and throat and strained to keep from shooting the two men nearest him.

"No!" he bellowed. "Get after them now!" He saw worried looks, more wary body movements in the way they looked from each other back to him, their facial features smothered in darkness. Rhouran pointed his weapon at the man closest to him, Guillone, and could barely form words through the rage swirling inside him. "Move. Now," he ordered and pointed in the direction the women had fled.

The man under the muzzle of his gun leapt to his feet and stepped warily toward their prey. After a moment the rest followed suit. Rhouran watched each man closely as the five misfits Obert Thoomba had left him with did as they were told. When they seemed to be following his order, he moved quietly off to the left of their line. Though woefully out of their depth hunting armed humans over dumb animals, Hassan Rhouran thought maybe he still might make use of them.

***

Victoria and Lilliana sprinted ten or so meters into the trees and dove under some low bushes. They gasped for breath, sucking the hot evening wind and dust while their hearts pounded in their chests.

"What is happening?" Lilliana was the first to say.

Victoria shook her head, "I don't know."

"Why are they after us?"

A man was yelling out in the night causing both women to crouch a little closer to the ground. It was hard to hear what was said but when Victoria stole a look at her partner, she saw Lilliana transfixed on the direction from where the sounds came, the whites of her eyes glowing in the darkness.

"No," she whispered.

"What?" Victoria asked.

"No," her voice cracked a little.

"What do you mean no, Lilliana? What is it?" Victoria hissed. She grabbed her by the shoulder to shake her out of it. When Lilliana focused on her, she looked terrified.

"It's him," she said. "He found me." There was a whimper in her voice, and she clutched at her necklace.

"Who is it?" asked Victoria, her insides growing cold.

"My husband," Lilliana whispered.

Victoria watched the scared woman for a moment then looked toward the fields they had just fled. She had no idea how much time had passed since they had called their situation in on the radio. It felt like an eternity. Victoria felt exhausted and jittery from an adrenaline spike all at the same time. They needed to think. "Swap out your magazines and lose everything but your weapons, lights and ammunition."

"Wh-what?"

"You heard me, do it. We are on our own, we need to be able to fight and move." *And screw your husband!* Victoria left that last part out.

CHAPTER SEVENTY-NINE

Obert let painful minutes tick off his watch. Each one was like a sharp stick jammed under his nailbed. A countdown against his soul. He tried doing the math in his head, but the variables were too much to deal with. What if the compound called police forces from Karoi, or worse, the military? He thought it a long shot, but he couldn't get the image of a convoy of police vehicles storming toward the ICPF encampment out of his mind. After all this time, all the planning and sweating over the damned table in his office, for him to be undone by something so simple as minutes on a clock was too much. Worse comes to worse, they'd hide the truck and adjust the transfer. Obert Thoomba was a smuggler and a hunter after all, it was part of the business... as long as Wei and his savages were found to be just as flexible. "Enough," he said, mostly to himself. "We go!" Obert smashed a meaty hand on top of the roof of the truck's cab and the heavy, abused engine ground to life.

***

"You know where she went?" Ty asked the gate guard whose English was as minimal as Ty's Shona--a Zimbabwean dialect. He pulled a map he'd swiped from the comm shed and held it out for the old man. "Do you know where Danner and the others went?"

He gestured strangely, even in his own estimation, trying to drive home the point. It grated being unable to aid the women he'd just spoken to a couple of hours ago. He was a badge carrier, even if not in his own country or jurisdiction, it didn't matter. He had a badge and a gun, and he should be on his way to help regardless. When the guard put his hands out and shook his head, Ty figured he was done. There was really no one else around to talk to. He noticed a couple of women lingering around the communications hut talking amongst themselves, but he doubted he would get much further with them, and as time went by, he was more likely to get lost in the Zimbabwean night than he was to have any real impact in helping the two rangers. Instead of pushing further he found himself wandering back toward his Jeep, disgusted.

He checked the safety on his long gun and dropped it across the driver's seat. He had just unclipped the side of his plate carrier when his phone buzzed. It was Kali back in Djibouti.

"Still grounded, I hope."

"For the night," Kali told him. "Looks like you get to stay a field agent for another twelve hours or so."

"Well, I'll try to make the most of it."

Kali scoffed, "I get why, Ty, but… going after an AD, really?"

Ty sighed. "He deserved it," he said after a moment's pause.

The line was silent, and he wanted to fill the pregnant pause with something, but he honestly could think of no other way to explain it. He was just about to ask about Boulden when the sound of an engine emanated from the distance. It grew in the darkness. As Ty opened the back gate of the Wrangler and slid his body armor over his head, Kali started to say something,

"Yeah, hold on a sec."

The old gate guard looked toward the comms hut, then out in the night. When he looked at the women sitting on the porch in front of the shed, they were all watching the front gate as well. Whoever was coming, they were not expected. He wondered if it was Maynard and his quick reaction force. Hopefully they were returning with Jurness and Cartwell safe and sound. Oddly and without any reference to go on, Ty thought it a little early for that.

He dropped the plate carrier in the rear of the Jeep and jumped as a shot cracked the silence of the encampment. Ty looked up just in time to see the sentry, the old man he'd just talked to, pivot and start running. The old man made it two steps before a volley of fire dropped him. Benhoff had trouble processing what he had just seen. He stood there looking at the still form of the gate guard as the roar of a large engine grew to a crescendo. Headlights bounced over the ground and the guard's body just as a deuce and a half crashed through the flimsy gate post.

Kali was saying something in the phone. "Yeah, I--"

More shots and now Ty grabbed his body armor. He threw it over his head with one hand and was reaching for the rifle in the front seat when a swarm of rounds pelted the Jeep. Projectiles bounced and snapped all around him, forcing him to dive behind the vehicle. As he did so the phone echoing Kali's now yelling voice smashed on the rocks and went dark.

"Son of a bitch!" Ty pulled his nine-millimeter and fired through the now shattered passenger side window and out the driver's side. This was his first opportunity to see what he was facing. The giant truck with a canvas-covered bed was belching men from its tailgate as it veered away from him. The fighters, each armed with an AK-47, or so it seemed, fired wildly around the compound. Ty holstered his Glock and yanked his Mark 18 free of the Jeep and crouched behind the engine block to check the chamber. He had one in the chamber and a full thirty-round magazine. He then swapped out the partial magazine in his handgun for a fresh fifteen-round load. Now what?

Rounds continued to pop off in a flurry, automatic weapons fire strafing the buildings, but what really took him aback was his previous thought. He was armed, he had to do something, right? But what? There was at least a dozen of them out there. When he heard a scream, he found himself moving. With his rifle up, he scanned from left to right and saw a woman, one of the rangers, who had a weapon of her own, sprinting as she tried to outrun an angry swarm of bullets that chased her heels and ate chunks out of the huts and trees around her. In an automated response Ty had never experienced, he traced the fire back to two men, backlit in the red brake lights of the deuce and a half. Without another stray thought or hint of question he loosed three rounds at the first man, and three rounds at the second before reassessing the first. He found the man on his ass but wheeling his rifle in Ty's direction. Three more rounds and the man sprawled flat on his back. Ty started moving then toward where he first noticed the woman running for cover. Muzzle flashes burst out of the periphery to his left but he for some reason didn't register any real sound. It was the headlight of his Jeep exploding next to his hip that let him know the bullets were meant for him. Turning toward the source while he continued to move, he found his target. The man he'd missed completely only a second ago fired at him while he hopped laterally from one foot to another like a cat on a hot plate. Ty fired six rapid rounds in his direction and the man flinched like a deer before stumbling and falling to the ground. Without thinking, Ty sent three more rounds into the man who was now no more than fifteen feet away. He saw his body jerk when two of the 5.56mm rounds found his abdomen.

More shots seemed to come from everywhere. Ty turned toward the huts, seeking cover more than to engage. He ducked between two huts where he'd seen the ranger running and in the dark, he found her, well, found the muzzle of her rifle pointing at his chest.

"Are you okay?" he asked.

"They go for the ivory," the woman said as she slipped to sit in the dust, her rifle falling to the ground.

***

Obert Thoomba watched the sentry fall under the cli-clack of an AK-47 as the truck passed by, barely missing the old man who clutched at his chest, his face a morass of fear and pain.

"To the left," he ordered the driver, gesturing down a row of wood and thatched-roof huts. Then he saw it. The building. A photo of the long, raised wood structure sat in the middle of his planning table at the shop, courtesy of the woman Fannel had located to obtain the necessary information to execute the plan. The image of the building and all the hope it held for him had been square in his mind for a month straight.

"There at the end." As he said the words, Obert wondered if his voice sounded as shaky as his hands felt. So close.

He looked out the rearview mirror to see how the men were handling themselves. A deafening maelstrom of gunfire echoed all around him which was what he'd called for. He honestly hoped those of the rangers that were still inside the compound would simply hide under all the bullets and destruction. That his ring of armed gunmen surrounding the vehicle and soon, his ivory, would keep even the bravest of these women at bay. He had no interest in killing them all. It would be their choice whether to fight his men and die or hide and live. As Obert thought this he was watching two men firing into one of the buildings. When one of them fell, then the other, he sat straight up in his seat. Just as he did so, the big truck lurched to a stop, and he had to brace himself against the metal dashboard. Maybe he had not seen things as he thought they were. Before dismounting, he looked once more out the rearview and saw one of his men still on the ground, lying in a cloud of dust. Then he watched the man's body jerk as rounds hit him. A blur flashed through his isolated view of what was happening behind him. Just as he opened the passenger door with a creak, Fannel was there waiting for him. The lethal fighter had his own rifle in his hands, his eyes stoically scanning the chaos surrounding them.

Obert gestured toward the body of his own fallen fighter. "They fight back?" he asked.

"The American," Fannel said without taking his eyes off the battle. "His rifle sounds different but there is only the one."

Obert looked at the storage building and breathed as he saw the first of his designated people hauling a massive elephant tusk toward the back of the truck. Three more quickly followed. "That is a very stupid American then. They must all think they are John Maclean."

Fannel looked at him, eyebrows arched, "Who?"

"Nevermind," Obert said as he watched the line of ivory coming from the building. "The American is yours, my friend. Finish him and get back here so we can get this over with."

Fannel nodded and disappeared down a row between the raised huts.

CHAPTER EIGHTY

The dense undergrowth she hid behind obscured her view through the night vision goggles. She could hear them coming, their legs swishing through the tall grass. She swore she could feel the impacts of their feet in the soft dirt.

"What do we do?" Lilliana whispered.

Victoria ignored her and instead looked around the little patch of trees where they'd taken refuge. It was dense inside their sanctum, but not thick enough to hide from half a dozen armed men. They would be found simply by being trampled on. If they tried to run, they could only flee to open ground, or worse yet stumble into Kanja's herd and be trampled to death by the panicked animals. There were a host of other dangers waiting for them in the darkness. Victoria put those out of her mind and chose to deal with what was in front of her.

"We wait," she whispered.

"Wait?" Lilliana's voice trembled and Victoria felt for her. She didn't deserve this, no one deserved to deal with something like this on their first patrol. Victoria had heard stories of rangers being ambushed before, but those tales were few and far between. They seemed so distant until now.

"They get close to us, we fire, get as many of them as we can at once. Don't shoot until I do." Victoria ended the discussion, leaving Lilliana to come to terms with what was about to happen on her own. Truth was whether Cartwell kept it together or not, Victoria Jurness meant to kill those men and get them home.

CHAPTER EIGHTY-ONE

Ty took one of the woman's hands and pressed it into the wound on her thigh.

"Keep pushing on it," he told her as he ripped a windlass tourniquet from the medical kit attached to his belt. As he pulled on what was nothing more than a nylon belt with a torque band running through it, he noticed the woman's head bounce just a bit.

"Hey," he said, loud enough to get her attention but quiet enough that he hoped none of the machine gun toting assholes surrounding them could hear. There was still firing seemingly coming from everywhere, but the volume had lessened. Ty hoped that meant everyone in the camp was taking cover and getting out of their way. The alternatives creeping around in his mind were too heinous to entertain. Her head bobbed again, and he snapped his fingers in front of her nose.

"Hey, I need you to watch my back, okay?" He had to snap his fingers in front of her face twice more before her eyes brightened. "Come on, there's a bunch of bad guys around here. You with me?" She nodded. "Good, I'm Ty."

"Allenda," the ranger said through clenched teeth.

"Nice to meet you."

Ty slid an end of the tourniquet under her wounded thigh and fed it through a loop on the device. "This is going to hurt, but it will slow down your bleeding, okay?"

Allenda nodded.

"Okay." The errant thought that she probably didn't want to know that he had only ever used a tourniquet on himself and a dummy during training made him wonder about his own sanity. He cinched the loop as tight as he could, about six inches above her wound, and wrenched on the black plastic dowel that constricted the band around her leg. Allenda yelped but he kept on wrenching until he could barely turn the dowel and locked it under a built-in plastic hook.

Allenda was biting her bottom lip as he secured the dowel with a Velcro strap. Her face crunched against the pain, but to her credit she remained quiet.

"Okay," he said, "now you get under there." He gestured toward the crawlspace beneath the hut at her back.

"You are not coming?" she asked, fear plain on her face, even in the dark.

Sure will! part of him wanted to scream and race her into the creepy darkness of the crawlspace. Instead, he shook his head. He couldn't... could he?

"What will you do?"

"I have no idea," he told her. *Get the ivory, catch the bad guys,* odd one-liners scrolled through his head like the cheesy sayings littering a Hollywood writer's floor. "Sit tight."

He rose and stood still in the dark corridor between buildings for a moment, absorbing the ambient sounds around the encampment. The odd two-stage crack of Kalashnikov rifles continued. In the distance he heard the steady rumble of an engine. The truck seemed as good a place as any to start. Ty felt the safety switch on his rifle but then had to force himself to take the first step in that god-awful direction.

Here he was safe, relatively anyway. He could still hide. This wasn't his fight. As a matter of fact, he had no idea what the hell was going on here. He forced himself to take that next step, then another, before freezing in place as a shadow flittered across the opening at the end of the short alley. He lowered into a crouch for a moment. There was no more movement. Ty put his rifle up to his shoulder and walked softly toward the end of the building.

CHAPTER EIGHTY-TWO

When the first man broke through the trees, Victoria Jurness felt her heart skip a beat. The urge to run was so great she wondered what her fresh-out-of-training partner was feeling but didn't want to risk exposing herself by looking at her. Instead, she trained her weapon on the center of the man's chest. She noted that he wore a Manchester United soccer jersey. The men were spread out in a line. Not long after the first entered their stand of trees, she watched the others, five of them, do the same. She tried not to think about how far apart they were. She committed herself to the plan. If Lilliana did not join in when she started firing, she would be killed. They were close now, a little over three meters she guessed. Just a bit closer. Victoria used Manchester as her gauge. She let her finger hover over the trigger and set her thumb on the fire selector switch. She did not like firing on fully automatic, the rapid rate of fire lacked control. But in that moment, she needed all the rounds she could put down range. Victoria eased the switch two stops. She swore the sound of the click, click was earth-shattering but the men did not pause. Manchester kept edging toward his destiny. She took a deep breath and started squeezing the trigger.

"Jurness, Cartwell, report," Danner Maynard's voice crackled through her earpiece.

Victoria startled, and she might have heard a yelp from Lilliana. Gathering her senses, she looked, and Manchester was suddenly frozen in place. Time slowed as she watched her target bob and weave as he tried to locate the sound, she was now sure the two rangers made.

"We are ten minutes out, what's your status? Report." She could hear the tension in Maynard's voice, and she appreciated it. But ten minutes might as well have been ten days.

Without another thought, Victoria Jurness loosed a spray of 5.56mm ammunition into the night.

***

Something was wrong.

Danner Maynard didn't say it, but he could feel something was off. Poachers did attack rangers, it happened, when the poachers were cornered or surprised, but they never sought out conflict with conservation units. He couldn't be sure that was what was happening now to Jurness and Cartwell, something just seemed off. Maynard had been around long enough to see through experience that poaching groups would always prefer to give up a hunt rather than go toe to toe with the rangers. It was simply a better business practice. You attack the rangers, you bring in the cops, such as they were. The cops meant attention, pressure on your area of operation. If Jurness and Cartwell had gotten in a scrape with a group of hunters, the comms shack would have known, and he would have known about it long before the shooting started. ICPF procedure dictated they call in a description--vehicles, people, weapons, kills, if the poachers already made one--before making contact. The first call he heard contained more gunfire than information meaning something went terribly wrong very quickly.

Maynard checked his watch. Three minutes since he last tried to contact the patrol. He keyed his radio.

"Jurness, Cartwell, report." He kept his voice calm as he broadcast. Not only for the patrol under distress but for the four women in the truck with him. He checked his watch to note the time of the call and started the mental countdown as he received nothing but silence from the handheld radio. For a moment he watched the grass and trees flash by as his driver, Mena, powered the SUV down the rough dirt road at an amazing rate and with great control. "ETA?" he asked.

"Seven minutes, sir," Mena answered without taking her eyes from the road.

Too long, he thought, too long.

CHAPTER EIGHTY-THREE

When the magazine ran dry, the sudden quiet shocked her. Lilliana shook herself out of it and changed magazines. She chided herself in the time she lost between emptying her weapon and reloading.

"Move! Just like we did before!" shouted Sergeant Jurness.

Lilliana scrambled to her feet and dashed further into the brush. After counting to ten in her head, she spun and dropped to a knee to cover her training officer.

Jurness was past her moments later. Lilliana scanned the area for what was in effect the first time since she and Victoria fired on their pursuers. Nothing moved in the darkness. Dim glimpses of light shone through the trees and nothing, not a shadow, not a bush or length of tall grass moved. It was eerie and in moments she felt a tension rise in her chest as her mind envisioned one of those men lying prone in the darkness, readying his shot the moment she moved.

"Hshhk!" Jurness hissed.

Lilliana swallowed her fear and repeated her bounding process, skirting right past Jurness's shoulder as she sped past. She again was counting in her head while trying to see in the darkness for anyone who might have circled around them. She took one final step as her internal countdown struck ten when a sudden whack across her left cheek made everything go white.

Victoria counted down once Cartwell was past. A wary confidence grew inside her when she did not pick up any targets moving in her field of vision. Her internal clock struck one and she rose and spun on her heel to run. A bright orange flash and a crack confused her only an instant before a great punch in her chest dropped her to the dirt. She couldn't breathe and her vision swirled as her body tried to recover from the sudden assault.

Your feet, get to your feet, she ordered herself, telling herself she'd been shot, she needed to move. Her limbs were like water-soaked logs, heavy and unresponsive.

She fumbled for her rifle in the darkness, anything to protect herself, to keep fighting. She managed to slap the receiver of the rifle with a numb right hand when a voice, cool with an exotic accent, broke through her befuddled mind.

"Do not touch that weapon," the voice said. "Do not move."

The order was clear and crisp, with an authority that carried a certainty that stopped her cold. She took a breath as she tried to focus on the man standing over her and wanted to curl in on herself as her ribs seemed to splinter as her lungs expanded.

The man approached her dragging the limp form of Lilliana Cartwell by the scruff. She dangled under the man's control like a ventriloquist dummy. He threw her down in a crumple at Victoria's feet.

"If you move, I will kill you," he told her. Then he kicked Cartwell in the stomach, eliciting a whimper.

"Lilliana," the voice said. "Lilliana, you should have known I would find you. You ran off with something very important. You took it from my safe." He kicked her again, causing her to cough and hack as she tried to catch her breath.

"Hassan," she cried. "Hassan, no!"

"Hassan?" Victoria choked as she slipped a hand around her chest and under her vest while this man was focused on Lilliana. To her surprise she found only sweat.

Hassan straightened his rifle at her with one hand and backhanded Lilliana with the other. "My name is Hassan Rhouran, this is my wife. I am here to collect what's mine."

Victoria focused on the barrel of the rifle, putting a hand up in capitulation.

"Please, no!" Lilliana cried as she also put her hand up to plead with him. He grabbed her outstretched fingers and twisted them to an obscene angle.

"I will not ask again. The flash drive or I shoot your new friend."

Lilliana's face was clenched under the pain and strain of her bones and tendons. She nodded her head franticly and reached in her shirt with her free hand to retrieve a small velvet bag on a string around her neck. For the first time, Rhouran let his rifle swing on its sling, and he let his wife go. He worked the bag open with one eye on the women. Victoria saw him breathe deeply as he felt whatever prize he sought in his hand.

A voice in her head screamed, *no!* To simply play along and he would let them go when he had what he wanted, though she knew that wasn't true. Like all the women of the ICPF, she had suffered at the hands of a man like this. Her hand started creeping toward her pistol while she watched the man's every move.

Then she felt it, the butt of her nine-millimeter waiting in its holster, so close. Another nudge and she felt the back strap of the rough grip along the web of her palm. Another centimeter.

In a flash, the rifle was up again and pointed at her head.

Victoria's breath caught in her throat as she saw the tenth of a second she needed to draw evaporate into the night. Time slowed inexorably as she watched him lean forward on his lead foot and push the rifle toward her. Even in the darkness of that moment she watched his shoulder tense and knew he was going to shoot her. She rolled just as he fired. Knowing she stood no chance of escaping the rapid fire of the AK-47, she refused to die like a victim. She felt a pull at her hip, and another at her back as she bounced into the bushes and kept moving, trying to reach her feet while clawing for her own weapon. She heard the firing then, shot after shot as she moved, tried to get away, tried to do anything to survive. When she rolled into a tree, she lost her momentum, though the shots continued. She cringed and curled into a ball and waited, knowing all her opportunities had been spent. At least she tried, she told herself as she waited for the inevitable.

But the final darkness never came.

After a moment she opened one eye, then two. She pulled her side arm and willed herself to face him and found her left leg protesting and grinding against her orders. She coughed and tasted copper. When she clawed her way back to a position where she could see, there was still a figure standing from where she'd fled. However, it was not Hassan, and she was the least of the dark figure's attention.

Lilliana Cartwell, nine-millimeter in hand, stood over her husband who writhed on the ground clutching his gut.

"Lilliana?" Victoria asked.

There was no response at first. Finally, without taking her eyes off of her husband, she asked through tears, "You are okay?"

"I'm good," Victoria lied.

Lilliana nodded slowly.

She seemed frozen in that moment, processing. Then she emptied her weapon into her husband. His body wracked and shook as the remainder of her magazine burned through him. When it was over, Lilliana ejected her empty magazine and smoothly reloaded her weapon as she studied what she'd done.

CHAPTER EIGHTY-FOUR

Fannel knew the compound. He had studied the location for weeks alongside Obert as the two planned the operation. He had a map in his head that he relied on to keep himself oriented while he hunted the American. Shooting continued around the compound, but it was random and all from the Kalashnikovs he and the rest of the men carried. Fannel paused on the perimeter of an open garden ensconced behind a collection of living quarters. He took a knee inside the inky black shadows of the night and absorbed the environment. He heard the crunching of gravel as people ran at various points around the ICPF. Most were his men, though he had no doubt some were rangers simply running for their lives. The women inside the base had not been ready for this. Fannel had always marveled at the arrogance these women and their lone do-gooder splashed around the preserves. These females thought they could be police, protect the herds from men such as him. Tonight, these women were being shown the reality of the game they thought they were playing, and if they did not interfere some might very well survive to warn the others.

Fannel heard heavy breathing coming from his left, diagonally across the garden, and watched as his quarry crept out of the darkness between two huts. He wore a baseball cap backwards, and carried what looked like a carbine, a lighter weapon than his own weapon chambered for a stout 7.62mm round. The man was careful, to a point, but as he moved out into the soft light, he could see the American policeman's focus was on the horizon, and he ignored the dangers right in front of him. Fannel considered his options. The rifle in his hands was the most efficient means of ending this man. Fannel tracked him over the front sight of his rifle, no more than fifteen, maybe twenty meters. To shoot now would accomplish his mission and get him back to the real objective: the recovery of their precious commodity. But it would lack the satisfaction Fannel so wanted. It was not often someone like him got to hunt an American. Every death he had seen at the hands of the Americans, from Somalia, to Libya, even to his days fighting with those lunatics in Syria screamed for righteous vengeance deep within him. Americans were able to kill so easily with their drones and their missiles. It seemed cheap to allow this one such a quick death when such a rare opportunity presented itself. Fannel continued to track the man in the baseball cap, but instead of eliminating him, he let the clumsy American police cross his field of fire and slip back into the darkness. There's still time, Fannel told himself. After a moment's pause, he rose from his hiding place and followed his prey.

CHAPTER EIGHTY-FIVE

Ty stuck to the darkness and tried to walk softly as he made his way between buildings. The random shooting had died down to cracks in the night every now and then. It seemed to him these assholes were content to let the ICPF personnel cower in their huts while they stole the ivory from what Ty deemed their evidence room. With every step there was a voice in the back of his head admitting that they were on to something. Not the bad guys but the ICPF folks hiding in their rooms. He paused as he came to a T intersection that accessed the main thoroughfare. He half-circled the opening between the two huts, slicing the pie as the term was, so he could get the best view possible while staying concealed in the darkness. He counted four men spread out among the rear of the big six-wheeled cargo truck. They meandered in a loose perimeter, rifles in hand, as a trail of men cycled through carrying the ivory Maynard had showed him only hours before.

This isn't your fight, that annoying voice in the back of his mind reminded him. He had to admit that was the truth. He had no jurisdiction, no authority. But he'd seen an old man killed by these assholes and a woman shot. Ty thought of them and any cares he had about his role in all this disappeared. Fuck these guys, was his final estimation. Immediately following that resolve came the natural question... now what?

Shoot out the tires. Ty figured that was an option. One that would result in him, and the others stuck inside a fenced off kill zone with up to a dozen men armed with assault rifles--not great odds. So, let them go and follow them? Follow the same dozen killers into the wilds of Zimbabwe and call in the cavalry with what? The radio in the comm shack? The stray thought of charging them guns blazing tried to form but he wasn't even crazy enough to entertain that idea. What then?

A sudden wallop in between his shoulder blades and Ty found himself stumbling and rolling into the open. Right in front of the throng of armed men. He kept rolling, not really sure what had just happened to him until he found himself standing between the rear of the truck and the man who had just kicked him out into the street. For a moment the perimeter guards just stared at him in shock. There was no one more surprised than he so they ended up staring at each other. Ty looked at the man who had ambushed him. He was taller than Ty, which was saying something in this neck of the woods. He was thinner but even in the dark, tight cords of muscles were evident and could be seen running through his arms and broad shoulders under a grimy, formerly white professional soccer jersey. Ty warned himself in that moment not to be killed by a guy wearing a soccer jersey. Hockey, maybe, soccer, definitely not.

"The American po-lice man!" a booming voice yelled.

Ty was leery to take his eyes off the man who had so easily snuck up on him. His eyes were dead, as if staring right through him. It was a look he'd seen before, and not one that ever ended in a peaceful resolution. The man in the soccer jersey held his rifle casually pointed toward the ground at an angle across his body. Ty still held his in the same way. He bladed his body slowly so he could keep an eye on the tall one with the predatory stare while at the same time address a giant of a man wearing of all things a Hawaiian shirt. He wondered for a moment which was worse, killed by a guy wearing a pro soccer jersey or a Hawaiian shirt? As he surveyed the rest of the ten or so armed men staring at him, he figured it was probably a wash. Most of them wore shirts that emulated a sport where the athletes wore more hair product than most American pop singers.

"That's me," Ty answered the giant who only carried a handgun. One of the biggest handguns he'd ever seen, too, by the looks of it a .50 caliber Desert Eagle; in chrome no less. The guy had a lumbering strut and was clearly the man in charge. "You are?"

"Reclaiming my property," he waved the gun casually in his direction. "This has nothing to do with you, why get involved?"

Ty shrugged, looking around at the hard faces boring through him. "Well, I'm here, right? You guys come in here and start shooting up the place. Like you said, I'm the po-lice, what was I supposed to do?"

"You made a poor choice, American, now what to do with you?"

"You guys could drop your guns, get on your knees, and put your hands behind your backs. I don't know if I read you your rights in this country, but I'd be more than happy to if that would make you feel better." Ty could feel his resolve drying up. None of these men looked amused in the slightest. His trigger finger rested on the lower receiver, just above the trigger, the muzzle way out of any functional range. Any move would result in his death.

"Oh, and if you know anything about the death of Albieto Cruz you should tell me now, otherwise things could go bad for you." Somehow Ty managed to cap off that statement with a grin.

"You make a joke," the big man chuckled. "You have style, but I have a timetable," the man hissed and gestured toward the taller man who'd bushwhacked him. "Fannel, finish this, we go."

Ty had already made up his mind. The tall one was the most dangerous man there, not that it mattered given the numbers against him. Ty was going to lose this fight, but he would take that guy with him. He tensed as the guy took a step toward him. He was raising his weapon when a loud explosion shattered the silence that had fallen over the camp.

Ty knew that sound: a flash grenade. Instructors at FLETC had rained flashbangs on them relentlessly during pre-deployment training. You never really got used to the stunning percussion, but with involuntary practice the effect became manageable. It still jarred his senses. He felt slow as he spun and fired from the hip toward the soccer fan, he now knew as Fannel. He missed and noticed Fannel was only a tick slower. Ty cranked on the trigger again and felt the firing pin click on an empty chamber. He let the rifle fall on its sling and in what felt like an excruciatingly long length of time transitioned to his Glock. Shots filled his still ringing ears and he could swear every weapon was firing at him as he punched the Glock out in front of him and fired over and over. Fannel was shooting, too, and the two of them circled each other, firing as they moved. Benhoff planted a nine-millimeter round in Fannel's right shoulder just as Ty felt an impact on his side. The impact to Fannel caused his rifle to falter under his damaged arm. Ty put two more into his chest, stitching him toward his midline until a final bullet stopped the man in his tracks.

In an instant Fannel's expression changed from one of cool resolution to confusion as Ty's bullet severed his aorta. The gunman dropped to a knee, his rifle falling to the dust at his feet. Ty continued firing, closing as he adjusted his sights for a final round between the eyes of the man who until only a moment before was certain he would kill him. Ty watched the impact snap Fannel's head back and charged past him for any semblance of cover in what had become a madhouse of flying bullets and stun grenades. Ty crossed back to the relative safety of the gap between huts where he'd been ambushed earlier and swapped out magazines in his handgun. He was doing the same for his rifle when three rounds splintered the side of the wood hut at head level, driving him back into the darkness. In the shock and pain of wood chips peppering his face he dropped the magazine and lost his balance as he fell to the ground. He scrambled as rounds bit the dirt and carved chunks out of the buildings around him. Holding his rifle one-handed, he gained a knee and slammed another magazine into the well as the flailing form of a madman with bushy hair, no more than a silhouette in the darkness, charged the gap firing wildly. The lunatic howled and yelled unintelligibly, rounds sizzled and popped in the air just over Ty's head. Benhoff squeezed off three rounds and the man collapsed on top of him, pinning his rifle to his chest. Benhoff clawed for his pistol and cranked off six contact shots into the shooter's torso until finally pushing him off of him.

"Fuck is wrong with you guys?" he huffed, examining the limp form. He kicked the man in the head, and he didn't respond. He kicked the man's AK-47 further into the darkness and turned to face the insanity rampaging through the ICPF compound. Instead of running toward the fight, he dropped to his knees as fire tore through his right side. Even through his gloved hand he could feel wetness soaking the pants over his hip. "No, shiiitt," he grimaced.

Shots continued from everywhere. Despite the screaming complaint in his side, he limped slowly back toward the main thoroughfare where it all began. He crouched and gritted his teeth as a couple of forms ran past the opening between the buildings, then he heard a rumble as the big truck revved its engine. He made for the gap and slid to a stop as yet another group crossed his line of sight. This one was in a formation, a steady line of four women armed with M-4s. They marched shoulder to shoulder, firing mercilessly at the attackers. He put his hands up as the nearest ranger scanned him over the muzzle of her weapon.

He blurted out, "I'm with you guys!" And had no idea if she was about to drop him. She looked him over dispassionately and moved forward with her team.

"Stay here," she said plainly.

Ty didn't quite know how to take that. He sure as shit wasn't going to let a woman fight in his place but as he watched, the line of rangers dropped the gunmen trailing the truck that was now picking up speed toward the perimeter fence. When the last straggler was mowed down, the four women broke off into teams of two and flanked the cab. It took a while for a machine like that to get up to speed so they were able to overtake it easily. Ty watched and winced as a flash of light and a loud crack ruptured all the glass in the cab. He saw two bodies spill from the machine and was amazed when one of the women buttstroked the passenger rather than execute him. He heard no further shooting and imagined the driver's side team showed the same restraint. Ty started limping forward when the screaming throb in his side finally overcame him and he slouched to sit on the front step of one of the huts. He tried to breathe smoothly and repetitively, trying to remain calm and gear himself up to study his wound. He safed his weapon and leaned back against a post.

For a moment Ty considered the noxious cloud of gun smoke settling over what only seconds before was hell on Earth. Then he commented to no one in particular, "This is going to be hard to explain."

CHAPTER EIGHTY-SIX

Danner Maynard heard the report come over the radio. All he said was, "Copy." There were people, his people, dead and wounded at the ICPF compound. Julius, the old gate sentry, Nissa Mallet was another, some had yet to be accounted for, others had faced the attack and apparently won the day… and he was driving in the opposite direction toward yet another attack on the ICPF. It was too much to comprehend. His first reaction to the totality of it was pure unbridled fury. Twenty years ago, he would be tearing the dashboard in front of him apart with his own hands, bashing anything readily available. That was a different Danner Maynard in a different life. Back then there was no one looking to him for guidance… for hope. Now he had four rangers, even Lyss, his driver, looking at him sideways as she flew down the dirt track toward Jurness and Cartwell.

He keyed the microphone. "Sitrep in five," he said in a voice he hoped sounded calm. He turned in his seat to face the women in the SUV.

"We put one foot in front of the other, handle one problem at a time. We can't help our friends back home right now. But we have two friends we can help, make that your focus." He nodded out the windshield, "How far out are we?"

"Thirty seconds, sir," Lyss responded.

"Get ready," he told them. "Anyone not ICPF holding a weapon, you put them down and make sure they stay down. We don't show an ounce of restraint until Sergeant Jurness and Ranger Cartwell are secure, understood?"

"Yes, sir," the three of them responded.

Maynard nodded and checked the load in his rifle and patted his body armor where replacement magazines, his hunting knife and pistol were secured. It was muscle memory, something he'd been taught decades ago by much wiser warriors than he. It was a comfort to see the habit had never faded.

***

Victoria Jurness gasped as her ribs ground together. She heard the motor coming from far off and told Lilliana, who stood motionless between her and the lifeless form of Hassan Rhouran, to get down.

"Load a fresh magazine," Victoria whispered as she slowly, and in agonizing fashion, went prone in the underbrush. "They have to find us. We hide until the others arrive. If they get close it is the same as before."

"Yes," Lilliana responded, her voice vague, distanced.

"Yes, what?" Victoria hissed.

"Yes, Sergeant."

"Better," Victoria stated and focused her sights on the movement of an SUV with its lights off approaching the watering hole. It stopped at a ridge just over the small pond, and five occupants dismounted quickly, forming a perimeter around the vehicle.

Victoria smiled, recognizing them instantly in the way they moved. She heaved herself to her feet. Her chest hurt so bad she could barely breathe. Lilliana appeared and supported her under her shoulder.

"Come on," Sergeant Victoria Jurness said. "Let's go tell them about your first day."

CHAPTER EIGHTY-SEVEN

Ty leaned on his right leg to try and assuage the burning wound on his side. Luckily, once he peeled his plate carrier off, he found the damage to his abdomen was nothing more than a half inch deep furrow across the side of his hip. It bled plenty but once he applied a pressure dressing, he was able to seal it up pretty good.

Once he'd realized he wasn't going to die any time in the near future, he pulled himself up off his ass and tried to help out. There were three Rangers killed in action, Julius, the old gate guard, and another two who had died fighting. The ICPF had a sort of field medic on staff, but the ranger was desperately ill-equipped to deal with Allenda, the ranger he'd treated during the fighting. Her leg was shattered, and another ranger, Xiida, had sucking chest wound from a bullet she'd taken just over her right breast. They had called for help from Karoi but the infrastructure in Zimbabwe being what it was left the two women's fate more up to chance and determination than true response capabilities. With no other option, Ty handed the keys to the Jeep over to the medic, Levona, so she could at least try to transport their two wounded. Just as they were about to leave, Danner Maynard and his rangers returned two heavier than when they left. They also had five bodies strapped to the hood and roof of the SUV.

The head ranger leapt from the vehicle and wandered, in utter disbelief, at the carnage surrounding him. Jurness, against the urging of Lilliana and the others forced her way out of the SUV and limped to Maynard's side.

"We control what he can, sir," she had said as she shuffled up next to him.

"Getting them to the nearest hospital is the best you can do for anybody right now."

Maynard looked at him like a wild animal for a moment before catching his breath. He took Ty's hand and shook it. "Thank you," he said.

"It was your rangers that saved me." Ty had told him. "Thank you."

Before they left, Ty handed the paper bag with Albie's hat to Jurness and asked her to get it to Captain Hanswei as soon as she was able. He wrote the captain's mobile number on the bag with a Sharpie.

She nodded slowly when he handed her the bag. "I will."

As Maynard and the wounded rangers drove away, Ty realized that kind of evidence handling really would have gotten him fired, if he wasn't on the chopping block already. But at least that way Hanswei would get what he needed a lot faster than Ty would have been able to get it for him.

That left Ty on pseudo guard duty with the other four ambulatory ICPF women, Nissa, Shari, Eve and Bella as they introduced themselves. Five of the attacking poachers had survived the fight, including the big man Ty found out was Obert Thoomba, a name that meant nothing to him but had quite an impact on the rangers. The man sat on his left side favoring an obviously broken leg. Thoomba's knee was clearly dislocated, the bottom half sitting limp in the dust and blood that flowed freely from a giant gash across the side of his head. The rangers had taken him out savagely while at the same time showing what was in Ty's estimation extreme control. The man had just murdered their own in cold blood and invaded their home. The fact he was still alive was incredible in Benhoff's opinion. Despite that the women would not go near him. They pointed and whispered amongst each other from time to time like he was the boogie man, all the while he sat frozen in place, staring blankly at the ground.

Ty took it upon himself to cover the big man, if for no other reason than he wanted to watch the man in charge, couldn't help but want to hear his side of the story. That and the fact the remainders of his merry band were either unconscious or whimpering while they suffered their last moments, lying in the dirt, gut shot, like so many of the creatures they mercilessly hunted and poisoned. They were nowhere near as interesting.

At first Thoomba wouldn't acknowledge him, much less talk to him. But that had never stopped Ty Benhoff before. That was half of his dating strategy all through college. Eventually Ty just took to asking him about the payday he was looking for. Rambling on about what a million plus in American dollars meant in Zimbabwe currency. That's when Thoomba chuckled.

"The money meant nothing to me, American."

Ty cocked his head. "Then why did you do all this?" he asked, nodding at all the destruction around them.

"Business, my friend. Business."

"Business. What kind of business doesn't include a payoff?"

Thoomba turned his head painfully from the ground, one eye was swollen shut, but the man fixed Ty with a measured stare with the other. "A dangerous business, my friend."

"Clearly." He looked at Fannel's body out of the corner of his eye. He knew the man was dead, Ty had checked his pulse while he looked into the man's wide lifeless eyes himself. But that man had scared him, and he only counted it as dumb luck that he was still alive. *So much dumb luck,* Ty reminded himself. Despite the fact that bastard was dead, Ty couldn't help putting an eye on him every now and then.

"Speaking of *friend*, what's up with the tall guy over there? What was his deal?"

Thoomba groaned as he moved gingerly to look where Ty was gesturing, "Him, Fannel." Obert nodded as if considering his words before looking at Ty again with his one functional eye. "He wanted to kill you very much. You should know I did not let him."

"Until tonight that is," Ty mentioned. "Still, I appreciate it. Why'd he want to kill me so bad? I wasn't even looking at you guys."

"Because you are an American. Fannel hated Americans."

"That's kind of general, what about the Navy kid, Cruz? He kill him?"

Thoomba looked back at the dirt. "No, no, another man," he snorted. "A boy killed your Navy man."

"Who?" asked Ty. Shit, he was on a roll all the sudden.

"Doesn't matter."

"Why not?"

"I killed him."

"For killing Cruz?"

"For threatening the business."

"Business again. I gotta be honest, I'm not so sure about your business practices."

Thoomba scoffed and cocked his head, then nodded slowly.

"So, I go back home and I can tell Albieto Cruz's mom his killer is dead?"

Thoomba stopped for a moment. He struggled to look at him again, "You can."

The way he answered him caught Ty a little odd. There was an odd inflection there. A sincerity maybe?

At that moment a phone chirped. Ty jumped too fast, out of habit, and bit down on his lip when his side protested.

Then he remembered his phone was smashed to bits when all the shooting started. He noticed a glow coming from Thoomba's front pocket. "Need to get that?" he asked the big man.

Thoomba studied his leg for a moment as if wondering if he could even maneuver enough to retrieve the device if he wanted to. "What time is it?"

Ty checked his watch, "Eleven-fifteen or so."

Thoomba's head dropped, "No, I have nothing to tell them."

Nothing good anyway, Ty didn't add.

In the distance, a rumble started to grow. A familiar chop and hum. Keeping an eye on the poacher, Ty watched as two Blackhawk helicopters swooped over the ICPF compound heading for the field outside the gate. He checked his watch and realized time had gone in fast forward since Thoomba had first struck. Three hours had passed.

"Worst response time ever," he mumbled as he started toward the helicopters. "Take care, Thoomba," he called behind him.

Ty put a hand on Nissa's shoulder as he passed her. The ranger was thumbing the safety on her rifle. "My people," he said.

She nodded and relaxed but watched him closely.

Ty left the gate as one of the two helicopters was easing toward the tall grass. As he covered his face from the blowing dirt and sand in the rotor wash, he noticed Lilliana standing over the body he had been told by Nissa was her husband.

"Everything ok?" he asked as he approached. He had to yell over the sounds of the Blackhawk.

Lilliana offered a weak smile and she nodded, "He was my husband," she said.

Ty didn't respond.

"And I killed him."

"You saved your friend and yourself, just like they taught you to."

Lilliana nodded again. More to herself than anyone else. When she turned to face him, she had a small black object in her hand. She handed it to him. It was a thumbdrive.

"I don't know what it is," she said, her eyes never leaving the device. "I know it is bad, and I know it is why he came after me."

"I, uh…" but she was already gone to join the rest of her rangers standing in a cluster by the front gate to watch the helicopters.

Ty watched the doors of one the helicopters slide open. The Blackhawk maintained a covering position over the field. A team Ty guessed was with some sort of Special Forces outfit leaped from the Blackhawks and formed a perimeter. One man, tall, black, and loaded with gear, approached him. He offered his hand, "Special Agent Benhoff?"

Ty shook the soldier's hand but before he could say anything they both turned as someone shouted, "That's the asshole we came to find!"

Kali, intimidating in her body armor and gloves, pushed by the soldiers and shoved Benhoff hard on the shoulder. "The fuck, Benhoff?"

Ty gasped in pain, doubled over, wheezing as fire raced up his side, "Owww."

"Couldn't hurt to call seein's how the last I heard from your phone was a shit load of gunshots."

Ty was still wincing as he held up his smashed iPhone as evidence.

Kali studied the ruined device for a moment before stepping toward him again, fist balled. Then she noticed his bandage and stepped back, "Oh… still, what was I supposed to think?"

Ty had caught his breath enough to form words. "Bring the cavalry? And I appreciate it, but your response time sucks." At that moment Boulden walked up, shaking his head at the both of them.

Ty looked at the soldier who was watching the interaction with a blank sort of disbelief. "Thank you for coming, Sergeant."

"Bailey," he looked from Kali to Ty, then back again. "Right, so you're good?"

"I'm good."

"Okay, dust off in five, got me?" The sergeant turned when one of the men called his name.

Ty gave a thumbs up before acknowledging Boulden was standing there. "Am I still in trouble?" Boulden looked at the camp over his shoulder. Ty followed his attention. There were several bodies under tarps that could not be missed, "I have no doubt."

"Sure, I get it," he said, cringing. He turned to go grab his gear when Bailey called his name.

Ty turned and the man was gesturing toward a row of bodies lying outside the ICPF perimeter fence. They were the dead men Maynard dumped outside the fence himself before leaving with Jurness and the other wounded. Maynard had made it clear before taking Jurness to meet an ambulance at the main road that none of the corpses were welcome inside the ICPF.

"They can stay out here and rot for all I care."

As Ty walked up to Bailey and one of his men, who was documenting the five bodies with a Biometrics scanner. Bailey asked, "Where the fuck did this guy come from?" He was pointing to Cartwell's husband.

"Ambushed two of the rangers out in the bush. The Arab was one of the women's husband. Why?"

"What kind of clearance you got?"

Ty's eyebrows bounced, "TS/SCI, why?"

Bailey shrugged. "Not enough." He turned to his soldier and said, "Bag this fuck, he comes with us."

To Ty, Bailey said, "Get your shit, time to go."

"Hold on." Ty handed the drive to Bailey. The solider looked at him, "One of the women he ambushed was his wife. She stole that from him before coming here. You got an exploitation guy?"

"I do, good stuff." Bailey pocketed the drive and moved on.

Ty nodded and turned back to Kali and Boulden.

"Dude's a heavy hitter," Ty told Boulden. "Has to be."

"Possibly," Boulden allowed.

A big grin spread across Benhoff's face, "Think I'm still on the NCIS shit list now?"

Boulden sighed, "Just go get your shit. Let's go."

CHAPTER EIGHTY-EIGHT

Captain James Hanswei, along with Inspectors Billa and Vong, pulled up to the gate protecting the palatial home of Gerald Thoomba just after dawn. Detective Matthew Tsunga was waiting for them.

Before saying a word, Hanswei took Tsunga's hand, the two bearing wide smiles.

"Finally," Captain Hanswei said.

"Yes, finally," Tsunga agreed.

Entering on foot, Hanswei kept his eyes on the wide, double front doors for any sort of movement, but the façade of the entire location was still. He had practiced what he would say to Hanswei upon meeting him. Rehearsed the lines he would use in the hopes he would not appear as nervous in front of such a powerful man. Even with the preparation Hanswei had butterflies in his belly like he'd not felt since his first year as a policeman in Harare.

At the front door he straightened his suit and tie before announcing themselves via a heavy wrought iron knocker on the left side of the two doors.

There was no response at first, so they waited patiently... then continued to wait patiently until Tsunga mentioned that Gerald had a full-time wait staff of two women in the home.

Hanswei knocked again, the heavy iron bashing against its companion plate affixed to the door. Moments passed in silence.

"Could he have fled?" asked Billa.

Less than twelve hours had passed since Hanswei received the call from Tyrone Benhoff regarding what had transpired at the ICPF compound. There is no way he could have known, was Hanswei's first instinct in response to the question. Then he considered the judge, and the judge's staff where he'd applied for an arrest warrant, notifications he made to his superiors, and he had his answer.

Grimacing, Hanswei tried the doorknob. It was unlocked.

The four men unholstered their side arms and Hanswei announced, "Police!" as he opened the door.

"Police!" he called again. "Gerald Thoomba, we have a warrant for your arrest. Come out! Now!"

His call and the announcements of the others were met by silence. Hanswei gestured for Billa and Vong to check upstairs. The two men took to the stairs off the expansive receiving room in unison.

Hanswei looked at Tsunga, who stood on his right flank. Tsunga nodded in return and the two men made their way into the house. He expected to find one of the housekeepers, or at least a fan running in one of the rooms they passed, but there was nothing. The silent house was unnerving in its utter lack of movement or sound.

He and Tsunga passed through a sitting room and through an archway where they were met by their first sign of any movement in the house. A light, almost translucent white drape lifted under a soft hot breeze blowing through an open door to the veranda. He ensured Tsunga understood his intention and pushed aside the drapes to exit onto the terrace. Hanswei sighed not two steps into the growing morning heat.

He felt Tsunga next to him in the next moment. Out of the corner of his eye he saw the man's shoulders slump.

"Down here!" he called for Billa and Vong.

They had found Gerald Thoomba. Though they faced only his back, the cloud of flies, thick as the clouds of a dust storm, buzzed around him in an angry flurry, each fighting for space around the body to lay their eggs amongst the fresh meat. Gerald was sitting perfectly straight in his chair. As Hanswei and Tsunga approached slowly, they could see why.

Gerald Thoomba was bound to his ornate cast iron chair with bailing wire. Lines of blood seeped from his neck and through his robe where the rigid bindings had cut his skin. As they came around to face the man they had worked so hard to bring to justice, Hanswei's breath caught in his throat. Tsunga turned away to stifle a sudden flood of bile in his throat.

Gerald Thoomba's mouth was frozen in a horrific, almost comedian-like grin, his teeth clenched tight, even in death. His eyes had been gouged out and sat before him on a porcelain plate. His wrists, bound to the metal arms of the chair, ended in cauterized stumps. His hands, fingers amputated, likewise sat on the plate before him.

"This is monstrous," said Matthew Tsunga through a forced breath.

"This is a message," opined Hanswei.

"To who?" gasped Tsunga.

"Everyone."

CHAPTER EIGHTY-NINE

Lilliana Cartwell left the comm shack to find Danner Maynard strolling down the gravel walk toward her. She immediately noticed the bags under his eyes. He was pale. She doubted he'd eaten or slept for the last two days.

"How are Sergeant Jurness and Allenda?" she asked. Despite his casual gate, she knew he was coming for her. Since the wounded were still being treated at hospital, she had become his special focus. He checked on her over and over, asking how she was, if she needed anything. It was a sweet gesture but there was nothing he could do. Nothing anyone could do. It was scary but Lilliana actually felt nothing about the death of her husband. In fact, she had felt nothing at all since waving goodbye to Victoria Jurness the night Maynard took her and the others to get medical treatment.

"Everyone is coming along," he answered trying to sound upbeat, but she heard the exhaustion in his voice. "How are you?"

She shrugged, "I must go to Harare." she said.

"That a good thing?" he asked.

"It is about my home. It caught fire earlier this month."

He grimaced and she could see him not wanting to pry.

"It will be good to have this all behind me. Dealing with this will get me one step closer."

"To what?" he asked.

Lilliana looked around the camp. "This," she said, "Where I can do my job without fearing every vehicle that comes through the gate is him coming to force me back."

Maynard studied her for a long moment. "That sounds like a good way of handling things," he said. "I would suggest one thing though if I may."

"Anything, sir."

"I can't think of any place I would rather be than here," he said. "But once your business is concluded and you put a cap on that life. Take some time for yourself. Spoil yourself, just for you, you know. Then come back to us. This place is great but there's always room for a little freedom here and there. God knows you've earned it."

Lilliana thought about it for a moment but could not think of what she could possibly do for herself. What did that even mean? The fact she couldn't think of anything was almost as off putting as having no emotion one way or the other about killing Hassan.

"Think about it." He tossed her a set of keys, "And take my ride. It could use the work out."

"I will take care of it."

"As long as you take care of yourself at the same time Ranger Cartwell," he said over his shoulder as he headed further into camp.

CHAPTER NINETY

Ty Benhoff slept like a dead man. The Blackhawk dropped them off on the tarmac aboard Camp Lemmonnier just after the sun started to breach the Gulf of Aden. Boulden, under strict orders to deliver him to NCISHQ as soon as possible. So instead of Ty heading for his house in town to at least try to pack, Boulden ushered him directly to the air wing. Ty scoffed when the petty officer manning operations told him no flights were scheduled for the day, and the one bird they did have on station, a C-47 so old Patton could have commandeered it to cruise the skies over Europe, was down with electrical issues. When Boulden turned and tried to send Ty to the commercial airport in Djibouti City he found nothing but empty air. Ty had commandeered a vehicle of his own, Boulden's assigned Land Cruiser. He drove straight to his rented house and dropped into bed bloody bandages, grimy clothes and all. He didn't even bother to take off his boots.

That was twelve hours ago.

Ty woke with a start, reaching for his gun that sat in the evidence vault at the office. Since he had discharged it in Zimbabwe, it was now evidence pending administrative review. He heard banging on his front door. He must have been in deep REM because he was so out of it, it took him a minute to be able to focus on his watch. It was 1900 hours, *FUCK!*

Ty pried himself clumsily from the bed and stumbled his way to the front door where no doubt SSA Thomas Boulden was waiting for him. Ty was still a little bleary eyed when he yanked the door open, but he was fairly certain the vaguely familiar black guy standing on his front step was not SSA Thomas Boulden.

"Bailey?" he asked. The Special Forces solider was in a blue polo shirt that strained against the man's musculature. A pair of 5.11 cargo pants and Salomon hiking boots finished his ensemble. Over his shoulder Ty noted a Toyota Land Cruiser, a short haired, deeply tanned, white male watched him through a dark pair of Oakley's.

"That's right Agent, get your shit, we need you."

Ty left the door open and let Bailey follow him in, "I'm supposed to be wheels up in two hours."

Bailey shook his head, "You know that thumb drive you gave me?"

Ty nodded, the world around him was finally resolving back into solid matter. "Thought I wasn't cleared for that stuff."

"You are now. It's a crypto wallet. It needs a key to unlock it. We're going back to Zimbabwe to talk to the girl."

"Why do you need me for that?"

"You know her, you know the case, you've got contacts."

Ty thought about the pending career apocalypse waiting for him at Quantico for a second. It wasn't hard to weight the two options, "Let me get my stuff."

Five minutes later Ty and Bailey were skipping down the marble steps of his quarters toward Bailey's Land Cruiser when Boulden and Kali pulled up to the curb in the office's beat up old Hillux.

"I told you to return my car," Boulden said, slamming the passenger side door. "What's this?" he gestured at Bailey and the other solider.

Ty tossed his body armor in the back of the SUV, "Back to Zimbabwe for a minute."

"The hell you are."

Bailey slapped a piece of paper in Boulden's hand, "He is, sorry you didn't get the memo."

Ty got in behind Bailey who took the driver seat. He winked at Kali. She couldn't help but snicker. Boulden stood between the two of them dumbfounded.

"What am I supposed to tell the Director?"

Bailey dropped the Land Cruiser into gear. "He already knows," he said pulling away.

Boulden watched them go for a second then unfolded the email Bailey had given him. All he needed to see was the line that read: "DIRNCIS (Director NCIS) concurs."

***

Fifteen minutes later Ty, Bailey, and five of Bailey's squad were aboard a C-130 headed for Zimbabwe. The five of them stood around a table while an Intelligence Specialist pulled a couple of slides up on her laptop. She was out of uniform like the rest of them. She wore a trim green polo shirt and 5.11 cargo pants. Her blonde hair was tightly bound in a bun on the back of her head. She had intense blue eyes that Ty found at once enchanting and intimidating, that seemed fun.

Before Wilson got started Bailey introduced him to the group, "All, Special Agent Ty Benhoff, you might have met him last night. He brought us the crypto wallet and has been on the ground in Zimbabwe for the last week. Benhoff, Spencer, Wheels, Briggs, Gates, and our Intel Specialist, Wilson," he said gesturing toward each one in order. Ty received a couple of nods in response. The majority of them chose to simply appraise him with practiced thousand-yard stares. Ty smirked and gave a subtle wave to the group.

Wilson took her que, "Lilliana Cartwell, 21 years of age. Originally from Zambia, married to Hassan Rhouran, a string of possible a.k.a.s, for approximately five years. Cartwell fled Rhouran earlier this year and joined the International Counter-Poaching Federation. As the majority of us know Cartwell killed Rhouran last night. He now sits in our cooler back at base. The thumbdrive Ms. Cartwell gave Special Agent Benhoff last night turned out to be a bitcoin wallet believed to hold substantial intelligence. It has been prioritized by the national command authority."

As she spoke her eyes flashed to Benhoff. He couldn't help but feel like she was taking a measure of him, and not in a good way. More like do you deserve to exist in the same world as me sort of way.

"We believe given Rhouran's past this wallet could be a major link to sponsors of international terror. The wallet requires a key, a string of sixty-four alpha-numeric characters to gain access to the currency and block chain associated with the account."

Bailey took over, "For Benhoff's benefit. Hassan Rhouran has a long history beginning in Afghanistan fighting coalition forces at Tora Bora. A Native Saudi, his family are known wahabists with ties to the royal family. He has been an extremist fighter since his early teens. Several years ago, he went dark, chatter brought him back to our attention last year when he emerged as a precious gems dealer working out of Harare. Given his familial status and the profile associated with the precious mineral market, there was speculation he had been promoted from cannon fodder to a more executive role within the extremist community. There was nothing solid to substantiate that until last night when you gave me the wallet. Rhouran's house burned down a couple weeks back. A couple of bodies were found in the rubble, but they remain unidentified. That's why need Cartwell. She's the only link to Rhouran we've got and the best lead at finding that key."

He pointed at Ty, "That's why Benhoff's here. We land in Zimbabwe, he talks to Cartwell. Hopefully she either has the key or she can point us in the right direction."

"Long shot," Ty heard himself say. When he looked up, he noted the squad staring at him with much the same look that Wilson had given him. It was cute when she did it, these dudes just looked like they were either practicing a Clint Eastwood impression or they had to take a shit. "She didn't know me. She handed it to me and only said that it was bad, and she didn't want it anymore. Pretty sure any of us here could have filled that role."

Bailey pointed at a photo of the drive taped to the table in front of him, "This device is one of the highest intelligence priorities in the United States. You know her better than anyone else in the American inventory. You know the local cops. We don't have time to get spun up on all that."

Ty nodded, "Works for me, I'm just telling you be ready if she doesn't even know what cryptocurrency is."

"We'll find out," said one of the soldiers standing around the table. Ty couldn't remember his name, but he was wearing a Goonies t-shirt which Ty found pretty cool. He was holding up a black iPhone, "She just got a call from the Police in Harare. They want to talk to her about the fire at her old home."

"You guys are up on her phone?"

The guy in the Goonies shirt returned his question with a blank stare.

"You're not Army, are you?"

Another blank stare.

"We own all the phones at the ICPF," said Bailey, "Gates you got a good read on her phone."

"She doesn't have her own, but I'll be able to track if she takes one with her to Harare."

"Make sure you do that, alright...."

"How long ago did her place in Harare burn down?" asked Ty cutting Bailey off.

"Couple weeks, why?"

"Why are they just getting a hold of her now?" Something wasn't sitting right.

Bailey shrugged, "It's Africa man."

Ty thought of the bottle cap he found in Albieto Cruz's case file and couldn't disagree with the Special Forces Solider.

Bailey gave him a second before asking, "Questions?"

There were none.

"Alright, gear up, low profile. We intercept her in Harare."

CHAPTER NINETY-ONE

Lilliana Cartwell stared at the mobile phone. It was a smartphone. One she could use to run apps, take pictures, read the internet. Compared to the ancient flip phone she had in her pocket the smartphone was like something out of a movie. She had the money. And now she had the freedom. So why was it so hard for her to take it to the purchase counter? The flip phone she had was anonymous. She had picked it up only as a possible lifeline to the police or something if she needed it. She never used it. She hadn't even turned it on since joining the ICPF. The smartphone though, a Samsung could not be so anonymous, especially if she truly were to join the world again. She had seen Head Ranger Maynard's phone, and some of the more senior rangers, and the way they had Instagram and Facebook pages. They interacted with the world as if it were all right there at their fingertips. That was something Lilliana could never do or thought she could never do until now.

She felt eyes on her and looked up to see the Indian shop owner eyeing her impatiently. She offered him a weak smile as she struggled with her decision. Keeping it in her hand she stepped to a cabinet that held various laptops. She had no idea what the markings or brand names meant. They made her wonder though. What could she do with a device such as that? Maybe schooling, neither her family nor Hassan had ever shown any interest in her education. It never made sense to them. In fact, when she asked Hassan about school, he had hit her and told her about the true path of a Muslim woman. Lilliana had no idea why, but she found herself smiling as she remembered his nostrils flaring and his eyes going wide with rage at her daring to better herself. She turned back to the shop owner who was still watching her intently,

"I wish to purchase both of these items, sir." She gestured with the smartphone in one hand and pointed to the laptop with the other.

The shopkeep smiled then, his suspicion melting to warmth.

Moments later and with a handful of accessories she had no idea how to use Lilliana Cartwell emerged, two heavy bags in hand onto the hot Harare night. She was smiling again, and the sensation was pleasing. Almost as much as the knowledge of how infuriated her actions would have made her husband if he were still alive. But he wasn't. She was free, just like Head Ranger Mander said. It felt good.

"Kilo has eyes on," Samm Heim heard out of his left ear. His right had been seized by yet another nervous assistant from the organization. He had been listening patiently, if not completely while this one. He didn't remember his name, so he simply designated him as the America blathered, reinforcing the importance, and insinuating the personal severity of his current mission. He watched Kilo's vehicle, a black Mercedez Benz pull into traffic as the target continued down the busy evening street headed presumably back to her hotel. The policeman they had contracted to draw her to Harare had done his job well, he thought. On the phone the American was silent. He must have asked him a question.

"Young man, if you are finished, I will tell you that all your information will be taken for advisement. The same way the call from your contemporary representing the Arabs will be. I will also point out that both of your messages are the same. Almost to the word. Before bothering me again do see your two factions coordinate your veiled threats."

The American stuttered, clearly exasperated. Heim had no time for this.

"Good evening," he said and disengaged the call. He keyed his comms unit, "X-ray status?"

There was a wisp of static, "Hotel secure, all units green," said a feminine voice.

***

Lilliana had made it to Harare Just before sundown. She checked in to the Meikles Hotel in downtown. It was a posh, luxurious place that she could not afford. But she had decided to take to heart Head Ranger Maynard's advice. Besides, what is there in the bush to spend her pay on? When she laid down on the bed in her room she might as well had fallen into a cloud. It was paradise compared to the cot she called her own at the ICPF camp. Hard as she tried; however, she could not manage to relax. She was edgy. She didn't know if it was guilt over splurging on such a hotel or maybe the fact she was meeting with the police tomorrow. Either way she could not get comfortable in such a glorious place. She had to get out. Exiting the hotel between the regal stone lions that guarded the entrance of the hotel she found herself standing under the portico with no idea where to go or what she wanted to do. One of the valets took pity on her aimless appearance and suggested and Indian restaurant a little less than a kilometer away. He offered to flag her a cab, but Lillian thanked him and chose to walk. She needed to burn off some energy.

The valet was not wrong. The Indian food was so flavorful and exotic, curried rice and vegetables seasoned in ways she had forgotten about since choosing her life in the bush. It was fully dark by the time she exited the restaurant though the streets of Harare were still full of people of all kinds crowding the sidewalks. Lilliana was in no hurry to get back to the hotel, so she meandered in and out of the many shops until she ended up with the two heavy bags of electronic equipment filling her hands. She was truly enjoying being there amongst all the hustle of a big city. It was amazing how quickly one could forget the energy of a place like Harare. Hassan did not let her out while she was with him, especially alone, but in her duties as the show piece wife she had been out socially with the elite of the city. Tonight felt different, honest maybe? She wasn't sure of course though she did know one thing. Head Ranger Maynard was a soothsayer. He was absolutely right about what Lilliana needed.

***

Ty, Bailey, Gates, and Wheels were in one Range Rover, Spencer and Briggs paralleled them a block over while they tried to hone in on Cartwell's mobile phone signature. Its last ping was on a tower near Inez Terrace, but it had gone dark by the time they reached downtown. The two teams drove around the busy part of Harare filled with pedestrians filtering in and out of stores and restaurants. Looking for a petite black woman, even a proven bad ass like Lilliana Cartwell was like searching for a needle in a truckload of needles.

"This search is looking low tech all of a sudden," said Ty.

"Maybe she switched her phone off," Gates said, monitoring the laptop and other classified gear that allowed them to sweep cellular traffic within a given area.

"Get off your ass and knock on doors," Ty said to himself.

"Fuck you say to me?" Gates spat.

Ty startled and looked back at him. He looked at Bailey who was staring at him with a dark look, "What, you guys never heard that before?"

They continued to stare at him.

"It means you can't solve a case from your desk. My squad Sergeant used to tell us that all the time. You can't police from the office. Get your asses out there and knock on doors."

Bailey crunched his eyes, "How is that relevant?"

"We're trying to find Cartwell on crowded city streets in an area full of hotels and stores. We got no visual electronically unless her phone pops back up. We might as well start canvassing," Ty explained.

"Canvas?" asked Bailey.

Not big on cop shows?

"We need to wander around to some of the hotels surrounding the last tower she pinged from. Show her picture to the desk people. See if they've seen her," Ty explained.

"That'll take forever," said Gates.

"It's better than sitting around doing nothing," said Bailey.

"You take the left; I'll take the right side of the street. Just show her pic to the concierge or registration people. Maybe we get lucky. Also give me a hundred bucks," Ty told him.

Bailey cocked his head back, "What for?"

"Good Samaritans are rare and we don't have any authority here."

***

"She's a block out," reported Kilo who paced Lilliana Cartwell from the opposite side of the street. He had parked his Benz a block back when his target entered a crowded plaza so he could keep up with her. He dodged random pedestrians while keeping the target in his peripheral vision.

"Roger," answered Delta, she turned to Heim who was appreciating the sights and sounds of a night in Harare. There wasn't much to see compared to other cities around the world and he'd worked in many of them. But every environment had its own uniqueness to it. He basked in the last, fleeting moments of peace and silence before the operation commenced. Chaos would soon envelope him and would not end until he completed his mission. He did not know much about the woman other than she had killed Rhouran. That alone was impressive and piqued his interest. He looked forward to meeting her. Movement in the window reflection caught his attention. It was beginning. X-Ray appeared in his window. He took the opportunity to straighten his tie as she briefed him,

"Charlie and Zebra are set; Kilo will cover our exit and provide rearguard once we are mobile."

Heim nodded, "Very well."

***

It had been a half hour. Ty had made his way around the three blocks that surrounded the last cell tower Cartwell's phone had connected to. He was just leaving his fourth hotel, a Holiday Inn of all places when Bailey keyed his earpiece, "Struck out for three quarters of a mile in either direction. Going back to the car."

"Copy," Ty said, careful to hold his phone up to his ear so as not to have all the Zimbabweans surrounding him thinking he was a crazy person who liked to talk to himself. "Copy that, I'm hitting up one more on my side. I'm a couple blocks down."

"We'll start that way."

Ty took in the fourteen-story building and the two lions guarding the entrance. It was a nice place. He was betting there wasn't a chance she would be there. His gumshoe cop work idea was turning out to be a loser. He pulled Lilliana's image up on his phone. When he did so he noticed the rack of notifications on his lock screen. One from Kayla, more than a dozen from Boulden. For whom the bell tolls, he found it odd that, that phrase was the one that popped in his head. Ty sighed and went in. The air-conditioned atmosphere engulfed him the second he walked through the door. Ty stopped for a moment just to enjoy it. He hadn't noticed the heat in the night air, but the cold attacked the places where his sweat soaked t-shirt stuck to him, especially down the center of his back. The sensation made him shiver as an avalanche of cold raced down his spine. Ty didn't care.

"Where you at?" asked Bailey.

"The Meikles," Ty answered.

"What's that?" a Brit, maybe a South African who was passing by asked him. The guy was pale, and kind of short, with a slick ponytail not quite shoulder length. He had a wiry frame and the inklings of a mustache which made him look, in Ty's opinion, like a C-list porn actor. He wore a black suit and had intense eyes.

"What?" asked Ty, realizing right at that moment he had been talking to himself as far as this guy knew.

"You said something," Brit, Ty caught enough to tag his accent that time.

"Nothin, just talking to myself, long day," Ty was talking to the man's back. The little prick was already walking toward the elevators. What an asshole.

Ty made his way through the cavernous lobby to the registration desk where a knockout Thai woman with long black hair, perky smile and instantly hypnotizing green eyes awaited him. Ty clocked a gold cross pendant hanging just below her neckline.

"Can I help you, sir?" she asked in clipped English. Her name tag read "Maggie." There was no way that was her real name. It always kind of irked him when hotels felt the need to westernize their employees. Even in the oddest parts of the globe.

Ty leaned in to try and keep his voice down, "Yeah, this might be an odd request, but can you tell me if you've seen this woman. She's part of my church group and we got separated out in the market."

"I'm sorry, sir. We are not supposed to give out guest information."

"I don't need her room or anything, I just need to know if she's here. I'm getting a little worried about her."

The receptionist, her name tag read Maggie, smiled, and tilted her head to one side. It was the international sign of, 'Aww, how sweet,' an expression every woman on every continent did exactly the same. She nodded her head and said, "You just missed her."

"I did?" Ty asked.

"Yeah." Then Maggie's eyes lit up. "Actually, there she is now."

Ty turned to see Lilliana Cartwell, surrounded by four people wearing matching black suits. A fifth was escorting her under her arm. Ty couldn't see either of her escorts' hands. He noticed a sixth member of the party as the rat faced little guy, he talked to earlier fell in at the rear of the diamond formation they had around her. They looked like a protection detail, and definitely not Zimbabwe National Police. Every one of them were white, immaculately dressed, an each wore an expression as warm as a T100. What the hell was this? Apparently, the United States weren't the only ones who wanted to talk to Lilliana Cartwell. He watched them like a guppy watching a Great White swim by, hoping they don't notice him,

"Bailey, where you at?" Ty remembered to hold his phone to his ear this time. He kept his eyes locked on Lilliana Cartwell.

"Still a block out in traffic, why?"

"Somebody beat us to her," he answered.

"What, who?"

"Don't know," Ty caught sight of Cartwell's facial features for a moment as she turned her head toward the interior of the lobby. Her eyes were wide, her mouth hung open like there was a question on the tip of her tongue, but she just couldn't find the words. Ty was already moving toward them, "You guys better haul ass."

"Ben...," Benhoff ignored him. He was more focused on what to do next. As he gained on the six surrounding Cartwell he noted bulges in the coats of three of them. They were wearing shoulder rigs. He fluffed his shirt out once to free up access to the borrowed Sig Sauer nine-millimeter Bailey had lent him. He had thirty rounds against, first guess, over one hundred and fifty between the six of them. But he couldn't let them get to their cars or whatever they had waiting for them. They were contained for now, on the roads there were too many variables to deal with. Not to mention the risk to thousands of people roaming Harare if they rabbited. His mind was spinning trying to think of something, even when he heard himself call out, "Lilliana!"

They all turned to look at him at once. The five on perimeter had hands under their coats in a subtle message that was breathtakingly clear. Ty completely ignored them, why would an art teacher from Syracuse on a mission trip pay attention to dirty scowls from well-dressed potential kidnappers anyway? He went in for a hug but received a stout stiff arm from a bearded man holding Lilliana's arm.

"Lilliana, thank the Lord I found you, we were all so worried," Ty suddenly had an odd lilt to his voice. He crinkled his nose and looked at the bearded man holding her arm, "Who's this?"

The man pursed his lips, "My name is Agent Edgar, Interpol. Step aside, sir."

He had an accent Ty couldn't place. The guy didn't show a badge either. He'd worked with Interpol before a couple of years ago and this wasn't their M.O. This guy was full of shit. "Interol, what's that?" Ty demanded, putting his hands on his hips. He was careful to keep from drawing tension on his shirt. The t-shirt he wore didn't do much to conceal the full-size pistol on the back of his right hip.

Agent Edgar started to speak, Ty cut him off.

"I'm not sure what's going on here, but I lost this woman once today, I'm not taking my eyes off her until we're singing hymns and sharing the good news out in the bush," Ty exclaimed raising his hands in pseudo spirit fingers.

"We're here." Bailey said in his earpiece.

Ty looked at Lilliana. He saw she recognized him. She was scared. She looked at him, speechless. Worry lines crinkled her eyebrows.

A strong hand suddenly took his wrist and bent it under his arm in a come along grip, "Hey!" Ty protested weakly while the rat faced little dude he'd talked to earlier cranked on him with an iron grip. Wrenching pain shot through his wrist. Ty went to his tip toes, the first thing he'd done that hadn't been a total act since jumping into this hornets' nest, "Ok, Ok!" Rat face turned him and shoved him further into the lobby while the others continued toward the door.

***

Bailey, Gates, and Wheels passed the stone lions guarding the entrance to the Meikles and took the stairs casually to get a look at the place. What they found was a handful of men and women in black suits, their target, Lilliana Cartwell, and Ty Benhoff being spun around by a small man with a black ponytail who had the NCIS Agent in an escort hold. Bailey had just reached level ground with them when a bearded man turned the target toward the door. Both men locked eyes for an instant. With an instinctive quickness, the bearded man pulled out a gun and fired. Bailey launched himself to the right into a set of lobby furniture. He felt the air pressure of the round meant for his head as it zipped passed him. All at once the hotel lit up in a gunfight.

***

Ty felt the torque on his wrist slacken as Rat Boy flinched at the sound of the first shot. Ty spun, rolling his wrist with the tension Rat Boy had on him. The move took away Rat Boy's leverage and Ty escaped his grip. Rat Boy turned back on him, a questioning expression on his face, like which way do I go, you or do I start shooting?

Ty relieved the man's confusion with a stunning uppercut to his jaw. As Rat Boy stumbled backward Ty drove the back of his head into a marble pillar, cracking his skull against the polished stone. Shots boomed and a screaming wave of panic washed through the hotel. Ty barely heard it, too focused on his immediate threat. But Rat Boy was done. Ty felt the man's body shudder before collapsing on the floor. A pool of blood began spreading from Rat Boy's head as he relieved him of an FN Five Seven handgun and two magazines.

He stood up after completing the robbery just in time for a bullet to ping off a massive stone planter next to his head. Ty dove behind the pillar that bore Rat Boy's hair grease and checked the load on the FN. The concussive boom of multiple weapons firing reverberated throughout the building. Dashing men and women fled in an uncoordinated insanity to get away from the hell that just exploded around them.

Ty poked his head out from cover to take stock of the situation. Bailey, Wheels, and Gates were just inside the main doors taking cover behind pillars similar to his own and flower boxes, whatever they could use against the extremely dangerous five-seven caliber ammunition being fired at them by Lilliana's captors. The black suited men and women were in a like position just passed the registration desk. He heard a woman bark an order in a foreign language Ty thought might have been Africanz. The bearded man yanked Lilliana into a crouch and they started moving while the others poured fire into Bailey's position. The bearded man, Agent Edgar, and Lilliana were coming right at him. He had her by the arm. She tried to pull away seeing an opportunity to fight him.

There you go, he thought.

Ty broke from cover and snapped off two rounds. Missing on his first shot Ty's second pierced 'Edgar's' right shoulder. He dropped his gun and looked up in time to see Ty, now within an arm's length put two more into his heart. 'Edgar' dropped with a wide eyed and dumfounded look on his face. Ty shoved Lilliana and the two of them toppled clumsily over the registration desk as rounds chased them, chewing up papers and shattering computer monitors. Maggie, the Thai registration clerk was cowering under the desk. She screamed when the two of them landed in front of her.

"You okay?" he yelled over the din of gunfire.

"You're the agent!" Lilliana yelped, "What is this?"

Maggie also answered in the affirmative.

Ty slapped the Sig in Cartwell's hand and she froze, "That drive you gave me has drawn a lot of attention." He said as he popped up and snapped off two more rounds at a female with a tight ponytail as dark as her suit. He dropped to a knee pretty sure he missed as a round cracked the air over his head. Lilliana was staring at him the gun still sitting in her open palm.

"I'm guessing you're not with these guys. Want to get out of here?"

She looked at the gun, then at him again. Her expression changed from one of confusion and shock to that of determination, blank, concrete determination. She checked the weapon he'd given her and settled in to a two-handed grip. Ty nodded, a grin on his face. He took two steps to his left and popped up to fire again. He noticed the woman he'd been shooting at before was on the ground writhing in the fetal position with a wound in her stomach. On the flip side, two of Bailey's men were down also.

"Is there a way out of here?" Ty asked Maggie.

She nodded, pointing to the back of the registration area to a door as if she had just realized it was there. It drew her like a siren's song, and she dashed forward no regard for the bullets flying through the air, smashing through the thin wood. In a moment she was gone, fleeing for her life.

"Bailey, I've got her. And I got an out."

"Take it, take it now. We'll cover. Two rendezvous and exfil."

"Two copies," said Briggs.

"Go!" Bailey commanded.

A burst of fire from Bailey's team pinned everyone in the lobby to the ground. Ty pushed Lilliana to the door covering her back. Lilliana stutter stepped in the back office before sprinting through an open door that led to a wide corridor adjacent to the lobby. Ty tried to keep up, but she was ten years younger than he was, and fast as a gazelle. He tried to remember the orientation of the hotel to the street as they sprinted passed door after door, but he sucked at cardinal directions. There was a steel exit door at the end of the hallway. He needed to give two their position, for the life of him he couldn't figure out if they were running East or West.

"We're coming out the West side door," he called his guess over the comms.

"East!" Lilliana yelled over her shoulder just as a shot from behind them planted itself in the wall beside his head.

"Correction East, with company!" Ty spun and dropped to a knee to see three of the black suited gunmen charging them from the lobby. A woman with dark hair was ahead of the other two. She fired just as Ty did. His first shot chipped through the tightly weaved brown carpet in front of her, his second caught her in his knee. Turned out she was a better shot. She fired as her leg gave out and caught him in his left forearm. The speed of the bullet filleted his arm splitting the meat from wrist to forearm and knocked him back on his ass. His eyes watered and a hot blast of searing pain overwhelmed his senses. Through his blurry vision he could see the other men still coming. Two rounds ripped through the floor next to him. From his back he raised the Five Seven with his right hand to return fire. Ty pulled the trigger, nothing happened. Tried it again, not even a click. A brief look at the weapon and he could see the round in his forearm had ricocheted off the slide. It was mangled and sat in an odd angle off kilter to the frame. Over the barrel the two men closed on him. Guns level to his head, he was done. That realization seemed odd, there wasn't any fear, no panic. He kind of had the same feeling as if he'd just struck out in little league.

BAM! BAM! BAM! BAM! BAM! BAM!

The concussion from Lilliana's weapon stunned him. Ty's ears rang, drowning out all sound. He watched with a sort of detachment as the two men dropped. The woman further down the hall slumped over after the third shot. He felt a hand take him under the arm.

"Come on!" Lilliana cried.

* * *

He was heavy.

Lilliana had seen him fall out of the corner of her eye when she was mere steps from the exit, from safety. Three rounds had pinged off the heavy metal door, but she had focused on the grey security bar. It was her salvation. When she saw the agent stumble everything changed. There was no thought, no weighing the odds. Cartwell simply reacted when she saw him in trouble. Two targets in black, there were no faces, she noted no expressions from them. She saw their weapons aimed at him and fired until they fell. Then she saw the woman down the hall, on the ground but gun in hand. She dropped her too, with all the care of a crocodile smashing a fawn between its jaws.

He stumbled to his feet, and she saw all the blood. His arm was a red mess of meat and shredded tissue. A steady stream of blood fell from him like rainwater cascading off the leaves of a tree. Despite all that when she looked at him, he had a smile on his face.

"Really glad I gave you that gun," he said through heavy breath.

She couldn't help but return the smile.

"Coming out the east side," he said when they reached the door.

Lilliana rammed the security bar with her shoulder, and they burst into the night. There waiting for them were three more of the black suited enemy. They had their guns trained on them. Two women, one with red hair and pale features, the other with dark brown skin and tight clipped hair flanked an older man, massive in stature. He wore a manicured grey beard with a full head of wavy hair. His skin was tan, healthy. Whereas the women to his left and right looked at her with unmitigated hate. The man's features were placid, almost sorrowful. He opened the door to a black Mercedez G-Class SUV,

"Ms. Cartwell, my name is Samuel Heim, please join me."

She said nothing in response. She squeezed the agent's wrist.

"What about me? I don't get a ride?"

Lilliana's breath caught in her throat. The American was very pale, a drop of sweat fell from his nose. His breathing was ragged. Still, he had an odd grin on his face. She wondered if he were mad or just going into shock.

"I don't know you, nor are you part of my contract." He gestured toward the idling vehicle, the sounds of sirens wailed in the distance, "Please Ms. Cartwell, time is precious."

"What do you people want from me?" she cried. Her feet locked to the ground she stood on.

"This is neither the time or place, but I can tell you there are some people who need to speak to you about an item that belonged to your deceased husband. I would offer my condolences but that doesn't seem to be necessary under the circumstances." Heim gestured toward the redhead, and she took aim at the agent and closed on them.

"Sorry Lilliana," she heard the agent say. His head hung low; his skin was almost white.

She felt her eyes well up, "No!" she cried, dropping her gun to the concrete walk.

The redhead stopped. Heim smiled warmly. He started to say something, but his words were muted by a burst of rifle fire. Lilliana watched the three of them jerk in an uncoordinated dance as the Mercedez and surrounding decorative bushes and potted plants were chewed up along with them. The roar of an engine and screeching tires followed. She watched in stunned silence as three men leapt from another SUV. These men wore polo shirts, ball caps, and cargo pants. They were armed with American AR-15's though much more compact than the weapon she carried in the bush. Two of them went to the three mangled bodies sprawled next to the Mercedez. They rifled through pockets and took photos while the third, a black man with stern hard eyes charged her making her take a step back.

He put a hand up, "Ms. Cartwell, please, my name is Sergeant Bailey. I work with Mr. Benhoff. Please come with us ma'am. It's for your own safety."

***

Ty wasn't real clear on what happened after Bailey showed up. He remembered getting in the SUV and seeing Lilliana's face. She was worried, maybe scared, it was kind of hazy. Then somebody popped him in the arm with a syringe and that was pretty much it until he woke up to the low thrum of turboprop engines.

It took him a minute to get his bearings. He lay on a gurney bolted to the deck of the plane and he wasn't alone. Two other gurneys, one on either side of him were fastened to the deck of the C-130. One carried a body bag. The other held Gates. He was unconscious, his shirt had been cut off, and his chest was covered in bandages and gauze. Monitoring leads, IV's, and a breathing line tethered him to an array of devices, an air tank, and a bag of fluid hanging off a rack above him. Spencer, the medic, was sitting on a net bench monitoring the machines display.

"Welcome back."

Ty looked at his left arm. It was covered in a pressure dressing and a bandage. He had an IV hanging from his right. He realized he did not feel a lick of pain. Spencer seemed able to read his mind.

"I loaded you up with Ketamine. Let me know if you start feeling anything."

Ty nodded but he couldn't get any words out. His mouth felt like a dust bowl, his tongue eighty grit sandpaper.

"Here." Lilliana appeared at his side holding a bottle of water for him. He sat up but paused, propped up on his good arm, while the world spun like he was a college freshman who'd just been introduced to tequila.

"Whoa," he said, taking things a little slower. He took the bottle of water and drained half of it. Lilliana watched him with no small amount of trepidation. His mouth and tongue softened a little bit, "Glad you're okay," he croaked.

"Me?" she scoffed, "I was so worried. You look so bad."

Ty raised an eyebrow, "Thanks."

She smiled, "You know what I mean."

"These guys treating you okay?" he asked looking past the vehicles likewise strapped to the deck plates to see Bailey, Wilson and the others huddling over a laptop.

"Yes, Sergeant Bailey and his men are very nice to me."

Ty looked at the body bag, then to Spencer, "Who's that?"

"Briggs," Spencer said quietly.

"Sorry, man."

Spencer nodded.

Ty went to stand up.

"I wouldn't." Spencer warned from the bench. He nodded toward the IV needle in Ty's arm.

"I really need this?" Ty asked.

Spencer Looked at him with a stoic expression, "You want to start feeling that arm?"

Ty looked at the saline bag laying on the net bench next to him. He took it in his good arm and looked at the medic, "How about this?"

Spencer didn't take his eyes off the monitors, "Don't start crying when you fuck yourself up."

"Deal," said Ty, he had to talk to Bailey, "How is he?"

"A pain in the ass. Took one in the lung and keeps trying to die on me, big pussy." Spencer looked up at Lilliana, "Sorry ma'am."

She smiled a wicked little grin, clearly entertained by the medic's apology. She took Ty by his good arm, "You have to see this."

Ty moved gingerly among the SUVs toward the briefing table. Wilson was sitting at the head of the table. She looked up with her severe, appraising eyes as if taking stock of him, "It's good to see you're okay."

"You, too."

Bailey turned from his computer and he and Wheels Looked at his arm, "You look like shit."

"Ketamine is awesome."

"Normally I wouldn't bother filling you in since you're so high you probably won't remember this anyway. But since you pulled this off more than anybody take a look."

Wheels transferred the screen from the laptop to a large monitor over their heads. Ty tried to make sense of the giant stream of numbers covering the screen. He gave it a minute then said, "I don't get it."

"It's a block chain."

"Right."

"You have no idea what I'm talking about do you?" she asked.

"Nope."

"These numbers are transactions between the biggest financiers of terrorism around the globe. And this shit dates back at least three years as far as we can tell."

The confused look on Ty's face didn't change. He turned to Lilliana, "You knew the key?"

She shook her head. Then held up a tiny clear stone. She produced a velvet bag and filled her delicate palm with more of the same.

Ty dropped the IV bag on the metal table and took the stone. He looked from her to Bailey, and back again.

Bailey pushed a magnifying ring light mounted to table his way.

"Take a look," he said.

It was hard to focus through the meds. It took him a minute to realize what he was even looking at. Finally, things settled and the diamond in his fingers came into detail. He turned it over and over in his fingers searching for something to jump out at him. When he finally noticed it, he couldn't believe it. A barely perceptible line of micro etched numbers scrolled across one face of the diamond.

"You're kidding me."

"No, and you're not going to believe this," Bailey said with a sly grin.

CHAPTER NINETY-TWO

The art of keeping an agent waiting was designed to make him or her sweat. Give an agent on the ropes time to consider their future and how much they needed their job. Time to think about how their actions and their words had threatened that future. Benhoff had given the subject plenty of thought over the fourteen-hour flight back to the U.S. According to big NCIS, he was a traitor. Eva, being the ruthless investigator she was, made sure neither NCIS or the DOD could cover what McClintock and Praetal had done by leaking her case to the national news. By derivative, he had embarrassed the NCIS on the national stage, no matter the fact that the case needed to come to light. The facts of the case, the elements of the crime, the corruption of one of NCIS's own assistant directors, or the damage done to Alexa Wilshire and her family. Thanks to McClintock, NCIS had victimized her all over again when he helped Pretaul skate on the investigation. None of that mattered in the face of going outside the ranks and spilling the agencies dirt. Ty had effectively committed professional suicide, that's what he'd decided while suffering through a string of pompous, so-called hit movies, and mediocre bourbon on the way back from Africa. He was at peace-ish. So, when the Director's Assistant told him to take a seat in the waiting area inside the Director's suite. Ty put his head back against the wall and fell asleep.

The day before had been the official policy review board where Executive Assistant Drapnier had hosted a panel of three other faceless NCIS 'senior leaders' as they discussed his 'evidence mishandling' and procedural violations related to the Albieto Cruz case. Making use of the Zimbabwean's national crime lab had been a particularly interesting topic. They had basically roasted him for using a substandard, third-world crime lab to analyze evidence in a DSI case. Benhoff hadn't even bothered to defend himself despite the fact he had added the lab's quality assurance procedures, and the certifications of the analyst who had done the testing on the casings, and blood stain as an addendum to his report. That bit never came up for discussion. Nor had the fact that Benhoff's actions resulted in the preliminary identification of a suspect.

The fact that he later learned from Obert Thoomba that his suspect had been killed by the man himself after confessing to Cruz's murder also did not come up. It was these things and the fact that they'd never mentioned the part where he'd saved several lives and kept over a million dollars' worth of illicit ivory from flooding the black market that made it clear to Ty the review board was nothing but a formality. When they did bother to ask him for a clarification on a particular point anywhere along the process, Benhoff kept his answers short and succinct without making much of an effort to defend himself. Even when they offered him a closing statement he'd declined. What was the point?

Two hours into his wait, the door to the director's office finally opened. Ty snapped his eyes open to see Drapnier exit the suite. The suit didn't bother to look in Benhoff's direction as he passed. A couple of stray entertaining thoughts of witty one-liners flitted through Ty's head but he decided he didn't care enough to make the man blush.

Benhoff watched him go then noticed a news flash stream over the suites wall mounted television. He watched as a Fox News anchor explained a tragedy in the Arabian Gulf where a Saudi Prince was believed dead after his superyacht sank overnight. This story was immediately followed by a report on the continuing search for an oil magnate who went missing from his Texas ranch the day before.

Ty wondered for a moment, *Nah, right? Even Bailey can't move that fast.* Then again, maybe their intel guys worked fast, and the powers that be had no interest in bringing either of those guys into a courtroom.

"The director will see you now, Special Agent Benhoff."

She watched him like she was waiting to see him crack. Like he really was being walked to the gallows. Ty grinned and said, "Thank you, ma'am."

Ty realized as he walked in the expansive office that he had absolutely no idea what the protocol was for getting called to the carpet in that particular situation. The director was an older guy, his bio said mid-sixties, tall with close-cropped grey hair, and a thick frame that gave credence to his history. According to his bio DIRNCIS Alexander Tenever played defensive end at the University of Tennessee before starting his law enforcement career. He had thirty years between the City of Memphis Police Department and what was now Homeland Security Investigations. He looked like he could still play on a defensive line or throw somebody through a wall if called upon. Tenever made Ty question his gym routine.

Tenever was leaning over his desk making a note. Ty wondered, *do I stand at attention? Do I take a seat in one of the two plush, leather-backed seats placed before the director's desk?* Somehow, he doubted he should kick his heels up, so he decided to place himself in between the chairs and wait. Tenever didn't even look up from his scribbling. He finally noticed how deep into his own thoughts he was when he realized there was a witness to his execution. In his defense she was slight of build with brown hair over a dark suit that blended with the couch she sat on to his right. Fact was he wouldn't have even noticed she were there unless he had caught a sharp toed shoe bob just over the rise of the coffee table that accompanied the couch. Despite all that it still took him a minute to recognize who he was looking at. Detective Eva Hill made her eyebrows bounce once and flashed him a quick somewhat malicious grin.

On instinct he turned toward her then snapped back to attention as the director said quietly, "Sit down, Agent Benhoff."

"Yes, sir."

Ty sat back straight, one hand resting on the armrest, another hanging in a sling across his chest, and took in the wall behind the man as the director's attention was elsewhere. He hoped it would keep him from turning and trying to engage Hill, or from chewing over the reason she was sitting back there. Compared to other executive offices he'd been in, Director Tenever was a spartan when it came to décor. There was a bookshelf loaded with volumes of what looked to Ty like a little bit of everything off to his left. A photograph of the director and who he guessed was the man's family, wife, a son and daughter, he guessed, both grown. Next to that was a painting of a dog of indistinguishable breed. Below and to the side of the dog was a framed pencil shadowing of a name Ty's eyes couldn't quite read. He recognized the shadowing though. He had one himself he kept in his own office. It was a name from the Law Enforcement Memorial in DC.

In Ty's estimation, the absolute void of a 'love me' wall was an interesting aspect of Director Alexander Tenever. Although the potential story related to a painting of a dog stirred in Ty's mind. He'd always valued a minimalist approach to depicting how important and accomplished you were in your career. A few things were cool but if you get to the point, you are framing and hanging your basic training certificate fifteen years after leaving FLETC, it's very possible you lead a really uninteresting life. Not that it mattered but Ty gave NCIS Director Alexander Tenever a couple extra points for his control over the need to show everyone who entered his office how awesome he was.

"You have a way with executive leadership, Special Agent Benhoff," Tenever stated while still focusing on his notes. "After that phone call the other day and the way you talked Drapnier and McClintock around in circles, I thought you would have had more to say at your panel yesterday." Tenever looked at him. His focus immediately fell from Ty's eyes to the sling supporting his left arm.

Was that a question? "No, sir," Ty stated.

"Still jetlagged? Or is it that you've got nothing left?"

"I think I understand where we're at sir, and I just want to look forward to what's next."

Tenever sat back in his chair and appraised him. After a moment he asked, "What is next for you, Agent Benhoff?"

Benhoff continued to look the director in the eye while he tried to decide if the man was playing games with him. He was also trying to keep focused, what the hell Hill was doing there? Ty felt a stirring in the pit of his stomach but reminded himself to keep in check. He wanted to see how this played out before blowing up. He gestured toward the papers on his desk, "I assume, sir, that Drapnier briefed you on the board's findings. I agree that I violated policy. I'm not going to qualify my reasons. I'm waiting for your decision."

Tenever nodded, "Drapnier is no fan of yours. He laid out his side pretty well. But we both know that the severity of his recommendation was biased."

"I imagine it was, sir."

"He thinks you betrayed the agency. He could give a damn about the evidence."

"And you, sir?"

Tenever took a slow breath, "I think betrayed is a strong choice of words. Did you lay our business out there for all the world to see? Yes. Was the way you went about it warranted? I don't know. It all went down before my time."

Benhoff didn't respond. He decided to let the silence stand for a moment.

Tenever did too. The two men watched each other, and Ty got the feeling there was something else at play. Tenever nodded toward Hill. *Finally*, Ty thought.

"Way I see it, you got a lead and wanted to follow it. Looking at the affidavit Detective Hill was so kind to deliver, it was a righteous lead. I spoke to your former chain of command. They chose their responses to my questions about what happened when you tried to get the case opened very carefully but couldn't give a real reason you kept getting a door slammed in your face. One of them tried to state their reason as operational readiness. But our charter has no operational readiness exemption. In my opinion, you did what you thought was best."

"I did."

Tenever held up a hand, "That's not what saved your job. The insubordination toward two senior leaders was enough in my book to kick your ass from this organization."

He still had a job?

"Then I look at the panel's review of the Cruz case. I read the statements of SSA Boulden, Drapnier, and I followed some email chains AD McClintock wrote discussing your insubordination, disregard for the chain of command, and a slew of other descriptors of your style, so to speak. It didn't help your case much. I noticed SSA Boulden states that while brash, sarcastic, insubordinate, and a general pain in the ass, I'm paraphrasing, he had never had an agent go to the lengths to close a case that you did. He detailed some of the steps conveniently left out of the panel's report. His words spoke highly of you. Then I received a call from Admiral Whillet who wanted to thank me not only for our hard work but for our discretion in the matter of his relationship with the ICPF. Unfortunately, I had to tell the Admiral that given all that has transpired I must have missed the details of his relationship. When he informed me of the incriminating facts and circumstances you willfully excluded from your report, I again started to wonder how you came to be hired by this agency. On top of all that JSOC has you seconded to their team. Within a day you are shooting up a hotel in Zimbabwe. I didn't get the details but according to the miniscule debrief I received that action is going to pay off big. So, there I am, torn, On paper kid you're at once Sherlock Holmes and an administrative tornado. I find myself at a loss of what to do. Finally, Detective Hill came to give me an update on the McClintock case." He gestured in her direction.

Eva Hill took her time standing, her composure one of utter grace and professionalism, "Sir as I informed you earlier, Mr. McClintock has been formally charged with obstruction of justice. He has also volunteered to cooperate and has since incriminated Mr. Ennis, and the Senator in a conspiracy to Obstruct. As of this morning the case has been taken by the Bureaus' Public Corruption section pending further investigation."

Tenever nodded, "And…?"

Eva fixed him with a slight nod of the head, "Yes, Sir, last night two things happened. The first was that Petty Officer Alexa Wilshire awoke from her coma. She will face a long road to recovery but from what the medical staff reported she was repeating the name Robert Pretaul before she could open her eyes. In all measures all her faculties are intact, and she would be damned if she didn't see Robert Pretaul the third in a courtroom."

Ty grinned from ear to ear for a brief instant then pulled his emotions back in check. He nodded in thanks.

"The second thing that happened last night was that upon taking Ms. Wilshire's statement I obtained a verbally approved warrant for the arrest of Robert Pretaul the third, currently stationed as a staff officer at the pentagon. I coordinated with the United States Marshall's Service to take him into custody, which they did while he was in the presence of the Chief of Naval Operations. He is being transferred to my custody as soon as I leave this briefing."

"That is fantastic," Ty stated flatly.

"Of course, it is Special Agent Benhoff. In fact, it was Ms. Hill here who convinced me to keep you on with us. Even with the whole administration against you, you moved forward."

Tenever studied him for a moment and Ty kept his posture as rigid as a dead man in full rigor. He looked at Hill, "Thank you for your great work on this Ms. Hill. May I have a moment with Agent Benhoff?"

"Yes, sir, thank you for your time."

Tenever and Benhoff watched her go. As she disappeared through the double doors, he couldn't help but feel she was the only thing keeping him from an epic ass chewing. When the door had closed Tenever cleared his throat and again looked Benhoff in the eye, "I only have two questions for you Special Agent Benhoff. The first, why did you work so hard on an assignment you knew was designed to get you fired? And two what made you think you could take on someone like Douglas McClintock and win?"

The lack of sudden shouting threw Ty off. He thought about it and finally shrugged after a minute, "I like working cases, Albieto Cruz deserved to have his story told. I wasn't going to let an ass-... sorry...."

Tenever cocked his head as if to say, come on, are you serious?

"I wasn't going to let McClintock win, sir. I knew it might cost me, but I learned a long time ago that even if you don't survive, you can still win."

Tenever nodded, thinking about his words, "I might need to hear that story someday Agent Benhoff."

"What story is that, sir?"

"The one that resulted in your take on survival."

Ty remained quiet. A couple of faces flashed in his mind that he hadn't thought about in a long time, "Maybe some day, sir," he said quietly.

Tenever wrote a note on the stack of papers on his desk. "Very well then, Special Agent Benhoff."

Ty took a deep breath, "Yes, sir?"

Tenever rose from his chair, came around the desk. Ty stood a bit slower, the close call with an AK-47 round still stinging under a thick bandage, and his arm screamed.

The two shook hands, "We've established you are unorthodox, brash, insubordinate, effective, self-sufficient, and resourceful. You cleaned a rat out of the agency using the only means available to you. You decimated the chain of command, caused the agency embarrassment, but you stuck to your oath and the agency will be better for it in the long run."

"Yes, sir."

"Good. One final question, how are you feeling?" Tenever said, guiding him to the door.

"What's that, sir?"

"You took a bullet to the abdomen one day, and another one to the arm the day following. Are you okay?"

Ty let slip a slight grin, "I'm good, sir."

"Good to hear, now go get settled in," Tenever said.

Ty turned to leave. Then he thought about it, "Where, sir?"

"What's that?" Tenever asked.

"Where do I get settled? What office am I going to?" He fought the image of the front gate of Twenty-Nine Palms Marine Corps Base that kept blinking in his head.

Tenever grinned. That unsettled Tyrone Benhoff. "Don't worry, Benhoff, I have just the thing for an agent like you."

***

Eva Hill was waiting for him. She leaned against the wall, hands in her pockets like an old west gunfighter lounging in the hot sun. She grinned as he stopped in front of her,

"That was a surprise."

She grinned, "For everyone here, I think. I was for sure you were toast. You okay?"

Ty smiled, "Thank you for what you did."

Eva stepped off the wall and the two made their way toward the elevator. A pack of four white shirt and tie wearing HQ types were quietly waiting.

"So, we taking the Pretaul case?" he asked.

She scoffed, "After how badly you guys fucked it up last time, not a Goddamned chance."

Ty watched the HQ nerds squirm. When the elevator doors slid open suddenly there were no RKB denizens to be found. Eva watched them scurry off from the elevator and raised one eyebrow, "You feds are kind of sensitive," she observed.

"You have no idea," fighting the urge to kiss her.

"You thinking of kissing me?" she called him out.

"No," he blurted. The two of them looked at each other for a moment.

"Better not, we've tried that. You're a terrible kisser. Buy me lunch and we'll call it square for saving your job."

"Deal, and I'm a helluva kisser."

"Sure," she scoffed.

The two cops stood next to each other another moment before Eva said, "Where do you think you'll end up now that this is all over?"

"I have no idea."

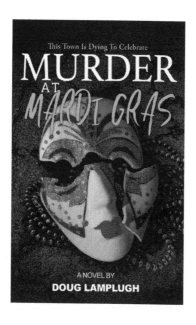

AVAILABLE NOW FROM CRAIG HOLT AND WILDBLUE PRESS

HARD DOG TO KILL by CRAIG HOLT

http://wbp.bz/hdtka